SWORD

OF

SHADOW

AND

STAR

SWORD

OF

SHADOW

AND

STAR

First Paperback Edition September 2024
First Hardback Edition September 2024
First Ebook Edition September 2024

ISBN: 978-1-7397126-3-1 (paperback)
ISBN: 978-1-7397126-4-8 (hardback)

ALSO BY ALLIE BRENNAN

The Ravenheart Series

Heir of Ravens and Ruin

DEDICATION

For you, Mum. My biggest fan and best friend.

TRIGGER WARNINGS

This book contains strong language, sexual scenes, intense fight scenes, violence, blood, torture, depression, PTSD.

Feel free to contact me through my Instagram (@authoralliebrennan). My DMs are always open for those who need someone to talk to.

PRONUNCIATION GUIDE

Characters

Rexah – *Reck-sa*

Kalen – *Kay-len*

Torbin – *Tor-bin*

Storglass – *Stor-glass*

Arelle – *Ah-rell*

Venrhys – *Ven-riss*

Sorana – *Sor-ana*

Valfae – *Val-fay*

Locations

Adorea – *Ah-door-ee-ah*

Kaldoren – *Kal-door-en*

Etteria – *Ette-ree-ah*

Brywen – *Bry-when*

Dorasa – *Dor-as-ah*

Savindeer – *Sav-in-deer*

Vellwynd – *Vel-wind*

PLAYLIST

Gangsta's Paradise – 2WEI
when the party's over – Billie Eilish
Colorblind – Counting Crows
Pieces – Red
Desire – Meg Myers
Find You – Ruelle
Exile – Taylor Swift, Bon Iver
Warfare – Katie Garfield
Rescue – Lauren Daigle
Viva Forever – The Butterfly Effect
Crossing Over – Lawless, IO Echo
My Sacrifice – Tommee Profitt
I Found – Amber Run
Up in Fire – McKenna Brienholt

ETTERIA
ADOREA
OAKHAVEN
TELLA'S MEADOW
BRYWEN
GR
DORASA
KALDOREN

SAVINDEER
VELLWYND
LOW
RELLE'S HUT
DARK FAE KEEP
THE DARK LANDS

I

KALEN

Cold, endless dark suffocated the light, engulfing it within its wicked embrace. The very air itself was hard to breathe, like a poisonous fume filling his lungs. Dark magic clung to him, oppressive and relentless, and the hand that curled around his arm and pressed into his skin promised no way out.

He was trapped.

As quickly as the darkness had consumed him, it dissipated like smoke in the wind, giving way to a terrifying sight. A range of black mountains stood before him, the jagged peaks reaching for the darkening sky like deadly sharp claws. Small windows were carved into the face of the mountains, candle-light flickering within. His blue eyes widened with fear. He knew then exactly where he was.

The Dark Lands.

The strong grip on his arm tightened before he could take a step. He moved forward, groaning slightly when Venrhys dragged him towards a huge set of dark stone doors where two Dark Fae stood in leather armour, hands on the hilts of their swords, their spines straight. These were soldiers of the Dark Army.

Both fae bowed their heads to Venrhys and turned to open the doors for them. The heavy stone creaked as it moved, revealing a large foyer. Concrete covered the floor, and the walls were like that of the mountain outside: untouched, jagged, and damp with rainwater that seeped through cracks in the structure. Kalen felt just how tough it was when he was shoved face first into it; he hissed in pain as the rough rock bit into the skin of his cheek.

"Hand me those," Venrhys ordered one of the soldiers.

The rattling of chains echoed through the room, and his stomach dropped. He wouldn't be chained. He began to struggle in the general's grip.

Venrhys turned him around to face him, shoving him harshly against the wall once more. "Don't make me do this the hard way, Kalen," he said. He grabbed his wrists in his hand and clamped the metal cuff around them. A soft click confirmed they were locked.

Kalen winced and looked down at his wrists; the bonds were made from iron and were already starting to burn his skin. He scowled; for reasons unknown, iron didn't affect the Dark Fae like it did normal fae, and a familiar bitterness compounded the pain.

When Venrhys let go of the cuffs, Kalen's eyes moved from his shackles to the chain attached to them that the Dark Fae General now held in his hand. He staggered forward as Venrhys yanked the chain, and another hiss escaped his lips as the metal pressed firmly against his skin. The pain was one thing, tolerable even, but shackles were an insult to the soul. With his agency gone, he pushed down an entirely new fear that threatened to devour him anew.

Kalen's eyes were everywhere as they made their way towards a rugged archway to the left of the foyer. Dim light emanated from the sconces dotted throughout the corridor, but thanks to his fae senses, he could still see perfectly. If the opportunity arose for him to escape, his only chance at succeeding would be to memorise every turn they took and anything that was notable enough to commit to memory; a particularly jagged rock, an undulation in the cement, he would do well to remember as much as he could.

Dark Fae soldiers lined the walls here and there as they walked, or dragged in Kalen's case, standing proudly on guard and ready for any trouble that may arise. Each bowed their heads in respect to their general who didn't so much as acknowledge them.

Counting each guard as they went, Kalen was pulled through another archway and down a set of stairs. At the bottom was a long corridor with multiple doors lined on either side. He knew this walk would end somewhere grim, but it wasn't until he walked by the doors and noticed the locks underneath the handles that the reality of imprisonment fully presented itself. The stickiness of the Dark magic around him seemed to worsen tenfold then, and his lungs begged for fresh air as intensely as his legs yearned to run.

Fuck.

"Come, Kalen Vidarr," Venrhys said, tugging forcefully on the chain.

Kalen stumbled forward; the iron in his shackles was weakening him. He just managed to stop himself from falling and continued down the dimly lit corridor with him.

Whimpers could be heard from behind one of the cell doors, groans of pain from another. Kalen tried to drown them out as they made their way down the corridor, but their sounds of discomfort sliced through any remaining hope that lingered. He desperately wanted to help them, but in his current situation he couldn't even help himself, and that thought alone terrified him.

The hallway seemed to go on forever, and when he thought that maybe it *was* a never-ending passageway, they halted outside a door on the left. A Dark Fae soldier stepped forward, the jingle of keys sounding as he pulled them from his pocket. No one spoke a word as he slid the key into the lock, unlocking the door before stepping back and bowing his head in respect to Venrhys.

The general stepped into the room, pulling Kalen forward with the chain and urging him roughly into the space. At first, he saw nothing, the shadows of the room dominating his senses for a moment, but his fae sight quickly kicked in and his eyes adjusted. He was saved from complete darkness only by a trickle of light that bled through a tiny, barred window high up on the wall, and with just one look at it he knew he would never fit; the thick bars would prevent anything or anyone getting through it.

The only item in the room was a bucket.

Venrhys walked towards the back of the room and crouched down to the floor. The chain's rattling echoed throughout the space, and after a few moments he stood to his full height, no longer holding it.

A small pull of the chain confirmed that he'd fixed it to the floor.

"Welcome to your new home," Venrhys said as he stepped towards his prisoner.

Kalen shuffled back but only moved two steps before the chain pulled taut, halting his movement and digging the iron shackles deeper into his already sensitive flesh. He gritted his teeth in pain as Venrhys drew near.

"You should make yourself comfortable. We've got a lot to talk about," he said as he studied Kalen's face. "We're going to have the best time together, you and I."

Kalen's gaze never left his as he glared at him. "Go fuck yourself."

Venrhys tilted his head slightly, the movement almost predatory. A sadistic smirk spread across his lips. Moments later, his fist connected with Kalen's jaw, sending him straight to the floor. Pain exploded across the side of his face, and he groaned with the heat of immediate swelling.

"You will learn to respect me, Kalen," Venrhys said as he crouched down to him. "That I guarantee."

Kalen lifted his gaze to meet Venrhys's glare once more, his eyes blazing with fury. "We will see about that," he replied through gritted teeth, a rush of hatred washing through him.

Venrhys rose to his feet as he brushed off his sleeves, his silhouette blocking out the moonlight flooding in from the small window above. "I will leave you to adjust to your new surroundings," he said as he turned and headed for the door.

Kalen peered over his shoulder as Venrhys pulled the handle and stopped in the threshold. Another evil smirk spread across his face giving his black eyes an even more haunting look. He didn't speak, he didn't need to; his eyes made a promise of pain and suffering before he walked out. The sound of the door slamming and the lock securing echoed throughout the cell.

"Fuck." Kalen sighed as he rolled onto his back, the cold from the stone floor seeping through his clothes. His body ached from the wounds he'd received in the fight at Grimhollow and now, thanks to the iron around his wrists, his fae healing abilities were dulled. Usually, his injuries would be at least halfway healed by now, but he could feel the slow progress of recovery in his blood. Soon, it would likely stagnate completely, and with his magic so muted there was no use trying to break the shackles.

Kalen always felt his magic flowing through his blood; now, bereft of that sensation, he felt utterly lost. His magic was like a presence all of its own, a companion of sorts, and it buzzed through him in a way he would never be able to explain to someone without magic. The feeling was unique to each Power Blessed, and for Kalen it felt like a ripple through his blood, ebbing and flowing like the waves in the sea. For Torbin it felt like heat spreading through his veins, like a wild-fire sweeping through a woodland. When they were younger, they had learned to control their powers together, experienced each magical revelation jointly, and Kalen would never forget that first conversation with his best friend about their gifts.

Torbin, is he alive?

One of the last things he saw before Venrhys ripped him away was Torbin screaming in agony as a Valfae tore its claws through his side. The last thing he saw was his friend, his brother, bleeding out.

Then there was Rexah. His beautiful Rexah with tears falling down her face as she made a deal with a monster. She was to find the Shadow Star and hand it over to Venrhys in exchange for him, alive but with no guarantees of being unharmed, and he would never forget the heartache in her eyes as she agreed to it – it would haunt him for the rest of his life.

Looking around the dark, damp cell, Kalen took a deep breath. He wouldn't intentionally jeopardise the deal by trying to escape, but if the opportunity arose, if it was handed to him on a plate, then he wouldn't let it pass him by, not if it meant he could be by her side once again and protect her. He could take whatever that monster threw at him. If it meant Rexah wasn't the one being tortured, he would do this a million lifetimes over.

For her, he would do anything.

Hours ticked by and Kalen hadn't moved from his spot on the cold stone floor. The burning on his wrists had numbed over time, but he knew that wasn't a good sign. There was constant movement in the corridor of his fellow inmates being pulled from their cells, some screaming, some pleading for their lives – for mercy – before being returned to their prison. Upon that return, nobody cried for help, and there was no shouting or pleading. There was instead a deafening silence to mark the return of one most broken and defeated, a silence that was enough to send a shiver down Kalen's spine like lightning forking across a darkened sky.

Gazing up at the rocky ceiling, he wondered when it would be his turn. Would Venrhys give him one night of peace before commencing his torment, or would he burst into the room at any moment to begin?

Kalen didn't have to wait much longer to find out the answer; it must barely have been half an hour before Dark Fae guards dragged him from his cell and took him to what he could only assume was a room specifically designed for interrogation and torture. Various knives, swords and other tools lined the far wall, and a dark stone slab sat in the centre of the space with four leather straps attached to it.

Perfect for tying someone down.

He was surprised when he wasn't immediately strapped down on the slab. Instead, Venrhys ordered the guards to chain him up and they did as commanded without hesitation. The iron shackles burned into the already tender flesh of his wrists as his arms were lifted above his head, his feet barely touching the cold floor. The guards left them to it, and Venrhys had his fun.

During this time with Venrhys – how long it had been in that room, Kalen didn't know – pain was all he knew. The stab of a knife to his stomach, a hammer to his side so strong he felt each one of his ribs shatter beneath his skin – the torture went on and on. He took everything Venrhys gave him, and not once did he let out a cry of pain. He wouldn't give him the satisfaction of expressing his affliction, but each agonising second dragged by like the knife Venrhys slid across his skin.

"Don't lose consciousness now."

The Dark Fae's voice echoed and reverberated, shaking Kalen's senses and pulling him back to reality. Blood dripped from the slice on Kalen's cheek, from the numerous cuts and gashes littering his chest and abdomen, splashing to the floor beneath him like crimson raindrops.

"You've done exceptionally well, Kalen," Venrhys said, making his way over to the wall of blades, placing the blood-stained knife onto the table. "I half expected you to pass out within the first ten minutes, but you exceeded my expectations. It's been two hours, so far."

Kalen answered by spitting blood onto the floor, the scarlet liquid landing an inch away from Venrhys's black boot. It was a little immature, but damn did it make him feel good for a second.

Venrhys looked at the stain before stepping over it and walking up to him. "I think we're all done for the day."

"What is the point in torturing me? I can't find the sword, there's no reason for you to do it," Kalen replied through gritted teeth as his body pulsed and shook with ebbing adrenaline. "You're wasting your time."

"Because when Rexah finds the sword and brings it to me, when she sees the pain and suffering you've gone through, the look of unmitigated agony and guilt on her beautiful face will be more pleasurable than what any woman could give me with the soft flesh between her thighs." Venrhys leaned closer. "And also," he whispered menacingly, "because I enjoy watching you writhe under my blade."

Rage flooded Kalen's veins as he glared at the Dark Fae. "You're sick."

Venrhys merely smirked at him. "Compliments won't give you any reprieve but are appreciated none the less."

Gods give me fucking strength, Kalen thought.

"Don't give me that look. You'll learn to enjoy feeling the pain as much as I do inflicting it," he said, his black eyes brightening, if that were possible.

"I can take whatever you throw my way. You won't break me, I can promise you that," Kalen told him, looking him dead in the eyes.

The Dark Fae grinned wickedly at him. "Time will tell if your words hold truth, but I look forward to proving you wrong."

Kalen shifted his gaze away from the sadistic bastard, unable to watch that sick, twisted grin spread across his face any longer. He could feel warm blood trickling down his chest and abdomen, and suddenly he felt weak – too weak.

"Rexah will fulfil her end of our bargain," Venrhys said as he walked to the table, pulling open the top drawer. "She isn't stupid enough to break the deal."

"Maybe … maybe you've got it all wrong." Kalen groaned softly as he shifted his weight, trying to stop the strain on his raised arms.

Venrhys looked over his shoulder. "What makes you say that?"

"You've put all your f-faith in what you believe she feels for me." He gritted his teeth. "What makes you so confident her feelings are strong enough for her to do as you ask?"

Venrhys stepped towards him again. "Rexah Ravenheart is irrevocably in love with you, Kalen. The look in her eyes when I took hold of you, it's one I will never forget. I witnessed the moment her world crumbled." He grabbed Kalen's chin, forcing their eyes to meet. "I know what she is to you, and it brings me so much joy to know how it tears you up inside to be apart from her."

"Stop." Kalen glared at him, baring his teeth. "Stop it."

The Dark fae studied him for a moment before chuckling darkly, roughly shoving Kalen's face away before stepping back. Kalen groaned at the pain that sliced through him at the movement as he swayed with the chains.

"She is the key to everything. She doesn't understand just how incredibly powerful and blessed she is," Venrhys said.

Kalen took a few deep breaths, shoving the agony aside as best he could. "She knows about the Raven God and that she's his Chosen."

"That may be, but she doesn't have the knowledge to access that power, *his* power," Venrhys replied, before lifting a cloth from the drawer at his side and wiping Kalen's blood from his blade.

"Rexah is smarter than you give her credit for," Kalen told him. "She'll figure it out one way or another."

Venrhys huffed a laugh before putting the knife back into its place on the wall, the set complete once again. "It will be too late by then."

"You … your *kind*," Kalen hissed with disgust, "you won't come out the other side of this war victorious." Kalen scowled as the Dark fae stepped into his personal space once more. "You won't win."

The Dark Fae lifted his hand and swept his fingers through Kalen's damp locks, pushing them from his face before he leaned in closer. "That's the beauty of it all," he whispered, the vicious smirk spreading across his lips once more. "We're already winning."

2

REXAH

"Bring me the Shadow Star, and Kalen will be returned to you." She replayed the events over and over, Venrhys's words echoing in her mind. "*The clock is ticking, Little Raven.*"

She saw over and over the dark magic that surrounded Kalen, smothering him with its malevolent embrace. It had filled the atmosphere making it hard to pull oxygen into her aching lungs. It didn't matter that she wanted to save him, thanks to the deal she had made, there was nothing she could do but watch as they disappeared before her eyes.

He was gone.

The branches and twigs in her arms dug into her skin as she gripped them tightly, her footsteps as silent as they could be. The Valfae may still be lurking, and drawing their attention was the last thing they needed right now. Without Torbin's fire magic it was up to Rexah and Storglass to light the fire themselves. She hadn't been keen to light a fire, but Storglass told her Torbin needed it, that they had no other choice. For the past two days they had watched over the injured Torbin, cleaning his wound as best they could and wrapping it with whatever cloth they had, but his condition was growing worse as the days went by.

As she neared their campsite, hidden by a large thicket growing next to a broad tree, Storglass came into view. He was arranging small rocks into a circle for their fire, close enough that Torbin would be kept warm too.

Gods, he looks worse than he did an hour ago, Rexah thought when her eyes moved to the fae. He was wrapped up in his cloak, his bag under his head for support, but what worried her most was the pallor of his skin and the sheen of cold sweat that coated it. Dark circles surrounded his eyes, and his lips were bloodless. It was clear the poison from the Valfae's claw was spreading through his system and working fast.

"Let's get the fire going," Storglass said quietly when he saw her approach. "The quicker we light it, the better."

Rexah nodded softly as she walked over and placed the wood she'd gathered into the centre of the stone circle. "He's getting worse. Are you sure there isn't anything else you can do for him?"

Storglass fixed the branches, ensuring they stayed within the circle. "I would if I could. I was so close to burnout at the end of the battle and my magic is yet to replenish itself."

He looked just as exhausted as she felt. Heavy bags hung beneath his dull hazel eyes, the spark they usually held gone for now, and his youthful features held a consternation that aged him. Warlocks never looked old, not really – it was difficult to tell their age simply by looking at them – and she sometimes forgot how old Storglass actually was. He was older than Rexah, older than her grandmother had been, but he didn't look a day over thirty.

"Burnout? Is that a condition of your magic?" Rexah asked as she crouched down next to him.

"Yes. Magic has its limits much like everything else. Getting as close to burnout as I did, it will take a few days for it to fully return," he told her as he picked up two rocks he'd kept separate from the circle and began rubbing them together.

"So, you can't do any magic until its fully returned?" she asked, watching as small sparks jolted from the stones.

The warlock nodded. "I can feel it coming back. It's like filling a bottle of wine a drop at a time. Think of it this way: a merchant can't sell it if it's half empty."

The first night they'd made camp, Storglass had seen to Rexah's wounds after making sure Torbin was okay. She'd insisted she was fine, but Storglass was so stubborn. With amazement, she had watched his magic stitch the skin of her arm back together. He'd healed the wound on her forehead too. *That must have drained the last of his magic,* she realised.

Smoke began to seep out of the branches, flames spluttering to life underneath the pile. "I'm sorry for the questions, I'm just curious about it all. It helps keep my mind off everything that's happened."

Storglass set the stones down and began blowing on the fire, the flames finally catching on the branches at the top. "No need to apologise. Like you, answering the questions keeps my mind off everything that's happened."

Rexah rose from where she crouched and nodded thankfully to Storglass before shifting over to Torbin. Kneeling by his side, she carefully peeled back his makeshift bindings. The sight of the wound made Rexah's stomach clench. Three deep gouges marked his skin. The bleeding had thankfully stopped, but the redness and the puss within the wounds were a true sign that infection had set in. Black veins slithered across his skin, spilling from the wound – Valfae poison. Rexah was no healer, but she knew that an infection and poison were not a good combination. Storglass had used his magic to keep the poison at bay as best he could but they needed to get to Arelle as soon as possible; his magic would only last for so long in Torbin's system.

Covering the injury back up, she moved his sweat-soaked hair from his face. "You're going to be okay, Torbin. I won't let you leave this world, not yet. Kalen would kill me," she whispered, huffing a pathetic laugh.

Tears pricked her eyes as she thought of him again. Only the gods knew what Venrhys was doing to him, what torture he was enduring all because of her, if he was still alive.

He has to be. Venrhys made a deal. Kalen, alive, for the Shadow Star. She ran a hand over her face. *I cannot give him that sword, but I cannot leave Kalen in his grasp.*

Torbin mumbled quietly, catching her attention.

"Shh," she whispered soothingly. "Sleep, Torbin. You're safe." The fae slowly relaxed at her words and slipped back into slumber.

Yes, he was safe for now, but how long would it be before they ran into trouble? They'd been extremely lucky so far, but that luck would surely run out. Rexah had no idea where Arelle, the Seer, lived, but Storglass did. Part of her questioned whether she could trust him or not, but he'd almost given his life for her, and he hadn't abandoned them. It didn't mean she wouldn't keep an eye on him though.

Rexah moved closer to the flames, remaining beside Torbin so she could monitor him. "How long until we reach our destination?" she asked as she turned back to Storglass.

"If the weather holds," he replied, warming his hands against the fire, "then we should arrive within a few days."

"It's that close?" she asked, bringing her cloak closer.

Storglass nodded. "It is, but it's not an easy place to find, not if you don't know where to look."

Fucking riddles.

Rexah sighed. "Okay, if you know where to look then that's fine. I will tell you this though, if you lead me and Torbin into a trap I'll waste no time sinking my dagger into your throat."

His hazel eyes slid to hers. "I understand but trust me when I tell you that I will not betray you. If I wanted to then you'd have been the one Venrhys took, not Kalen."

She saw the truth in his eyes. "Everything is a mess," she whispered, pushing a hand through her tangled hair. "My mind is running at a million miles an hour, and I just don't know what I'm going to do to get him back…or if Torbin is going to live."

"Take it one step at a time, Rexah. All we need to focus on right now is getting to Arelle," he replied, rubbing his hands together near the flames. "Once we are there, we can give Torbin the treatment he needs."

Rexah nodded slowly, holding her hands out to the fire. *It's easier said than done, but he's right. One step at a time.*

"I should have been faster. Maybe I could have gotten to Kalen before Venrhys managed to lay a finger on him," she said, staring into the fire.

Storglass shook his head. "No. Venrhys is very powerful. There's nothing any of us could have done to prevent what happened."

"He wants the sword, Storglass. A sword that has been missing for centuries that apparently only I can find. He can't be allowed to get his hands on it, but the longer Kalen stays in his presence the higher the chance he won't be given back to us alive, deal or not." Hot tears spilled down her cheeks, and she quickly wiped them away. "I don't trust him. Despite what fae customs say, I wouldn't be surprised if he twisted the deal to benefit the Dark Fae."

The warlock shifted closer to her and gently placed his hand on her back. "I know it's hard, but we will get through this, together. We will figure out a way to get Kalen back without you having to give the sword to Venrhys, I promise."

Rexah met his gaze, his hazel eyes almost shining in the firelight. "I'm scared," she whispered.

Gods, I'm pathetic.

Storglass studied her for a moment. "I'm scared too," he replied. "It's only natural to feel this way, but I promise that I won't let any harm come to you. We will get through this."

Rexah dipped her head to hide the bulging tears in her eyes. Storglass was kind to offer his support and sword, but her sadness was unreachable. She cared not for her own safety, not really, and the realisation caused a grief to swell in her heart for a hopefulness she'd once felt. "Get some sleep, Storglass," she said softly. "I'll keep watch first."

The warlock nodded and gently patted her back before shifting over to his bedroll and getting comfortable.

Rexah looked down at Torbin. She watched his chest rise and fall, each breath crackling like the fire before her. He looked nothing like the fae who'd saved her life. Watching him deteriorate in front of her eyes, knowing there was nothing she could do, killed her inside.

Soon, Storglass began to snore softly; he'd drifted off to sleep with no issue. She was glad, he would need all the strength he could get.

Hopefully when he wakes his power will be at full capacity, she thought. *Gods, I hope we reach Arelle in time.*

Torbin began to move restlessly under his cloak. Rexah slid closer to him, gently running her fingers through his dark hair comfortingly.

"Shh," she soothed. "Everything's going to be okay."

"Rex," he whispered through chattering teeth.

Tucking the cloak closer around him, she whispered, "I'm here. We're close to Arelle. We'll be there soon."

Torbin's eyes opened a fraction, those once bright amber eyes now as dim as an ember. "K-Kal…"

Rexah's chest tightened. "I know. We will get him back, whatever it takes," she said, gently stroking his cheek. "Rest, Torbin. Save your energy."

Not able to resist, Torbin's eyes fluttered closed and he fell back into unconsciousness, his chest rattling once more.

Rexah moved her gaze to the fire, watching the flames dance as more tears burned her eyes. Hugging her knees to her chest, she prayed to the only god who could help her.

I don't know if you can hear me, but I have no one else to turn to. Guide me to the sword. Help me find it so I can make those monsters pay. Rexah paused as if allowing time for the Raven God to answer. Feeling a fool, she bit her lip and continued. *There is one more thing I ask of you. One important thing,* she prayed silently, projecting her thoughts as strongly as she could. *Keep him safe. Until I can reach him, I beg you.* Rexah closed her eyes, the hot tears sliding down her cheeks. *Keep him safe for me.*

The snapping of twigs caught Rexah's attention, and her eyes shot open as her hand moved to the hilt of her dagger. She pushed herself to her feet, scanning their surroundings as she unsheathed the weapon.

"Put that blade down before you hurt yourself, little girl," a male voice resounded to her left.

Rexah spun and saw a group of four men. Quickly measuring them up, she surmised they were human and didn't have much in the way of possessions.

"I suggest you keep walking," she replied, gripping her dagger. "We don't want any trouble."

"What happened to him? He doesn't look so good," one of them said, motioning to Torbin behind her.

"He's none of your concern," she responded coldly. "Now leave."

The men chuckled. "Not going to happen, sweetheart, not until we take everything you've got, maybe have a bit of fun…" the leader of their group remarked.

"You can try, but I don't advise it," Storglass said, appearing beside her, green energy swirling in his hand.

Rexah was surprised to see him using his power, and she felt a nauseating cocktail of gratitude and wariness.

"This is your last chance to walk away now."

Rexah saw panic fill two of the men's eyes, but their leader seemed unflustered. "Your cheap tricks don't scare me," he said, pulling out a small blade. The others followed suit, pulling out their weapons albeit hesitantly.

All four rushed forward with well-practised synchronicity. Storglass wasted no time and threw the energy at one of them, hitting the man straight in the chest and sending him flying back into one of the trees. Rexah brought her dagger up, blocking the leader's attack. She planted her boot into his stomach, kicking him hard, forcing him to stumble back. His friend took a swipe at her – that, she easily dodged. She slashed her dagger down, ripping the sleeve of his shirt – a warning, not enough to cut his skin.

Storglass stepped out the way of an attack before punching the advancing plunderer square in the face, and the man fell to the ground in an unconscious heap.

Rexah shoved the man with the ripped sleeve away from her as the leader came back for more. She grabbed his wrist as he attempted to stab her and quickly thrust her head forward, smacking it against his. Pain exploded through her head, but it was worth it to see him clutching his bloody nose.

"You bitch!"

"Take your men and leave," she commanded.

"It's not worth it, boss," the other man said, clutching his stomach in pain. "Let's just go. There'll be others."

The leader scowled at him before looking to Rexah. "This is your lucky day, girl. You get to live."

Rexah watched as the two men grabbed their unconscious comrades and dragged them off back through the trees. Her shoulders slumped with relief as she sheathed her dagger. "That was far too close," she breathed.

"Are you hurt?" Storglass asked as he walked over to her.

She shook her head. "I'm good. Are you okay?"

Storglass nodded. "Go sit down. I'll stay here and make sure they're gone."

She walked over to Torbin, sat back down and checked him over. Thankfully, he hadn't been harmed in the attack, but he still didn't look any better. She looked over to Storglass and saw his eyes were glowing green. Maybe he was using his magic to track the men?

She frowned, confused. "You said your power was slowly coming back, how are you using it now?" she asked him.

The green in his eyes slowly faded back to their normal hazel as he looked to her. "I had enough back to defend us. My source has almost depleted again, but so long as I don't use any more I should still be on track to being at full capacity in a few days."

She nodded and took a steadying breath before looking down at Torbin. They had to get to Arelle, and they had to get to her fast.

A few days later, Rexah watched as Storglass stood before two tall trees that curved towards each other, creating a natural archway. His hands were raised as his green power danced along his fingertips, and he was muttering to himself. Just as he'd predicted, his power was now back to its full strength, much to Rexah's relief. Torbin lay beside her. His condition had deteriorated, and he hadn't opened his eyes since he'd spoken to her by the campfire days ago. Her anxiety was deepening by the hour.

Rexah looked down at Torbin, fixing the cloak wrapped around him. "Almost there," she whispered to him. "Hold on. Just a little longer."

Just as the words left her lips there was a shift in the atmosphere. The hairs on her arms and the back of her neck stood on end as an electrical charge zapped through the air. Rexah held Torbin close, covering him with her body as she looked over to Storglass, watching as the warlock stepped back a few paces.

The space between the bowed trees began to ripple like air in a heatwave, power shimmering like moonlight on a lake. Magic hummed as their surroundings began to melt away like sugar dissolving in hot water, revealing a meadow filled with pink and white flowers and blossom trees scattered in the expanse, swaying delicately in the soft breeze. A white stone cottage sat within the centre, grey smoke billowing from its chimney.

Rexah's eyes went wide with awe as the once hidden environment was revealed to her. She'd never seen anything like it in her life.

"Wow."

Storglass made his way over to her. "Welcome to Arelle's abode."

Rexah got to her feet and helped Storglass lift Torbin into his arms. The fae made no noise at the movement, and it did nothing to ease Rexah's concerns. "Let's get him inside."

They wasted no more time; they stepped through the tree archway and onto the dirt path, crossing the meadow towards the cottage. As they approached, the light-green door opened for them, and Arelle appeared in the doorway.

Her mint-green eyes flooded with worry as they drew closer. Her pastel pink chiffon dress fell to below her knees and swayed lightly in the cool breeze. "Bring him in," she said, stepping back and opening the door further.

Storglass didn't hesitate as he stepped through the threshold with Torbin. Rexah followed close behind, the dark hardwood floor creaking as she stepped onto it. Lilac curtains hung over archtop windows that bled warm light into the open space. A pristine, white sofa with a grey woollen blanket folded over the top of it sat across from an unlit, brick fire-place along with two grey armchairs. A soft blue coated the walls, where one could spot it; shelves full of trinkets covered one wall completely, and dreamcatchers in various sizes and designs hung from the ceiling to draw the eye. In the open plan space, the kitchen was situated towards the back of the room, clean and elegant with white wooden cupboards and counters. There was much to admire, but what drew Rexah's eye was an area to the left of the kitchen where sheer violet curtains hung from the ceiling, separating this part of the room from the rest.

From where she stood, Rexah spotted floor to ceiling cupboards filled to the brim with jars of unknown substances, liquids and materials of differing colour and texture.

Is that...

Her mouth parted to find that sat atop a circular table in the centre of the space was a crystal ball.

"Put him in here," Arelle said, pulling Rexah from her thoughts.

She looked over as Storglass followed Arelle into a room at the back of the cottage. Rexah quickly followed behind and stepped into the room in time to see Storglass placing Torbin down as gently as he could on the bed.

Arelle was by his side in a flash with folded cloths and jars in her arms that Rexah hadn't even seen her pick up. "How long has he been like this?" the Seer asked.

"Almost a week," Rexah told her, hugging her arms as her body gently shook. "We did what we could to help slow the poison, but it's not been enough."

The Seer looked at Rexah, her eyes warm and sympathetic. "It *has* been enough. Both of you kept him alive." The Seer moved a hand to Torbin's torso, hovering over it as though attempting to sense his afflictions. "You got him to me in time, just."

Storglass pulled off his cloak. "He will live?"

Arelle nodded as she inspected his wounds. "It's a nasty injury, but yes, I can heal him."

Rexah's shoulders drooped as the tension of the last few days washed off her shoulders like a raging waterfall. A deep breath left her lips as relief flooded through her. "Thank the gods," she whispered.

"One more day and he would have been beyond even my healing capabilities," she said as she picked up one of the jars filled with something that looked like ash.

"Thank you for this, Arelle," Rexah replied quietly.

Arelle shook her head dismissively as she unscrewed the lid of the jar. Suddenly, she stilled, and the markings on her forehead creased as she frowned, looking between Storglass and Rexah.

"What? What's wrong?" Storglass asked.

The Seer looked down at Torbin before moving her eyes to Rexah. "Where's the other one?"

3

KALEN

rip, drip, drip.

It was the only sound Kalen could tolerate. He kept his mind fixed on the small droplets of water falling through the tiny crack in the stone ceiling; listening to it splash into the small puddle it was creating in the corner of the room was easier than listening to the screams and cries of agony echoing through the dungeon halls.

If he had to guess, he'd been imprisoned almost a week. The days all bled into one another, and the incessant darkness made it difficult to keep track. The sun never shone on the Dark Lands; it was kept a permanent prisoner behind thick stormy clouds. The only indication that it was a new day was when the moon would disappear; the sky would barely brighten, and one would have to make the effort to check for the absence of the stars.

More often than not, Kalen made no such effort.

Aches pulsed through his battered body as he sat up, his bare back pressing against the cold wall. His clothes had been taken from him during his first round of torture. Where they were now was a mystery to him. The only scrap of clothing now on his person was a pair of knee length threadbare shorts. The chains fixed around his wrists clinked as he moved, biting into his already tender skin. He'd tried many times to call upon his magic in attempt to break free, but as he fine well knew, the shackles shackled his power too.

Everyone loves a trier, he thought.

Moving his gaze to the window, Kalen found it was the moon that poured light upon that fraction of cracked floor and that the stars were twinkling somewhere behind dense grey clouds.

As much as it pained him not to be in Rexah's presence every second that passed by, he knew that he had made the right decision to let Venrhys take him instead of her. The memory of her violet eyes strained with the agony of that decision tore him apart inside, so he'd made it easier for her. He'd been the one to make the decision, told her it would be okay. But when their opportunity to say goodbye to one another was stolen from them, it unearthed a pain he'd never felt before. What he would have given to see her smile one last time, to run his fingers through her silky raven hair, to kiss her and tell her everything was going to be fine.

Kalen's head fell, his dark hair tumbling around his face as the absence of her became all too real once again. He could not have allowed her to make this choice, but what of the choices she faced now?

She cannot give him that sword, he surmised silently. If it meant imprisonment, if it meant he was to die here, then he would gladly accept it. *I won't let the lives of everyone in the realm be put in danger just so I can be freed.*

Leaning his head back against the wall, he sighed. Was she

safe? Was she alive? She had to be. He'd have felt it if she weren't.

Gods, I should have told her when I had the chance.

What about Torbin? The injury he'd witnessed him suffer from the Valfae was a horrific one, a wound that would guarantee death if not treated right away. Was his best friend, his brother, still alive?

Just as his thoughts were about to devour him once more, the lock on his cell door thumped loudly. Every unhealed wound burned in response as though they each anticipated more.

The wooden door creaked and groaned as it swung open. Footsteps echoed around the room as the Dark Fae entered, kicking the door closed behind him. Sauntering towards Kalen, Venrhys held a tray with a cup of water and a plate filled with horrible, thick looking mush in his hands.

"Good evening, Kalen. How are you?" he asked as he knelt, placing the tray on the floor and sliding it towards Kalen.

Kalen glared at him. "Living my best life," he replied sarcastically. If the chains were a little longer he'd wrap his hands around his neck – or try at least. He'd imagined it so many times, but the chains only let him move so far and were bolted to the floor next to the far wall.

Venrhys grinned at him, his black eyes close to brightening, almost as if he knew what Kalen was thinking. "That's what I like to hear. It brings me great joy when our guests are happy."

"No, it doesn't," Kalen mumbled.

The Dark Fae rose to his feet, laughter leaving his lips. "You're right, it doesn't."

Kalen knew from first-hand experience that Venrhys loved

nothing more than hearing someone in pain, watching as their body writhed in agony. The wounds Venrhys had inflicted on him had only just been healed the day before by one of the Dark Fae healers. At first, he'd assumed them lacking in skill, as many of his wounds remained unhealed after their treatment, but his suspicions grew to suspect that maybe all the Dark Fae intended to do was defer death.

Kalen lifted the cup of water before kicking the tray of food away. The water cooled and soothed his dry throat as he drank it.

"Not hungry?"

Kalen finished his drink in one go and set the empty cup down on the floor beside him. "You try eating that shit."

The Dark Fae's laughter echoed loudly through the room, bouncing off the walls so crisply that Kalen was sure everyone nearby would hear it. "I don't blame you. I wouldn't feed that muck to my dogs."

"If you've come here to annoy me to death, I'm not in the mood," Kalen muttered, swiping the back of his hand across his mouth.

"I've merely come to give you food. Wouldn't want you to starve to death now, would we?" Venrhys stood to his full height, towering over him.

Kalen didn't answer. He only willed the monster to leave the room and let him get lost in his thoughts once more. Suddenly, he was dragged to his feet and slammed against the wall, Venrhys's grip on his throat tight. Kalen tried to grab his wrist, but the chains wouldn't allow him.

Venrhys leaned in close to his face, his breath dancing across his cheek. "We are going to have so much fun, you and I."

Kalen's lungs burned, begging for air to be let back into

them, and a pained sound left his lips. Venrhys chuckled as he released him, letting him slump to the floor in a wheezing heap.

"Pathetic," he spat.

The Dark Fae walked to the door, the hinges groaning as he pulled it open. Stopping on the threshold, he looked at Kalen over his shoulder. "Eat. You'll need your strength for what I've got in store for you," he said, a sick, masochistic smirk spread across his face before he walked out. The door slammed shut followed by the sound of the lock being slid back into place.

Kalen gulped down a lungful of air as Venrhys's footsteps echoed down the corridor, before another door was opened and closed, signalling his departure. His heart pounded in his chest; only in solitude would he allow himself to look so weak.

Leaning his head back against the cool stone once again, he let his mind wander back to her. The way her smile lit up the room, her gorgeous eyes brightening every time she laughed. How soft her lips felt against his and the taste of her.

My Rexah.

A door slamming shut woke Kalen from his slumber. Sitting up, his eyes moved to the door, and realisation quickly set in that it wasn't his. Rubbing his eyes, willing his tiredness away, he sighed softly in what could have very well been relief.

He didn't fear them, not exactly, but he felt dread at the

thought of being caught off guard. Whenever he would be taken for his slice of torture, he wanted to be ready, to have prepared himself beforehand as much as possible for what he was to endure. Without that, he dared not think of how he would survive with his mind unbroken.

Growling and snarling emanated from the cell next to his. There were sounds of a scuffle, feet shuffling, and then a thud.

"Alright, alright," a male voice groaned softly. "Don't get too excited."

Chains clinked, and what Kalen could only assume was a Valfae huffed and grumbled. Loud, heavy footsteps followed, making their way to the door, and it left the room, closing the door with such force that dust trickled down from the ceiling in Kalen's cell.

It seemed only the more intelligent Valfae dealt with prisoners. He supposed the others were too monstrous and rabid to follow orders other than to kill. The smarter beasts couldn't speak, but at least they were perceptive enough to understand commands.

The man in the next cell groaned again in agony. If Kalen could have moved closer, he would have.

Curse these godsdamned chains.

"Are you alright?" Kalen asked, so hushed that only the individual in the next cell would hear him.

"I'll live," the male replied after a moment of silence.

Kalen spotted a tiny crack in the wall and shifted as close as the shackles allowed. "What did they do to you?"

His fellow inmate let out a pained chuckle. "I think the easier question to answer would be what *didn't* they do to me," he replied, his hoarse voice seeping through the fracture in the stone. It wasn't broken enough for Kalen to see the man in the cell next to him, but he could imagine how beaten he looked.

"What's your name?"

"Does it really matter? We're all dead here anyway," the man replied.

"We're going to be stuck here for a while, I just thought it would be nice to talk to someone. Take my mind off everything," Kalen said. *Off her* was what he really wanted to say.

"You can call me Crow," he told him.

Kalen's lips lifted into a soft smirk. "That's what you're going with?"

"You got a problem with that?"

"Absolutely not," Kalen replied.

"What's your name?" Crow asked.

He leaned back against the wall. "I'm Kalen."

There was a moment of silence before Crow spoke again. "It's nice to make your acquaintance, Kalen. Although, I wish it were under better circumstances."

Kalen chuckled softly. "It's good to meet you too."

Silence fell between them once more, and soon Kalen heard the gentle snores of his companion in the next cell. He'd let him sleep; he needed it to heal from whatever horrible things they'd done to him.

Kalen looked down at the injury on the inside of his arm and flashbacks of the serrated knife Venrhys had dragged along his flesh filled his mind. It was a nasty wound, and it hadn't healed well.

Kalen shifted his gaze to the window. The sky was beginning to lighten ever so slightly; morning was on its way. As always, his mind went back to the one person he could never get out of his head. Would she be sleeping right now or was she wide awake like he was, wishing to be with him as he did her?

Only Rexah could stop the constant ache in his chest. It felt as though his heart was trying to tear itself from his body to get to hers.

I will see her again, whether that be in this life or the next, he thought. *I'll find her again.*

He closed his eyes to see her again. He would spend a hundred lifetimes in the underworld, in the very depths of the darkest pits, if it meant she were safe. He would endure the torture, suffer being torn limb from limb to be put back together only to be torn apart again, so she could be free.

She's not safe. She will never be free. Are you really that much of a fool? You fool. You should be out there, by her side, protecting her. Instead, you're here in chains, like a dog. As helpless as you were the day you let your mother and brother die.

You let your mother and brother die.

Pathetic excuse for a fae. All that power and yet you did nothing, you still do nothing but lay down in surrender. She deserves better than you. Someone who will be by her side every step of the way. Not a fae who couldn't even protect his own family.

You are not worthy of her.

"I am worthy of—" His eyes flew open, wild and unfocused. His chest heaved as he breathed heavily, and when his eyes adjusted, he was met with the jet-black stare of Venrhys.

"What were you dreaming about?" The Dark Fae stood above him, a wicked grin spread across his face. "No need to tell me. I have a pretty good idea of what, or I should say *who*, you were dreaming of," he said, chuckling softly.

Kalen eased himself up into a sitting position. "To what do I owe this pleasure?" he asked as two Dark Fae guards entered the room.

"It's your turn," Venrhys told him, watching as the guards changed Kalen's shackles in the blink of an eye with a set that weren't connected to the floor.

The guards took him by his arms, pulled him to his feet, and began dragging him towards the open door, and as they crossed the threshold, Kalen heard Venrhys say, "It's playtime."

4

REXAH

"What the hell is that?"

"You never had one of these at the palace?" Storglass asked as he leaned past her and turned a brass knob. When he did, water flowed like rain from the lump of metal above their heads.

"No," Rexah replied whimsically, staring at the running water in absolute awe as she reached out to touch the warm liquid. "We didn't." Gods she would have loved it if they had. It would have made bathing a lot easier and quicker.

"Well, here you are. It's called a shower. They're wonderful."

"They're a relatively recent invention. Only a handful of homes in the realm have them," Arelle shouted from the next room before popping her head around the door. "Think of it as consumer research," she said. "Would you put an invention into the home of royalty if you didn't know it was completely safe first?"

It was a very good point, one that Storglass seemed satisfied with.

"Consider me absolutely fine with being their test subject." The Seer fixed eyes with the warlock then, and with a cock of her head she ushered him out of the bathroom.

The shower was amazing. She'd never experienced anything like it and couldn't wait to take another one. For the hour she'd spent under the hot spray, all her fears and worries washed away with the water down the drain, and she felt a little better. Some of the tension left her shoulders, filling her with much needed relief.

Unfortunately, solace didn't follow her out of the water, and as she sat on the top step of the front porch, a cup of hot lemon juice warming her hands, all of those worries came flooding back. Here she was, enjoying hot showers, cups of warm soothing drinks, and later a soft bed with fluffy pillows. All the while Kalen was enduring only the gods knew what, all because of the deal she had made with that monster. The guilt of making that bargain ate away at her, like woodlice chewing through rotten wood, but she'd had no other choice. Kalen hadn't allowed her an alternative. The fight in Grimhollow had gone south so quickly and making that deal with Venrhys was the only thing she could do to ensure they all got out of there alive, especially Torbin.

"I'm so sorry about what happened to Kalen," Arelle said softly behind her.

Rexah looked up over her shoulder, watching as she stepped closer and took the spot next to her on the porch holding a large glass filled with what looked like some sort of delicious looking fruit juice. Gazing down into her cup, Rexah replied, "I wish things had gone differently."

"Don't we all, some time or another." Arelle stared off into the trees, a look of guilt flashing in her eyes that disappeared as quickly as it had appeared before she turned to meet

Rexah's gaze. "What happened wasn't your fault. There was nothing else you could have done. I would have chosen the same path you did," the Seer told her. Arelle's features, like Storglass's, were youthful. Seers lived longer than warlocks, often longer than fae too. Arelle looked around the same age as she did, but Rexah couldn't help noticing how tired she looked, her skin ashen and her eyes dull.

"Are you okay?" Rexah asked, concern thick in her voice.

Arelle nodded. "I haven't used that much magic in a long time. Torbin's wound was serious."

Burnout, Rexah thought. She sipped her juice, savouring the warmth of the liquid as it slid down her throat. "I know I've already said this but thank you for saving his life."

"No need to thank me, Rexah," she replied, her voice as gentle as a summer breeze. "He will wake tomorrow. It will take a few days for his wounds to fully heal, but he will live. It would have been different if not for your effort and Storglass's magic. You both played a part in saving his life."

Rexah nodded and set her now empty cup down beside her. It was so peaceful here. Knowing that Arelle's home was protected and hidden by her magic made her feel safer, but she knew now more than ever that she'd never be completely out of danger.

Not until I get my hands on that sword.

"I see so much of her in you," Arelle whispered, pulling Rexah from her thoughts before they could completely consume her.

Rexah turned her gaze to the Seer, her eyes softening. She knew she spoke of her ancestor, Riona. "You do?"

Arelle's mint-green eyes were filled with grief and heartache. "Very much so. The way you hold yourself, the dimples that appear on your cheeks when you smile, and your complete and utter devotion to others."

Rexah's chest tightened at her words. Everyone compared her to Riona all the time, her legendary ancestor and former queen of Adorea, but it was the emotion on Arelle's face, in her voice, that made this occasion more sentimental and pulled at Rexah's heartstrings more than usual.

"That is, of course, apart from your hair and your eyes." Arelle smiled sadly.

She had lost her best friend – the one person she could talk to and spend time with, who wouldn't judge her and who she made so many memories with – and Rexah's heart twinged at the thought.

So did I.

"I wish I could have met her," Rexah said. "I could sure use her advice right now."

"How about relying on the advice of her best friend?" Arelle suggested, reaching out to tuck a loose strand of Rexah's dark hair behind her ear.

Rexah's violet eyes connected with Arelle's. "I'd like that very much."

"You are not alone in this fight. You never will be," Arelle told her. "When times get hard, just remember, you were born for this."

Rexah's eyebrows knitted together. "But what if I don't want any part in this? Don't I get a choice?"

"Fate works in mysterious ways. The gods never give reasons for the things they do, but their actions are never meaningless," Arelle explained. "Everything will still be so raw for you. I understand how hard it is."

"No, you don't. No one will ever understand how it feels."

Arelle reached out and gently took Rexah's hand. "I saw

Riona go through this exact journey. I saw how it tore her apart inside, especially when she found out she was pregnant. She never wanted any of it, but she knew how great an honour it was to be Chosen."

Rexah didn't flinch or pull her hand away. She was too engrossed by Arelle's words to do anything other than listen.

"All Riona wanted was to be the best mother she could be to her little girl. To provide her with a safe home and watch her grow into a strong, beautiful woman. She wanted a better world. Instead, she was taken from this life when her daughter was only two years old, Arius left an orphan due to her father's passing before she was born," Arelle continued.

"Every day when Riona would retire to her chambers, I'd be waiting for her so she could cry into my shoulder. I was there to help her through every agonizing emotion. I was the one who picked her back up, fixed her crown, and reminded her just how strong she was. So please do not say I don't know how you feel," Arelle said, her voice breaking towards the end.

"You're right, please forgive me," she said softly. "I didn't mean to be so insensitive."

Arelle gently squeezed Rexah's hand and wiped away her tears. "It's okay. Like I said, I understand."

"Will it ever go away? The grief? The pain?"

"No," Arelle told her simply, "but you'll learn to cope with it. You'll learn to live with the absence of those you lost."

Rexah nodded slowly. She wished there was a potion she could drink or a spell that could be cast that would take it all away, but sitting here talking with Arelle was helping. Simply knowing she had someone by her side who had already lived through this lifted some of the weight off her shoulders.

"I know this will be a silly question, but how are you feeling?" Arelle asked as she studied her as though she could see right through her.

Rexah let out a breath. "In all honesty? I'm feeling so many emotions right now that I don't know which one is the strongest."

Arelle nodded. "That's natural," she said before she gently squeezed her hand again. "We will find Kalen, I promise you."

"I know this sounds foolish, but it's like something is trying to tear my soul from my body. I haven't known him for very long, but I've never felt this way about anyone before," she said, her guilt kicking her in the gut again for feeling this way about someone and it not being Ryden, her fiancé before Adorea fell.

"It's not foolish at all, Rexah. The heart wants what the heart wants."

Rexah sighed deeply and closed her eyes. "I need to locate the sword first, that was our deal," she said, shaking her head. "I don't know where to start. It could be anywhere. It's like trying to find a needle in a haystack."

Arelle let go of her hand. "Take tonight to rest. I know it's difficult, but sleep will do you good and we can start fresh first thing tomorrow morning."

Rexah slowly nodded. "Okay."

She watched as Arelle rose to her feet. "I need to check on Torbin. I'll see you in the morning," the Seer said before walking inside.

Lifting her violet eyes, Rexah watched as the stars began to sparkle in the darkening sky. They winked their greeting, but it didn't feel the same without Kalen by her side asking what secrets they whispered to her. Nothing was the same without him.

Rexah picked up the empty cup as she rose to her feet and

headed back into the cottage. The warmth from the fireplace seeped into her skin as she walked to the kitchen to wash the cup. Storglass stepped out of the bathroom down the hall. He wore a pair of dark-green cotton trousers and a night shirt to match.

He probably conjured them with his magic, she thought.

His hazel eyes softened when he spotted her, and he ran his fingers through his damp hair as he made his way over to her in the kitchen.

He gently placed his hand on her shoulder. "I'd enquire as to how you're feeling, but I'm guessing Arelle already covered that."

Rexah nodded. "She did, but I appreciate the thought. I'm as well as I can be."

"You need to get some rest, Rexah," Storglass said quietly. "It won't magically make everything right in the world again, but you'll feel better."

"I appreciate your outlook on life," she replied with a tired smile as she rinsed the cup in the bowl of water.

Storglass gave her a sympathetic smile before leaning against the worktop and looking out into the room. "This part of the journey is going to be tough, but we will get through it together."

"Thank you, Storglass," she whispered.

The warlock nudged her shoulder comfortingly with his own. "Goodnight, Rexah," he said before walking down the hall to the back of the home and into the room he'd claimed as his own.

Rexah placed the clean cup on the drying rack and moved to the room where Torbin's room was, gently pushing the ajar door open further, the hinges squeaking quietly. Her heart ached to see him lying in the bed, unconscious and vulnerable, but she swore a little colour had returned to his pale cheeks.

Arelle looked over her shoulder to her. "Everything okay?"

"Yes," Rexah nodded. "I was wondering which chamber I should sleep in."

The Seer smiled. "The room to the left of this one."

Rexah thanked her and took one last look at Torbin before stepping away and into her designated room. It was small. White paint covered the walls with soft curtains to match. The bed called to her like a lullaby, and she sat down on the edge of it, kicking her boots off. They thumped softly against the wooden floorboards as she lay on top of the covers and blankets, closing her eyes. Taking a deep breath, she willed herself to fall asleep.

An hour passed and slumber never came to her. No matter how hard she commanded herself to drift off, she couldn't. She'd heard a little movement outside her room, but nothing that should have kept her awake. She'd heard Arelle leaving Torbin's room to go into her own about ten minutes ago, but silence since.

Rexah sighed in defeat and got up from the bed. There was no point in lying there staring at the ceiling, so she shuffled out of her room as quietly as possible.

The hallway was illuminated by the moonlight pouring in from the window. Torbin's room door creaked softly as she pushed it open and stepped inside. Tiptoeing over to him, she silently pulled the armchair to his bedside. "Sorry, Tor," she whispered to him as she lowered herself into the chair, "I just didn't want to be alone."

The fae didn't flinch, didn't move a muscle, as she reached over and gently took his limp hand in hers. Rexah got herself as comfortable as she could, facing Torbin. She watched as his chest rose and fell, slow and deep. It was the only comfort she took, knowing that he was still breathing.

He's still alive.

"Once you have recovered, we will find Kalen," she whispered. "We will bring him back. Sword or no sword." Rexah's chest tightened as she spoke of him. Every minute she sat here, he was suffering. "For every mark they make on him, every drop of blood they spill, I promise I will make each and every one of them pay in kind."

Tears stung her eyes as the silence pressed in on her. As she closed her eyes and tears slid down her face, she willed her panic away, back into the cage she kept it in along with the grief she had yet to fully process. A lot had happened in such a short space of time, so much loss and pain; she could barely comprehend the memories she would have to unpack and work through.

That's if I'm still alive after all this to do so.

5

KALEN

Sunlight from the barred window glinted off the numerous knives, pliers and other metal instruments that hung on the stone wall to Kalen's left. Some were still stained with his blood, while others had yet to taste it.

The knives weren't the only tools he'd used on him; he'd brought his power into play to inflict pain too, malicious swirling energy that spread agony throughout his nerves, sinking deep into his bones. Kalen could still feel the remnants of dark magic skittering like ants along his broken skin, but the pain had disappeared, and he wasn't sure if that was a good sign or a bad one.

Leather straps held him down at the waist and legs, and heavy chains still encircled his wrists so tightly that any movement was an arduous task.

Laying his head back against the hard, cold stone slab he was strapped to, a heavy sigh left his lips. He had every faith that Rexah would find the sword. His only wish was that she wouldn't hand it over to Venrhys for the sake of his freedom. He wanted her as far away from Venrhys as possible.

A sound pulled him from his thoughts. It was small, but thanks to his fae senses, he heard it clear as day. There was a soft creak, and his gaze slid to the door. His heart was in his throat at who he saw standing there, at who he watched close the door with utter silence behind them.

"R-Rexah?" he croaked.

Her violet eyes shone in the sunlight pouring in like a beacon. A look of relief washed over her beautiful face as she hurried over to him.

"N-no … no, you shouldn't be here. You can't be here," he said as panic blossomed in his chest. "Get out … now. Leave before he comes back."

"Shh, it's okay. It is going to be fine. I'm getting you out of here," she whispered as she reached out and stroked his cheek with her soft fingers.

"I don't understand. How did you—"

"Everything is going to be okay, my love."

Kalen couldn't help himself; he closed his eyes as he leaned into her touch. It felt surreal, as though he were caught up in a dream.

"You're safe."

Everything he felt but had never said to her came to him; it eased the pain that lingered everywhere. He would tell her everything.

"Rex …" His exhaustion and the true weight on his heart threw the room into a haze. "I …"

My love.

An icy realisation spread through him like the roots of a tree stretching through the earth.

She's never called me that before. He opened his eyes and looked up at her once more only to be met with Venrhys's smug face.

"You really thought it was her, didn't you?"

"Fuck!" Kalen flinched away from him as though he had been burned and strained against the bindings holding him in place. "Stay the fuck out of my head!"

"It's far too easy to mess with you, Kalen. I thought you were a fierce fae warrior?" Venrhys chuckled deeply. "She is your weakness, Kalen," he said before he surveyed him further. "Should you witness her death? or shall I let her watch you go first? I haven't decided which I'd prefer to see. Either way, I will enjoy ending you both."

Kalen growled as his gaze followed Venrhys around the stone slab and over to the wall of torture devices.

Venrhys crossed his arms over his chest and cocked his head to the side as he studied them. "Hmm, which one shall I use this time?"

Kalen glared daggers into his back, cursing him.

Venrhys turned, a mischievous look settling across his features. "Only joking." He laughed. "I've had my fun with you today."

As if on cue, the door swung open and two Dark Fae guards stepped into the room, bowing their heads to their general.

"Escort Mr Vidarr back to his cell," he ordered in a bored tone.

The guards moved forward and untied the leather straps before hauling Kalen to his feet.

"Wait."

The guards halted at the command causing the chains of his shackles to clink together. Kalen mentally rolled his eyes. *What now?*

"No need to be gentle with him on the way there," Venrhys said.

Kalen heard the smugness in his voice, could feel it radiating off him before being tugged out of the room.

Halfway down the corridor Kalen's legs gave out, but the guards didn't care. They continued to pull him, letting his limbs drag along the stone beneath him. Kalen gritted his teeth when his knees caught on the rougher parts of the floor. It wasn't until the guards threw him into his cell that the pain from his wounds began to make themselves known once again. One of the guards changed his cuffs and secured the chain to the floor once more, and he kicked Kalen hard in the side as a parting gesture. The guards left, slamming the door shut behind them.

Kalen groaned in pain, spitting blood onto the floor as he curled up in agony. The guard had managed to land his kick straight into one of his lacerations.

I am a godsdamned fool, he internally cursed himself. Of course, it hadn't been Rexah. He'd have scented her before she entered the room. At the time, in his exhausted state, he'd been so convinced it was her. He took slow, deep breaths as the pain in his side eased slightly.

"I'd ask if you are okay but that would be a stupid question," Crow's voice emanated from the tiny crack in the wall. "Don't worry. You'll learn to switch off the pain in no time."

"Thanks for the advice," Kalen groaned as he shuffled across the floor and sat back against the cold wall.

There was a moment of silence before Crow spoke again, "Venrhys seems to like you."

"What makes you think that?" Kalen asked as he inspected his wounds. The injury to his side was the worst and was still bleeding slightly, thanks to the guard.

"Well, for starters he's visited your cell more times in the week you've been here than he has mine, and I've been here for months."

"That doesn't mean anything. It's probably because I'm fresh meat," Kalen replied dismissively. "He'll get bored of me eventually."

Crow chuckled softly. "Or you're special to him for some reason."

Kalen didn't respond. The less anyone knew about Rexah, the better. Not that it seemed like Crow was getting out any time soon, but Kalen couldn't be too careful.

"How did he capture you?" Crow asked him.

"On the road as I was on my way home," he replied, the lie rolling off his tongue with ease. "I guess you could say I was in the wrong place at the wrong time."

Crow chuckled, the sound crackling in his chest. "I suppose we were all in the wrong place at the wrong time."

"Is that how he captured you?" Kalen asked.

"No. I was exactly where I was supposed to be, but the gods had other plans for me it turns out," Crow replied.

Kalen ripped off a small section of his shorts and folded it up before placing it against his bleeding side, his teeth clenching against the sting. His shorts were dirty, so it wasn't the best idea, but he had nothing else.

Leaning his head back, hissing softly at the contact of the fabric against his injury, he gazed up at the cracked stone ceiling. He hadn't been here for long, but it already felt like an eternity had passed. It was worth it though; every slow second that ticked by knowing it wasn't *her* that sat in this cell was worth it.

"Where do you hail from, Kalen?"

"Vellwynd," he answered.

"Interesting. I went to Vellwynd once. It's a beautiful place," Crow told him.

Was, Kalen thought. *It was a stunning place.*

He missed his home terribly. He missed his mother and his little brother. Kalen shook his head, shoving the memories of the day he'd lost them to the back of his mind before grief could drag him under. "What about you? Where do you come from?"

"Ah, that doesn't matter. My home is likely nothing but ruins now thanks to those monsters." He sighed.

Kalen closed his eyes as a pulse of exhaustion washed through him. It felt as though he were on a ship traveling through rough waters, and for a moment he wobbled and moved with the current, lost in imagining he was free.

Opening his eyes, he peeled the scrap of clothing from his wound. It had thankfully stopped bleeding, so he tossed the bloody material across the room. The air stung his uncovered laceration, but he didn't care. The fact he could feel the pain again was a good sign.

It means I'm still alive.

"Has anyone ever escaped?" Kalen found himself asking.

Crow was quiet for a moment. "Yes. The person who occupied your cell before you managed to get out," he answered.

Kalen shifted his gaze to the tiny crack in the wall. "Did he make it all the way?"

"They let him think he'd outsmarted them, let him think he'd done it. Just as his foot crossed the threshold and touched the dirt outside, they crushed his skull," Crow told him. "At least that's what the guards said."

"Why would they tell you?"

Crow huffed a laugh. "To warn me what would happen if I was ever dumb enough to try myself, I guess."

Unease settled in his gut. Escape wouldn't be easy in his current condition even if he could somehow find the strength to burst out of his shackles. He wouldn't make it far, and he didn't doubt for one second that Venrhys wouldn't go back on his word to Rexah and kill him, deal or no.

"One day, Crow," Kalen said, slumping down the wall, "one day, we'll get out of here."

"Of course we will," Crow said with a booming laugh, "when it's time for them to bury us."

His fellow inmate certainly had a strange sense of humour, one that in different circumstances might have been entertaining, but Kalen couldn't laugh – not when there was a good chance Crow was right.

Kalen managed to stop himself from groaning as he lay down on the freezing ground. Crow's laughter grew louder, seeping eerily through that small gap in the cell wall, and for the first time Kalen pondered if his neighbour was close to losing his mind.

6

CROW

is new friend must have fallen asleep. Crow had muttered a few things to him, but the man hadn't answered. He wouldn't bother him any longer; he'd let him sleep. The gods knew he needed it.

It wasn't difficult to imagine what the Dark Fae General might have in store for the man. Sure, he'd already enacted some torture, but that was only the beginning. The poor guy didn't know what was coming, and Crow wasn't about to be the one to tell him.

He'd learned quickly to keep himself to himself, to look out for number one. That's the only thing that kept him going each minute, each hour, each day. Just before his friend had arrived, he'd started to make peace with the fact that he was going to die here. In the cell or the torture room? he didn't know. All he knew for certain was that there was no escape other than death, and the quicker Kalen came to terms with that the better and easier it would be.

Laying his head back against the stone wall, he fixed his gaze to the ceiling. If anyone had asked him a year ago where he saw himself in a year's time, it certainly wasn't in this cell. Everything had turned to shit in the blink of an eye, and there was nothing he could have done to stop it, no matter how much he'd tried to convince himself otherwise in those first few weeks.

Even if he did somehow escape, there was nothing left for him on the outside world. No one would be waiting with open arms for him. No home with a roaring fire to greet him. He'd made peace with life as it was now.

All he could do now was wait patiently and count down the days until the sweet touch of death released him from this prison.

7

REXAH

The chirping of birds singing their morning songs was what woke Rexah from her slumber, and the pain in her neck told her that she'd fallen asleep in an armchair. Groaning, she slowly shifted to a more comfortable position, and when she opened her eyes, she was met with familiar amber orbs that burned into hers like an open flame.

The realisation of what awaited her was slow as she blinked away the remnants of sleep, but when it hit her, her eyes opened wide. "Torbin?"

The fae smiled at her. "Good morning, Rexah."

She scanned her eyes over him excitedly. The colour had come back to his cheeks, and all signs of a fever had gone. Once she convinced herself she wasn't dreaming, once she stared and assessed him deeply, she leaned forward and wrapped her arms around him. Torbin chuckled and held her close.

"Thank the gods," she whispered.

Torbin's hand ran up and down her back comfortingly. "I missed you too."

Rexah buried her face into his shoulder as tears burned in her eyes. "We almost lost you."

"Don't worry, Rex, I'm not going anywhere," he assured her.

She slowly pulled away to look at him. "You don't know how happy I am to see you sitting up and awake. I was so scared."

"I woke up and you were holding my hand," he said before a mischievous smile spread across his lips. "But it was your snoring that woke me."

She gasped. "I don't snore!"

He chuckled deeply. "I hate to be the one to tell you this, but you do, *very* loudly."

They stared at each other for a moment, neither one of them speaking, before they burst into a fit of laughter. It struck her then that she couldn't remember the last time she'd laughed. The thought sent a sudden wave of sadness through her, a sorrowful nod to what once was.

Rexah found his gaze once more. "It's so good to have you back, Tor," she whispered.

Torbin reached out and took her hand, squeezing it gently. "It's good to be back."

"How are you feeling? Are you in pain? Do you want me to get Arelle?" she asked, fussing over him.

"No, I'm fine. I'd love some fresh air though," he replied, his gaze moving to the window.

Her eyes softened, and she nodded. "Fresh air sounds good."

Rexah rose from her chair as Torbin pulled the covers off himself and moved to a sitting position. She offered him her hand. "Take your time," she said as she helped him slowly stand on his feet.

Torbin held onto her, trying not to put too much weight on her. "Thank you," he said softly.

The door creaked slightly as she pulled it open, and she guided him down the hallway, moving at a slow and comfortable pace that Torbin had set.

"What happened?" he asked apprehensively. "I don't remember much."

Her eyes saddened as she looked up at him. "We can talk once we're outside. I'll explain everything."

Torbin's eyes filled with concern, but he nodded his head slowly and they continued down the hallway and through the living area.

The air was cool, and the crisp morning breeze that floated by was soothing. Goosebumps flooded her skin as she sat beside Torbin on the back porch. The pink and white flowers swayed back and forth gently, rippling like a wave. The sun was shining brightly in the clear blue sky.

Rexah went back to that awful day in Grimhollow and began to tell Torbin what happened and how they came to be in Arelle's home, about how Venrhys took Kalen, the deal that had been made, and their escape into the forest.

"I was so worried about you, Tor," Rexah said quietly, nausea bubbling in her stomach at the memories. "Your skin grew paler with each hour that passed. I felt so helpless, just like I did when Adorea was attacked."

Torbin gently rubbed her back. "You'll never feel that way again, not if I can help it. I'm sorry I worried you."

Sliding her purple gaze to him, Rexah shook her head. "No, don't apologise. You didn't intentionally get yourself hurt. If anything, *I* should be the one apologising."

"Why?" he asked as his brow furrowed.

She hugged her arms as the breeze grew stronger. "If it

weren't for me then you wouldn't have been injured, Kalen would still be here with us and—"

Rexah was cut off by Torbin pulling her close, her head instinctively resting on his shoulder.

"Don't put any of this on yourself. Your shoulders already bare too much," he whispered to her. "You saved my life, Rex."

The words sunk into her like a stone sinking to the bottom of a lake. They soaked into her bones, heating them. She felt that warmth, that compassion of a dear friend, spread throughout her body, and she felt herself relax too deeply for it to be regular. "Did you just use your healing powers on me?" she asked softly.

"Maybe," he replied coyly.

Rexah smiled. "Thank you. Also, just for the record, Storglass saved your life too. He did more to help you than I could."

A chuckle rumbled through his chest. "He did, indeed. And Arelle too."

Rexah saw a sparkle in his eyes, and his cheeks glowed a soft pink colour when he mentioned Arelle. She smiled before sighing softly. "I don't know where to begin to look for the sword," she said, her chest tightening. "Every second that goes by is another second Kalen is trapped with the Dark Fae. Only the gods know what they've done to him already, what *he's* done to him. But now you're awake, we can at least begin to figure something out."

Torbin pulled away slightly and looked down at her, his fiery eyes full of dark determination. "I will help you, we all will, no matter what it takes. We will free Kalen, you will find the sword, you will kill every single one of those bastards, and

I will be by your side every step of the way, striking them down with you."

Rexah's eyes softened as she absorbed the comforting sound of her friend's voice once again. "This road we've taken is a dangerous one, Tor. I don't know if any of us will survive."

"Then at least we'll go together," he said with a smile that didn't reach his eyes.

A chill slid down Rexah's spine like paint dripping down a canvas. Torbin was trying to be positive, and while she appreciated his attempt at lifting the morale, she knew they couldn't take any further steps down this path without a solid plan.

How do I plan for a journey when the destination is a mystery?

"Good morning."

Both Rexah and Torbin turned to the Seer who leaned against the doorframe. Her teal locks were pulled back into a loose braid that disappeared down her back. The knee length, lavender silk dressing gown she wore swayed slightly in the light breeze making her dusty-pink silk pyjama's visible, the bottoms stopping at the top of her thighs.

Rexah glanced at Torbin whose cheeks were flushed once more. She grinned as she got to her feet. "Good morning, Arelle."

Arelle's mint-green eyes lingered on Torbin for a moment longer before she looked at Rexah and smiled. "Breakfast is ready. Although, Storglass was the one who prepared it, so we have yet to see how good his cooking skills are."

Stepping through the threshold, Rexah looked over her shoulder to see Torbin rise to his feet, the blush on his cheeks still apparent. Grinning, she walked further into the cottage and followed the delicious smell of eggs and sausages that made her stomach growl. Storglass was humming a tune to himself as she rounded the corner. Rexah halted in her tracks as she took in the sight before her.

Storglass stood behind the island counters, a large white chef hat on his head and a stained, white apron wrapped around his body. Various pots and pans littered the counter as well as half a dozen eggshells and other cooking ingredients.

He looked up, mid hum, and grinned when he saw her. "Your Highness!" he said. "Or is it Your Majesty now?"

Choosing to ignore his question, Rexah replied, "Good morning, Storglass. You're rather chipper this morning."

"I had the most wonderful night's sleep! Also, my magic has fully returned, and I can sometimes get a little buzzed when that happens … so please, forgive me," he said as he stirred the contents of one of the pots.

Rexah shook her head. "No need for apologies. It's refreshing to see someone so upbeat. Is there anything I can do to help?" she asked as she eyed the ingredients laid out on the counter.

"Absolutely not. Please, take a seat. Your food will be with you momentarily," he told her.

She smiled and nodded as she headed to the dining table next to the window on the other side of the room. The chair creaked slightly as she sat down, and she waited patiently until Torbin and Arelle walked in a few moments later.

"It would be a shame if after all the work Arelle has done I die from food poisoning. Are you sure you've done this before?"

Storglass turned abruptly and smiled widely. "Torbin!"

"Storglass."

"It's … wow. It's good to see you." Storglass nodded and sighed happily. "A little strange, actually. We were worried."

Torbin nodded grimly before taking in the sight of Storglass in his chef attire with a smirk. "Where did you get the hat?"

"For the record, it's not mine," Arelle said as she made her way to the dining table and sat down beside Rexah.

Storglass smiled widely. "I conjured it. Do you not think I suit it?"

"It compliments you very well, Storglass," Torbin replied. "Do you need help with the food?"

Storglass shook his head, the chef hat wobbling on his head like jelly. "Please, take a seat."

Torbin nodded and walked over to the table, sitting across from Rexah, giving her a smile as he lowered himself into the seat.

"It's good to see you up and about, Torbin," Arelle said.

Torbin shifted his gaze to the Seer. "I want to thank you for everything you did for me. You saved my life, and I will never forget that."

Arelle opened her mouth to speak, but it was as though the words became lost. They sat staring wordlessly at each other, and Rexah thought she might stop breathing with the tension that lingered between them. Thankfully, Storglass chose that moment to present them with their food, and Arelle and Torbin took to looking anywhere but at each other.

In true Storglass style he didn't bring the plates to the table himself. Instead, he snapped his fingers and their food materialised in front of them. The smell of the eggs and sausages filled her nostrils instantaneously, and she felt her stomach grumble more aggressively.

Rexah grinned as she watched him walk to the table and sit down on the other side of Arelle. With one final snap of his fingers the chef hat and apron vanished.

"Dig in everyone," he said as he picked up his fork.

No one wasted any time in tucking into the freshly made food. The only sounds were forks scraping against plates and Storglass chewing his food.

"Storglass, would you mind using your magic to conjure us some fresh orange juice please?" Rexah asked, gritting her teeth.

The warlock studied her for a moment. "Of course, are you all right?" he asked as he clicked his fingers. A large jug of orange juice and empty glasses appeared on the table, clinking together slightly.

Rexah nodded. "I'm fine."

Arelle smirked. "I'll say it if you don't want to," she said before shifting her gaze to Storglass. "You chew loudly, and it is incredibly annoying."

Torbin burst out laughing at the look of shock on Storglass's face. Rexah felt her cheeks burn softly.

"My apologies, I didn't realise," he said, his hazel eyes sliding to Rexah. "No one has ever told me I chew loudly."

"I hope you don't take any offence, but it's something I've never been able to withstand. Even when it was my grandmother," Rexah replied as she poured herself a glass of orange juice.

"No offence taken," he said, grinning playfully before he shoved a forkful of fluffy eggs into his mouth, chewing much quieter this time, much to Rexah's relief.

"We have more important things to discuss," Rexah said, the cold drink soothing her throat as she sipped it. Placing it back down on the table, she looked at them. "I know we need to find the sword, but I cannot let Kalen stay in Venrhys's clutches any longer."

Torbin's eyes softened. "I will be at your side whatever

path you choose, but we need to think about this carefully. We need a plan."

"I agree with Torbin," Storglass said. "We need a backup plan, a backup plan for our backup plan, and so on and so forth."

"We need to find out where they are keeping him," Rexah said, pushing the food around her plate with her fork. "Gods, none of this is going to be easy."

"No, it won't, but you have me," Arelle said, smiling wickedly at her, "and I know how to find where they're hiding out."

Rexah stared back at her, dumbfounded. "How?"

"You saw my crystal ball." She smirked at her. "I can find Kalen through it. All I need is something of his."

"We should have known better than to think you hadn't already devised a plan, Arelle." Torbin looked to the Seer as though in awe, but he soon caught himself and coughed away the moment. "Very good."

Rexah set her fork down, hiding a smirk. "I have one of his daggers, will that do?"

The Seer nodded. "Yes, I can work with that. Like you said, it won't be easy, but I will find him, whatever it takes."

"Thank you," Rexah whispered, the back of her throat tightening. Feeling Torbin's eyes on her, she looked over to him. He gave her a look of understanding. *He's going through this too. It must be worse for him,* she thought. She nodded her head softly at him, letting him know she knew and that everything would be okay, even if she didn't fully believe it herself.

"Have you had any other dreams?" Arelle asked her, pulling her attention from Torbin.

Rexah shook her head. "No, but I had ... I think I had some sort of vision. It was strange."

Arelle's eyes filled with intrigue. "Go on."

"I was in a book shop in Dorasa browsing the shelves when one fell to the floor close by. It had no title, but the Shadow Star graced its cover," she told her. "When I picked up the book, I was in a different place. It's hard to explain."

"You're doing well," Arelle encouraged her gently. "What happened next?"

"Someone was standing before me. It was like he was made from the night sky. Stars and shadows swirled all over him. I couldn't see his face, but he spoke to me, told me that war was coming and that I needed to find the sword," she continued. "Black raven wings sprouted from his back, and he called me his *Chosen*."

"The Raven God," Arelle whispered.

Rexah nodded. "It couldn't have been anyone else."

"Did you find anything of use in the book?" Storglass asked.

"No. It was about the history of the Raven God and how he made the sword," she replied, finishing off her food.

Arelle sipped her orange juice. "The gods rarely show themselves to anyone. I suppose for you it's different because you're his Chosen, but it's still amazing nonetheless when it happens."

Sitting back in her seat, Rexah sighed. "The gods never interfered when my kingdom was being attacked or when Vellwynd fell, so why did he come to me?"

"It has always been the goal of the Gods of Light to keep their creations safe from harm, but they can only do so much; what's left of their power is limited. That's why they want to one day return to this dimension. But for every God of Light, there is a Dark God," Arelle explained. "As you know, the

Dark Gods want to destroy the Gods of Light and claim our dimension for their own."

The food in Rexah's stomach turned sour and threatened to come back up. "I cannot let that happen."

"*We* cannot let that happen," Torbin said. "I cannot speak for Arelle and Storglass, but, as I said before, I'll be by your side to whatever end awaits us."

Arelle gave Torbin a heart-warming smile before turning her gaze back to Rexah. "I am with you too, Rexah Ravenheart."

Storglass grinned and lifted his glass. "As am I. So, it's settled. *We* will not let it happen. *We* will stop the evil bastards in their tracks, no matter what," he said, lifting his drink higher in a toast.

Torbin and Arelle lifted theirs too and said in unison, "No matter what."

Tears burned the back of Rexah's eyes, but she managed to blink them away as she raised her own glass.

"No matter what."

8

VENRHYS

It was exciting, having a new plaything. Especially when they meant so much to your enemy. It was the best kind of leverage, the ultimate advantage. He would never get tired of watching how Kalen flinched and winced when he dragged his blade across his flesh. He relished in the way Kalen refused to cry out in pain and struggled to keep his wailing at bay.

Everything was going exactly to plan, and soon the Elder would be strong enough to leave his chamber and take the realm for his own, to spread evil and chaos and help the Dark Gods prevail.

The corridor was dimly lit, just how the Dark Fae liked it. As much as Venrhys enjoyed his visits to the castle, his nerves always managed to worm their way through him. He was a devout follower of the Elder and would do anything to appease him. It had been a great honour to be chosen as one of the Dark Army Generals. He was one of five, and they were a powerful and terrifying bunch of great distinction.

The walls of the passageway were bare and painted a deep

blood-red – the Elder's choice. Dark wood covered the floors throughout the castle, complimenting the walls perfectly. Everything here felt refined, more in keeping with the elegance of the Dark Fae agenda; the castle held within its own right an air of superiority, more so than the Keep. It was menacing, certainly held its own as a Dark Fae hold – the mountains were as demanding for attention as their cause – but within it they kept scum. *Let them experience the abrasions of our disgust,* he thought. *Let them rot within the dark, cruel mountains and reflect on their fate.*

Venrhys stopped outside the large double doors, waiting to be granted access. The two Valfae at either side of the entryway ran their crimson eyes over him, confirming he wasn't a threat.

"Come on, boys. You really should recognise me by now," he told them.

The creature to the right let out a huff before both beasts straightened their spines and stepped aside just as the doors shuddered open. Venrhys grinned at the Valfae before he continued inside.

His footsteps echoed as he descended the short staircase and walked across the obsidian floor. The chamber was colossal. Tall bookcases filled the walls to the left and right, both separated in the middle by two stained glass windows depicting the Dark Gods – each more frightening than the next – and on the far side, a huge fireplace graced the wall, the flames within burning high, filling the room with a soft glow. In front of the fireplace sat two tall-backed armchairs, both dyed a beautiful wine-red colour – and sat in one of those chairs was the Elder.

The coppery scent of blood filled Venrhys's nose as he drew closer.

You came at feeding time, you fool.

"Please accept my apologies master, I did not realise the time. You are busy," Venrhys said softly.

Quiet sounds of choking emanated from the other side of the chair. First, a struggle, the gasping for air, then a breathy sigh of release. Venrhys watched as the body of a young fae woman hit the floor with a sickening thud, bleeding puncture wounds in her neck. The trickle of blood on the floor twinkled in the firelight.

"That's quite alright, General. I'm done now," the Elder said in his croaking voice. "Come, take a seat beside me."

Venrhys followed his orders and stepped to the empty chair next to him. He bowed deeply in respect before sitting down. "Thank you for seeing me on such short notice."

"You have an update for me I take it?" the Elder asked, sitting back in his chair.

Venrhys took in the sight of him. The last time he'd visited a month ago, the Elder looked horrific, nothing but a reanimated corpse. Now, the colour had come back to his pale skin, and his black hair, once short and wispy, fell to just below his sharply pointed ears. The Elder's eyes were different to that of the other Dark Fae. Where their eyes were completely black, the Elder's irises were pure white. They were uniquely haunting, and it always sent a slither of fear flowing through Venrhys's body. He revered that power, that leadership; there was nothing else that made him feel this way, so full of purpose.

The fae blood must have been working. The Dark Fae's blood was too impure to allow him vitality, so he relied on the blood of normal fae for the healing magic within their lifeblood. It would never be enough to sustain him forever, nor would it return him to his full power, but it would suffice until they could get their hands on the Shadow Star.

"I do." Venrhys nodded.

The Elder wiped the blood from his chin. "Go ahead."

Venrhys squared his shoulders slightly. "I have captured the Chosen One's favourite. He sits in a cell in the Keep. She has made a deal with me. She will find the Shadow Star and hand it over in exchange for Kalen."

The Elder surveyed his general, his eyes scanning over his features, searching for something known only to himself. "You're certain this plan will work?" he asked.

Venrhys nodded. "I am very confident. He means a great deal to her, and she will do anything to have him back."

The Elder leaned back against his seat. "How close is she to obtaining the sword?"

"I'm afraid I cannot answer that, my lord," Venrhys replied. "But I will keep a close eye on her movements."

"It is imperative that she finds the sword, but we cannot let her activate it, not yet at least. She will be harder to kill if she taps into the sword's power," the Elder said, drumming his fingers against the arm of the chair. "Keep me up to date with her progress. If she makes any significant development, I want to know about it."

"Of course. You will be the first to know," Venrhys confirmed.

"Anything else?"

Venrhys shook his head softly. "That's all, for now at least. We have Kalen and we made a deal for the sword. Now we wait and see what her next move is. We have the perfect motivation for her to do as we desire, and I doubt it will take her long to find the sword."

The Elder nodded, seemingly satisfied with things as they

were. He snapped his fingers and a Dark Fae guard appeared, almost slinking out of the shadows. "Clean this up," he ordered, motioning to the body of the fae woman on the floor.

The guard didn't speak, only bowed to his master before moving forward and picking her up. Her body was limp in his arms, her lifeless eyes trained on Venrhys. Even he found it quite haunting, and it sent a familiar thrill through his spine as the guard turned and headed for the doors.

The power here was immense.

Venrhys turned his gaze back to the floor where a small pool of blood was soaking into the dark wood. "Do you require any more fae?"

"My stock has recently been refilled," the Elder told him. "Thank you for the offer though."

The general tipped his head to him. "Always, my lord."

"I don't know if I've ever told you this, Venrhys," he started, "but of all my generals, you are most certainly my favourite. Do you know why?"

His words made Venrhys's heart pound with pride. "I do not."

"You follow your orders without complaint. The work is done efficiently and on time. The best results are always obtained when you oversee the task I set out," he responded. "The others have their grumbles. They still get the work done, but not as well as you."

"Those are very kind words. Thank you, my lord," Venrhys said. "But if I may, if you're unhappy with their work ethic, why are they still in your employ?"

The Elder slid his gaze to meet his. "It's something I've been considering these past few months myself. If there are any guards you rate highly, send them to me. I think a change in the ranks is in order."

Venrhys nodded. "There are a few who have proved their loyalty to the cause in the past couple of weeks. I'll be sure to send them to you."

They sat in a comfortable silence for a moment. The only sound was the crackling and snapping of the fire burning bright in the fireplace.

Venrhys watched the Elder. He could see he still had a lot of healing to do. The wound Riona had inflicted on him in the Battle of Adorea had been a terrible one. It had been an awful blow to their side of the conflict and had pushed them thousands of steps back. They'd been so close victory, to snuffing out their enemies, only to have it ripped away in mere seconds. It had taken time and effort to get back on their feet, but they were getting stronger by the day. Soon they'd be back to their full strength and would be ready to attack once again, and this time they would not fail.

"Our efforts this time will not be in vain."

A sinister smile cursed the Elder's face. "Indeed. They might have won the battle that day, but they will not win the war. They will be bowing at my feet, one way or another."

"The soldiers are stronger than they were before. Our army has more than doubled in size," Venrhys said, a smirk spreading across his face. "They won't know what hit them."

The Elder nodded. "Continue to ensure your soldiers stick to their regime. We cannot afford for any of them to fall out of line. If they do, eliminate them. Only the best will do," the Elder instructed.

"As you wish."

The Elder shifted in his seat, crossing one leg over the other. "Go, Venrhys. Return to me when you have more news."

Venrhys rose to his feet and bowed deeply at the waist. "My lord."

He turned and headed to the small staircase. He would make certain that their army was at its strongest. The only prospect more exciting than his new plaything was killing the Chosen One and bringing the realm to its knees once and for all.

This was going to be so much fun.

9

REXAH

The familiar weight of Kalen's dagger in her grasp made Rexah's chest tighten with sorrow. She recalled the day he'd given it to her, the first time she held it in her hand. She knew how much it meant to him and kept a silent promise to handle it with care, to keep it safe until she could return it to him. His absence filled her with a different kind of grief as she rubbed her fingers along the hilt, one she never knew was possible to feel, and it clawed at the cage she kept it locked in, begging to be released so it could devour her.

Rexah's stomach flipped with nerves. What if this didn't work? What if the dagger wasn't enough for Arelle to make the connection? So many thoughts, what ifs and buts swirled through her racing mind. They had to try at least, for Kalen's sake.

Leaning against the wall, she watched as Arelle moved back and forth across the space, hurriedly preparing and setting everything up at her alter. She knew exactly where everything was on the shelves; she could probably do this with her eyes closed, and Rexah found it fascinating. The only light in the area emanated from the candles Arelle had lit on the table and around the area she used for rituals and blessings.

"I'm proud of you," Torbin whispered to her.

Rexah looked up at him, confused. "Proud of me? For what?" she whispered back.

His amber eyes met hers, almost glowing in the darkness. "After what happened in Grimhollow, most people would have fallen apart, but not you. You never gave up."

Her violet eyes softened. "Well, I think we can agree that I'm not like most people. For better or worse."

Torbin chuckled quietly and nodded. "You certainly aren't, Rex."

Having Torbin at her side was a comfort Rexah welcomed. It felt almost as though Kalen were nearby, simply in another room.

"Okay, I'm ready," Arelle announced, wiping her hands on her dress.

Rexah took a deep breath and walked over to her, holding out Kalen's dagger, which she accepted with a "thank you". She took a few steps back to give the Seer some space and once again felt some relief when Torbin was by her side. Storglass stood at the other side of her fae companion, studying everything his friend did.

Arelle cast her gaze across the three of them. "I need complete silence whilst doing this. Any distraction, no matter how small, will break my concentration and the connection will be lost."

"Our lips are sealed," Storglass said, nodding softly.

The Seer shifted her gaze to Rexah. "Are you ready?"

"As ready as I will ever be," she replied with a small nod.

Arelle shifted in her seat, straightening her spine as she clutched the hilt of Kalen's dagger in both hands and held it to her chest. Closing her eyes, she began to whisper a chant in a language Rexah didn't understand, but she recognised it. It was Seer Speak. Never in her lifetime did she ever think she would meet a Seer, never mind hearing the ancient language first hand from one.

Soft wisps of pink and light-green energy began to swirl through her fingertips and around the dagger. Rexah didn't dare move or breathe in fear of distracting her, but her eyes widened as she watched the blade begin to glow blue, just like it did whenever Kalen summoned his power into it. The cobalt energy seeped into Arelle's fingers before it dissipated completely. Arelle opened her eyes and set the weapon down carefully on the table next to the crystal ball. She took another deep breath, grounding herself before lifting her hands to the mystical sphere before her.

Rexah watched in amazement as Arelle pressed her fingers against its surface, the light within glowing a little brighter as she sank her fingers in, only stopping when it reached her knuckles.

The hum of magic filled the air, flooding Rexah's skin with goosebumps and making every hair on her body stand on end. She watched as the crystal ball pulsed once with power, and Arelle jerked. Pink and mint-green veins spread over the backs of her hands and stopped above her wrist. The Seer gasped as another surge of energy passed through her, and when Arelle opened her eyes, they were completely white. No colour and no sparkle.

No one moved.

No one breathed.

Arelle was as still as a statue. She was so motionless that Rexah feared she'd stopped breathing altogether. Her heart was pounding fiercely like a drum in her chest as she willed the Seer to do something, anything, to show she was still with them. The heavy silence in the room only added to the suspense.

Just when Rexah opened her mouth to speak, she noticed Arelle begin to shake. The Seer's body trembled and the white of her eyes flickered like a flame. Rexah slid her worried gaze to Storglass who met her stare with a concerned frown, his hazel eyes filled with unease.

Suddenly, Arelle gasped loudly. Cracks spiderwebbed through the crystal ball before it shattered, and Arelle was thrown back by an invisible force. She flew and her back slammed into the cabinet behind her, sending a few jars crashing to the floor, spilling their contents. Before Rexah could make an effort to move, Torbin was by Arelle's side.

"Are you hurt?" he asked fearfully, checking her for injuries.

Arelle shook her head as she stood up with his help. "No, I'm fine," she confirmed despite groaning, "I can't say the same for my crystal ball though," she said, looking down at the broken pieces of glass littering the floor at their feet.

Storglass dragged one of the chairs from the dining room over, and Torbin helped her to sit down.

"What happened?" Rexah asked, stepping forward. "Did you see Kalen? Did you see anything?"

A warm hand on her shoulder made her look up, and she was met with Storglass's chestnut gaze. "Give her a moment," he said softly.

"No, I didn't get far enough to see anything. Wherever he is, there are magical wards up to conceal his location." Arelle sat back in her seat trying to catch her breath. Her gaze fell on Rexah, and upon seeing the panicked look in her eyes, she smiled sympathetically. "Do not fret, princess. It just means I need to grab a bigger hammer to break through, that's all."

Torbin handed the Seer a glass of water that Rexah hadn't seen him retrieve. "I know you want to help but that'll take a lot of power. Don't burn yourself out."

Arelle took the glass from him, studying his face. "I'm well aware of the consequences of magic overuse," she said with a hint of playfulness to her voice that made Torbin's cheeks pink.

"Thank you for trying," Rexah said. "But Torbin is right, your wellbeing comes first."

Arelle dismissed her words with a wave of her hand. "I'm more powerful than I appear, Rexah. I've been doing this a long time, remember?"

The corners of Rexah's mouth lifted into a smile that spread across her face. She loved Arelle's attitude and could see why her ancestor chose her to be her best friend.

"Everything is going to be alright," the memory of Nesrin's sweet voice rang in her ears. *"I promise."* The grief monster scratched its claws along the bars of the cage she kept it in deep within herself. Shoving the heartache down, she nodded. "Of course."

"Give me a few days. I'll break through those wards, and I'll find him," Arelle assured her before taking a big gulp of water.

"But your crystal ball shattered, how will you search for him now?" Rexah asked as she eyed the shattered glass spread across the floor.

"Do not worry." Arelle's lips tugged up in a soft smirk. "I have plenty more where that came from."

Pink and white flowers rippled in the gentle morning breeze. Petals freed themselves from branches of the surrounding cherry blossom trees, floating on the wind, dancing around Rexah and Torbin like soft snowfall as they sparred. The land surrounding the abode was spacious enough that they could spar without worry of hurting anyone or damaging any of Arelle's property.

An entire week had gone by, and they were still no closer to locating Kalen. Arelle had broken another handful of crystal balls, at least, trying to source him. Every failed attempt had dampened Rexah's hope, but she wouldn't show it. She had to stay positive and strong, not only for Arelle but for Kalen, though that was easier said than done.

The space he left behind was suffocating. Of course, she wasn't alone – she had the others – but they did not fill the crater in her chest his absence made. Every day, whenever Rexah failed to hide her hopelessness, they would attempt reassurance that everything would work out for the best, but her doubts that it would multiplied by the day. There were only two outcomes: she would locate the sword and kill the Elder Fae once and for all, or she would be too late, every living soul in Etteria would be doomed, and darkness would be king.

The stakes were overwhelming, and she cried every night under the weight of them.

As if sensing her growing apprehension, Torbin had suggested they go out into the fresh air to train. At first Rexah was hesitant. She hadn't trained since that day in the forest with Kalen, and she hadn't fought since that day in Grimhollow. She feared she may be too rusty now, but Torbin wasn't taking no for an answer.

Sweat glistened on her skin, coating her back with its slickness so much that her clothes stuck to her. The sun shone in the sky, but white, fluffy clouds hid it from sight now and again, providing them with short intervals of much welcomed shade and a soft, cooling breeze. They'd been sparring for over an hour before Rexah called for a short rest.

She rolled her already aching shoulders. "Gods, I didn't realise I'd become so unfit. It's quite embarrassing."

"I think you're doing great given everything that's happening right now," Torbin told her, running his fingers through his damp dark hair.

"Thanks." She smiled softly at him as she caught her breath. "I'd like to continue these sessions going forward to keep up our strength."

While Rexah was aware of her own need for practice, after the horrific injury Torbin had suffered at the hands of the Valfae, she knew he too would need some sparring and exercise sessions to bring him back to his full warrior self, both physically and mentally.

Torbin nodded. "I'd like that too. Now, let's go again," he said as he moved into position opposite her. "And this time try not to lower your left elbow."

A stab of grief pulsed through her at the memory his words brought flooding back. Zuko always told her to stop dropping her left elbow. Gods she missed her old instructor terribly. She would never be able to get the sight of his bloodied clawed corpse from her mind.

Shoving that gut wrenching grief aside, she took a deep breath and widened her stance, gripping her dagger tighter in her hand. "Don't go easy on me this time, Tor," she said.

The corners of his lips lifted in a soft smirk. "As you wish, Your Highness."

Torbin stuck to his word and didn't hold back. They danced around the space, the sounds of their blades clashing against each other singing in the air along with their groans and heavy breaths. The tip of Torbin's blade swung dangerously close to her throat, but Rexah blocked it with her own just in time; she ducked under his arm and shoved her boot into the back of his knee, sending him stumbling forward with a curse falling from his lips. But the fae was quick. Before she could celebrate her small victory, Torbin moved so fast she could have sworn he'd teleported.

"Never hesitate around fae," his voice rose from behind her.

Rexah quickly spun on her heel, swiping her blade across nothing but thin air. Frowning, she scanned her surroundings for him. *Where is he?*

"Fae are blessed with enhanced speed. If you manage to take one down," his voice echoed around her before she was knocked off her feet, the cool edge of a blade at her neck, "make sure you finish them off."

Rexah gazed up at Torbin who had pinned her to the ground. "There's one thing you seem to have forgotten about humans," she replied, her breathing heavy.

"And what's that?" he asked, his eyes shining with curiosity.

"You should never underestimate us," she said, her eyes trailing to Torbin's side where her dagger pressed against him.

Torbin's gaze followed hers before a grin spread wide across his face, pride shining in his amber eyes. "Well done, Rex," he said in approval as he moved the blade away from her neck. He helped her sit up before he sat down in the grass across from her, discarding his weapon at his side.

The sun reflected off the purple jewels adorning the hilt of her dagger; she studied it as they sparkled like stars in the night sky. "I'm not sure if the lightning is contained within the blade or if it lies within me."

"Given what Arelle has said about Riona, it lies within you," he said. "Although, there's a chance that some of the power could have been passed to the weapon too."

"How do I tap into the power in my blood? Is there some sort of ritual I need to perform?" she asked as she shifted her gaze to her fae companion.

He chuckled softly. "No ritual is required. All that is needed is a clear mind and the determination to unlock the magic within."

She sighed. "Every answer at the moment seems so basic in theory but annoyingly complicated to achieve." A clear mind was surely attainable, but for her it felt an impossible task.

Torbin chuckled under his breath. "Isn't that just life, though? Like with anything, you just have to start at the beginning ... and do as a wise fae tells you."

Rexah shook her head in amusement and studied him for a moment. "Is that how you tapped into your magic?"

"It is," he said, nodding softly. "It didn't happen overnight. Magic is very sensitive and can be unpredictable. You must learn to control it and not let it control you."

"How did you master it?"

"Meditation," he replied as he sat back on his hands, stretching out his powerful body. "Like I said, a clear mind is key."

"Will you teach me?" she asked quietly.

Torbin's lips tugged into a pleasant smile. "Of course. We can start with the basics and gradually build it up."

Warmth spread through Rexah's chest as her eyes softened. "Thank you, Tor. How grateful I am to have such wise fae guidance at my disposal."

"Please. What good is my brilliance if I can't share it with those less … refined."

Rexah snorted a laugh. "I am serious, though, I'll be forever in your debt for this."

His brown hair fell into his eyes slightly as he shook his head. "Friends don't keep debts."

Rexah grinned. "Are you sure?"

Torbin chuckled and nodded. "Positive."

"Okay, let's give this meditation a try then," she said, sheathing her dagger at its place on her hip.

"Sure. It'll be a good way to cool down," Torbin replied as he picked up his own weapon and put it away, shifting to sit on his knees.

Rexah quickly followed suit and moved to copy his position. She'd never meditated before, and butterflies fluttered erratically in her stomach in anticipation. "What happens now?"

"Patience, Rex. Meditation can't be rushed," he explained. "Every step needs to be calm and relaxed. Close your eyes and take a deep breath."

Following his instruction, Rexah closed her eyes and took a slow, deep breath, and when he praised her and told her to take another, she did. Torbin breathed with her, setting the pace, and slowly the energy surrounding them softened into a soothing atmosphere. Soon, the calming sounds of the birds and breeze dominated where once thought and feeling reigned.

"Now," Torbin's voice spread through her like gentle

waves in a calm sea. "I want you to picture a place that makes you feel safe and happy."

Rexah instantly found herself in the forest under a star filled sky in Kalen's strong arms, completely content in his embrace as she leaned back into his chest. This was where she felt unreservedly safe.

"Savour every little detail. Sound, smell, taste," Torbin continued. "Memorise it."

She could never forget Kalen's scent or the sound of his laughter, and she certainly could never forget the taste of his lips, not even if she tried.

"When you're in that safe place, you need to reach into yourself. Imagine a long tunnel before you."

Rexah saw the tunnel. It was dark and filled her with unease, but when his voice echoed for her to follow the path, her legs moved with his command. Each footstep reverberated off the walls, matching every rapid beat of her heart. It felt never ending, but her blood began to tingle in her veins, the pull of an unseen force tugging her forward, beckoning her to come closer.

Suddenly, at the end of the tunnel, a large wooden door appeared before her, and she stopped in her tracks as she surveyed it. The wood was painted a deep purple, the handle made of iron. Light flickered through the space beneath it, and she swore she heard the faint, delicate sound of tinkling. *What in the world is that?*

Rexah reached out her hand and grasped the handle. It was cold to the touch, and both excitement and trepidation dripped down her spine like a rain drop sliding down a windowpane. Taking another steadying deep breath, she twisted the handle and pushed the door open. The hinges made no sound as she stepped over the threshold.

The interior was dark, and she was immediately met with a staircase leading down into a lower chamber. She took her time descending them, listening out for any sounds of people, animals or creatures that could be lurking – for she was sure in this place they could be – waiting at the bottom for their next meal to appear. Despite her surroundings, despite the darkness of the chamber that oozed danger, she felt calm and utterly in control as she reached the lower chamber.

The room was circular and made from dark grey stone. Cracks spread like spiderwebs on the walls and throughout the concrete floor. It felt beautiful and chaotic, both thoughtful and random. But what held her attention was the purple energy swirling like a storm in the centre of the space, and hovering within the core was a sword.

The tinkling sound she'd heard was louder now, and she stepped closer. The energy seemed to hum and glow a little brighter as she drew nearer, hypnotised by its very presence. Her movements seemed to outpace her mind's direction then, and Rexah watched as she closed the gap further. She halted as she reached the edge of the energy, the atmosphere pulsing, and she felt it everywhere.

Rexah lifted her arm and slowly pressed her fingers into the wall of power. Lightning sparked and crackled through it as she reached in, sending ripples of magic washing over her flesh. And when her fingers wrapped around the hilt of the sword, a jolt of pure, undiluted power shot through her. She stumbled back a few paces, ripping the sword from its place. Forks of lightning flashed down the blade, snapping and cracking against the steel. Now she was closer to it, she noticed the purple energy swirling around the lightning in a terrifying dance of raw power.

Her eyes snapped open, and she was met with Torbin's amber gaze.

"Rexah, I need you to breathe," he said, his voice thick with concern.

Her chest felt tight, and she could hear her erratic heart beating in her ears. Her lungs screamed at her, her body rebelling, but none of that mattered in that moment. Not as she looked down at her right hand, at the lightning sparking in her palm and licking up her fingers.

"Look at me," Torbin commanded, and she couldn't deny him. Her eyes shifted to meet his. "Breathe or you'll pass out."

Nodding softly, she took steadying breaths until her body calmed, her lungs thanking her, and it resulted in that flicker of power in her hand disappearing.

Rexah looked at her hands, amazed by the electric power she possessed. "I can't believe I did it," she said, her voice shaking slightly as her body continued to relax. "I did it."

"You did." Torbin grinned widely. "This is a huge step in the right direction."

"And I … I saw it," she panted softly. "I saw the Shadow Star."

Torbin's eyes widened. "You did? Rexah, this is incredible."

She nodded, taking another deep breath. "I don't know where it is, but I saw it within a storm of power, like it's being protected."

"So, it is not entirely lost."

Rexah ran a hand over her forehead, exhausted. "It's as good as lost to me, Tor. But I do appreciate your optimism."

Torbin's shoulders slumped in relief as Rexah's breathing returned to normal. "I've never seen anyone tap into their power that quickly before. It took me at least two weeks to produce embers in my hand."

"But did you have an oh-so-wise fae guardian to help you?" she asked, trying to lighten the mood, but the gut-wrenching feeling in her stomach gave her the answer.

Kalen.

"Did I ever." Torbin stood and collected his weapon, watching her carefully. "There is hope, you know."

Rexah scoffed and rose from her aching knees. "You think so?"

"I do think so. Between your power, which is clearly stronger than we realised, and Arelle's thousand crystal balls…"

Rexah waited for him to finish, but nothing came. Instead, Torbin stood, staring off into the breeze and the floating petals, lost in thought.

Rexah shook her head and smiled, and as she collected her weapon and took for the house, leaving him to his daydream, she finished Torbin's thought.

We'll find everything we need.

IO

"*It calls to you; all you need to do is listen.*"

The memory of the Raven God filled her mind. Their meeting had been too brief for him to elaborate, his advice nothing more than a riddle, but her success with Torbin had animated something in her. It wasn't quite understanding, but when she'd meditated, she had felt that undeniable pull: the Shadow Star was calling out to her.

As for Kalen, there was nothing, no hint of his whereabouts. Arelle's innumerate attempts had all been for naught, and it was clear that she was beginning to slowly lose hope as well. Torbin had tried to keep the positive energy flowing – unrelenting was his faith in Arelle's abilities – but as everyone stood silently around as Arelle searched for Kalen once more, the mood between the four of them was overwhelmingly thick with despair.

As if hearing Rexah's thoughts, Torbin slid his fiery gaze to her. He nodded his head softly to her in reassurance, and she returned the gesture before turning her attention back to the Seer.

Arelle's fingers slid into the crystal ball as she took a deep breath, and the scrying spell began. The now familiar hum of magic in the air surrounded them, sending floods of goosebumps over Rexah's skin.

Please, let this work, she prayed silently to the Raven God. *I beg you.*

The Seer jolted, her spine snapping straight, causing Rexah to jump in fright. No matter how many times she'd watched Arelle perform this, it never got any easier. This was how far they'd gotten with the spell each time. Rexah held her breath in anticipation of the disappointment she was beginning to become accustomed to.

All was eerily quiet, as it always was, and the time passed so slowly that the wait felt torturous.

"It's dark," Arelle said cooly, haunting voices cooing alongside her own.

Rexah's head snapped up, her breathing immediately erratic.

Hope.

"The rain is beating down heavily outside."

That could be anywhere, she thought.

"It's so poorly lit … I'm struggling to see anything that could give away a location," Arelle continued.

Rexah snuck hold of Torbin's hand for support, gripping it tightly. Torbin didn't make a sound as he gave her hand a gentle squeeze back.

"Give me a moment to try and see if I can push through the shadows," she said, taking another steadying breath. Minutes passed like hours before Arelle spoke once more. "I can hear water, like lapping waves, and I think I can see something. Gods, it's so difficult to make out."

Rexah kept her eyes on her, watching for any signs of

discomfort or confidence, but the Seer was hard to read, and it made Rexah's anxiety spike.

"It's the ocean," Arelle said, her first words in over an hour. "And I see a bridge."

Storglass leaned forward in the chair he sat in, his elbows resting on his knees as he listened intently.

Arelle's eyebrows knitted together in a frown. "The wind is so loud, like wolves howling to the moon."

Rexah shifted her gaze to Torbin next to her. He was so focused on her that he never met Rexah's eyes. His jaw was tense, his free hand curled into a fist as if he were prepared to spring into action should the worst happen.

"The … the magical wards … I can feel them," Arelle stuttered. "Gods, they're powerful."

As soon as the words left her lips she cried out in pain, removing her hands from the crystal ball and clutching the sides of her head. Rexah watched with wide eyes as the markings, the scars, on Arelle's face glimmered white before everything went dark. The light from the crystal ball and the markings on her face blinked out, and every candle hissed as they were snuffed out by an invisible wind.

Torbin darted forward, his hands outstretching to Arelle in the darkness. "Arelle? What's wrong?" he asked, concern thick in his voice.

"The magic," she said, moaning in discomfort, "it attacked me."

Rexah squinted in the darkness but could only hear Arelle's panting. Suddenly, Torbin's palm emitted a glow, a familiar soft green magic, and the pair came into view; Torbin kneeled by a pained Arelle, gently moving his hand to her cheek as he used his healing powers. After a few moments

Arelle slowly lowered her hands, her tear-filled eyes meeting his.

"Better?" he whispered, his eyes searching hers.

"Better," she whispered back.

Rexah's heart melted at the sight. "Are you alright?"

Arelle looked to her and nodded. "I'm fine." Arelle stood, slowly and carefully, and walked into the darkness of the room. Moments, later, the striking of a match filled the room, and Arelle's face came to life in the dark. The glow from the flame flickered against her skin. "But I can't do this. I'm so sorry, Rexah. I have failed you."

The words stung. It felt like she'd been punched in the gut, but she shoved the feeling down. "Don't apologize, you tried your best, and I'll be forever grateful for everything you've done."

The Seer gasped in surprise when the rest of the candles roared into life on their own. Rexah looked to Torbin; flickering fire now danced between his fingers.

"Sorry if I startled you," he apologised.

Arelle smiled at him. "No apology needed, Torbin. Thank you for your assistance."

Everyone quietened and shared in collective rumination.

"You should get some rest," Storglass told Arelle.

She nodded and looked at Torbin once more. "Would you mind helping me to my room?" she asked kindly. "Getting up was more difficult than I thought it would be."

"Not at all," he said as he walked over and wrapped his arm around her waist, securing her to his side.

As they passed, Rexah gently squeezed Arelle's arm, and she replied with a tired smile. Rexah watched them both disappear into the house and stared at the door for what could have been hours.

"We will find him," Storglass said, pulling her attention to him.

"It was never going to be an easy task," she replied, pushing her hand through her hair. "But I cannot lie, I thought we had it that time."

Storglass nodded. "There are some other things that we could try. It's not a guarantee that they'll work either, but there are options."

"Like what?" Rexah asked, intrigued.

"There are a few spells I could cast. A locator spell to be precise. It's similar to what Arelle tried but given the outcome of her spell, I don't think it will work either."

Rexah sat down in Arelle's chair and leaned back with a sigh of defeat. "We will try your other methods once Arelle is feeling better."

"Agreed, but for now, I think you could use some rest too," he said, his eyes full of sympathy. "You've been training with Torbin nonstop these last few days. In the meantime, I'll make a list of other things we could try."

She stood up and nodded. "Thank you, Storglass. If it weren't for you I would have gone insane."

The warlock smiled at her. "If not for you then I too would have gone insane."

Rexah returned his smile and bid him a good night before she headed for her room, and as she closed the door behind her, the smile dropped from her face as the realisation struck that they might never find him before she found the sword.

The heat from the cup spread through Rexah's hands as she lifted it from the tray.

"I've been thinking." Arelle sipped her tea before she continued, "what was the first thing I said to you, the first thing I saw scrying for Kalen?"

In just two days Arelle's magic had fully replenished itself. Despite how hard it had been on her, she was full of energy and eager to get straight back to work and continue the search for Kalen.

The three looked to each other before Torbin spoke up. "You said 'it's dark'."

"I did," she confirmed, smiling sweetly. "Before the magic attacked me, I was struggling to see anything, it was like wading through a fog it was so dark. It got me thinking, maybe he's in the Dark Lands, but with how little I could see I wouldn't be able to say that with any certainty. Nothing to base a plan on, for sure."

A chill slid through Rexah's body when she heard the name of that godsforsaken place. The Dark Lands lived up to the name, a country where the sun didn't dare shine and darkness was king. From her studies growing up, Rexah knew that nothing good ever came from The Dark Lands, only evil and death, and that's where Kalen was potentially being kept.

"It would make sense," Storglass replied grimly "The ocean, the bridge…"

"Maybe now that I have a direction, an understanding of what I might be looking at, I could—"

"We need to try a different method," Rexah told her. "As much as I appreciate your help, I hate seeing you hurt and weakened."

Arelle's eyes softened. "What other methods would you suggest?"

"Storglass, you mentioned something about a locator spell, something similar to what Arelle's been trying to do?"

"We could do that."

Torbin turned to face the warlock, a quizzical eyebrow raised. "Why do I feel like you're about to say something ridiculous?"

"There is something else we can try," Storglass said, turning to Torbin. "Although, it would be, as you have so astutely precepted, quite ridiculous to try."

"What is it? I'll try anything," Rexah said, not caring how desperate she sounded.

"It's called Dream Walking," he told her.

Arelle almost spat out the tea she had been drinking. "Are you serious?"

Rexah looked between the two of them. "What is Dream Walking?"

"Exactly what it sounds like," Torbin replied before looking at Storglass, "and it's a completely stupid idea."

"I agree," Arelle nodded, setting her cup down on the coffee table.

Storglass sighed and moved his attention back to Rexah. "There is a spell I can cast that will allow you to appear in Kalen's dreams," he explained. "You would fall asleep once the spell is cast, as would Kalen, and you would share a dream."

Rexah's violet eyes widened. "Would I be able to talk to him? Touch him?"

Storglass nodded. "Yes, but like all magic, the spell comes with risks."

"Such as?"

"When your subconscious travels between planes, it's extremely vulnerable. Monsters and demons sometimes dwell in the spaces between, and if they sense you, there's a chance you could be trapped by them," he told her.

"*Forever*," Arelle finished.

"I'll do it," she said without hesitation.

"No," Torbin said sharply.

Rexah's head snapped to him. "No?"

"Absolutely not. The risk is far too high."

"I'll be the judge of—"

"It's not happening," he said, anger coating his voice.

Rexah stood up from the armchair, disbelief coursing through her. "I'm sorry, Torbin, but you don't get to tell me what I can and can't do."

Torbin rose to his feet and walked up to her, so close she could feel the heat from his body. "I made a promise to Kalen that if anything happened to him, I would protect you. I swore to him that I would keep you safe, and that is exactly what I'm doing."

Their eyes met, and she saw then the pain of Kalen's absence in his gaze. Torbin had lost not only his best friend, but someone he considered a brother. Rexah reached out and gently took his hand.

"I didn't know. I'm sorry, Torbin," she whispered.

His shoulders slouched as the tension in them dissipated. "No, I shouldn't have been so harsh with you."

"You love him, don't you? You'd do anything for him?" she asked.

Torbin nodded. "I'd give my life for his."

"I feel the same way. Every minute, every hour that goes by without him here is killing me. I'll do whatever it takes to free him, no matter the risk, because he would do the same for either of us," she said.

For a few moments, the room was silent. All the while,

Torbin pinched his nose and squeezed his eyes shut as though his thoughts pained him. "He's going to kill me for this when we find him."

Rexah's eyes softened as she squeezed his hand. "I'm sure he'll make an exception," she said, smiling faintly.

Torbin lightly pinched Rexah's chin and looked into her eyes. "If you're showing signs of distress, I'm getting Storglass to pull you out of there no matter what, okay?"

She nodded. "Deal."

"I'll need ten minutes to prepare," Storglass told her flatly, standing from his seat. "I will call on you once the spell is ready."

"Thank you," she replied as she watched him walk to his room.

Rexah looked up to Torbin once more before making her way out to the back garden. She needed to ground herself, get some fresh air. The wood felt cool underneath her as she sat down on the porch.

This was dangerous and most likely stupid, but she couldn't leave him there. She couldn't let him suffer any longer. Any chance of bringing him home, she'd take.

He'd do the same for me.

Running her hand through her hair, she sighed.

"I know it's tough," Torbin said softly behind her.

Rexah looked up at him, watching as he sat down in the vacant space beside her. "Never in a million years did I ever think this would happen."

"No one expects anything like this to happen."

"My grandmother is gone. My people are gone. My home is gone. Kalen ..." she said, her voice breaking as she looked up at the stars.

"Kalen is not gone," Torbin whispered as he slid closer, the side of his body touching hers as he gently pulled her against him in comfort.

Rexah lay her head against his shoulder. "Thank you," she whispered back.

"No need to thank me, Rex. It's what friends do for each other," he replied.

No matter how sad and helpless she felt in that moment, she couldn't stop the smile that spread across her face. "Best friends?"

Torbin chuckled softly, looking out onto the encroaching grey clouds. "Absolutely."

II

Rexah had never seen so much concentration on Storglass's face before as she watched him prepare the spell that would allow her to walk in Kalen's dream. She willed time to move a little faster before her nerves got the best of her, and just when she thought they would, Storglass finally opened his eyes.

"It is ready," he told her, looking up from the spot where he knelt on the floor.

Taking a deep breath, Rexah rose from the armchair, crossed the living area and walked into the bedroom. Her stomach flipped with nerves as she lay on top of the covers, the others entering the room as she settled herself.

"This is your last chance to reconsider this option. Are you sure you want to do this?" Storglass asked as he set a lit candle down on the bedside table.

Rexah nodded. "Yes, I'm sure," she replied quickly before she could change her mind.

"We will be right here," Arelle told her. "We won't leave you."

Storglass pressed his hand to her forehead, and her eyes shifted to Torbin who watched her with a worried expression painted across his usually soft features. Despite her ever-present doubts, Rexah tried to tell him with her gaze that everything would be okay.

"Clear your mind and think only of Kalen. Imagine his hair, the colour of his eyes, and the feeling that consumes you when he is in your presence," Storglass told her. "Concentrate on him and him alone."

Rexah sucked in a breath before slowly closing her eyes. Kalen instantly came to mind, the memory of when he'd saved her from those bandits on that dirt road outside of Brywen presenting itself; his blue eyes pouring into hers like a waterfall, the annoyed expression on his face when he'd accused her of stealing his horse.

Her mind moved to another memory, one that lit a fire within her every time she thought about it.

"You're a vicious little thing, aren't you?"

The smirk that had spread across his face had made her feel so hot in her own skin that she was sure the stars themselves would melt from the sky. And when she brought forth another memory of his voice, of him cupping her face in his strong hands, she felt again that fire he set alight within her.

"I will always save you, darling."

D*rip, drip, drip.*
Rexah frowned as every noise faded away until nothing remained but that sound.

Drip, drip, drip.

The sound echoed, bouncing off walls she couldn't yet see, and she knew before she opened her eyes that she was no longer lying in the bed in Arelle's home; she knew that Storglass's spell had worked.

Rexah's eyes fluttered open.

Wherever she was, it was dark and cold. She could see now that the dripping was from water seeping in through a fracture in the ceiling, splashing onto the cracked stone floor just inches from her feet.

A clinking sound pulled her attention, and her head snapped forward in the direction of the noise. A shadow loomed at the bottom of the opposite wall, but it was difficult to make out what it was from where she stood. She took a few steps forward, moving slowly and willing her eyes to adjust to the darkness as she squinted.

"It … it didn't work the last time," a rough but familiar voice grumbled. "What m-makes you think it will this time?"

Her mouth opened to answer but no words left her lips, not as she registered who it was. She couldn't see his face; she could only see the outline of his body in the shadows, but it was him.

"K-Kalen?" she whispered.

"Are you deaf as well as stupid?" he asked, anger coating his words.

Rexah watched as he leaned forward, the moonlight shining in from the small window illuminating the side of his beautiful face. She didn't notice she was crying until she felt the hot tears slide down her cheeks.

"Crocodile tears, nice try," he mumbled. "Get out and leave me in peace. I'm not in the mood for your games right now."

"Kalen," she whispered brokenly. "It's me."

He shook his head, a muscle ticking in his jaw. "This is getting old. Where is your c-creativity?"

"Ask me anything," she blurted, pleading with him. "Ask me something only the real Rexah would know."

Kalen was quiet for a moment before he spoke once more. "All right, I'll humour you. What did I say to her on the dock when she asked me if I still wanted to be with her?"

She remembered that day like it were only yesterday. Licking her lips and taking a deep breath, she replied, "'Nothing will ever send me away from your side, not even death itself.'"

Kalen was quiet, the silence almost deafening, and it sent her already pounding heart into a fierce rhythm. "It's me," she whispered, praying he would see the truth in her eyes.

The clinking sound filled the air once more as he slowly rose to his feet, clutching the wall behind him as his legs buckled slightly. It was then she noticed the chains. Her chest ached and her blood boiled with anger all at once. Venrhys had chained him up like a dog. But the chains weren't the only thing that made Rexah's heart feel like it had cracked in two, it was the marks littering Kalen's body. The evidence of the abuse he'd suffered, and was still suffering, was unmistakable on his skin. The look in his once beautiful blue eyes was haunting, dark like a night-time sea.

Kalen's strong shoulders seemed thinner, just like the rest of his body did. Were they not feeding him or was he not eating what they brought for him? So many questions ran through her mind, distracting her from the reason she was here, that she flinched slightly when she felt his hand cup her cheek. His usually warm touch was cold. It was then she saw that the chains had disappeared from his wrists and were nowhere in sight. Dreams could change in the blink of an eye, Storglass had told her, each detail melting into another.

Rexah's eyes trailed up his face, stopping when they

connected with those dark ocean ones. For what felt like an eternity, neither spoke, but it was Kalen who eventually broke their silence.

"Am I dead?" he whispered.

"No," she whispered back. "You're dreaming. We both are."

Kalen's eyes scanned every inch of her face like he was committing every detail to memory. "Then why do you feel so real to me?"

Rexah's hand gently went to his wrist. "Storglass cast a spell that let me dream walk."

His eyes widened in fear. "No, please tell me you didn't. Dream Walking is dangerous, Rex."

The use of her nickname sent her stomach into a fluttering mess. "I understand that, and I knew the risks before we did it, but I had to see you."

"I almost forgot how reckless you can be," he said, a small smile tugging at the corners of his lips. "So, it really is you?"

"It really is me." Laying her other hand gently on his bare chest, Rexah's expression remained calm for him. "I'm getting you out of here, one way or another. We've been trying to find you. Arelle has used her magic more times than I can count, but she said the magical wards wherever you're being kept are hard to break through, keeping you hidden. Dream Walking was our final option. Where are you Kalen?"

"I'm in the Dark Lands."

"We thought so." Rexah swallowed the pain of his confirmation. "How do we get to you? Which way?"

"South of the bridge. They call it the Keep." His finger gently stroked her cheek. "Does that mean you've found the sword?"

"No, not exactly. Torbin and I have meditated. I saw the

sword, but I don't recognise its location. I haven't begun to figure that part out yet," she said, shaking her head. "But I can't leave you in his clutches any longer – I won't."

"I'm fine, Rex. You need to keep your focus on finding that sword," he told her as his other hand came up to cup her other cheek. "The sword is the only thing that matters. It should be your main priority."

"*You* matter, Kalen. I cannot do this without you," she said, her voice breaking as unshed tears burned in her violet eyes. "I won't leave you to rot here, no matter the deal I made with that monster."

"He won't kill me. I'm his leverage, remember?"

"Yes, but what's to stop him from killing you as soon as he knows I have the sword? What's to stop him from killing you anyway and pretending that you're alive and well?" she asked.

The list of possibilities was endless, a mere handful of outcomes were positive but the majority ended in Kalen's death, and she would rain hell down on this world before she ever let him leave it without her.

"I would do anything for you, darling, you know that. So, I'm going to request one thing from you and one thing only," he said as he leaned closer to her, his eyes pouring into hers. "Do not come here. Stay as far away from this place as you possibly can."

"What if the roles were reversed?" she asked, never breaking their gaze. "What if I were trapped in a cell within the enemy's walls? Would you stay away and leave me there whilst you searched for a weapon that you hadn't the faintest clue how to find?"

"That's not fair," he whispered.

"Of course it is, and you've given me your answer. You

wouldn't stay put; you'd do whatever it took to rescue me," she replied, "and that's exactly what I'll do."

"I love you with every part of me, body and soul," he said quietly.

His words sunk deep into her bones, washing over her like a wave. "I love you too, with every part of me, body and soul." Rexah's eyes fluttered closed, more tears cascading down her cheeks as Kalen closed the distance between them and pressed his mouth to hers.

Despite his injuries and the neglect that he'd suffered, his lips were soft and exactly as she'd remembered. Kalen's hands slid from her face to her waist, bringing her against him. She slowly wrapped her arms around his neck as the kiss deepened. A few moments later, Rexah pulled away to catch her breath, and Kalen leaned his forehead against hers.

"I will rescue you," she whispered.

Kalen's thumb gently swiped across her cheek, wiping away the tears that had fallen. She savoured that touch, savoured the lingering feeling of his lips on hers.

"The mountains, darling."

When she opened her eyes, she was met with darkness, and Kalen was gone. She was no longer in his cell. She was alone and surrounded by emptiness. Rexah looked around at the dark, vast expanse of nothingness. From what she could tell, it went on forever and there was no way out.

A horrific screech pulled her attention. She spun around but saw nothing. Her pulse quickened as the sound surrounded her, and that's when she saw them shifting out of the darkness. Wraith-like creatures emerged with melted, rotten flesh on their faces, their eyes black like endless voids. Their skeletal bodies were barely covered by scraps of thin clothing. Some had hair that danced on an ethereal wind, others were completely bald, and as they slid closer to Rexah she noticed that they did not walk but float, their toes brushing against the ground.

The horrendous noise continued to emanate from them, a cacophony of wails and shrieks piercing her eardrums. Rexah winced at the sound as she covered her ears. Her eyes darted from side to side, desperately searching for an escape route. There was none.

Shit.

Before she could conjure another thought, one of the creatures was upon her, slashing its wickedly sharp nails across her chest. She gasped and stepped back just in time for the claw to tear through only her shirt, barely missing her skin. Adrenaline flooded through her veins as fight mode kicked in. Rexah brought her leg up and planted her foot in the creature's stomach, kicking it so forcefully it stumbled backwards a few feet. Its arms flailed as it howled; the sound was like a cry for help, and she noticed the other creatures' heads snapping to attention.

Rexah's stomach sank as she watched three of them fly towards her, their arms outstretched, claws ready to rip her to shreds. Then, she felt that familiar tingle in her core that quickly spread to her limbs, flaring with more vehemence until it reached her fingertips. She looked down to see little bursts of lightning licking between her fingers, the purple energy beginning to glow in her palms, and her eyes widened in surprise. The screeching creatures pulled her attention, and she looked up to find them dangerously close. Her breath caught in her throat as she threw her hands up to protect herself from the impending blow.

But it never came.

Horrible shrieking resounded, and as she slowly lowered

her arms, she watched with wide eyes as her purple energy engulfed the beings, lightning burning through their forms as they crumbled to the ground, nothing but piles of charred bone and ash.

More wraiths appeared from the darkness, appearing from pockets of space beyond sight. One suddenly materialised beside her, and she had no time to react. Its bony fist connected with her face, and it sent her to the ground with a hard thump. Pain radiated through her jaw and cheek. Blinking a few times, she willed her power to resurface once more, and it flashed into life in her hand.

Rexah thrust her hand forward and blasted the creature. But no sooner had her magic appeared than it spluttered out, lacking the control and training to keep hold of it.

That's when she heard it.

A voice echoing in the darkness, calling out her name from a haunting distance. But when she focused on it, she recognised instantly who it was. Her stomach fluttered.

Torbin.

Shifting her gaze over her shoulder towards his muffled voice, she saw nothing but the same ever-present darkness, but it was now or never. Leaving the remaining monsters behind, Rexah shot to her feet and raced towards Torbin's voice. As she drew closer, his voice grew louder and louder; occasionally when his voice wavered in volume, she would adjust her direction until his voice became crisp again.

She barrelled through the shade, pushing her legs to move faster no matter how they throbbed in protest. The demons snapped and howled behind her, but she placed her sole focus on getting back to her friends.

With one final push, demons snapping at her heels, a flood of magic washed over her skin.

. . .

Her body shuddered and her eyes snapped opened as she sucked a gasping breath back into her burning lungs.

"Thank the gods." She heard Torbin sigh, watching his shoulders slouch with relief.

It was then she felt how hard her heart was beating, her chest heaving. Looking down at herself, she noted the cold sweat that coated her skin; it glistening softly in the firelight from the burning candle on the bedside table.

"Torbin," she rasped as her gaze flickered to him.

He moved some of the damp hair from her face. "It's okay, Rex. You were convulsing so we had to get you out. What happened?"

Rexah forced herself into a sitting position, Torbin and Storglass helping her. "Those demons you were worried about," she said as she felt Arelle's eyes on her from the foot of the bed, "I ran into them."

"Did they hurt you?" Torbin's eyes bulged with concern. "Arelle, how would that work?"

"I'm fine, Tor," she said, her hand pressing to her chest where the fabric was whole, no sign of any claw marks.

"She's okay. If she weren't she'd still be there," Arelle confirmed softly. "Did you see Kalen? Did you speak to him?"

Rexah nodded as she took calming breaths, willing her body to stop trembling. "It was one of the strangest experiences of my life. It didn't feel like a dream. It was so real."

"Did he tell you where he is?" Torbin asked quietly as he sat down on the edge of the bed next to her.

"Yes, he did," she said before moving her gaze to Arelle. "You were right: he's in the Dark Lands."

It was then she felt it, she felt what it was like to see Kalen so broken. In the dream, she was so focused on her goal that she hadn't the time to feel. But now, back in Arelle's house, she couldn't comprehend his suffering, and by extension her own.

Rexah swung her legs out of bed, sitting up and squeezing her eyes closed. "Over the bridge and head south toward the mountains." Rexah stood and walked to the door. Fatigued, she stumbled and grasped onto the frame.

"Wait, Rex." Torbin stepped toward her. "Is he …"

Rexah looked over her shoulder, a tear rolling down her cheek and over her lip. The chains, the scars, the dullness of his eyes: she saw it all. How could she tell Torbin how broken his brother was?

She looked to her friend, and with one look, she knew he understood.

"Forget the sword," she said sniffing away her melancholy to make way for determination. "We're out of time."

She walked out of the bedroom, making for the porch. And just as she opened the door and felt the evening breeze chill the wet lines trailing down her face, she heard the crashing of splintering furniture, the cursing of a forlorn brother, and the soothing words of a solicitous Seer.

12

Mashed potatoes and pork smothered in gravy was served for dinner along with some delicious cherry wine. The food was tasty, but it sat in Rexah's stomach like lead. It still churned at what she'd encountered, her ears ringing from the screeches and howls of the demons that had attacked her. Unease rooted itself deep within her bones as the sight of Kalen, battered and bruised and chained like an animal, continued to flash in her mind. The look in his eyes when he'd realised it was her filled her heart with the most agonising guilt that she couldn't bring him back with her. She had to leave him there in that place of pain and torture. The sadness ran so deep, hurt so keenly, that she could feel a defensive wall building itself. If it didn't, she would surely sob into her meal, never sleep or eat again.

Torbin sat to her right. His amber eyes had dimmed when she finally told them what she'd seen. The guilt she felt shone in his eyes, but there was also something else in his fiery gaze, something smouldering beneath the surface. He did well to keep it contained but Rexah knew at one point or another, if left unchecked, his anger would erupt like a volcano.

Rexah gently placed her hand on his forearm, squeezing comfortingly, letting him know that she was there for him and knew exactly how he felt. The smile he gave her was tight, but when he bowed his head slightly, she perceived that he was grateful for her support. They would always be there for each other, through the good times and the bad.

"The food was excellent, Arelle. Thank you again for preparing it," Torbin said as he shifted his gaze to their host.

Arelle met his stare and smiled warmly. "It was a pleasure, Torbin Farren."

A small smile tugged the corners of Rexah's lips. Even if they would never admit it, there was an attraction there that couldn't be hidden if they tried. It was in the little looks they shared when they thought no one was watching. It was also in the way Torbin turned into a teenager every time Arelle walked into the room, his attention fixed on her as his cheeks grew rosy.

"I enjoy cooking," Arelle told him.

"I enjoy eating," Torbin replied.

Rexah chewed her lip to stop the playful snigger that threatened to escape and stood up, gathering the empty plates. Storglass rose from his chair and helped her, chuckling softly as he followed her to the kitchen area across the room.

"I wonder when he last lay with a woman," Storglass murmured to her.

Rexah nudged him in the ribs. "Storglass!" she hissed quietly as she turned on the tap.

"What? I'm curious. His flirtation skills need the cobwebs dusted from them, that's all I'm saying," he replied, grinning as he stacked the plates.

Shaking her head softly, she picked up one of the plates and held it under the running water. "He's nervous, that's all," she said quietly. Although, she knew Torbin would hear every word they said thanks to his fae hearing.

"I'm not judging," he replied, grabbing the dish cloth, ready to dry the plates. "Maybe I could help him."

Rexah slid her gaze to the warlock. "You want to give him relationship advice?"

His mouth widened with a smile. "I would like to give him a few pointers that I feel would be beneficial in his pursuit of Arelle."

"My advice for you," she whispered as she leaned closer to him, "leave Torbin be."

He sighed softly, taking the plate from her. "Ah, I suppose you're right," he said wiping the cloth over the small dish. "The man just needs a bit of confidence."

"He'll be fine," she told him. The warmth of the water pouring from the tap sent goosebumps skittering along her snowy skin. "If he wants to be with her, he will. It's his choice."

Storglass nodded. "It is indeed."

"Do you have a wife?" Rexah asked. They'd spent a lot of time together, but she realised she didn't really know much about him. And when she'd been in his home, she hadn't noticed any pictures or portraits of a significant other, or any family members for that matter.

"No, I don't have a wife," he replied, setting the plate down on the wooden counter.

"I'm sure your soulmate is out there somewhere waiting for you," Rexah said as she continued to clean.

"There is someone special in my life. Someone I care about more than anything in this world," he told her.

"Where is she now?"

"*He* is far away from any danger. I sent him away when things got too dangerous. I had to make sure he was safe from the Dark Fae. If harm was to ever befall him ..." Storglass stiffened and dipped his head. "I would cease to exist in a world he did not," he confided in her.

Rexah's eyes met his, her heart beating faster against her chest as her stomach filled with a million butterflies. His words conveyed how much his partner meant to him, and her mind wandered to Kalen, her heart aching. "What's his name?"

"Jaroz." A look of absolute adoration washed over his face, admiration shining in his hazel eyes.

"Do you keep in touch with him?"

"Yes. We communicate through fire messages when we can."

She smiled at him. "Is he a warlock too?"

Storglass shook his head. "No, he's human."

Rexah's eyes softened. Warlocks and witches didn't live as long as the fae, but they lived longer than humans. It was a sad realisation, and not one that would have escaped the warlock. It didn't bare a mention.

Rexah smiled, putting the clean dish she held aside. "One day you will be reunited," she whispered. "The Dark Fae will be destroyed, and peace will once again fill the realm. I promise."

Storglass gently squeezed her arm, his chestnut eyes rimmed with tears. "We will win this war for those we love, for those we've lost, and for the heirs to come."

Rexah nodded her head, unable to form words for fear of falling to pieces. She swallowed her grief down and they continued to wash up the remaining dishes and cutlery in comfortable silence.

Rexah watched the fire dancing in the fireplace, the flames crackling now and again. The woollen blanket wrapped around her supplied her with additional warmth, but it was more for comfort than anything else. They'd been sitting in the living area discussing the next plan of action for two hours, and they were no closer to a solid stratagem.

Storglass carried maps in his pack from his travels throughout the realm. He was fascinated by how different each town was, all the different cultures and people. So, when they'd started to discuss their options, Storglass had pulled out the map of the Dark Lands and spread it across the table using candles and other trinkets Arelle had on the surface to keep it from curling in on itself, giving them a better idea of the terrain they would face.

Rexah watched as Storglass trailed his finger along the map, over the bridge and through the woodland south toward the mountains.

"As one might expect, the Keep itself isn't marked so obviously on here. But thanks to Kalen we know it must be near or within this cluster of mountains." During his visits to the Shadow Market, many clients and friends talked about the Keep, some even claiming to have spent a short time in the cells, but Rexah had her doubts. "It shouldn't be too far from the bridge, and the woodland should provide good cover for us on our approach."

"The Dark Lands are minacious," Arelle warned from

where she sat on the sofa next to Torbin. "There is no room for error. One tiny slip and you will all be dead."

"How insightful of you," Storglass murmured from the armchair opposite Rexah.

"I'm being realistic, Storglass. This isn't a game," she said sharply. "If the Dark Fae catch you then death will be a mercy." Arelle wasn't accompanying them. For her own safety it was best she stay in her home, available to help where she could, but it didn't stop her being the spokesperson for every-one's wellbeing.

"A portal would be the best mode of transportation," Stor-glass suggested. "Time is of the essence, after all."

"I can create one to get you as close as possible without being detected. The Dark Fae Keep has magical wards protecting its walls, so I won't be able to portal you straight into Kalen's cell," Arelle explained. "The bridge too is enchanted in some way. You may have to cross the bridge on your own."

"I didn't expect it to be that simple," Rexah smiled sympa-thetically. "If you can portal us as close as possible it will be greatly advantageous."

"Speaking of, we do have an advantage here, dare I say it," Storglass said. "See this map. The Keep isn't on here. They believe themselves hidden. Heard but never seen. One can only hope their perimeter security is lacking as a result, but once we're inside, it's a different story."

"Agreed," Torbin chimed in. "When we get inside, we need to be conscious of the guard patrols. It will be difficult to slip by unnoticed, especially with their fae senses. They will smell us a mile away."

"That's where I come in." Storglass grinned. "I can mask our scents with a spell."

"Won't they smell the magic?" Rexah asked.

Storglass shook his head. "Only certain Power Blessed can smell magic."

"My next question is, how on earth are we going to find Kalen's cell?" Rexah moved her gaze to meet Torbin's, the fire reflecting in them making them look like they too were ablaze. "When I dream walked there was nothing in particular that stood out to me. It seemed like a standard cell. I never saw the corridor outside of it."

Torbin cursed. "I'm assuming all the doors are going to be the same, and there's a strong possibility there could be more to the Keep than cells," he said, his eyes scanning the map. "Barracks, interrogation spaces …"

That thought turned the food in Rexah's stomach sour. "So, we get lucky with correct turns, or we fail."

Everyone was quiet for what seemed like an eternity, silently contemplating every possibility. It was a suicide mission built on things out of their control, but she couldn't leave Kalen there no matter what bargain she'd made with Venrhys. She would deal with the consequences of breaking their terms so long as she had Kalen back by her side.

Suddenly, Arelle shot to her feet, and Rexah's heart stumbled in her chest at the abrupt movement. She watched the Seer hurry over to her shelves of witchy goodness – as Arelle had put it when they'd first arrived – and rummage through her stock, jars clinking together as she searched. Rexah sat up a little, curious as to what Arelle was looking for.

"Got you," Arelle said victoriously before she shuffled back to her seat.

"What is that?" Torbin asked as he studied the object in her palm.

"Azurite," she answered. "This crystal opens up the senses

and enhances communication. I can enchant it and attach it to a small chain – I'm sure I have a spare necklace around here somewhere – and all you will need to do is thread the chain between your fingers and walk. The closer you get to Kalen, the faster the crystal will spin."

Rexah stared at the Seer in awe. *Magic is so fucking fascinating.* "That's incredible."

Arelle smirked proudly. "You pick up a lot of tricks when you live as long as I have."

"Can we go through this plan step by step one more time?" Torbin asked. "I want to make sure it's crystal clear."

Arelle laughed softly. "Torbin, love, you have such a witty sense of humour."

Torbin's cheeks pinked as he smiled shyly at her. "I truly didn't mean it as a joke. I'd like to go through the plan one more time."

Storglass chuckled. "We gear up and Arelle opens a portal which will take us to the bridge that connects the mainland to the Dark Lands."

"Unfortunately, I can't get you into the Dark Lands directly, so you'll have to cross it," Arelle added.

Rexah continued. "Then, once we cross the bridge, we head south toward the mountains, through the woodland, until we find the Keep. We assess the danger throughout and determine a good time for Storglass to mask our scents with his magic. Then, we sneak inside, dealing with any guards in our path as silently as we can."

"And you, Rexah, will hold the crystal that will guide us to Kalen's cell, and then, we'll just ... break him free," Storglass said nonchalantly.

"Gods, that is a gross oversimplification of the task, one that excludes all of the thousand potential problems we could and likely will run into," Torbin finished, squeezing his temples.

"Once we have him, how are we getting him out?" Rexah pondered aloud, ignoring for the most part Torbin's concern. "We can't exactly carry him out the front door."

"Arelle isn't the only one here who can create portals," Storglass announced. "If I don't use any magic, other than to mask our scents, I'll be able to create a portal out of there."

"That's all very well and good, but what about the wards? Surely, they'll prevent us from leaving?" Torbin countered.

"We will have to get him out of the Keep before we can portal away," Storglass confirmed, a grim look washing over his features for the first time.

"Then we fight our way out if we must," Rexah said.

"It's too dangerous to fight our way out," Storglass replied.

"And Kalen will be weak," Arelle added sadly.

"We will try to enter and leave quietly, but if needs must, we will fight. Hopefully we can find another way once we're there, but if I have to kill every Dark Fae in the Keep to rescue Kalen, I will," Rexah told them with determination. "This is an improvisation dense plan, but I trust us enough to navigate it."

Storglass and Torbin shared a look, knowing they wouldn't change her mind. The former sighed. "I am at your command."

Rexah looked at Torbin. His eyes shone with conflict, his body tense, before he too let out a breath. "I promised that I would be by your side every step of the way. I also vowed to Kalen that I would keep you safe in his absence, and I don't go back on my word. I will be by your side, Rex."

Her eyes burned with tears, but she refused to let them fall. "Then it's settled. Rest up," she said as she rose from the armchair. "Tomorrow, we bring Kalen home."

13

The quill slid across the parchment with ease, the sound of its point scratching against the surface as Rexah wrote down every little detail of her nightmares. Arelle had asked for it, requested that she leave nothing out no matter how insignificant it may seem. It had been a while since she'd last written anything and her handwriting was a little shaky, but she soon got used to the feeling of the quill in her hand again, and the words flowed freely and neatly onto the page.

Setting the stationary on the table, Rexah read over what she'd jotted down. The scene replayed in her head as her eyes scanned each word, bringing back the familiar tightness of terror in her chest. The raven's eyes scorching through hers as it perched on her bloody chest, the sky brightening with the lightning that forked across it. It was curious; the nightmare hadn't haunted her sleep for the last month or two, and she'd failed to make note of it until now. She hadn't gone without the bad dream for any longer than a week for some time. What was different now?

The chair scraped across the wooden floor as Rexah rose to her feet, parchment in hand. She crossed the room and set it down on Arelle's altar. The wood was made from dark oak with a large crescent moon and star etched into its centre. Witch runes were carved about its circumference, and, if she wasn't mistaken, it looked like tiny specs of glitter had been soaked into the wood. It was a stunning piece of craftsmanship.

Rexah's father appeared in her mind, standing inside his workshop in Dorasa, chiselling and sawing to his heart's content. Remembering the way his smile lit up his eyes made the ache in her sternum intensify. She missed her family terribly, but it was best for them if she stayed away until the Dark Fae and their beasts were destroyed.

"What's that?" Torbin asked as he approached from behind her.

"Oh, Arelle asked me to write down the nightmare that I've been suffering with. She thinks Riona may have had the same one."

Torbin nodded softly. "Hopefully she has some answers for you."

The wistful tone of his voice made her study him for a moment. His hair was slightly dishevelled, dark circles smudged under his eyes that seemed full of trepidation.

"How are you feeling?" she asked him quietly as she turned to face him. "Did you sleep at all last night?"

"An hour here and there," he told her, running a hand down his face. "I'd be lying if I said I wasn't anxious about this whole plan."

"I know, but we cannot leave him there," she said, hugging her arms.

Torbin leaned against the wall as he nodded, his brown hair

falling into his eyes. "I get that, but everything about this is extremely dangerous. One hair out of line, one breath taken too deeply, and we are done for."

"We will take our time to make sure the plan goes as smoothly as possible. Do I think the plan is going to go off without a hitch? Absolutely not," she said, shaking her head, "but like I said yesterday, I'll do whatever it takes to get him back."

Her fae companion ran his long fingers through his hair, pushing it out of his face as a small smirk spread across his lips. "I almost forgot how stubborn you can be, but sometimes that's not a bad thing."

Rexah smiled warmly at him. "One of us has to be."

Closing the space between them, she gently wrapped her arms around his waist, pressing her face against his chest, hugging him. "It's okay to be nervous. I am too."

Torbin wrapped his arms around her, returning the hug. "We only get one shot at this, and we need to make it count."

"Don't worry," Rexah replied, her voice thick with conviction, "we will."

A few hours went by, and everyone had gone to their respective rooms to prepare themselves for what lay ahead. Rexah secured the strap of her weapons belt as she went through the plan in her mind step by step over and over again. Her gaze moved to the corner of the room where the sword Storglass had given to her in the battle at Grimhollow stood against the wall.

To bring you or not?

Trying to be stealthy with a huge sword strapped to one's back felt a bit too risky for her liking, and Kalen's dagger was so familiar, a comforting weight in her palm. The dark blue gem in the centre of the hilt reminded her of his power, that mighty energy he'd been gifted with, every time she caressed it with her finger. She did so again, and that soul wrenching feeling washed over her like a tidal wave. She struggled to shove it back in its prison knowing that she would see him soon. She would take him from that wretched place and bring him home, back where he belonged.

Sheathing his dagger into her belt, Rexah reached over and lifted her own – the Ravenheart dagger wielded by her ancestor, Riona. Power thrummed in the handle like a caged animal waiting to be released on its prey. She still didn't fully understand the magic that lay within the blade or how she'd managed to activate it the few times she'd been in combat, but she felt drawn to it all the same.

Maybe it's something else Arelle can help me figure out.

Once the blade was secured on her other hip, she walked to the floor length mirror. The black fighting leathers she wore hugged her curves generously. She pulled her raven hair into two braids on her head, the ends sweeping down the small of her back. Rexah had watched Nesrin braid her hair enough times to know how to do it herself. It would never quite be as neat as Nesrin's work, but she looked every bit the warrior all the same, just like Riona had in the portrait that once hung so proudly in the gallery in Adorea.

With her weapons strapped to her belt, her spine straight and her intent clear, she was ready.

This was it. Now or never. No turning back.

The door clicked closed behind her as she walked down the hallway and into the living area. Storglass was sat on one of the armchairs inspecting his weapons. Arelle and Torbin stood by the kitchen counters talking in hushed voices.

As Rexah appeared, everyone looked up, and she gave them a soft nod as she made her way further into the space. "Is it time to go?" she asked.

Storglass nodded stiffly. "Everything is ready."

Anxiety clung to the atmosphere. Everyone knew the risk that this rescue mission posed.

"Before we go, I'd like to thank you all for what you have done, for what you're about to do for Kalen," Rexah said. "I'll never forget it."

"If this is the heroic pre-battle speech, can I kindly ask that you don't give it?" Storglass asked.

Arelle and Torbin turned to him and narrowed their eyes in what was undoubtedly confusion and surprise at the warlock's rudeness.

"I don't mean that in a bad way," he continued, softening his voice to appease the surrounding frowns, "it's just, usually when that happens things don't go to plan, and I don't know if I've got the—"

"Storglass, you're doing that babbling thing you do when you get nervous," Arelle chimed in, her frown softening to reveal a more sympathetic expression.

The warlock rubbed the back of his neck and laughed slightly. "Apologies."

Rexah smiled softly. "That's all right. It's good to have some nerves. Maybe we can use them to strengthen our fortitude – no pre-battle speech intended."

"Before we leave, one thing I forgot to mention yesterday," Torbin said, "the bridge we need to cross is full of mist and fog, and demons are said to lurk within it. We will need to be on our guard as soon as our feet touch the ground on the other side of that portal." Torbin shifted uncomfortably on his feet. "I'm sure you would have assumed as much danger crossing the bridge, but just so you know exactly what we're up against."

"Good to know." Rexah nodded, her hand gripping the hilt of her dagger.

"Once I open the portal everyone should step through with haste. It will deplete my energy quickly, and I want it to remain stable. You can never be too careful," Arelle told them.

Rexah nodded and looked to her companions. "Are you sure you still want to do this? I won't judge you if you change your mind."

"We made a promise, Rex. We do this together, no matter what," Torbin reminded her, and a wink from Storglass confirmed he agreed with her fae friend.

Arelle stepped forward and took her hand, regarding her keenly with sympathetic eyes. "I know you're too head-strong to admit it, but I understand your feeling of dread. I saw the same look in Riona's eyes. Trust me when I tell you that every-thing is going to be okay."

"Have you received a vision of what's to happen?" Rexah asked the Seer curiously.

Arelle laughed quietly. "Not quite, but I have a feeling that even though the task ahead is treacherous, this isn't where the story ends."

Rexah's eyes softened. "Did you always give Riona words of encouragement before she went off to combat?"

"I did," she said, the corners of her lips tugging up into a smirk. "Now, let's get you on your way." Arelle turned her back to them and raised her hands as if she were surrendering to an enemy. A phantom breeze blew into the room, lifting Arelle's hair in sweeping motions. Her hands began to glow that familiar pink hue Rexah had seen on several occasions now, and the atmosphere started to hum as Arelle whispered in Seer Speak.

Goosebumps flooded Rexah's skin as she stepped closer to Torbin. He placed his hand on the small of her back in a comforting gesture, and she lifted her worried gaze to his. Those fiery eyes were calm, like the embers of a dying flame. He was no longer the kind, gentle fae she was used to. No, standing before her was a warrior of Vellwynd, and he was ready for battle.

A few moments later, tearing through the very fabric of reality, the portal opened. It shimmered like the full moon on a lake, pink and light-green energy swirling within. It was one of the most beautiful things Rexah had ever witnessed.

"Go!" Arelle yelled over the sound of the portal's energy.

Storglass was the first to step forward, and he moved through the gateway as if disappearing under water, the power within rippling like waves.

"Together?" Rexah asked Torbin, her voice trembling.

Torbin moved his hand from her back and slid his palm into hers, lacing their fingers together. "Let's do this," he said looking down at her. "For Kalen."

Rexah took a deep breath to ground herself, nodding once. "For Kalen."

Before she could talk herself out of it, they both stepped through the portal.

Time itself felt as though it didn't exist. Gravity lost its pull, and Rexah was certain she was floating in a vast expanse of nothingness. The sensation made her stomach turn, but before she could empty its contents, gravity sucked her back to the earth, her feet firmly planting themselves on the solid ground. It took her a few moments to gather herself, to make sure she wasn't going to throw up, before she was able to take in her surroundings.

Their mode of transportation had blinked out of sight as soon as all three had popped out the other side, and in its wake she espied a clearing in the middle of nowhere, with thick, thriving trees reaching for the stormy sky behind them. The grass beneath her feet was soft and spongey, the air damp and humid like they'd just missed a downpour of rain. There was nothing too foreboding about the sight of it, but as she turned and saw the bridge, her heart sank.

Made from stone and steel, the structure stretched out before them, wide and dominating. Rexah couldn't determine its length thanks to the dense fog that spread across its path, and dread dripped down her spine as she failed to comprehend how one might defend oneself in such low visibility. She knew the Dark Lands were called the Dark Lands for a reason, but there was a difference when you were reading about them in books, tucked up in bed with the fire roaring in the fireplace, from standing metres away from its sinister entrance.

"Do not take your eyes off your surroundings for a second. That's all it takes for them to be upon you," Torbin said quietly, pulling Rexah's attention to him.

Rexah nodded. "I'm ready when you are."

Torbin studied her for a moment before he inclined his head to her. "As long as you're sure."

"Positive," she said. "Kalen is waiting."

Rexah didn't wait for a response from either of them before she stepped forward into the gloom.

14

er boots clicked against the rough stone as she took a few cautious steps forward, the fog swirling around her like a tornado, almost as if it were greeting her, analysing her. Rexah shrugged off the eeriness as she gazed over her shoulder in time to see her companions stepping into the smog.

Torbin already held one of his short swords in his hand, his grip firm on the hilt. Storglass also held one of his daggers, ready for anything. Rexah followed suit and unsheathed her dagger, the weight a reassurance in her grasp.

"One step at a time," Storglass whispered encouragingly. "We can do this."

They continued across the bridge at a snail's pace, listening out for any signs of danger. Torbin led the group as he would hear everything better than Rexah and Storglass could; warlocks did have better hearing than humans, but out of the three of them, Torbin's hearing was far superior.

They walked for minutes upon minutes, every one that passed without danger an unbelievable blessing, and each moment Torbin went without indicating anything out of the ordinary, they continued on, grateful to be covering ground unscathed.

Suddenly, Torbin threw his arm out, stopping Rexah dead in her tracks and sending her heart into a panicked rhythm. She looked up at him, watching as his amber eyes scanned for danger.

Torbin looked at both of them, placing a finger to his ear, signalling that he'd finally heard something. Rexah felt a tremor in the handle of her weapon and sparks of lightning flickered. She knew what that meant, and it only confirmed Torbin's suspicions.

Nodding her head in acknowledgement to Torbin, she tightened her grip on the dagger. They all turned and pressed their backs against each other, covering all angles and readying themselves for what was about to happen. And just when Rexah thought maybe Torbin had misheard, a familiar growl pierced through the fog, sending goosebumps skittering across her skin.

Moving through the murk, the hulking shape of a Valfae appeared. Its red eyes brightened when it saw them, its maw dripping with drool, a hungry look on its face. Her stomach sank when she heard multiple snorts and huffs around them from all directions.

They were surrounded.

It was time to ground herself, just like Zuko taught her, and so Rexah took a steadying breath as her gaze settled on the beast before her. "No turning back now," she said, her voice smooth and low. "Leave none of them alive."

The Valfae threw itself at her, but she was prepared. Rexah dove forward, shooting out of the monster's way before rolling expertly back onto her feet. She whipped around and sank her blade into the nape of the Valfae's neck. The hilt of the dagger vibrated in her grip before forks of lightning licked down her fingers and shot down the steel, striking the beast.

As one beast fell another took its place, and Rexah did not falter. Her determination to get to Kalen sent wave after wave of adrenaline rushing through her body, giving her the edge she needed to cut through the brutes like butter. Black blood sprayed as she sunk her dagger into the neck of another Valfae, piercing a vital artery, and she let it fall to the ground choking on its own blood.

Out of nowhere a Valfae slammed into her back, sending her to the ground. Rexah's ears rang, and her vision blurred as her head smacked against the stone with a sickening crack, stunning her.

"Rexah! Move!" Torbin yelled from somewhere behind her.

Ignoring the almost blinding pain in her skull, Rexah rolled, throwing herself out of the way just as the Valfae's claws raked through the stone where she'd been only seconds ago. The creature roared in anger and swiped at her again but missed as she stumbled to her feet, knocking into the side of the bridge. She looked down, surprised she'd managed to keep a firm grip on her dagger.

Okay then.

Focusing her attention on the Valfae stalking towards her with murderous intent, she slid Kalen's dagger out of her belt and flipped the weapons round so the blades were angled towards her elbows. With a cry, she launched herself forward and buried the steel into the creature's chest. It howled in pain as it crumbled back onto the ground. Rexah went with it, twisting the blades to make sure the thing was dead.

Rexah pulled the weapons free and rose to her feet, trying

to spot her friends through the mist. Her body sagged slightly with relief when they appeared a few seconds later. "Are you both all right?"

Storglass nodded. "Just peachy." He panted heavily as he leaned his hands on his knees, trying to catch his breath.

"We have to keep moving," Torbin said, wiping the black blood coating his sword onto his sleeve. "There will be more of these brutes ahead."

They walked side by side, faster now, constantly on edge as they anticipated the inevitable danger for what seemed like an hour. Surely, they would arrive at the end of the bridge shortly.

It couldn't go on forever, could it?

Imagining them wandering endlessly down the bridge for all eternity was something that didn't comfort her in the slightest as they carried on, and she quickly dismissed the thought.

It will end.

As predicted, another group of Valfae were waiting for them. As before, the three worked in tandem, taking out the monsters.

"I won't lie," Torbin said through heavy breathing as he finished off the final beast nearby. "It feels so fucking good to kill monsters again."

Rexah grinned as she tried to push oxygen back into her burning lungs. "That's the spirit, Tor."

"It's been a breath of fresh air not using my magic in a fight for once," Storglass said as he ran his hand through his hair, black thanks to the sweat and blood that coated him. "I'm surprised I'm still rather good at it."

Rexah opened her mouth to speak but was silenced before

she could as a horrific shriek filled the air. She spun on her heel, frantically looking around.

That was no Valfae.

"What ... what the fuck was that?" Rexah croaked as she looked up at Torbin. The look on his face was one of pure horror and she swore the blood had drained from his face. "Torbin?"

"Run," he commanded. When she began to protest, he looked her straight in the eyes, leaving no room for argument. "Get out of here! Run!"

The shriek pierced the fog once again, freezing her in place. Rexah looked over her shoulder as a gangling figure floated out of the mist. The creature hovered a foot in the air, it's long black hair dancing like a den of snakes. It was barefoot, its body skeletal, and when it lifted its head to them, Rexah cringed at the cracking sound its bones made. It's eyes, or lack of, were petrifying; they were nothing but black bottomless pits, no eyeballs in the sockets, and its face was more skeleton than flesh.

A Howler.

Howlers were wraith-like creatures enslaved by evil, and their sole purpose was to alert their master to intruders. If one of them got their bony hand on their skin, a simple touch, they'd suck the soul from their bodies as payment for trespassing.

"Oh, this is not good." Storglass shook his head. "This is not good at all." He moved forward and wrapped his fingers around Rexah's upper arm, tugging her in the opposite direction, pulling her from the trance-like state she'd been in as she studied the Howler.

"No, wait! Torbin!" she yelled as she struggled against Storglass.

Torbin didn't acknowledge her. She watched as he sheathed his sword on his back. His hands came together as if in prayer, and he mumbled something that Rexah was too far away to make out. In one swift movement, Torbin's hands shot out by his sides, igniting with orange flames.

The wraith flew towards him, mouth opening to emit another cry, but before it could, Torbin thrust both of his hands forward and his fire exploded, engulfing the Howler. The roaring of the magical fire smothered the shrieks and cries of the looming creature, and it became lost in the magnificent light of Torbin's magic.

Rexah continued to fight against Storglass as he dragged her in the opposite direction. She couldn't leave Torbin to fight the Howler himself, but Storglass wasn't letting her go. "Storglass, I swear to the gods, if you don't let me go right now—"

Before she could finish her sentence, the thick fog suddenly disappeared, the air clearing in an instant. The bridge wasn't endless after all; they'd made it out of the smog and out onto the other side of the bridge.

"We have to go back in there! Torbin needs our help!" she protested.

Storglass shook his head. "No. Torbin told us to run, so we did. I don't know about you but from what I saw, I think he can handle himself."

Rexah was about to give him a scalding when Torbin rushed through the fog, and much to her relief, he wasn't any worse for wear since they'd left him. She stepped forward and put her hand on his arm. "Are you all right?"

Torbin dipped his head as he panted, trying to catch his breath. "I'm fine. I can't say the same for the Howler." The corners of his mouth tugged up into a smirk as he slicked his hair back from his face, but Rexah could see in his eyes that the beast had shaken him.

"You scared me," she replied, letting out a breath as her shoulders slumped with dwindling adrenaline.

"I hate to break this up, but we're in the open here," Storglass interrupted.

Rexah's gaze lifted. No flowers or plants flourished from the dirt. Dead trees littered the land, their bare branches spread like claws. The earth was scorched, the sky was gloomy, and large boulders were scattered here and there, some so tall she swore they touched the stormy clouds. To their left, there was a road. To their right, a scantly trodden path led to an expanse of decaying trees, and behind those trees, mountains.

Rexah wondered if the sun would be capable of shining on such an atrocious landscape even after the Dark Fae were defeated.

Out the corner of her eye she noticed Torbin trembling. Turning her head to him, she asked, "Are you okay?"

Torbin looked down at her, a haunting look in his eyes. "I can feel everything. The insects skittering, the creatures lingering in the shadows; the magic this place holds is so thick it's coating my tongue," he told her, his skin paling. "This land is cursed."

Rexah took his hand and gave it a comforting squeeze. She hated seeing her friend like this, forced to carry the burden of presences she could barely comprehend, but she knew there was no changing his mind. Kalen was his friend, his brother, and he would go to the very depths of hell for him if he had to.

As they carefully made their way toward the mountains, keeping behind the trees and rocks, Rexah spotted more than one skeleton. Animal or human? she didn't know, and it made her pulse thrum in her veins. She forced herself to keep moving, focusing on the task at hand and staying close to Torbin and Storglass.

"There's nobody nearby," Torbin said as they found themselves deep in the dead forest. "Nothing interested in us, anyway."

It certainly seemed so to Rexah. No owls hooted; no animals ducked behind shrubbery. Everything there was to see was dead, and the only sounds were that of crunching twigs underfoot.

"I say we push on, for now." Storglass nodded. "Get through the woodland. It doesn't look too far to the mountains."

Rexah stopped at Storglass's side and placed a hand on the hilt of her weapon. "After you, then."

With their success at the bridge and the uneventful trek through the trees, Rexah felt, at least for a small moment, hopeful. But as the trees became sparser and they entered the clearing, her spirit weakened. The wind began to pick up, sharper and more piercing than any wind she'd ever known. It was like a thousand needles threatened to pierce her skin.

"I should cast the cloaking spell now. I don't want us to go any further without its protection," Storglass murmured as he kept his eyes on what could have been the horizon.

"Come on." Torbin nodded his head to their left. "That rock over there looks best for coverage."

Once safely behind the huge rock, Storglass closed his eyes and held his hands out in front of him, palms facing the sky. Rexah didn't dare distract him as he began to whisper an incantation, but it always fascinated her when others used their magic. Everyone had their own rituals and their own way to tap into and use their power. It was no different now as she watched the warlock's hands begin to softly glow green, the magic slithering through his fingertips like a snake in the grass.

"Take my hands now," he ordered them, and they obeyed without question.

When their skin touched, Rexah felt a jolt through her body like an electric shock. Storglass's green power engulfed her and shimmered away before she could process what was happening, but a lingering warmth spread throughout her, heating her chilled bones.

"It is done." Storglass opened his eyes, and they slowly faded from green back to their original shade of hazel. "Our scents are masked. We have two hours until the magic fails, so we must make haste."

Torbin nodded. "We need to get closer." He checked the area around them closely before turning back to Rexah and Storglass. "Follow my lead."

They crept from shadow to shadow until they settled behind a cluster of large boulders with good visibility of the mountains. Distant yelling bounced through the air around them.

We're near.

"You see there?"

The Dark Fae Keep was located within a group of mountains around fifty feet to their right. Its dark stone blended well with its surroundings. Iron bars covered each of the tiny windows, ensuring there was no escape for those trapped within.

"I see it." Rexah surveyed the building. The perimeter wasn't too heavily guarded, but a few Dark Fae were patrolling the area. Storglass was right; they clearly didn't expect anyone to travel to this godsforsaken place and attempt to sneak inside. Surely people would be running in the opposite direction of this place. Rexah would wager that the Dark Fae had their sights on keeping everybody inside in, rather than the other way around.

The easy part is over.

"Right there," Torbin said, motioning to the right side of the mountain so far that Rexah could barely see what lay there. "There is an unguarded door."

"We need to wait and see if that Dark Fae passes by again before we move," Storglass added.

As if on cue, the figure marched around the corner with a hand firmly on the sword at his hip. Even from here Rexah could see the black pits of his eyes as he kept watch. The guard paused for a moment, causing them all to duck behind the boulders, and Rexah was certain he'd spotted them.

After a few moments she slowly peeked her head up, and her body relaxed slightly seeing the guard had continued on his path, having walked past the door and out of view.

Checking their surroundings one last time, Storglass was the first to go with Rexah behind him, followed by Torbin watching their backs. Their steps never faltered as they hurried towards the wooden door.

Storglass hissed a curse when he tried to open it. "It's locked," he told them.

"Move," Rexah ordered as she gently shoved him aside and crouched down. Quietly freeing her dagger from her belt, she carefully began to pick the lock. Victory flooded her veins a few seconds later when she heard it click.

Storglass and Torbin both gave her surprised looks.

"What?" She shrugged as she rose to her feet. "Sometimes I got bored in the castle and I'd go snooping."

Torbin smirked at her. "I'm impressed, Rex."

She smiled at him before she looked into the doorway. "Let's go get Kalen."

Once they'd shuffled quietly inside, Storglass closed the door behind them. It was dark and damp, and Rexah swore she felt something scurry across her boot but chose to ignore it, suppressing the shiver that threatened to wash over her.

They'd entered a room used to store chains and other horrific contraptions. Bear traps lined one of the shelves on the wall to her right, some of them stained with dry blood, and rustling crates were stacked up in the corners – it turned her stomach when she imagined what could be inside them.

The quicker we get Kalen out of this fucking pit, the better.

Torbin stepped silently up to the door on the opposite end of the room and pressed his ear to it, listening for anyone on the other side.

Rexah could feel herself trembling, both with fear and adrenaline; she shoved the trepidation aside and clung to the adrenaline like a lifeline. She had to keep it together for Kalen's sake.

Once Torbin confirmed the coast was clear he pulled open the door. It squeaked quietly but thankfully didn't draw any attention. Rexah peered out of the doorway, double checking that it was clear before she stepped out into an empty, dimly lit corridor. One lantern bolted to the wall was their only source of light.

Rexah dug into her pocket and pulled out the crystal Arelle had given her, letting the chain thread through her trembling fingers. Whilst the others kept a look out, Rexah took a deep breath, closed her eyes and emptied every thought from her mind, every thought apart from Kalen. She pictured his dark hair, his stunning blue eyes and that smirk that always sent a tingle straight to her core.

My Kalen.

The chain began to pulse in her grasp, and when she opened her eyes, the crystal was spinning ever so slightly. Hope filled her as she looked to Torbin who gave her a small, reassuring smile.

I can do this.

We *can do this.*

Rexah took a few quiet steps to the right, passing by Torbin, but halted in her tracks when the crystal stopped moving. Spinning on her heel, she retraced her steps and went the opposite way, this time passing Storglass, and this time the crystal spun a little faster.

"This way," she whispered to them as she neared the corner of the corridor.

Before she reached it, Torbin stopped her with a hand on her arm. He snuck ahead and looked around the bend, and a squeeze of his hand confirmed that it was clear to move.

Torbin led the group, using his enhanced senses so not to lead them into danger; Storglass stayed at the rear, watching their backs; and Rexah padded between them, directing them to Kalen. They kept on this way through every passage and past every door for what felt like a lifetime.

The Dark Fae Keep was like a maze, made up of endless

twists and turns. The lanterns were sparce, but even when they were present, they didn't provide nearly enough of a glow for human sight. With her free hand, Rexah kept her fingertips to the wall, lightly brushing its surface to keep her steady, and occasionally she reached forward to brush Torbin's back.

Still there.

As they progressed through the building, the sounds of screams began echoing around them from all angles, spiking Rexah's nerves.

Suddenly, Rexah gasped as Torbin grabbed her and pulled her into an alcove to her left. Storglass followed suit. It was a tight squeeze, but they all fit. Rexah had her back to the wall, her chest pressed against Torbin's and her hands resting gently on the front of his fighting leathers.

Rexah didn't know what had startled her fae friend, but she trusted his senses so strongly that she stood there silently, soothing her mind in anticipation of the unknown. Then, just as expected, she heard something: the unmistakable sound of heavy footsteps.

The dull light aided the shadows to swallow them whole within the alcove. As the footsteps grew louder, closer, Torbin placed his slender finger to his lips, and Rexah complied, keeping her mouth firmly closed. A few seconds later, a Dark Fae guard stomped by with his sword clinking at his hip. Rexah gripped the front of Torbin's fighting leathers a little tighter when the guard's pace faltered, and he came to a stop just ahead of where they were concealed.

Rexah watched in horror as he began sniffing the air like he'd caught scent of something unusual.

Just as she was about to slip into full panic, the guard huffed before continuing his patrol. Once he was gone, and they were sure no one was following behind him, they squeezed out of their hiding place.

"That was *far* too close," Rexah whispered, running her hand over her chest to ease the anxiety building underneath.

Storglass nodded. "Let's keep moving," he whispered back.

Rexah gripped the chain tighter and started walking, watching as the crystal began to spin once more, praying they weren't too far away from Kalen.

Keeping her gaze on the blue crystal, she guided them through a few more corridors, and as she turned into the next one, she ran into a wall and fell straight to the floor with groan.

"Woah!" an unfamiliar male voice said. "What the—"

Rexah looked up, and to her horror, it wasn't a wall she'd smacked into, it was another Dark Fae guard. Her violet eyes went wide.

Fuck.

The guard's eyes widened in shock before they narrowed in recognition, his face twisting with rage. "It's you!" he exclaimed, the steel of his sword singing as he unsheathed it. "You little b—"

His head twisted sharply to the side, a sickening crack echoing through the space, and as he crumpled to the floor, Torbin caught him from behind. The sword slipped from his grasp, but Storglass was there to catch it, preventing it from hitting the floor and making further noise.

For a long moment they waited, listening for any inkling of alarm raised, but there was nothing. When Torbin gave a nod to confirm, Rexah watched as Storglass dragged the dead guard into one of the alcoves that would keep him out of sight of any other nearby patrols before laying the sword on top of him.

Far, far *too close.*

Rexah took Torbin's hand gently when he offered it to her and got to her feet. Her heart fluttered as she squeezed his hand. "Thank you," she whispered.

"No one talks to you like that," he said quietly, his voice thick with anger.

She brushed herself off and looked back to the alcove. There was something about it; knowing what lay dead within its shadowed confines was more haunting than seeing him dead at her feet, somehow.

"Let's go," she said before looking to the crystal for guidance once more.

Storglass appeared at her side and found her gaze with a sideward glance. "After you."

15

The passing of time seemed warped in this horrible place, and she didn't know how long they'd been searching for Kalen. It could be the dark and dank conditions that affected Rexah's perception of it so, and with no idea of how much longer the spell Storglass cast would last, time may have already been spent and she wouldn't know it. She pushed herself to walk a little faster whilst remaining as quiet as possible.

A strange feeling flooded her skin, washing over her like an ice-cold breeze, throwing her off balance for a moment. As soon as it hit her, the crystal dangling on the end of the chain began to spin uncontrollably. It swirled so violently she feared it might snap off completely. Her heart pounding and her eyes wild, Rexah looked up, taking in the corridor before them.

As with the others, it was dimly lit, but her eyes had adjusted somewhat, making it easier for her to make out the doors along the walls on either side. These doors were different from the one they'd entered through. A tiny, barred window had been built into the top of them.

Cells.

Gazing to her companions over her shoulder, she whispered, "He's in one of these rooms."

Torbin didn't waste another second and headed for the nearest door, peering in through the small window. Storglass went to the opposite door and did the same.

Rexah pocketed the chain and rushed to the door next to Torbin, leaning up onto her tiptoes, straining her neck to see through the opening. The moonlight revealed a small figure sitting in the corner, huddled against the wall. From what Rexah could tell this was a woman, and the maggots squirming around her eye sockets confirmed that she was dead. She stepped away from the door, willing her stomach not to empty itself on the floor, and she thanked the gods when Storglass's voice pulled her attention away.

"Rexah," he whispered, now standing at the next door. "Over here."

She was by his side before she realised she was moving. Storglass stepped out of her way as she stretched up and looked into a familiar cell.

Dropping to her knees, she snatched her dagger from its holder and picked the lock with impatient, shaking hands. Sheathing the blade as she rose, the door slowly creaked open, and she slipped inside.

It was exactly as she remembered from her dream, the moonlight pooling in from the tiny window high up on the wall and the emptiness of the room apart from a bucket and *him.*

His back was against the wall, his legs stretched out before him with his head hung low. Dirt and blood caked his sickly pale skin and the ripped shorts that fell to just above his knees. Iron shackles circled his wrists, and even from here she could see the damage the metal had done to his skin. If it weren't for the shallow breaths rattling in his chest, she would have thought he was gone.

Rexah's boots clicked lightly against the stone floor as she hurried over and knelt beside him. Her fingers trembled as she reached out, gently cupping his cheek and tilting his face up to her.

His face was covered in bruises in various stages of healing, scratches and cuts littered his skin and his left eye was swollen to the point where he could hardly open it. Tears burned in her eyes. She could hardly bare the sight of him like this.

Bloody.

Broken.

"Kalen," she whispered once she found her voice again.

When he didn't answer or respond she called his name again, the word nothing but a faint breath from her lips, a silent prayer for him to say something, anything.

Kalen's chest rumbled softly, the words not leaving his mouth. He moved, trying to sit up, and she helped him as best she could.

"N-no … stop … cruel …" he managed to say. His voice was hoarse and raw, and it sent a new, sharp pain straight to her heart.

"This isn't a trick, I promise you," she soothed. "Look at me."

With some difficulty, Kalen lifted his head, leaning it back against the wall. Venrhys may have hurt him, took away his dignity, but those beautiful ocean eyes were still his.

"There are those stunning eyes," she whispered, mirroring what he'd once said to her.

Kalen stared at her for what felt like an eternity, analysing every inch of her face as though he were trying to decipher its realness, and when tears cascaded down her cheeks, he lifted a quivering hand to wipe them away. "Darling," he croaked.

She almost fell apart right there as both relief and heartbreak washed over her like a tsunami, threatening to pull her under. If it were not for Torbin appearing at the other side of Kalen, she might have curled up beside him.

"Brother," Torbin said, his voice wavering as he tried to keep it together.

A heart wrenching sob escaped Kalen when he saw Torbin, and Rexah's tears continued like a waterfall down her cheeks.

"You … you shouldn't … be here," Kalen told them.

"I told you I was coming. Now stop being so stubborn and let me rescue you," Rexah replied.

She swore she saw Kalen's lips tug up into the smallest smirk as she reached for his wrist, carefully lifting it. Her stomach twisted as she inspected the ruined flesh under the iron.

"I'm going to take these off, and it's going to hurt," she warned him as she pulled out her dagger.

A few moments later, both chains clinked to the floor. Rexah pulled the shackles away slowly, careful not to snag his skin, and she watched as Torbin took Kalen's right wrist and placed his hand over it as gently as he could.

"I've got you, brother," Torbin reassured him.

Familiar green magic emanated from his palm, and minutes later, the wound was nothing more than a red blotch. As Torbin tended to as many of his injuries as he could, Rexah studied the way Kalen's expression slowly relaxed. The tension in his body eased with each passing second as the pain he felt slowly lessened.

Torbin reined his power back within himself. "That's all I

can do without burning myself out," he confirmed, breathing a little heavy.

"Thanks, Tor," Kalen said, sounding a little more like himself. "I can feel my magic returning now the chains are gone; my own healing should kick in soon."

Rexah couldn't stop looking at him, afraid he might disappear. One thing she didn't notice before was his hair. The top was long, but the sides were shorter, almost shaved to his skull.

Storglass appeared in her peripheral. "It's good to see you again, Kalen," he said, sympathy shining in his hazel eyes.

Kalen nodded his head to him. "As it is you. Help me to my feet, would you?"

Rexah moved out of the way as Storglass and Torbin gently brought Kalen to his feet. A gasp almost escaped her as she took in the sight of his body. His muscular arms had shrunk in girth, his torso so much thinner than she recalled, and it made her chest tighten with sorrow.

"Will you be able to walk?" Storglass asked.

Kalen nodded. "With some assistance, yes."

Torbin looked to Rexah. "You'll need to guide us out of here."

That was a long shot. This was the most ambiguous part of the plan, a part that would rely mostly on luck and fortitude, but they couldn't stay here a second longer, so she turned and walked over to the door. As soon as her hand touched the handle, voices sounded on the other side.

Rexah pressed her back against the door like it would stop the Dark Fae from entering, but they didn't try to come in. Instead, they lingered outside the cell.

"Another one died on the torture table," one of them said.

"Good, one less vermin taking up space," the other huffed.

The first guard sighed. "It's our turn to patrol the tunnels."

The tunnels.

Rexah looked over to Torbin, her intentions obvious and his eyes lit up as he nodded in silent agreement.

"Urgh, those tunnels make me uneasy."

"Tough. It's General's orders. Let's go, the quicker we do this the quicker we can go on break."

The sounds of their footsteps echoed down the corridor once more, and Rexah peered her head out to see them turning right at the end of it. She started to turn back to the open door when a thought stopped her in her tracks.

"Rexah?" Torbin whispered. "What's wrong?"

"Our scents are cloaked, but Kalen's isn't," she replied, worry etched into her features.

"I could cast the spell again on him, but I'll need to do it with less magic. It won't last as long as it has on our spell," Storglass explained. "I've put most of my power into my reserve for the portal. I can spare only a small amount."

"It's a risk we have to take," Rexah replied. "With any luck we'll be out of here soon anyway."

Storglass moved his gaze to Kalen. "Do I have your consent to cast this spell?"

"Yeah, do it," he said. "I'll do whatever it takes to get us all out of here in one piece."

Storglass nodded and held his palm open to the ceiling.

"Wait."

The warlock looked at him. "What's wrong?"

"There is a man in the cell next to mine. He's been here longer than I have, and I cannot leave him here," Kalen told them.

"There are a few people in the cells in this corridor, but we can't save them all, Kalen," Rexah replied. As much as her words stung, it was the truth. "Plus, Storglass doesn't have a lot of magic to spare."

"I can do it, but only to one more person," Storglass confirmed.

"Are you sure?" Torbin asked.

"Yes, but we have to hurry. Our cloaking spell doesn't have long left either," he said.

"Go get him," Rexah said to Torbin as she walked over, carefully taking his place at Kalen's side to support him.

Torbin nodded softly and quietly left the room.

Rexah placed Kalen's arm gently around her shoulders, her hand resting on his bare chest. Ignoring the wild beat of her heart, she looked up at him, soaking in every little detail.

"Storglass, ready your spell," Kalen said, his voice rumbling through his chest underneath Rexah's palm.

Storglass nodded, and his eyes turned green to match his power once again, a colour she was beginning to get used to seeing on him.

There was the sound of muffled voices in the next cell, as well as a short scuffle. Rexah cringed, hoping the noise wouldn't alert any of the guards. She buried her nose into Kalen's neck, taking a moment to relish in the closeness of him. His arm tightened slightly around her, holding her close, sending the butterflies in her stomach into a fluttering mess.

The door to Kalen's cell creaked open again, followed by Torbin's quiet voice. "In you go. It's not a trap, I promise you."

Rexah lifted her head from Kalen, shifting her gaze to the two figures stepping inside.

All the sounds around her muted. Shock wrapped itself around her like thorn covered vines, slicing their way through her flesh. Her lungs burned, begging for oxygen, as her breath caught in her throat.

No, this cannot be. The Gods surely aren't this cruel. It's a trick; it must be.

His dark hair was longer and tangled, coming to rest just below his shoulders. A beard covered his jaw, and like Kalen, he was caked in blood and dirt. But through all that, she still recognised him. She still recognised the boy who stole her heart when they were children. The man who was her first kiss, her first everything.

When she finally spoke, the word scratched at her throat as it left her mouth in a broken whisper.

"Ryden?"

16

Ryden was standing before her, a shocked expression on his face as they stared at each other in disbelief. The man she was due to marry, the man who she thought had perished along with her grandmother, and kingdom, was alive and breathing. Her heart punched against her ribs, her pulse drumming.

"How … how is this possible?" she asked, confusion coating her words. "You're dead."

"As much as I hate to break up this reunion," Storglass cut in. "We *must* leave *now* if we want to catch up with those guards."

How?

Torbin guided Ryden forward and once they were close enough, Storglass cast the cloaking spell on him and Kalen.

"It is done. The spell will only last for half an hour at most," Storglass told them.

"Then we best make haste," Torbin said. "Lean on me, Ryden. I'll help you."

"Storglass has me, darling," Kalen assured Rexah. "You lead the way."

Rexah forced herself to move from Kalen's hold, her legs trembling slightly. Her mind still racing.

Ryden is alive.

She slowly opened the door, checked the corridor was clear, and then guided them out. Guilt ate away at her as they walked by the other cells, but they couldn't take all the prisoners with them, not without alerting every Dark Fae in the Keep. She made a silent prayer to the gods to keep the ones left behind safe until she could return for them.

It was surprising how quickly they managed to catch up with the guards. Ensuring they kept a good amount of distance between them, they stalked the Dark Fae's movements and stuck to the shadows. Despite Kalen and Ryden's injuries, everyone's footsteps were as light as a feather.

The guards stopped at the door at the end of the hallway. One of them pulled out a large, circular keyring from his pocket filled with keys of varying sizes. The metal pieces clinked against each other as he searched for the right one.

"Give it here," the other said, snatching the keys from him. "Utterly useless so you are."

The door squeaked open a moment later, and the soldiers disappeared inside. Much to her astonishment, they didn't lock the door behind them.

Reliable guards indeed.

Rexah led her group through the door to find that it led to a stone staircase that sloped downwards into a pit of darkness. She took her time descending the steps; she hoped everyone would see this as necessary caution, keeping as far a distance as appropriate from the guards, but in truth she was near blind in the darkness and sick to her stomach with fear.

How far would she fall if she stumbled?

The Dark Fae's footsteps echoed throughout the tunnel as they reached the bottom of the staircase. Rexah looked behind her to check on the others as they reached her, and a nod from Torbin told her they were okay to carry on.

Lanterns fixed to the walls lit their path as they moved down the enclosed passageway. The Ravenheart dagger thrummed at Rexah's hip at the proximity to the Dark Fae, and she placed her hand on the hilt as they walked as a precaution. They weren't out of the woods yet, and she wasn't taking any chances with these monsters.

As they followed the path through the tunnel, Rexah noted that there weren't many corridors, and unease settled low in Rexah's stomach. If there was only one way in, did that mean there was only one way out and the guards would have to walk back this way to get back into the Keep?

It felt like they'd been walking for an hour when a fork in the path appeared before them. They had three options to choose from. Left, right or straight ahead.

"Left," Kalen whispered. "I can still hear their footsteps. They went left."

Rexah slowed her steps to look back at them. "Should we go left too?"

The group came to a stop. Ryden leaned against the rocky wall with Storglass's help. Kalen patted Torbin's shoulder, indicating he was okay to stand on his own.

"The exit isn't to the left," Ryden said softly. "We need to keep going straight. There is a door at the end of that corridor that will grant us our freedom."

It had been so long since she'd heard his voice. It was a voice she never thought she'd hear again, and she gulped the emotion down along with every memory of him that begged to resurface.

How?

"H-how can you be so sure?" Rexah asked.

Ryden slid his gaze to her, his light grey eyes almost shining in the darkness. "Because this is the way I was brought into this hell hole. I wasn't brought through the front door and given the grand tour like Kalen here."

Kalen's eyes narrowed, but he didn't respond.

"I marked every subtlety of these tunnels when I was dragged through them – trust me, we go straight until we reach the door," Ryden confirmed.

"Then we should keep moving whilst the guards are heading in the opposite direction," Storglass said as he helped Ryden up off the wall.

Rexah looked at Kalen who gave her a reassuring nod. She held her hand out to him, and when he took it, her heart tingled at the contact of their skin. Kalen's eyes flickered, and she knew he felt it too.

All was silent as the group made their way down the path straight ahead. The silence did nothing to ease the worry brewing in her stomach like a storm. As they passed another tunnel to their left, something caught Rexah's attention, so much so that she slowed to a stop as the others kept walking.

Rexah squinted her eyes as she peered into the darkness, blinking and willing her sight to adjust, and that's when she saw them.

Red glowing eyes trained on her.

A pulse of fear pushed through her. Before she could make a sound or move out of the way, the hulking form of a Valfae rushed towards her, smacking into her chest and sending her flying into the opposite wall.

Rexah gasped for air as the breath was knocked from her lungs. Now, under the dim light of the lantern, she could see the Valfae clearer. This one was different to the others. It was larger, its claws longer and sharper than any of the others she'd seen, and its face was twisted with rabid hunger. Drool dripped from its fang filled maw as it snarled at her.

The creature didn't waste any time and launched itself at her again, fangs and claws ready to pierce her flesh. Rexah had no time to unsheathe her weapon and could only lift her arms to shield herself. As she did, a surge of power swelled from deep within her, spreading through her very being. It set her blood alight as it exploded from her hands, that familiar purple energy intertwined with lightning.

Her power slammed into the Valfae, halting the beast in its tracks as her power coursed through its body. The Valfae convulsed as forks of lightning sparked along its skin, and it roared in agony as the purple energy smothered the life inside of it. Finally, the hulking form slammed to the ground in a lifeless heap.

The power flowing through Rexah's hands slowly diminished as she stared wide-eyed, trying to process everything that just happened.

"Rexah? Rexah, talk to me," Kalen said, suddenly beside her.

She lifted her gaze to meet his worried expression. "It … it all happened so fast. I …"

"It's all right, are you okay? Are you hurt?"

She shook her head. "No, I-I'm okay."

Rising to her feet with Kalen's help, she stared down at the now smoking form of the Valfae.

"Your power has surfaced," Kalen said, a wondrous

expression on his face. "We don't have time to talk about it now, but once we're safe I want to know every little detail."

"Yes." Rexah nodded, dipping her head as she smiled bashfully. "Let's keep going. Those guards will have heard that, no doubt."

Rexah could feel her body begin to tremble. While her power had surfaced, it drained her quickly, and she had less control over its surfacing than she would have liked. All she wanted was to get out of there and back to the safety of Arelle's abode.

Apprehension sat like led in her stomach as she gripped the handle of her dagger tighter where it was still sheathed in her belt, and just then, the door Ryden had spoken of appeared in the distance; everything they'd worked towards was suddenly so close.

"Hold it right there!" a male voice boomed behind them.

Rexah cringed as she turned around to see the two Dark Fae guards they'd followed now standing ten feet away.

"Where do you think you're going?" one of them asked, his dark eyes brightening as they roamed over Rexah. A nasty scar cut through his top lip and ended underneath his chin.

A guttural growl sounded to her left and she shifted her gaze to see Kalen seething beside her. His hands were balled into fists at his sides, and if looks could kill, the two guards would be cold on the floor by now.

"You thought you could come in here, take two of our prisoners, and leave without a care in the world?" the other asked. This one had snow-white hair pulled back into a braid.

Rexah squeezed Kalen's hand as she turned her attention back to the monsters before them. "It was too easy to break in. You really should see about stepping up your security," she said with a boldness that took her by surprise. "It's quite embarrassing actually."

The man with the scar chuckled at her response. "Our general told us you had quite the mouth on you."

"It was a valiant attempt, I'll give you that, but no further." The white haired one smirked sadistically. "Our general will be thrilled when we deliver the Chosen One to him."

"Run," Kalen told her, never taking his eyes off the guards.

"Absolutely not," she replied stubbornly.

Torbin unsheathed his short swords, handing one to Kalen. "Do as he says, Rex. We'll be right behind you. Get Ryden out of here."

"I'll go with you," Storglass told her.

Rexah moved her gaze between Torbin and Kalen.

Kalen winked at her. "We've got this."

There he is.

Rexah knew they wouldn't take no for an answer and turned to Storglass, helping him guide Ryden quickly towards the exit as the sound of steel against steel rang out behind them. Ryden stumbled a few times, but with Storglass taking most of his weight, he managed to stay on his feet.

The door, as expected, was locked when they got to it, but Rexah broke the lock and yanked the door open.

"Go!" she yelled, ushering them out.

Storglass moved without argument and pulled Ryden over the threshold.

Rexah looked over to Kalen and Torbin in time to see them both expertly deliver killing blows to the Dark Fae guards. She watched as their headless bodies slumped to the floor, their black blood staining the wood a darker shade. Kalen might have looked different to when she last saw him, but the warrior within him was still as fierce as ever. He handed the sword back to Torbin as they jogged towards her.

She took Kalen's hand again. "Are you sure you're all right?" she asked worriedly.

He smiled down at her and nodded. "I'm fine. My healing has kicked back in. I'll be okay. I promise."

They rushed out the door, Torbin slamming it shut behind him. Storglass was already chanting, his hands raised similarly to the way Arelle's had been when she'd created the portal that brought them here.

Torbin moved to Ryden's side where he leaned against the trunk of one of the dead trees. From where they were, the bridge they'd crossed could be seen, the swirling fog within giving it a haunting look.

I can't believe we crossed over that.

Moments later, a portal made from green swirling energy materialised. Storglass kept his trembling arms raised as he looked over his shoulder.

"Hurry! I cannot hold it for long! The wards are powerful!" he told them through gritted teeth.

Torbin assisted Ryden to the magical gateway, holding firmly onto him before they both disappeared through it.

Rexah felt Kalen's comforting touch on the small of her back that she hadn't felt for so long. She turned to him as they stopped at the portal and wrapped her arms around his waist, burying her face into his bare chest.

Storglass moved his gaze to Rexah and Kalen. "Your turn."

"What about you?" Rexah asked hurriedly.

"I'll be right behind you." He grinned at her. "Now, go!"

Kalen wrapped his arms around her, holding her against him briefly before pulling away and squeezing her hand. "It's you and me, darling."

She tightened her grip on Kalen's hand as they stepped into the portal. The familiar feeling of weightlessness washed over her, and she fought to hold on to him through the force of magic pushing them through the gateway. The sensation was gone as quickly as it had come, and she felt her feet hit a solid wooden floor. When she opened her eyes Arelle's living area came into view.

Rexah had no time to take a much-needed breath of relief as she felt Kalen's body begin to collapse. Before she could call out or attempt to catch him, Torbin was there in a flash, grabbing him before he could hurt himself.

"What … what's going on?" Rexah asked, her violet eyes wide.

"His fae healing might be working again, but he still overdid it back there. He needs to rest," Torbin told her.

"Take him to my room, please," she whispered.

Torbin nodded softly and picked up his brother with ease.

The sound of boots thudding against the floor pulled Rexah's attention, and she looked up in time to see Storglass appear through the portal. The magical gateway sealed shut just mere seconds after the warlock stepped through. Storglass swept across the room, taking note that everyone was in one piece, before he helped Ryden into his room to rest.

Arelle appeared at Rexah's side. "Are you hurt?" she asked, scanning her for injuries.

Rexah shook her head. "No, I'm completely fine."

"The bruising surfacing on the side of your head says otherwise," she said with a deepening frown. "Let me have a look."

"No, check Kalen and Ryden over first," she said. "They are in a worse state than I am."

"Very well, but please go and sit down on the sofa and take

a moment to breathe. And no sleeping until I've checked your head," she said before turning her attention to Storglass as he walked back into the room. "Make her a cup of tea with extra sugar. Make one for yourself too. I'll be back shortly."

Rexah watched as Arelle walked into her room to see to Kalen, and only when she heard that he was conscious did she follow the Seer's instructions.

We did it. We rescued Kalen.

She sat on the sofa, sinking into the cushions with a sigh of relief as she closed her eyes.

And Ryden.

17

Sunlight poured in from the window, the warm rays touching Kalen's bare chest as Rexah lay beside him. She had woken up before him and watched him sleep for the last hour, scared to move for fear of waking him. She watched every single deep breath he took as he slept peacefully and wondered when the last time was that he'd had a good, restful sleep.

When Arelle had finished checking him over and helped speed up his recovery by offering him an interesting, silver potion, Rexah had made her way into the room, kicked off her boots and pulled off her clothing before sliding in beside him. She hadn't left his side since.

"It's rude to watch people sleep," he mumbled. "We've already had this conversation, if I recall."

"You were awake then just as you are now, so there is no rudeness in my watching," she replied quietly.

Kalen opened his eyes and gazed down at her, a small smirk spreading across his perfect mouth. "Indeed."

Rexah slowly reached up and pushed the hair on the top of his head back, her fingers tracing over one of the shaved sides. "They cut your hair."

"The ends were matted with …"

"You can tell me."

Kalen sighed. "Venrhys ordered them to cut it a few days ago after one of our sessions in the torture room," he told her. "Despite everything, I quite like it."

Sorrow and rage filled her all at once, but it was the touch of his hand on her bare waist that brought her back down to a calmer level.

It was then that everything she'd wanted to say in his absence surfaced, and it became such a jumble of words in her mind that she couldn't think straight. "You wouldn't have been taken if—"

"Listen to me."

"But I need to say that—"

"We're not doing this," he said sternly. "You did what you had to do. He was going to take me one way or another. Besides, I was the one that made you choose that option, and I would go back to that cell right now if it meant that you were safe," he said.

Her eyes met his dark blue ones. "Our actions yesterday … they will have severe consequences, and I'll pay the price if I must, if it means you're safe." Rexah dipped her head, her heart breaking for a terrible thing that had yet to happen because of this. "I couldn't leave you there any longer."

"What you all did for me, I won't forget it," he whispered, gently rubbing his nose against hers. "You rescued me."

"I will always rescue you," she whispered back.

Kalen pressed his mouth to hers, his lips soft and warm.

His hand moved to the small of her back, bringing her closer to him. She let herself get lost in his embrace, savouring the way his mouth moved on hers, how his body pressed against her. Just being in his arms again was everything.

Rexah turned to lay on her back as he hovered above her. His tongue slid against her bottom lip, and she opened for him without question or resistance. As the kiss deepened, Kalen nudged her knees apart and settled between her legs but kept his body from crushing her.

A soft gasp left her mouth when his lips moved to her neck, and her legs wrapped around his hips. Seeming to like the noise that left her, Kalen groaned softly against her skin, grinding his hard length against her. It sent a thrill of pleasure through her body.

"Kalen," she breathed heavily. "We … we shouldn't."

He lifted his head and looked down at her, the fire in his eyes slowly melting as the lust-filled haze dissipated. "I'm sorry, darling. I'm just so fucking addicted to you."

Her cheeks flushed. "I don't think this would be appropriate considering … you know."

Something flickered in his eyes briefly, something she couldn't place as he wiped his thumb along her temple, scanning her face. "Have you been to see him yet?"

She shook her head softly. "Not yet. I needed to make sure you were all right first, and I must have fallen asleep. Arelle was checking on him when I came to see you."

Kalen moved to lay down next to her again. "It must have been such a shock for you to see him standing there."

"It was. It still is. Between that and having you here, I feel I could still be Dream Walking," she admitted.

"That's understandable. It'll take some time for the shock

to wear off," Kalen said as he gently traced his fingers along her bare stomach. It was then she remembered she was in nothing but her underwear, and the realisation must have been clear on her face as Kalen smirked at her. "Not that I'm complaining, but why *are* you in nothing but your under-wear?" he asked, his eyes roaming her body appreciatively before meeting her gaze once more.

Swallowing the lump in her throat, she replied, "My clothes were a mess and changing into my night clothes wasn't a priority in the moment, so I stripped and got in beside you."

"I like this," he told her, reaching up to move a strand of raven-coloured hair from her face. "Maybe you could come to bed like this again tonight."

Her toes curled. A familiar ache of longing begged to be assuaged as she thought of what could happen if she did just that, but her guilt lingered in the shadows of her conscious-ness. The more lustful she felt as she lay next to Kalen, the more nauseous she felt knowing who was next door.

"I should go and see if Ryden is awake," she said, sitting up and throwing the covers off. She rose from the bed and grabbed a pair of leggings and a thin jumper from her bag, pulling them on. "You should take it easy today and get as much rest as possible."

"I'm feeling much better now. I might go and see what Torbin is up to," he said as he stretched out, his abdominal muscles bunching and shifting with the movement.

Rexah walked to the door, forcing herself not to go back on what she'd said and do all the delicious things she wanted to do to him. She stopped in the threshold and looked over her shoulder; she was almost afraid to leave him alone lest someone take him away again. Her heart fluttered when he chuckled.

"Go, darling." He grinned at her.

She smiled at him before walking out the door.

She stood outside Ryden's room for some time. Her palms were slick with sweat and her pulse jumped underneath her skin.

What am I supposed to say to him? Where do I even begin?

Giving herself a peptalk and taking a deep breath, Rexah gently knocked on the door and slowly turned the handle, quietly pushing it open. Ryden was lying on the bed with pillows placed around him to keep him as comfortable as possible. He was awake and staring right at her as she slipped into the room.

When she didn't speak or move, Ryden offered her a soft smile and said, "Close the door, princess."

It clicked shut behind her before she stepped further into the space. Ryden looked completely different to what she remembered. The dark circles of his eyes stood out against the paleness of his skin. It was also the first time she'd seen him with facial hair, and much like Kalen, the muscles he'd worked hard most of his life to obtain weren't as bulky as she recalled. To see how their imprisonment had eaten away at them physically must have been nothing against what it had done to them mentally.

"How are you feeling?" she asked him.

His shoulder lifted as he shrugged. "I'm better than I was yesterday, but my body is going to take a bit longer to heal than Kalen's."

Rexah nodded softly. "You're safe here. If you need anything at all let me know."

A silence filled the room, and it brought Rexah's attention to the goings on in the house. She could hear the soft clattering of pots and pans, a whistle of a boiling kettle and somewhere outside, a laugh. Torbin's laugh.

"Ask me what you're really here to ask," Ryden said. "You must have a lot of questions as I do."

How are you alive?

"I guess I'd like to start at the beginning of all this, if it's not too difficult for you," she said softly, walking closer and sitting down on the edge of the bed. "What happened in Adorea?"

Ryden gently took her hand in his. "I was awoken by my father. He was shouting about the Valfae and that the castle was under attack. We went through the dining hall to try and escape, that's when I spotted Nesrin hiding under the table."

The mention of her best friend flooded her eyes with tears. "Is she alive?" The hope filling her voice was pathetic, but she needed to know. If Ryden was alive, then maybe Nesrin was too.

"I pulled her from under the table and we took her with us. I wasn't going to leave her there," he continued, ignoring her questions. "We managed to make it outside, but ... but parts of the walls started crumbling.

"My father was behind us, told us to keep running, so we did. He was crushed by a falling piece of stone. I don't know how but I kept running, pulling Nesrin along with me ... but she tripped. I turned back to help her but I-I was too late," he said, his voice breaking. "Another huge block of stone fell ... there was nothing I could do."

Hot tears slid down Rexah's face as she listened to his side of the story, the events that happened to him and her best friend that fateful night. Her heart shattered all over again for his father and for Nesrin.

"I ran into the forest, but I ran straight into those monsters."

"Oh, Ryden," she whispered.

He reached out and wiped away her tears. "I thought you'd died. I didn't think I'd ever see you again. Gods, I've missed you terribly." The horrors of that night still shone through his eyes, like they played repeatedly in his mind.

"I barely managed to escape, but my grandmother ..." she trailed off, unable to speak the words.

Ryden opened his arms to her. "Come here, princess."

She carefully lay down in his arms, burying her face into his chest. Her sobbing began all at once, all-encompassing and uncontrollable, but Ryden didn't try to stop her, instead he cried with her, sharing his grief. She'd thought she'd gotten it under control weeks ago, but her body shook violently with sorrow, the weight of her loss let loose, and she released it more fully than any of those nights alone crying into a pillow.

Ryden's fingers gently threaded through her hair, soothing her as her tears slowly faded. It felt strange being in his arms again, but Rexah was over the moon that he was alive.

"You've been in that keep since they captured you," she said, her throat raw from crying.

He nodded, his eyes pained and glossy. "In all honesty, I can't believe I'm alive. It was unbearable most days, Rex," he said, wiping the tears from his face. "Until Kalen arrived."

Her pulse jumped at the mention of his name. "You talked?"

Ryden nodded. "We kept each other company for sure. Venrhys took a particular interest in him, and I didn't think anything of it, but now I know why. It all makes perfect sense." He smiled sweetly, his grey eyes staring off into nothingness. "It was because of you."

Rexah tensed in his arms and slowly looked up at him. "Ry …"

"It's okay, Rex. You don't have to say anything." He squeezed her gently and rested his head on hers. "Don't say anything."

Her eyes softened. "You know I—"

"I know." He smiled down at her and nodded. "I love you too." He sighed deeply then, as though releasing his worries through a single breath.

Rexah sat up and wiped the lingering wetness from his cheeks. "I know you said you're okay, but how are you feeling after Arelle checked on you?"

"That woman is a miracle worker. The medicine she has stocked is incredible. Last night was the best sleep I've had in so long."

"You must be starving," she said as she sat up. "I'll go and see if breakfast has been made yet."

When she stood up, Ryden gently took her hand again. "I've been thanking the gods since we left the Keep that they brought you back to me," he said.

Rexah smiled softly. "Rest up, Ry," she replied before walking to the door and opening it softly. "We can talk more later."

Ryden was alive. The man she'd mourned and let go of wasn't on the other side, he was here. The man she was promised to marry not so long ago. She had spoken to him, cried with him only moments ago. Had she lost her mind? If she went back in there, would he be gone? Dead still?

"We don't have a choice." The memory of his words to her returned. Everything it meant so long ago, everything it led to as his grey eyes had connected so deeply with hers. *"But if we did have a choice, I would still choose you, Rex."*

She remembered how her heart had answered, thumping in her chest as he'd said the words, and she mourned that feeling once again. That longing she'd once savoured was lost to the past, and as she made her way to the kitchen, following the delicious scent of Storglass's cooking, she fought away the memories of her own words, ones she no longer felt so connected to.

"I would choose you too."

18

VENRHYS

The words left the guard's mouth, but Venrhys couldn't believe what he was hearing. His guards wouldn't dare lie to him, not if they valued their lives, but he refused to accept it as the truth. He studied the Dark Fae before him as he sat behind his desk, watching the sweat drip from his brow, taking in the way his body trembled no matter how hard he fought to keep himself still.

"I'd like you to repeat that one more time," Venrhys said, his voice eerily calm.

Salrius, the guard before him, audibly gulped. "We … we've had a breech in our security. Two prisoners have … escaped, and three guards were killed. Two were found in the tunnels along with a Valfae and the other was discovered in an alcove."

"Which prisoners have left us?" Venrhys asked.

"Kalen Vidarr and Ryden Crowfell," Salrius answered.

Venrhys ground his teeth in frustration and tapped his knuckles impatiently on the desk. "How?"

"We don't know, but they had to have had help."

Venrhys pondered for a moment. Had Rexah Ravenheart been here, and he hadn't sensed her? Surely he would have known the second she stepped foot into the building. Her unique scent was one he could never mistake. But who else would come for him? His fae friend? not alone, at least. No, it was Ravenheart; he knew it. So, how exactly had she managed to enter and escape without being sensed by anyone? Venrhys's hand clenched into a fist.

The Warlock.

He must have had something to do with it.

He grabbed an inkwell and threw it against the door, the ink spilling down the wood and dripping into a pool of black on the floor. "How many guards were patrolling the dungeons and tunnels?" he asked.

"Six total. Two in the dungeons, two in the tunnels and two on perimeter duty," Salrius replied. "With the war preparations in full swing, we don't have enough soldiers to spare to keep guard here."

Venrhys felt his anger building higher and higher. "You think that is a good enough excuse? You are all Dark Fae. The strength within one of you is equal to that of ten men. Whether there were four or just one guard, this breech should never have happened," he said through gritted teeth, trying to keep his rage at bay, but that was easier said than done.

"I-I understand ... but—"

"I'm tired of hearing your excuses." Venrhys rose from his seat and walked around the desk, stopping in front of Salrius. His eyes burned into the guard's orbs.

"Please ... give me the opportunity to make this right. I'll go after them. Their trail will still be strong enough to follow," Salrius pleaded.

Venrhys didn't answer him, at least not with words.

Instead, he let his magic seep out, his hand morphing into a wickedly sharp claw. Before the guard could respond, Venrhys swiped. Salrius grabbed his bloody throat, his eyes wide as he choked, his mouth agape with the gurgling of blood. He dropped to his knees before collapsing to the floor, black blood pooling beneath him.

Venrhys shifted his dark gaze to the other two guards in the room. "Let this be a lesson to you. This cannot happen again. Increase the security, double it. Gather some soldiers and track down Rexah Ravenheart and her companions. Fail and you *will* suffer the same fate as him," he said, giving Salrius's corpse a kick. "Do I make myself clear?"

Neither guard spoke. They simply bowed their heads in both respect and understanding.

"Good. Now, go," Venrhys dismissed them with the wave of a hand. "Oh, take him with you. Feed him to the dogs."

They stepped forward, lifted the dead guard and left the office.

Once the door was closed Venrhys let out a deep growl of frustration, shoving everything off his desk, the items crashing to the floor. He pressed his hands on the now empty surface, leaning forward as he cursed. The only leverage he had on Rexah had been taken from him.

The Elder wasn't going to be happy about this.

"They escaped," the Elder said, repeating Venrhys's words.

Venrhys looked down at his clasped hands, lightly rubbing the spilled ink that stained his fingertips. "Unfortunately, yes, my lord. Kalen Vidarr and Ryden Crowfell."

The chamber was eerily quiet; the Elder's sangfroid compounding the fear in Venrhys's heart. Never in the history of the Dark Lands had any prisoners escaped. No prisoner could possibly leave of their own accord, many had tried and failed, but nobody had ever tried to break in before. In doing so, the little bitch had found a weak spot.

The wretched Chosen certainly is a bold one.

"Well, this is not good at all," the Elder said, sitting back in his chair. "How did this happen?"

"The guard suggested that the prisoners had help escaping."

The Elder's eyes fixed on him sending a shock of fear through his system. "The Chosen."

Venrhys nodded. "I believe so, and I also assume the reason no one sensed her was thanks to her warlock friend," he said, bitterness oozing from his voice. "He must have cast a spell to cloak them from us."

"I see." The Elder walked over to the window. He wiped his finger along the frame and felt with his thumb and forefinger the dust he collected. "To say I am disappointed is an understatement," he replied. "This cannot be allowed to happen again."

"I will do whatever it takes to ensure it doesn't," Venrhys promised.

"Double the search efforts. I want her found and brought to me," he ordered. "She will find the sword one way or another. I'll make sure of it."

"Yes, my lord. I already have soldiers on their trail. It won't be long before they're found," Venrhys told him.

"For your sake, I hope that is true."

The words sent a chill through Venrhys's bones. It wasn't just a threat; it was a vow. One that he wouldn't allow to come to fruition. Rexah would be found, even if it meant he had to go and look for her himself. "I will not fail you," he assured.

"I believe you." The Elder moved his gaze to the crackling fireplace. "Go now. Fix this."

Venrhys bowed deeply before walking to the double doors. Adrenaline coursed through him. He enjoyed the thrill of the hunt, but the promise of disappointment if he failed outweighed his exhilaration. Or maybe it fuelled it?

His master would return, and he would play his part dutifully.

Rexah Ravenheart had to be found sooner rather than later, and with that thought swirling in his mind he began to construct his plan.

The hunt begins, Little Raven.

19

REXAH

A few days passed and the rescue mission had taken its toll on everyone. Arelle made sure they were well fed and took the medicine she provided where needed, and Rexah thanked the gods for bringing her into their lives. She also thanked Riona, knowing her ancestor had something to do with their meeting.

Kalen was almost back to perfect health, his power nearing full strength once again, and it filled Rexah with joy to see glimmers of his old self slowly resurfacing. The heated kiss they'd shared in bed hadn't stopped playing in her mind either. The sensation of his lips lingered, a reminder of how close she had been to giving herself fully to him, but now wasn't the time, especially when her previous betrothed was sleeping in the room across the hall.

Her lungs burned as she bent over her knees, forcing much needed air back into them. Sweat slicked her palms and coated her body, and her legs felt like jelly.

"Remind me again when you became such a weakling?" Torbin taunted playfully as he twirled two daggers expertly in his hands. "I didn't expect you to be this out of shape already, especially considering all the training we've been doing. You're getting lazy, Rex."

Gritting her teeth, Rexah growled and swiped her dagger at his chest which he evaded with embarrassing ease. It was all the movement he needed, and he kicked the back of her knee, sending her tumbling to the grass, her weapons falling just out of her reach.

"You need to reign that anger in. It will get you killed if you don't keep it in check." He circled her. "If your opponent catches even a glimpse of that anger they will use it as another weapon against you, and they won't need to lift a finger. You'll do all the work for them."

Rexah rolled onto her back and stared up at him. "Even Zuko was never this harsh on me."

Torbin stopped at her head. "I'm not trying to be harsh on you, Rex. It's a dangerous world out there, as you are fully aware. Your enemy won't go easy on you. I need to know that you are more than prepared for what's to come, that I did everything I could to help you, and so I know you are more than capable of taking on any threat yourself if Kalen and I aren't there."

None of them knew what was to come. From experience she knew she could handle the Valfae and Dark Fae, but there was a greater evil in the realm, one she could not underestimate the power of.

The Elder Fae.

"Hopefully I won't have to fight him." She breathed heavily as she stared up at him, seeing his eyes soften at her words.

"We all hope it doesn't come to that, but you need to be prepared regardless," he said. "Now, get up."

Rexah smirked at his authoritative tone. She enjoyed the way Torbin spoke sometimes. Depending on whose company he was in, she noticed he would speak in a different way. When they'd first met, he was polite and a little shy, but as they grew to know one another she noticed how informal their conversations had become; he spoke to her confidently, how one would speak to a best friend.

The way you used to speak with Nesrin, the little voice in her head so kindly reminded her.

She shook away the pain of that newly reopened wound and did as Torbin ordered, pushing herself to her feet, gripping the hilt of her daggers tighter as she rolled her shoulders. "Do your worst," she taunted back.

Two could play this game.

Torbin chuckled as he shifted his stance. "As you wish."

In twenty minutes Rexah was done. Her body had made the decision for her. She lay on her back in the grass, staring up at the fluffy white clouds, her body refusing to do her bidding. She successfully connected with a few carefully placed strikes before deciding she'd had enough for the day.

Torbin sat beside her, discarding his weapons. "I didn't mean what I said earlier when I called you a weakling. You're the exact opposite of that. It was only meant to push you."

She smiled at him. "I know," she said through deep breaths. "Thank you for training me. I really appreciate it."

He shook his head. "The pleasure is all mine. It keeps me in my own routine, and it's nice to have someone to train with."

From nowhere, a tingling sensation bloomed to life on the back of her neck before it slid down into her chest, and by the time it reached her core, it was a pulsing ache of need. When she looked over to the back porch of Arelle's home, she saw the cause.

Kalen stood there, his shoulder leaning against one of the wooden beams and his arms crossed over his chest as he watched them. His eyes burned into her, intensifying that ache between her thighs, the white scar down his brow striking in the sunlight.

Rexah sat up and pushed the damp hair from her eyes, trying her hardest to push away her desire. "Kalen, you shouldn't be out here. You should be resting!"

"I heard the clashing of steel, and my curiosity got the better of me." He smirked as his gaze moved to Torbin. "It's nice to still see you in one piece, brother. I feared she may have bested you."

"Don't joke about that until you've fought with her your-self." Torbin chuckled. "She could take you on."

Kalen's eyes lit up at the idea, and Rexah shut him down instantly. "Absolutely not, so don't even think about it. I'm not training or sparring with you, not until you are a million percent healed."

"Spoil sport." Kalen grinned.

Rexah managed to get to her feet, her muscles protesting at the movement. "Thank you again for an amazing session," she said to Torbin before she headed in Kalen's direction.

"Same time tomorrow?" he called out after her.

"Sure! If I can actually move in the morning!" she replied over her shoulder.

Once she was within his reach, Kalen gently pulled her close, kissing her tenderly. She cupped his face as she returned it, melting against him.

"Get a room!" Torbin yelled before making fake gagging sounds.

Rexah giggled against Kalen's mouth as she pulled away.

"I'm going to take a shower," she said, and when she saw the wicked gleam in his eyes, she finished, "alone."

Kalen laughed and kissed her forehead. "Enjoy, darling."

Rexah made a promise to herself that once the evil in the world was destroyed, and it was time for her to settle down, she would have a shower installed in her home. It would be one of the first things she did. Baths were still one of her favourite things in the world, but since experiencing a shower, she wouldn't be able to give it up. It was a luxury she didn't want to live without.

The hot water flooded from the showerhead, hitting her back and soothing her aching muscles. There was something about the shower that made her thoughtful, and it was there, alone in the shower that she ruminated over Ryden. For the first time, she allowed herself some honesty.

Life never played out the way she thought it would. In her royal world she was to marry Ryden, produce heirs and one day rule over Adorea and Kaldoren. Rexah never did find out what the exact details of her married life would entail. The Dark Fae and those monsters ensured that fairy tale never came true, but another thought crossed her mind.

If the events in Adorea had never happened, I probably wouldn't have met Kalen.

Guilt instantly slammed into her like a kick to the gut. Ryden didn't deserve any of this. She'd assumed he was dead and had moved on. It was a choice she had made, and she didn't regret it, but it still saddened her. She didn't like being the cause of someone's heartache and sorrow. Ryden hadn't admitted it, he didn't need to, it was all there in those steel eyes of his; he was hurting and it was all because of her choices.

The cascading water soon turned cold, sending a flood of goosebumps over her wet skin. Rexah wrapped a soft cotton towel around herself as she stepped out. The glass of the mirror squeaked slightly as she wiped off some of the condensation that had gathered on it.

Her violet eyes shone brightly against her milky skin. The woman staring back at her wasn't the same as the one that had stared back in Adorea. That girl died along with her grandmother and her people.

Rexah was still learning how to stand, how to fight and how to defend. Zuko had already trained her, yes, but the fae fought differently to men, and Rexah was fascinated by their methods, almost like a ballroom dance except instead of a kiss, this waltz ended in death. She still had to learn how to tap into the magic that lay dormant most of the time and command it; she still had to learn control. It had burst forth in her time of need multiple times, but she had to master it. She had to know she could rely on herself; she could no longer rely on little more than a magical reflex.

Rexah cupped her hands and ran them through the roots of her wet hair.

"I am going to be the luckiest man alive because you will be my wife."

Ryden's words haunted her, replaying relentlessly over the image of his grey gaze, but as she gazed into her own eyes, she could see the fighter within ready to charge into battle, she could see the power simmering, waiting to be called upon and unleashed. There was something else in her unique gaze that held strength above everything else, pacing back and forth like a vengeful predator.

The princess whose birth sent shockwaves across the realm.

The heir who patiently waited to take her seat on the throne.

The queen who was ready to take back her kingdom.

"Torbin said you've started to meditate. That's good," Arelle said.

Rexah sat on the front porch with her legs crossed under herself, Arelle sitting opposite her in the same position. As excited as Rexah was to get started, to learn more of her own power, she was also terrified of the unknown. What would happen when she embraced her magic? Would she be able to control it, or would she cause untold destruction?

Magic was something Rexah had been fascinated with since she was very young. Magical studies was one of her favourite classes taught to her by the royal tutor. It wasn't a necessary subject for a human princess, but Rexah had begged her grandmother to let it be included in her curriculum.

It was surreal to her knowing that she had power rooted deep within, power that lay dormant in her blood. It had been there her whole life and she'd been none the wiser. The anger she felt about her grandmother keeping it a secret was still raw in her chest, but she understood why she was never told.

"Take a deep breath, love," Arelle said softly. "I can feel fear rolling off of you. There's nothing to be afraid of. I will guide you."

Rexah inhaled deeply, taking the crisp morning air into her lungs, squashing the nerves rolling in her stomach enough for her to straighten her spine. "I'm ready."

Arelle smiled at her. "The first thing I need you to do is close your eyes."

She did as she was instructed.

"Lay the back of your hands on your knees, palms facing up towards the sky," Arelle instructed in a soothing voice. "Good, now I want you to clear your mind until it is an empty void."

Just like she had with Torbin, she tried her hardest to erase every idea, notion, and belief. Each thought that presented itself, each anxiety and rumination, she pushed aside until there was nothing but the breeze and the steady rhythm of her breathing.

"I want you to picture that magnificent power. There are no wrong answers here. You could see smouldering embers or a raging ocean," Arelle instructed. "Tell me what you see."

Rexah saw nothing, and her heart dropped with disappointment.

"Your mind is filling again," the Seer said. "There is no room in the void for ruminations of failure. Be patient. Try again."

Rexah sighed, and with it she expelled that disappointment. Again, she pushed aside each thought, faster this time, and when her mind was empty, she worked on visualising her power.

Finally, there it was: emptiness.

A flicker of light appeared in that dark space within her.

"I ... I see a well ... made of stars," she whispered, her voice coated with emotion. "It ... it's absolutely stunning."

"That's perfect. You're doing so well," Arelle said and Rexah could hear the smile on her face in her voice. "Now what you need to do is reach into that well and grab onto your power."

Rexah pictured herself standing before the beautiful, twinkling structure. Warmth radiated from it as she reached her hand inside. She strained as she tried to latch onto something, anything, but the space she moved within felt humid, the air thick and oppressive. She imagined she were in a storm cloud, finding her way through the vapour to return to clearer skies.

Then, her fingertips grazed something.

It scared her, but Arelle's soothing voice pierced through her fear. "Hold onto that feeling, Rexah. Imagine it filling every nerve and every cell of your being. It doesn't control you; you control it."

Rexah willed the power to move on her command, ordered it to do her bidding and infuse itself within her, and to her amazement, it did. The electrical charge zinged through her, and the energy skittered along her flesh like ants rushing to a nest. When she moved her gaze back down into the well, she could see her magic slowly beginning to rise.

"Open your eyes, love," Arelle encouraged gently.

When she did, Rexah squinted at the brightness of the sun. She looked down at her upturned palms and her eyes went wide as she let out a surprised breath. Purple energy swirled in her hands, lightning snapping within it and crackling along her fingers painlessly. It brewed like a tempest, waiting for the order from her to erupt. She stared at it, completely enraptured. A laugh of disbelief and shock left her lips as she looked over to Arelle who stared back with pride shining in her light-green eyes.

"I did it," Rexah whispered.

Arelle grinned. "You did it."

Rexah began laughing as tears built up in her eyes. When she was a little girl, she would pretend that she was one of the warriors from her favourite book, fighting off evil with her magic. That story was now a reality.

Suddenly the power disappeared from her palms, and she frowned.

"You must maintain focus or else your magic will fade back into that well," Arelle told her. "But for your first proper attempt at harnessing, it was amazing, Rexah. I am so proud of you."

"I have the best teacher," she said, smiling as she wiped away the tears that had managed to escape down her cheeks.

Arelle gently took her hands. "I wish Riona could have met you. The similarities between you both are staggering. She knew you would be the next Chosen."

"How? How could she know that?"

"She dreamed of you," she replied.

Rexah's heart thundered against her chest. "She told you of her dreams of me?"

Arelle nodded. "We didn't know why she was having them. At first, I thought she was maybe dreaming about forgotten memories, but then she said your name …"

"What happened?" Rexah whispered.

"As soon as your name left her lips, I had a vision of you," Arelle told her. "I saw your wedding day. You looked so incredibly beautiful, a younger version of Riona, and I knew instantly what that meant."

Grief wrapped around her heart for the moment that never happened. Her wedding to Ryden was to be a lavish affair full of love and alliance, but instead it was crushed before it could take place by the Dark Fae.

For the thousandth time that day, she shoved the Ryden memories aside. "All my life I've been compared to her. The girl who resembled Queen Riona the most in our whole family.

I look more like her than her own daughter did. I've always found that unnerving," Rexah admitted.

"I understand, but that's how fate works," Arelle replied. "You are alike in more ways than one. The Raven God chose you both. Renvian's blood, his power, runs through your veins, just as it did in Riona's."

"But why did it skip generations? Why weren't there other Chosen in my family if he favoured my bloodline so much?" Rexah asked.

"The gods, much like fate, work in mysterious ways. We will never know the reasons for their actions, but they don't make decisions lightly," she said. "For reasons unknown he's taken an interest in your bloodline, and that's nothing to fear." Arelle unfolded her legs and moved to sit on the porch steps. "Now, I wanted to talk to you about your nightmares. I read what you wrote."

Rexah stood too, stretching out her legs before taking a seat next to the Seer. "What do you think?" she asked, her heart fluttering with anticipation. "Am I going crazy?"

"Of course not." Arelle let out a hearty laugh. "Riona often had a similar dream to yours. She only spoke of the dream she had of you once, but more often than not, she dreamt of storms and death. I consulted with the spirits, and they confirmed it was a side effect, if you will, of having the Blood of the Raven."

"The Raven God is the reason why I've been having the same bad dream over and over again?"

"Yes. The dream you describe seems to have been a warning of sorts, about what was to transpire in Adorea," she replied.

"I should have taken it more seriously. If I had then maybe

I could have warned my grandmother … maybe we could have evacuated the kingdom," Rexah began to babble.

"Rexah, love, there was no stopping what happened to your home and your people. As hard as it is, it was going to happen whether you stepped in or not."

It was a bitter pill to swallow, but Arelle was right, and the sooner she stopped blaming herself for what happened, the better. It was easier said than done, but she wouldn't let the crippling grief take charge any longer. She would grip it tight and turn it into the strength she needed to defeat the darkness, and she would be a force to be reckoned with.

"I don't mean to intrude."

Rexah and Arelle turned to find Ryden stood behind them holding a tray of tea and a blanket over his shoulder.

"Ry …" Rexah responded, moving to stand up. "You didn't have to—"

"Please, carry on. I just saw you both out here and thought it might be getting cold. I'll just leave these." Ryden bent, grimacing at the unhealed wounds that niggled when he moved. "There you go."

"Thank you."

Ryden smiled timidly. "You're welcome, princess."

Rexah reached for the tea and the warmth from the cup seeped through her skin comfortingly. "How is he?" she asked Arelle quietly, motioning to Ryden as he walked away.

"He was in bad shape, but he's doing really well. The medicine is working a treat on his injuries," she said as she picked up her own mug. "There's still a lot of healing to do emotionally and mentally, but overall, he's doing great, all things considered."

Rexah nodded. "It means a great deal to me that you welcomed him into your home. I feel like we've taken over."

"Don't fret. It's been a long time since I've had company. I've missed it. It got lonely for a while here." Arelle met her gaze and smiled. "How are you? Don't say you're fine, because I know you're not," Arelle said, gently blowing on the hot brew. "Tell me how you're really feeling."

"To be honest, I don't know how I feel or how I'm supposed to feel," she told her. "Right now, all I'm trying to do is hold it together and get through each day as they come."

"It must have been such a shock seeing Ryden in the Keep."

She should have known better than to think Arelle wouldn't know exactly what her worries were; the Seer's conscientiousness in that moment astounded Rexah, and not for the first time. "Is it that obvious?"

"To me, always," Arelle said before sipping her drink. "Have you spoken to him about everything since you brought him back?"

Rexah shook her head. "We had a very brief conversation, but we need to sit down and have a proper talk about what's going to happen going forward."

"What do you want to happen?"

The tea soothed her throat as she drank it. "I want my best friend back. I love him, but I'm not *in love* with him. I don't want to lose him because of it."

Arelle leaned forward and gently placed her hand on Rexah's knee. "I understand."

"You do?"

"Of course. You love Ryden as a friend. He's one of your best friends after all, but there's another that you love more, and that's okay."

"If it's okay then why do I feel so fucking guilty?" she

whispered, trying to hold back the tears that were threatening to fall.

The Seer's eyes softened. "Because it's in your nature to put other people's feelings before your own. Did you know that your great, great grandfather wasn't Riona's true love?"

Rexah's eyes went wide, and she shook her head. "He wasn't?"

"After Riona's husband died, she met another. The soul that was made for hers. It wasn't love at first sight; they hated each other, but I could see it wasn't hate at all." Arelle's lips tugged up into a smirk before sadness filled her features. "But as fate would have it, she met Kane four months before she died. He survived the battle, and when he learned of her death, it was too much for him to bare. He gathered his things, along with some rations, and left. No one heard from him or saw him again."

"Kane," Rexah whispered. "Another K."

"Riona and Kane," Arelle said with a grin. "Rexah and Kalen."

The world felt like it shifted beneath her. That couldn't be a coincidence, could it?

"That's not all that happened," Arelle continued.

Rexah took another sip of her tea, preparing herself for whatever Arelle might say next. "Go on."

"The Battle of Adorea is a day I will never forget. After the battle was won and Riona lay in my arms, I noticed a change in her. It was so subtle, but it was there," Arelle said, her voice wavering with grief. "As I held her close, my magic could feel her heartbeat slowing, along with the heartbeat of the baby growing in her womb."

"She ... she was pregnant?"

Arelle nodded, wiping her eyes. "She didn't know. I didn't

tell her. How could I tell my dying best friend that she was with child? How could I tell her that she was carrying her mate's baby? I've never told another soul until now.

"I've regretted it every single day since her passing. Sometimes I wonder if it was the right thing to do, but the spirits tell me it was. They told me that she forgave me and that her and her baby were together on the other side."

"I'm sorry you carried that with you for so long," Rexah said, her voice nothing more than a whisper as more tears fell.

Arelle reached for the blanket and wrapped it lovingly around Rexah's shoulders. "I have been gifted a second chance at this, with you, by the gods," Arelle told her. "For that, I'll be forever grateful."

Rexah held her cup close to her chest. Riona had been pregnant with her second child when she died. Her heart broke for her ancestor and for the Seer sitting across from her. "Thank you for being comfortable enough to confide in me. I won't breathe a word of this to another soul," she promised her.

Arelle nodded her thanks and picked up her own cup of tea. Together, they sat in peaceful silence, leaning into each other's shoulders.

"I need to find the sword," Rexah said finally, her thoughts too much to keep to herself. "We can't move forward without it. The only time I got close to discovering its location was during the meditation session with Torbin. It was behind a purple door, and I've been trying to figure out if I've seen it before, but I can't do it alone. I think I might need your help. Is there anything you can do?"

"I will help you, but I fear you will continue to fail in finding the sword while you are still beginning to harness your power. Not to mention it could be dangerous. You told me that you woke your power and saw the sword simultaneously, and I am not inclined to ignore that. Your power and the sword are clearly linked, and so we must be cautious. We will work together with your power, then we will go back to that place in your mind together. Patience will get you the sword, I promise."

"Thank you, Arelle. I wouldn't be able to do this without you, or them."

"We all have our part to play in the war to come. We're all soldiers of the gods in one way or another. I'd like us all to be as prepared as possible when it counts the most," she told her.

"Once we find the sword everything is going to change, the gods know things already have, but it's going to get worse, and I'm scared that we're not all going to get through this alive." Rexah ran her fingers through her dark hair. She didn't know what was going to happen, no one did, and it was the unknown that terrified her the most.

Arelle leaned forward and gently took Rexah's hand. "They will never admit it, but even the fiercest warriors are scared before battle. Any that tell you otherwise are liars," she said. "Fear is one of our most basic instincts. It's how our bodies cope and it's nothing to be ashamed of."

A painful cry caught Rexah's attention, and she looked over to see Torbin shaking his hand, his sword discarded at his feet.

"Everything okay over there?" Arelle called out to them.

Kalen chuckled. "Torbin got his finger caught. He's just being a big baby."

Torbin playfully shoved Kalen. "Let's get your finger caught and see how you like it."

"It's a good job we're done with meditation for the day." Rexah smiled. It was nice seeing them like this, without a care in the world, even if it was only for a short time. Rexah's grin deepened as she watched Arelle stare at the now shirtless Torbin.

Finally, Arelle turned to find Rexah smirking. "*What?*"

Rexah smiled a toothy grin. "Isn't Tor the best?"

Arelle narrowed her eyes and failed to hide a smile.

"Is he not?"

Arelle sighed extravagantly. "Okay …"

"And look at him. You'd be mad not to notice those muscles. Good guy, too. The whole package if you ask me."

Arelle scoffed as she stood and placed a hand on Rexah's head. "Maybe you and Riona weren't so alike after all."

"No?"

"No," Arelle said, winking at Rexah before planting a kiss on her head. "Riona was funny."

20

KALEN

"Come on, brother. I told you not to go easy on me," Kalen said to Torbin as he swung his sword expertly. "I'm not going to break."

For days he'd been training with Torbin to get his strength back up. If they were going to be taking on the Dark Fae and the Valfae, then he needed to get back into shape, and fast.

"You don't want to overdo it. The last thing we need is you pulling a muscle," Torbin told him, rolling his strong shoulders, the tattoos on his arms shifting as he moved. The ink was stunning and had been applied by the same artist who'd tattooed Kalen. The intricate patterns started at his shoulders and ended just below the bend in his elbows. Within the centre of the pattern on his right shoulder was the fae rune of fire. His other shoulder was decorated with a black and grey rose, a stunning dream catcher flowing from under the flower.

Kalen burst into laughter. "I've never pulled a muscle in my life, Tor. I'm not about to start now. Come on, fight me like you mean it, like your life depends on it. Like old times."

Torbin swirled his blades. "As you wish."

It felt like so long ago since it was just the two of them. When they'd found a dying princess on a dirt road in Adorea, they knew their lives would never be the same again. Kalen hadn't realised *just* how different his life would be.

Kalen hadn't appreciated how much he'd missed this, and he grinned as he ducked and dodged out of harm's way. He'd missed spending time with his best friend. He brought his sword up to block both of Torbin's, the steel singing through the air like a song of battle as they clashed together.

"Is it just me or are you getting a little sloppy, Tor?" Kalen teased.

Torbin growled and shoved him back before continuing his assault. This was the fighting Kalen loved. They weren't best friends, they were two warriors, and they weren't holding back. "I'm not sloppy," Torbin said through gritted teeth, thrusting one sword forward, aiming for Kalen's right side.

Kalen jerked back, the blade missing him by an inch. He took the opportunity that his friend handed to him on a plate; he punched Torbin in his left side, and when he doubled over, Kalen swiped his feet from under him, sending him to the ground.

"I win," Kalen grinned, the tip of his sword pointing to Torbin's throat.

The beaten fae glared up at him for a moment before his features smoothed and a laugh broke from his lips. Kalen held out his hand and helped him onto his feet.

"You're recovering well," Torbin told him, patting his bare back. "You'll be back to your old self in no time."

The cool breeze brushed by, cooling the sweat that dripped down his torso. "Thanks, Tor. Let's take a five-minute break then I'll let you try and redeem yourself from that embarrassing loss." Kalen chuckled when he playfully punched his arm.

"Got room for one more?"

Kalen looked over to see Ryden standing at the porch, leaning against one of the wooden pillars. It took a huge amount of energy to keep the green-eyed monster in its cage, and for Rexah's sake he would, but he was curious as to what would happen if he let it out to play, even just for a moment.

Rexah would kill me for intentionally hurting him, that's what would happen.

Forcing a smile to spread across his face, Kalen replied, "Sure, the more the merrier." He watched as the prince of Kaldoren descended the steps and made his way towards them with a hint of a swagger.

Cocky prick.

"How much training have you had?" Torbin asked him.

Ryden pulled his shirt off and discarded it at his feet. The hard muscles of his abdomen and biceps answered Torbin's question. It was clear he'd been taught to fight from a young age, just like they had. Even though he'd been in that cell for months, Ryden looked fit enough.

"One handed or two?" Kalen asked.

"Either," Ryden replied. "I'm proficient in both."

Torbin handed him one of his short swords. "You can use this for now."

Ryden thanked him as he took the weapon and studied it. "It's beautifully crafted."

Kalen wasn't just jealous that Ryden had been Rexah's first, her everything, but now he could feel that jealousy spreading to the compliment he'd just given *his* best friend's blade.

Get a fucking grip of yourself, Kalen.

Reining in his bitterness, Kalen took a deep breath. "Who do you want to fight?"

"After the time we spent in the Keep, I'd like to see what you've got," Ryden told him, a grin spreading across his face.

From the corner of his eye Kalen saw Torbin smirk, but he chose to ignore him as he nodded. "Very well."

Torbin walked over to the porch and sat down on the steps, getting himself comfortable to watch the fight.

"Are there any rules?" Ryden asked, giving the sword a few practise swings.

"Only one. No attempts to kill or seriously injure," Kalen told him. He got into his fighting stance, preparing himself for whatever Ryden was about to throw at him.

Ryden nodded in understanding and readied himself. "Ready when you are."

Kalen quickly scanned him for weaknesses before he shot forward with speed, swinging his sword. Ryden blocked the attack, knocking the blade away before shoving his shoulder into Kalen's chest, sending the fae stumbling back. Ryden tried to take advantage of Kalen's little tumble, but he recovered quickly and spun out of the way of Ryden's sword, the edge of the blade slicing through the soil beneath their feet.

Kalen ducked when Ryden spun, the sword missing his head by inches. Kalen kicked his foot out, taking his opponent's legs out from under him. When Ryden hit the ground, he managed to use his momentum to roll backwards onto his feet in one smooth motion.

"You're good, considering how long you were kept in that cell for." Kalen panted, a wide smile plastered on his face. "Very good."

"You're not too bad yourself," Ryden replied, smirking

softly. "Maybe there was more to that shit they classed as food than we thought."

Kalen huffed a laugh. "I don't ever want to think of that horrible stuff again." He sheathed his weapon and without warning, his mind bombarded him with images and memories he truly never desired to think of again. The feeling of starvation, the agony of a knife across his chest, and the sight of Venrhys's disgusting grin. "You're welcome to train with us to keep your strength up," he offered, forcing his mind elsewhere as he rubbed his eyes.

"That's much appreciated." Ryden nodded softly, assessing Kalen curiously before turning his attention to Torbin. "You want to show me what you can do?"

Torbin smiled and rose to his feet. "Sure, let's go."

Kalen picked up his shirt from where he'd discarded it earlier as Torbin and Ryden began to spar. After he pulled the material over his head, his eyes instantly went to the porch. An angel now stood there; raven-coloured hair danced lightly in the breeze, violet eyes taking in every inch of him, and it sent a thrill through his body.

"I hate to break up your training session, but dinner is ready," she told them, smiling as her eyes never left Kalen.

"Good, I'm starving," Torbin said, grinning from ear to ear.

Kalen laughed quietly as he made his way over to Rexah. "How was your session with Arelle?" he asked her as they entered the home.

"It went well. It's still early days, but I'm getting there. Arelle said I need to familiarise myself with my magic, like when you first meet a dog and it sniffs your hand," she told him with a chuckle.

"I love that example." He grinned. "It's very cute."

Rexah playfully hit his arm as they turned down the corridor. The smell of various meats and gravy hit his nose, and his mouth instantly watered. The dining table was filled with platters of pork, beef and potatoes smothered in creamy butter. A large bowl of mixed salad sat beside a gravy boat shaped like a cauldron.

"Take a seat and help yourselves!" Storglass said enthusiastically from the kitchen area.

Kalen looked over to see him plating some garlic bread wearing an apron that said *Kiss the Witch* on it, and he couldn't contain his laughter. He pulled out a chair for Rexah as Torbin and Ryden walked in.

"Smells great in here," Ryden said cheerfully. He walked over to the table, lightly patting Kalen's shoulder as passed. "You good?"

Kalen turned to Ryden, unsure of how to react. What was this for? The gesture felt genuine, but all he felt was a building frustration.

"Yes. I'm good."

Ryden eyed him as he pulled out his chair, scrutinising Kalen with such intensity that it quickly became irksome.

What the fuck does he want?

"Okay," Ryden said, his tone dubious. "Good."

Once everyone was seated and their plates full to the brim, Arelle said, "I've never had all the seats at this table taken before. It brings me great joy to have my home filled with such wonderful company."

"We are all extremely grateful and are in your debt for letting us stay here," Torbin replied, a gentle smile on his lips, and Kalen swore he saw Arelle's cheeks pink slightly.

Storglass lifted his glass. "To Arelle, for everything she has done for us all and still continues to do."

Everyone followed suit and raised their drinks, toasting the Seer.

Arelle shook her head. "No need for any of that. I'm just glad I can do my bit. Now, dig in before the food gets cold."

No one needed to be told twice; everybody tucked into the delicious meal. The food was incredible, and for the most part, the evening was too. But it all seemed to go out the window when Kalen looked up to see Ryden assessing him across the table, for once not with jealousy in his expression, but sympathy.

"What's on your mind, Kalen?" Torbin asked, reaching down to pick up another branch.

Kalen walked through the forest with Torbin, gathering wood for the fireplace. It seemed a strange request for him to join at the time, but his intentions now were clear.

Torbin wanted him to talk.

"What makes you think there's something on my mind?"

Torbin looked over to him. "I know you. You forget I can read you like a book, so spill it."

Kalen smirked. He loved how blunt Torbin could be sometimes, a side he rarely showed to anyone else. The smirk slowly faded from his face. "I've been having trouble sleeping."

"I'd be surprised if you weren't, brother. Tell me."

"I know you think you want to know, but you don't. Trust me." Kalen bent over to pick up more wood, groaning as he did. "What's done is done."

"It's not about what I want to know. It's about what you should tell someone. And this someone is asking."

Kalen sighed deeply. "Every time I close my eyes to sleep, all I see is that torture room. All I feel is what he did to me. It's like I'm reliving it over and over again in the quiet moments of my day. Sometimes it's so vivid that I wonder if I ever left. It's only when I look down and see Rexah sleeping peacefully in my arms that I know I'm safe."

Torbin was quiet as he took in his words. His eyes were soft and sympathetic as he replied, "What you endured was horrible, unspeakable. It'll take time to process and what you're feeling right now is completely natural. No one expects you to go through something like that and come out the other side unscathed, physically or mentally."

Kalen watched as Torbin walked over and placed his hand on his shoulder.

"You're no longer in that hell hole, I promise you," he said.

"It's that look too." He thought back to that moment with Ryden, about the softness of his eyes. How he felt sorry for him. "I hate the pity."

"People care about you," he replied with a shrug. "Comes with the territory."

"I didn't want to burden Rexah with this, didn't want to burden any of you."

"We're all here for each other. It's not healthy to keep things bottled up." Torbin squeezed his shoulder. "We'll get through this, brother. Together. Whatever you need, I'm here."

"Together," Kalen echoed, feeling some of the heaviness retreat. He could push through this; it would take some time, but he would get there. He always did.

Torbin shifted the weight of the wood in his arms. "Rexah

would support you one hundred percent if you were to tell her, regardless of what's going on right now."

"She would, but I don't want to add this to her growing list of worries," he replied, adding another piece of firewood to his pile. "She's lost a lot of people. Experienced a lot. Nearly died too many times. She's struggling."

"I tried my best to support her while you weren't here, but she can be so internal." Torbin's eyes were sad as he turned to meet his gaze. "It's been difficult. She wasn't the same without you here."

So, she felt it too?

A few moments passed while they each ruminated silently, staring out into the trees as though they might whisper their own secrets.

"I don't know about you, but I can't carry anymore. I think this will be enough," he said, motioning to the bundle in his arms.

"Let's head back."

"You know I'm here for you, Kalen. It doesn't matter what it is, you'll get no judgement from me," Torbin told him as they made their way back to Arelle's home.

"I really appreciate it, Tor. The same applies to you; I'm here if you need anything at all," Kalen said, and he meant it more than anything.

Torbin began opening and closing his mouth as though battling with indecision. To say or not say.

"Out with it," Kalen said finally, unable to stand the lip smacking anymore.

"You know who would be a *great* person to talk to about—"

"Don't even go there." Kalen scoffed. "Like things aren't weird enough."

He had nothing to be envious of, he knew that, but it didn't mean he wouldn't go green with envy over the relationship Ryden and Rexah had shared. Before, he was Crow, his fellow inmate who he'd shared many a conversation with, who had helped him through each day in the only way he could. Now he was Ryden, *the* Ryden, and he was still trying to figure out how to process that information and what that meant for him and Rexah going forward.

"Yeah, you don't say," Torbin said through a chuckle, "but seriously, if you can get past—"

"Parring me off already, brother?" The anger rose quickly, and he regretted his tone the moment he spoke with it.

Torbin rubbed a hand over his jaw, dropping some wood as he did so, and sighed. "No."

"He can be my shoulder to cry on the moment he stops looking at her like … that. And when is that ever going to fucking happen."

"I get it," Torbin said, reaching down for the wood. "I get it. I'm not saying don't talk to me. I want you to talk to me." Torbin walked round to face Kalen, forcing him to stop walking. "I'm saying that if you need to talk to someone who went through what you went through—"

"You've been through stuff too, Torbin."

"Not like this," Torbin said, his eyes pained. "Not like you."

They shared a look that said everything; it told Kalen that what he'd been through was truly terrible, and that his brother could see his turmoil. For the briefest moment, he could have broken down, not because of the pain of his imprisonment but from the gratitude he felt to have Torbin by his side.

"Fuck off, Tor."

Torbin grinned and sniffed. "So, tell me about this dream."

They continued to walk through the woodland, and Kalen recalled his most recent nightmare, sparing no detail of the horrors he'd endured in the torture room of the Dark Fae Keep; the knives, the blood, Venrhys's laugh; and with each word that left his lips the pressure eased in his chest. Talking about it helped tremendously, and he was so thankful to have a best friend like Torbin to confide in. But there was a moment that passed, fleeting as it was, where he wished he could ask the one person that had seen it all what they dreamt of, so that he might feel less alone in it; he wondered how it might feel to talk to the person who would know without so many words the weight of his nightmares.

He wished in that solitary moment that he could once again talk to Crow.

21

REXAH

"Where are we going? I can barely move after that last round with Tor."

"After where I've been staying, I'll take all the fresh air I can get," Kalen replied as he took hold of her hand. "Not to mention Storglass is being incredibly strange this morning. He's all … giddy."

Rexah chuckled lightly. "Oh, he gets like that. He sings too."

"Gods, take me back." He squirmed, seeming to hurt himself with his own joke, as though it encouraged memories of the Keep to return unwarranted.

Rexah ran a hand over his bicep comfortingly. "You know, Torbin and I wouldn't have made it if it weren't for Storglass," Rexah told him as the leaves crunched underneath her boots. "We would never have found Arelle on our own, not to mention saving Torbin's life. He healed him as best he could, and there was no way he'd have survived the road to Arelle's without it."

Kalen looked ahead into the trees. "I feared the worst. The

last I saw him, before Venrhys took me, he was dying. I could feel it," he said, his voice fading to a whisper.

Rexah gently squeezed his hand, sympathy shining in her eyes as she gazed up at him. "You felt it?"

"When we were younger, before we began our training, Torbin and I took an oath. Sure, we'd been training since we were small, but when we turned sixteen and were considered men, we swore to be each other's swords and shields. The oath is sealed with blood. We cut our palms and pressed them together.

"I can't read his mind or anything like that, but I get these little feelings from him, like he does me. We are bonded in a way," he explained to her.

"That's incredible. You're blood brothers then?"

Kalen grinned down at her. "Yeah, I guess that's a good term to use for it. Blood brothers, Torbin will like that." His eyes grew thoughtful. "And how he loves to use it against me," he said with a playful sigh, as though he both loved and hated it. "So, is the dog used to your scent yet?"

Rexah laughed heartily. "We're getting there. I'm supposed to give in to the process, but it's tough. I can't stop thinking about that first time meditating with Torbin. I saw the sword, and I swear it was real. Where I saw it is where it is, I'm sure of it. Arelle says I need to give it time to take further control of my power, but all I want to do is go back and look around again."

"And nothing was familiar to you? Nothing that we can go off? The place you saw the sword?"

"Just a room with a purple door," she replied.

For a short time, they walked in silence, and the rustling of surrounding trees lulled her into a state of rare serenity. She looked up to Kalen, but his face had a stiffness to it, one she saw often in these quiet moments. The same one she saw on Ryden's face when he spoke of what had happened to him.

"Kalen."

"Yes?"

"You will talk to someone if you need to, won't you?"

"My Rexah." Kalen stopped and pulled her in front of him. He leaned down and gently pressed his lips against hers. The kiss was tender and full of love. It was the softest kiss they'd ever shared, like he needed her to know how much she meant to him. After a few moments, Kalen slowly pulled away and leaned his forehead against hers. "Don't worry about me." He kissed her nose before taking her hand once more and continuing down the dirt road that led into the forest. "Would you like to know what is on my mind today?"

"Always."

"I often wondered if Venrhys would go back on his word and kill me," Kalen admitted. "There were a few times I would have embraced death. When the pain got to the point where I couldn't take much more, I would have welcomed it with open arms."

"We will make him pay for everything he did to you and Ryden," she said with conviction, her voice coated with anger. "They won't get away with it. They've ruined so many innocent lives. It has to end."

Kalen stiffened at the mention of Ryden's name. "Have you spoken to him yet?"

Rexah nodded. "Briefly, but I do need to talk to him again. We've got so much to discuss."

Kalen grew quiet. Too quiet.

Here we go.

Rexah's lips curled into a smirk, the smirk she knew would

send him wild. "Do I sense a hint of jealousy in you, Kalen?" she asked, her voice full of mischief.

He scoffed. "Absolutely not. I'm not *jealous.*"

"Okay, okay."

He kicked a rock and it clapped against a nearby tree. "I would never ask you to change. I know how much he means to you. He was a huge part of your life, your history, and when all is said and done, I am so fucking thankful for him."

Rexah's eyebrows came together in surprise. "Thankful for him? What for?"

"He protected you. He made sure you were happy. He gave you his love, his heart," he said. "He did all that when I could not. He will always have my respect for making you happy and keeping you safe."

Wow.

"I've never thought about it like that," she replied.

"I just have one question."

"Ask it."

"In light of everything I've just said." Kalen took a big breath in through his nose and expelled it slowly. "Do you think there's any chance of rekindling your relationship, your marriage?" Kalen asked.

Like Kalen had done earlier, Rexah stopped walking and pulled him so close that their chests touched. She knew the answer to his question unequivocally, and she wanted, needed him to know it. It had been the cause of all the guilt and pain of seeing Ryden again. It was the thing she begged herself for forgiveness for.

"No."

"No?" Kalen repeated, a laugh of disbelief escaping his lips. "Just, no?"

Rexah lifted her arms and put them round his neck. "A part

of me will always love Ryden, and that's something I can't change. He's my best friend. Like you said, Ryden has his space in my heart, and he always will, but the rest of it belongs to you."

Kalen gently wrapped his arm around her, tugging her closer to his body. "You mean that?"

"I do. I know things haven't exactly felt normal since we got you back. And there's not really been much of an opportunity for me to show you how I feel in a way that felt … appropriate, given the circumstances," she said. "But you make me feel safe. You make me feel like nothing is impossible. When I'm with you it's like we are the only two people in the universe. I've never felt this way about anyone before, and when it's this strong and it feels this right, no one can deny it."

Kalen's arm tightened around her, and he smiled, unable to hold back his relief. "Not even when past fiancés come back from the dead?"

"Not even then." She lifted her eyes to meet his once again so he could see absolute sincerity in them. "I'm saying that I'm yours, Kalen."

"Tell me," Kalen whispered. "Say the words."

Rexah searched his eyes for a moment. "I love you, Kalen. From the moment I first lay my eyes on you in Merin's home, I've loved you."

He gripped her by the waist and pinned her to the nearest tree, a gasp leaving her lips when her back connected with the trunk. His lips were suddenly on hers again, and this time their kiss was full of passion and need. It was a promise of protection and devotion.

Pure, undiluted love.

He pulled away, his eyes ablaze with adoration as he swept

his gaze over her face. "I love you too, Rexah Ravenheart. I always have, and I always will."

She kissed him; it was all she could do. Her tongue brushed his lips, and it coaxed a delicious moan from his mouth that set her blood alight. His hips pressed into hers, showing her exactly what she did to him, how she drove him crazy, and a moan fell from her own lips in response.

His hand went to the button on her trousers, popping it free with ease, along with the other two beneath it. "Tell me to stop." His chest heaved as he breathed heavily. "Say the words, and I'll stop."

"Kalen," she said, her own breathing erratic. "Don't stop."

His eyes connected with hers, searching for the permission he so desperately wanted and needed, and she gave it to him with a nod of her head. "Touch me."

He would never deny her.

Kalen's hand slid into her waistband and into her underwear. As soon as his fingers brushed against her already soaked core, Rexah gasped.

"Gods, Rexah," he said, letting out a shuddering breath. "I've hardly touched you and you're already so wet." His finger slowly ran up and down her centre, teasing her. He chuckled deeply when her hips rolled forward, trying to take more from him, and when he pushed his finger inside of her, he leaned into her ear and whispered, "Is this what you want?"

Rexah's moan was all the confirmation he needed as he slowly moved his hand, stroking her. His other hand gripped her waist to keep her steady against the tree as he worked her, adding a second finger to which she responded with a desperate call for more.

"Kalen," she moaned, her hand going to his arm, digging her fingers into it. Her hips began to move against his hand,

and he let her find her rhythm. She arched her back, inhaling sharply when his thumb found the sensitive little bundle of nerves.

"That's it," he praised. "You're so fucking beautiful." Kalen curled his fingers inside of her, bringing her closer to release with each stroke. He watched as she rocked against his fingers, chasing her high. "Come on, darling. Give it to me," he commanded.

When she finally let go, her body shuddering uncontrollably, his name fell from her lips again, this time in nothing more than a breathless whisper. He was completely enraptured by her; she could see it in his eyes that sparkled with arousal and adoration.

Her eyes fluttered closed and her mouth fell open. All she wanted to do was kiss him, to relive the moment until she was trembling once again.

The hardwood floor was cold underneath her bare feet as she padded down the hallway. She'd managed to slip out of bed without waking Kalen up. He seemed more tired than usual over the past few days. She'd first put it down to the amount of training he'd been doing with Torbin and Ryden, but something told her it wasn't that; the initial relief of being away from the Keep had worn off, she surmised, the reality of his trauma now fully set in.

As she moved through the living area, the soft glow of the lantern on the coffee table illuminated her path. Arelle wanted to keep it on in case anyone got up during the night for a drink, and Torbin was more than happy to provide some of his fae fire that would burn longer than a normal flame. A soft smile tugged at her lips as she thought about the Seer and the fae.

They would make the cutest couple.

Rexah went to open the back door as quietly as possible which was easier said than done in the complete silence. Her hand reached for the lock, but the key wouldn't turn. Her eyebrows pulled together. *Why is the door unlocked?* The tingle of her power surfaced, ever more present for her when she needed it, and she slowly opened the door, her free hand poised to release her power if necessary.

She peeked her head out the door and her eyes settled on a shape sitting on the porch steps.

Thank the gods.

"Couldn't sleep either?" she asked gently as she closed the door behind her.

Ryden looked over his shoulder. "No matter how hard I tried, I just couldn't seem to drift off. I thought that maybe some fresh air would do me good."

"I thought I was the only one," she said, taking a seat beside him. "Anything I can help with?"

"I was in that Keep for months. It's strange to be out. Not having to endure days of hunger and thirst, not having to sleep on a cold floor wondering when it was going to be your turn to be Venrhys's plaything," he told her, his voice wavering slightly. "Sometimes it feels like another one of his tricks, like it's all one big dream and I'm going to wake back up in that cell with him grinning down at me with that sick grin spread across his face."

Rexah's eyes saddened. She hated seeing him like this. "I can only imagine what they put you through, but you will never be back in that cell, not if I can help it."

Ryden met her eyes. "You don't know how relieved I was when you and the others rescued us."

"I'd do it all again in a heartbeat if I had to," she said softly. "You're safe now, Ry. I promise you."

A small smile spread across his lips. "I am. It'll take some adjusting to get used to normal life again." The smile faded. "Just to live, again."

"How do you mean?"

Ryden ran a hand through his hair before scratching the back of his head nervously. "There was no hope. I was in there for so long that I made peace with it. Now that I'm not in that position, there's something about that acceptance I felt that is difficult to live with … I was okay with dying, Rex. How do I go back to being okay with living? How do I forget that I was ready to die?"

"There were a few times I would have embraced death." She remembered Kalen's words only a few days ago. *"I would have welcomed it with open arms."* They sounded like the brave words of a warrior at the time, but she saw them differently now.

"Ry—"

"I know."

"I cannot imagine how you felt in there, and when I try it hurts so much." Rexah turned her gaze to him and urged him to look at her with a light nudge to his chin. "But for what happens now, you keep talking to me. You don't keep this to yourself. I'm here for you. The rest is a time thing."

Ryden met her gaze as though he'd forgotten how to do anything else, his expression lost to a sea of thought.

I cannot stand it.

Rexah smiled sadly and nodded before lifting her gaze up. The stars blanketing the night sky winked at her in greeting, sending a wave of comfort through her. She missed her spot by the lake in the forest of Adorea, but that was the beautiful thing about stars, they would always be with her wherever she went.

"Do you remember the last time we sat under the stars?" Ryden asked her, pulling his blanket tighter around himself.

"I snuck out to go and sit by the lake, and you turned up and scared the life out of me," she said, giggling quietly.

"You weren't very good at being sneaky." He chuckled. "I watched you leave, and I followed you. I wondered what in all of Etteria you were doing up at that time of night."

Rexah shook her head. "I'll need to up my stealth game if that's the case."

Ryden gently nudged her shoulder with his. "You were sat on a log in nothing but your night dress and a robe, looking up at the stars like you were having a silent conversation with them."

"Stars cannot talk, Ry, but if they could, oh the secrets they could tell," she said as she stared up at them in wonder, hugging her arms.

Ryden moved closer and put his arms around her, wrapping the blanket around them both. "You're cold."

"Thank you," she whispered.

They sat in a comfortable silence for a few moments until Ryden broke it. "Life is so unpredictable, isn't it? You think you know what's ahead of you, you plan everything out, and then before you can even comprehend it, all your plans are turned on their head."

"Fate works in mysterious ways," she said. "That's what I keep telling myself. The gods can be cruel, but once they make a decision, there's nothing we can do other than adjust."

"You truly believe that? You're fine with a god paving your destiny?"

Rexah looked up at him, those grey eyes almost glowing in the darkness. "I make my own choices, but those choices will all lead to the same end, no matter what."

He was quiet for a minute that felt more like an eternity. "Do you think that we were doomed from the beginning?"

She'd never thought of it like that. His words cut deep, but she looked up at him sympathetically. "No, I don't think we were. I believe we were two young royals in a life that we knew we would never be able to control thanks to noble tradition," she said. "You and I are so alike. From the beginning I believe we were destined to be best friends, no matter what has happened in the past and what is yet to come."

"You know that I am always going to be there for you. The Dark Fae may have destroyed our families, our homes, and our wedding day, but they can never break the bond we have," Ryden told her, gently kissing her head.

Her stomach was doing backflips. The last thing she wanted to do was hurt Ryden, but he deserved to know exactly where her heart lay. "I need to talk to you about Kalen," she said.

"I told you; you don't have to say—"

"I do. So long as it goes unsaid, we can both go on pretending things are different. You can go on hoping things could be different."

"Rex ..."

"I know."

He looked at her that way again, his eyes full of longing in a way she could no longer bare to suffer. It hurt too much when she could not return his gaze.

"Just know I don't hold any grudges," he said finally. "I'd

be lying if I said I wasn't jealous, if I said I didn't feel *it* anymore, but I can see how much you mean to each other, and I'm not the type of person to get in between that kind of love."

"I want to apologise," she whispered.

Ryden shook his head and moved the hair from her face. "There's no need. You're my best friend, always will be. I love you. But he's your one, and it's okay. The sooner you let go of the guilt you feel the better everything will be."

Hot tears slid down her cheeks. "You're really okay with all of this?"

Swiping his thumb across her wet cheek, he nodded. "I will be, I promise. But if he breaks your heart, I'll break his nose."

Rexah laughed softly as she lay the side of her head against his shoulder. She could see the truth in Ryden's eyes when he spoke. She could read him like a book, and she knew he was hurt by the circumstances, but he didn't hold them against her. She didn't know what she would do if he did.

"You don't know how incredibly happy I am that you're alive and that you're here." She sniffed softly, rubbing her nose with the sleeve of her robe.

"I do, because I feel the exact same way about you. It tore me apart inside when I couldn't find you that night in Adorea. I heard the guards talk about the attack every time they did their patrols. They said no one made it out alive, they joked about it." Anger and disgust were thick in his voice. "I prayed to the gods every day, begging them to give me a sign that you were still alive, but none came, and I lost hope."

"They will pay for what they've done, not just to us, but to the realm," Rexah promised.

"I will be by your side; my sword is yours. If you'll have me?" he asked as he gazed down at her.

Rexah nodded. "Of course. I'm not letting you go anywhere. You're stuck with me."

"I'm never *stuck* with you, Rex," Ryden said. "Believe me."

Ryden looked into her eyes then, forgetting the promise of propriety. He showed everything in that glazed expression: this wasn't over for him, not yet.

"I'm sorry," he said, embarrassed as he dipped his head. "I'm working on it."

"It's okay. Maybe work on it extra hard around Kalen?"

"Got it."

Despite everything, they laughed, and when the moment ended, she smiled at him lovingly. "Do you remember when we used to play in the grounds of Kaldoren?"

"I'll never forget the first time I told you monsters lived in the mist. You were so scared, and I felt awful, but it was just too funny." He grinned. "My father gave me a scolding for frightening you."

Rexah giggled quietly. "My grandmother had a hard time convincing me to come back on our next visit. She said you were a silly boy making up silly stories."

"Well, she wasn't wrong," he said and sighed happily. "Those were the good days. We didn't have to worry about any grown-up things. We were innocent."

"I will cherish the memories we made together for the rest of my days. You made royal life fun. It was never boring when you were around," she told him.

"We will have days like that again. Once the darkness in this world is snuffed out, everything will be better. That's what you told me that day by the fountain. You said we all crave a better world," he said, "and it's the godsdamned truth."

Rexah grabbed Ryden's hand and squeezed it. "The Dark Fae have had their fun," she said, lifting her gaze to the sparkling stars. "Now it's time for them to go."

22

With five solid days of practice, Rexah was making good progress with both her combat training and controlling her magic. It was still such a surreal thing knowing she had power. Now that she'd tapped into it, she could feel it simmering below the surface, slithering through her veins, waiting for her command to unleash itself. It scared her, but she was also increasingly thrilled by it. The power was a gift from the gods, the Raven God, and she would never be ungrateful for it.

In the two weeks since they'd rescued Kalen and Ryden, both had gotten stronger and were both looking amazing. Their muscles had filled out again, the colour returned to their skin, and they were much healthier and refreshed. The difference in them from being in the Keep and now was like night and day, and she was glad.

To Rexah's relief, they seemed to be getting on well. She found it amusing that Kalen, a fae warrior of Vellwynd, had been jealous, and most likely still was, of Ryden. It was a side to him she'd never seen before, but she understood why he felt that way and had reassured him that what used to be between her and Ryden was done, they were just friends, best friends. Ryden had proved his word true; he seemed to work on himself more with each passing day, especially around Kalen. The doleful looks, the longing in his expression was overshadowed by an unwavering attempt at moving on, at being the best friend that he could be to her, and Rexah could not have been prouder.

She loved them both very much.

Winter was now truly upon them. The temperature had dipped, the days were getting darker quicker, and each morning the windows were covered in frost.

"I love listening to fire crackling," Kalen said as she lay in his arms on the sofa, the fireplace lit, its flames the only light source in the room. The others had gone to their rooms an hour prior, but Rexah was too comfortable to move, and when Kalen made no attempt to get up, she guessed he was cosy too.

"There is something soothing about it," she agreed, snuggling closer into his chest, inhaling his scent.

Kalen gently kissed her head. "Are you okay?"

Exhaling deeply, Rexah replied, "I'm not sure how to answer that question. I'm getting by, but I don't know if I'll be okay for a long time, at least not until everything is over." She turned her head to look up at him. "Like you?"

"Like me." Kalen looked to the dancing flames. "Is Ryden okay?"

"Not even a little bit."

"He seems strong. I understand why you like him. Why you would choose him as a friend."

Rexah looked up, the surprise she felt surely apparent in her expression. "What makes you say that?"

Kalen huffed a laugh and shook his head like he couldn't

believe his own thoughts. "When you think you're going to die, and that the only person you can talk to will soon die as well, you don't care what you say to them. Because none of it will matter soon." Kalen smiled faintly. "He was good at being my friend. Even if he wasn't really. He helped." A devilish look took over his expression, then. "I still hate him, though, obviously."

Rexah batted him in the stomach and scowled jocularly. "No, you do not!"

"Okay, maybe I don't." He chuckled deeply, and it warmed Rexah's heart. "The point is, you've been through so much, we all have," he said quietly into her hair. "We will get through this together, no matter what. All of us. Weirdness or no weirdness."

She nodded against his chest, her eyes heavy with gratitude. "We will, but the future feels so uncertain right now that it's difficult to picture what it would look like."

"Give it a try," he said softly. "Take a moment and tell me what you'd like to see in your future."

What *did* she want?

"Once the darkness has been snuffed out of the world, I want to rebuild Adorea. I want to rebuild the realm and give every living soul a place to call home, a place where they feel safe. I want to get married and have children. And once all of that is done, I want to sit in a rocking chair with a blanket in my library reading my favourite books for the millionth time until the end of my days," she told him, gazing into the fire like she could see that future dancing within its flames, and for a moment she let herself believe it was real. When she pulled herself back to reality, she asked, "What about you? What do you want in your future, Kalen?"

He was quiet for a moment before he spoke. "I want to

rebuild the realm, restore Vellwynd to its former glory. I want to get married and have children. And once all of that is done, I want to be in the rocking chair beside yours until the end of my days."

She lifted her gaze to meet his and was met with his heart-stopping smile. "You really mean it?"

He nodded softly. "Every single word."

Rexah snuggled in closer, wanting to melt as far into his embrace as she could. Being in his arms was something she would never, ever, take for granted again. His familiar scent surrounded her, adding an extra comfort.

I could stay like this forever.

"Sleep, darling. I'm right here," Kalen's voice soothed, and when his fingers began to thread through her hair, she couldn't refuse.

A noise woke Rexah. It wasn't loud enough to startle her, but it did pull her from the depths of her dream. Her eyes opened just enough to see the light from the fireplace was a little dimmer, but the fire was still burning. Assuming it was just the crackling of the flames that had woken her, she closed her eyes again, trying to settle back into the dream.

Clink, clink, clink.

That wasn't the fire.

Rexah's eyes shot open, and she pulled herself from Kalen's grasp as she moved quickly to a sitting position. Before she could register the person standing in front of her, she was grabbed by the neck and thrown across the room. Rexah's back slammed into the side of the kitchen island, and she crumpled to the floor, groaning at the agony spreading up her spine.

"Rexah!" Kalen's panicked voice filled the room.

Looking up, she saw her attacker wasn't alone. There were at least ten of them, and they bore the same armour the Dark Fae from the Keep did. Three of them surrounded Kalen.

These were Venrhys's monsters.

"You didn't keep up your end of the bargain, princess. Now it's time for you to pay the price," her assailant said, grinning from ear to ear, showing off his sharp and pointed canines, a side effect from the dark magic that was used to create them. His hair was dirty blonde, and his eyes were a murky shade of dark grey.

"Venrhys sends his dogs to do his dirty work rather than face me himself," she said, wincing in pain as she used the island to pull herself to her feet. "Did you know your boss is such a coward?"

Grey eyes glared at her. "He said you had a mouth on you. He didn't say you weren't to be harmed before being brought to him," he said, unsheathing a dagger from his hip.

Rexah didn't have her dagger, but that didn't mean she was unarmed; never again would she be helpless. She flipped the switch within herself, turning on fight mode, and darted around the island, grabbing one of the large frying pans. Turning quickly, Rexah ducked out of the way as Grey swiped his blade at her throat before she swung the pan and hit him square in the face. The Dark Fae groaned, stumbling backwards as he clutched his nose.

The sounds of fists smacking and steel clashing filled the room; Torbin and Storglass had joined the brawl. Rexah pulled her focus back on those menacing grey eyes; he was stalking towards her once more. She gripped the frying pan tighter before she swung at him again, but this time he anticipated her strike and grabbed it with his free hand. He yanked it from her grasp and smacked her across the face with it.

Rexah hit the floor with a thud, blood dripping from her nose. Rage built up inside her, magic swirling in her blood like a storm, begging to be released. The air around her charged and a phantom wind lifted the ends of her hair in a silent dance. Curling her right fist, forks of lightning licking around it, Rexah twisted and punched her fist into Grey's chest. He howled in pain as lightning flashed through his body. Rexah watched with wide eyes as he convulsed, and as she rose to her feet, he collapsed to the ground, his body smoking from the current. When Rexah looked up, her gaze caught the mirror on the wall, and she swore her eyes were glowing a lighter shade of purple. She'd tapped into her power with little to no effort at all.

Kalen's cry pulled her attention, and she looked over in time to see him drive his dagger through one of the Dark Fae's eyes before kicking him to the floor. Rexah grabbed Grey's blade and rushed around the counter, stabbing one of the Dark Fae who'd managed to get behind Storglass in the neck.

The warlock spun on his heel, his hazel eyes wide. "Thank you!"

Rexah looked around and saw that more and more Dark Fae were pouring into the home like a never-ending stream. "Shit," she cursed. *How the hell did they even find us here?*

"Rexah, catch!"

Turning, she spotted Ryden on the other side of the room, her dagger in his hand. Ryden tossed the weapon to her, and when the handle was firmly gripped in her palm, she felt the vibration of power within it.

Arelle suddenly broke through the skirmish, anger pooling

in her eyes. Witch Word left her lips, and she clapped her hands together before throwing them out to her sides. She felt the power push past her, but it didn't do any harm to her or the others. Instead, a wave of energy slammed into the Dark Fae, sending them hurtling through the air and into the walls.

"Get ready!" Arelle called out.

Kalen moved to stand beside Rexah. "For what?"

"To run!"

She began chanting again and her palms started to glow with pink energy. Waving her hands in front of her, a shimmering pink and light green portal soon appeared.

Rexah's eyes went wide. "Arelle, what are you doing?"

"That spell only knocked those Dark Fae on their asses; it won't have them down for long. We need to go, *now*!" she yelled over the sound of the magical gateway.

"But—"

"We don't have time to talk about this, Rexah. They're already getting back to their feet, and I can't hold this portal open for long," Arelle told her through gritted teeth.

Looking around, Rexah saw the enemies getting back to their feet, and it was in that moment she realised just how outnumbered they were and how pissed off the Dark Fae looked. She quickly secured her dagger in the waistband of her leggings.

"There's no point in running, little princess," one of them hissed. "We will find you eventually, and next time we won't be so gentle."

"Enough of this talk – get her!" another yelled.

Rexah felt as though time itself had slowed. Adrenaline kicked in, flooding her veins, and taking over every single thought in her head. Her hands reached out, one grabbing hold of Kalen, the other seizing Torbin. Both fae looked down at

her with confusion in their eyes but she didn't give them time
to process. Before she could talk herself out of what she was
about to do, Rexah turned and yanked Kalen and Torbin
forward, pulling them with her through the portal and into the
unknown.

<h1 style="text-align:center">23</h1>

Rexah was quickly beginning to realise that she didn't like portals. The more she used them the more she loathed them. She hated the feeling of weightlessness and the nausea they gave her, and the feeling was only made worse once it spat you out on the other side and gravity caught up to you. She collapsed to the dirt as her legs gave out, and she willed her stomach not to empty itself right there and then, taking in a deep lungful of air.

"Easy," Kalen said as he kneeled beside her, his hand rubbing those small circles into her lower back that she'd come to love, easing the pain in her spine from hitting the counter.

She brought the back of her hand to her tender nose, and when she pulled it away blood stained her skin. "Bastard got me good," she mumbled. She hurriedly ripped a piece of her shirt and placed it against her bloody nose.

"Take a moment," Kalen soothed her, gently kissing her head.

"Where are the others? Why aren't they here?" Torbin

asked, his sharp tone reflecting his disquietude. "Why didn't they come through the portal?"

"Portals can be unpredictable," Kalen said, catching his breath. "It wouldn't surprise me if they've ended up some-where else amidst the panic."

Torbin nodded softly, a frown creasing his brow before he looked around. "Where are we?" he asked.

Rexah glanced around. Her heart began to beat fiercely in her chest as she took in familiar surroundings. Slowly lowering the now crimson stained cloth, shock spread across her face as she processed the scene before her.

The gate that was once welcoming now lay in two pieces in the dirt. The flowers that once bloomed in beautiful bright colours were now nothing but ash on the wind. The oak tree nearby was in a state of ruin; it leaned, dying and leafless, the stench of charred bark wafting in the breeze. And the cottage that belonged to her family was almost completely destroyed.

The wave of nausea came back like a tidal wave, crashing into her with force, but she somehow managed to keep it at bay. Her body began to tremble, and when Rexah finally found her voice, it came out as nothing more than a murmur. "We're in Dorasa."

Forcing herself onto her trembling legs, Rexah stumbled forward until she was jogging up the now broken path to the wrecked cottage. Her mind was spinning.

Please ... please let them be okay. Please, don't take my family away, not again.

The front door had been smashed to smithereens, the broken wood from it scattered on the ground at her bare feet. The wind picked up, its icy temperature slicing through her skin like a sharp blade as she stepped through the threshold into what was once a charming home. Glass littered the floor, and the sofa was split in two, white stuffing protruding from the ripped edges. Claw marks raked down the walls that were still standing and the shredded curtains floated on the wind, blowing through the shattered windows.

"M-mother? Father?" Rexah called out as she stepped further into the space. "Xandyr?"

The sound of shuffling feet behind caught her attention, and her shoulders sagged when she found it was only Kalen and Torbin who had followed her inside.

"They aren't here," Torbin told her, his voiced edged with compassion. "By how faint their scents are, I'd say they've been gone for at least four days."

Rexah looked up at him, horrified. "Gone? Gone as in—"

"Oh, no Rex." Torbin's eyes widened. "I didn't mean it like that."

"He means their scents aren't as strong as they were the last time we were here. Your parents and your brother aren't here. The only heartbeat I hear apart from Torbin's in this home is yours," Kalen explained.

Rexah looked around, hugging her arms to try and retain what little body heat she had left. "How did we end up here? Did Arelle set the course of the portal for this location?"

Kalen gently pulled her close to him, mindful of her tender back. "Like I mentioned before, gateways are unpredictable, and the panic of the situation made it unstable. Portals will take you to your most desired location, or in this case, the place you feel safest."

"If that's correct then why am I not here alone? I can't imagine Dorasa being a place of safety or significance for both of you," Rexah said, shaking her head. She couldn't help but move closer to Kalen, the warmth from his body drawing her in.

"When you grabbed me," Torbin said. "I felt your power surge."

"I felt it too," Kalen acknowledged. "Dorasa is a safe place for you, but you feel safest when you're with us."

Her eyes softened. It was the truth. They'd been through so much together since the moment they first met in Oakhaven. There was no one else she'd trust more to guard her back than the two fae before her. "We cannot stay here," she whispered.

"What we need to do first is find some more appropriate clothing. You're freezing," Kalen said as he ran his hands up and down her bare arms. She'd jumped through the portal wearing a pair of black leggings and a thin-strapped top.

"There's a tailor shop in town. We should head there with caution," Torbin said. "Danger could still be lurking."

They took their time as they headed down the dirt path towards the town proper, and when it came into view, Rexah gasped. The once vibrant and lively square was now nothing but soot and broken buildings. The air was thick with the scent of charred wood and ash. The fountain baring the statues of Arentious and Nadvika were now nothing but a pile of rubble, apart from their faces which remained intact; the haunting way their lifeless eyes stared back at her made her uneasy, and she gripped Kalen's hand a little tighter.

"Be careful, there are bodies up ahead," Torbin warned them quietly, his voice low and woeful.

Rexah's stomach sank but relief quickly followed when she saw it was the bodies of two Valfae. When she took a moment to look around, she noticed there were more than a few Valfae lying dead across the square.

The people of Dorasa didn't go down without a fight, but where the hell is everyone?

The thought set her on edge. As much as she didn't want to

see any dead Dorasians, it was strange to her that none of their bodies lay amongst the monsters.

Scorch marks smudged the cobble stones here and there, as well as some of the buildings. Rexah was cautious of where she placed her bare feet as they proceeded through the town square, not wishing to stand on the broken glass or sharp pieces of broken stone.

The tailors had been hit hard during the attack, and thanks to a huge hole in the shop front, it was easy for them to get inside. Most of the items within were damaged by fire, but by the luck of the gods, the storage room to the back had remained untouched and the stock inside looked brand new.

Rexah grabbed a black, long sleeve tunic, tugging it over her head before she grabbed a pair of fur-lined leggings. She didn't bother to take off the pair she already wore; they'd be an extra help to keep her warm. Sliding her feet into a pair of socks that matched her leggings, she almost let out a groan of relief at their softness. The boots she pulled on were a little on the tight side, but they would do. She finished off her outfit with a simple black cloak.

Kalen and Torbin were the perfect gentlemen and let her have the stock room to herself first to get changed. When she stepped back into the main area of the shop, after checking her dagger was held against her hip by the waistband of her leggings, both fae had found clothes of their own. She observed a weapons belt buckled around Kalen's hips with his dagger fixed to it, and Torbin had a bandolier secured around his chest, his sword strapped securely.

Part of her felt guilty for taking the clothes, but the reality was that no one was there to take the coin that they didn't have, and no one was there to stop them.

"Are you ready to go?" Kalen asked her quietly.

She looked up at him, searching those stunning ocean eyes she loved to drown in. "What are we going to do? Where are we going to go?"

"There's only one place that we will be safe," Torbin said, pulling her attention to his fiery stare. "Savindeer."

Rexah shook her head. "No, I won't lead danger to your people's door. They've been through enough and worked too hard to build that safe haven. I won't have their efforts be in vain."

"Their wards will keep the Dark Fae and the Valfae from entering," Kalen reminded her.

"What if the wards aren't enough?" Rexah asked.

"You underestimate the fae of Vellwynd. When we took you to Savindeer and passed through the wards, we felt the magic. We felt just how powerful they were. Trust me when I tell you, they're enough," Kalen replied with conviction.

Rexah took a deep breath. "You're absolutely sure about this? What about my family? I need to find them."

"Once we get to Savindeer, we will regroup and take it from there," Torbin said, his eyes scanning their surroundings. "We're like sitting ducks out here and I don't like it. We need to start moving."

"Very well," Rexah said, her eyes moving between the two of them. "Lead the way."

Walking through the forest brought back memories of travelling to Savindeer and Dorasa, the conversations by the campfire and the times they'd encountered the Valfae and Venrhys. Despite those encounters with the enemy, Rexah had enjoyed spending time outdoors, and now was no different. She had missed this.

Kalen walked to her left and Torbin to her right, both fae using their keen eyes to scan the area as they went. Rexah swore she saw shadows creeping between the trees, but she put it down to her eyes failing to adjust to the dark. The moonlight shone through the canopy now and again, but it wasn't enough. Shaking off the apprehension, Rexah focused her attention on the path ahead. The last thing she wanted to do was trip and fall flat on her face. Her injured nose was enough. She pressed on, her hand rested on the hilt of her dagger, prepared for anything.

Signs of the Dark Fae and Valfae's destruction was apparent throughout the woodland. Trees that once stood tall and proud now lay splintered and broken on the forest floor. Areas where the wildflowers grew were now nothing but ash and degraded soil. All the devastation brought sorrow to her heart. Was there any part of the realm that hadn't been touched by those monsters? If so, how long would it stay that way? If they didn't do something and soon, the whole of Etteria would be in ruins.

An owl hooted from high up in the trees, accompanied by the incessant chirping of crickets. Rexah concentrated on those noises and took comfort in the fact that they reminded her of the lake she often visited in the woodland of Adorea. Part of her anxiety eased, the tension lifting slightly from her shoulders.

I will sit on that log by the lake again one day, she silently promised herself. *I will sit under the stars without fear of the darkness, with nothing but the light in my heart.*

Rexah had no idea how long they'd been walking. Her boots squeezed her ankles so tightly she feared they might cut off her blood circulation. The boots were most certainly a bad idea, and she mentally scolded herself.

"How much further do we have until we reach our destination?" she asked her companions quietly.

Kalen took her hand and laced their fingers together. "Another two hours, give or take."

Two hours, just two more hours and she could take the godsforsaken boots off. Rolling her shoulders slightly and wiggling her toes, she told herself once more that she could do this.

Kalen leaned down to her, his hot breath brushing against her ear. "Something is bothering you. What is it?" he whispered.

Ignoring the feeling that settled low in her stomach, Rexah whispered back, "I anticipate that my toes will be nothing but mush by the time we reach our location."

Kalen huffed a soft laugh. "Well, if you require me to carry you at any point during our journey, please don't hesitate to let me know."

"I'm fine," she dismissed. "Let's just keep going. The quicker we get there, the better. I need to come up with a plan to find my family."

He gently squeezed her hand. "We'll find them, but let's take this one step at a time. The first step is getting to Savindeer in one piece. We can figure out our next one from there."

He's right. One step at a time. I can do this.

Rexah took a steadying breath as she continued walking. She tried her hardest to keep her movements quiet, but nothing she did prevented the twigs snapping and leaves crunching beneath her feet. Every cacophonous step brought fresh fears that the enemy would discover them.

After another hour of travelling, they took a short break;

the ache in her feet subsided a little as they did, but nobody wanted to hang around for too long in the open, so ten minutes later they were back on the road again, her feet screaming to have more of that blissful rest.

Kalen and Torbin halted in their tracks, and Rexah felt the familiar buzz of her dagger. Rexah didn't know how long it had been this way, but the forest seemed quiet, a little too quiet; the wildlife had stopped their calls, the crickets ceased their chirping.

Danger was lurking.

Kalen and Torbin drew their weapons silently, encouraging Rexah to do the same. The Ravenheart dagger juddered slightly in her hand as the lightning licked up the steel. She shoved her brewing panic to the back of her mind, locking it away, and readied herself for whatever was about to spring out at them.

Nothing happened.

No one attacked.

No creatures sprung from the trees.

Unease sank its roots deep within her. Goosebumps flooded her skin as the sensation of a dozen eyes on them creeped over her body. They were being hunted. They were being toyed with.

The moment of stillness didn't last long. Bodies shot out from between the trees, weapons gleaming against the moonlight, pouring in from the clearing in the canopy and heading straight for them.

Dark Fae soldiers.

They were so ruthless in their attack that Kalen and Torbin were separated from Rexah within seconds, but she didn't let it affect her. One of the Dark Fae smirked at her, licking his lower lip as he twirled his dagger. Rexah wasn't waiting for him to come to her; she rushed forward and lifted her blade, slicing it down toward his chest. The Dark Fae was quick and moved backwards, but he wasn't fast enough; her steel slashed through his fighting leathers, but not deep enough to cut into his flesh.

Rexah groaned in frustration and brought the dagger back, attempting her attack again, but the Dark Fae anticipated her move and grabbed her wrist, twisting it sharply. She cried out in pain before he smashed his fist into her face. She collapsed to the forest floor, momentarily dazed from the blow. Kalen's voice echoed through the haze, and she looked over through blurry eyes to see him struggling with three Dark Fae.

Get up, she told herself. *Get up and fight!*

Blinking rapidly to try and clear her vision, she forced herself up onto her feet. Her legs almost buckled but she managed to hold herself up. Torbin disposed of two Dark Fae he had been fighting before rushing to aid his brother.

You can do this.

Rexah took one step forward to help when a hand appeared out of nowhere; it latched onto her throat before she was slammed against the trunk of a tree. Her gasp of surprise was cut off as the hand around her throat squeezed tighter.

"There you are, Little Raven." The Dark Fae General's lips tipped up into a smirk. "It's so good to see you again."

Her wide eyes met the black pits of Venrhys's, and anger gripped her heart. Remembering the weapon in her hand, she grasped the hilt tighter and thrust it towards his stomach, but Venrhys caught her wrist with ease. His fingers dug into her skin as he twisted it until the dagger tumbled from her grasp and onto the ground.

"It's nice to see you've missed me too," he said, sarcasm dripping from his words. He leaned in closer and whispered into her ear. "You broke our deal. I don't like it when I'm lied to."

Rexah felt his hot breath on her ear as he spoke. She clawed at his hand, trying to pull it from her neck, but it wouldn't budge. "Did I … hurt your feelings?" she taunted through gasping breaths.

Venrhys chuckled darkly. "I've missed your spirit."

"Rexah!" Kalen called out, and when she moved her gaze to him, she saw he and Torbin were fighting off six Dark Fae soldiers.

"I will take you with me this time. You will find the sword and activate it and you *will* give it to me – with force, if necessary," Venrhys told her. "Your white knight won't be able to save you, not from where we will be going."

Rage flashed through her veins like lightning forking through a stormy sky. Her power rumbled through her body like thunder, and when her eyes met his she knew they were gleaming with magic.

"I don't need anyone to save me."

Her hand shot out and slammed into his chest, and Venrhys growled in pain as her power crackled through him. He let go of her throat as he stumbled back, convulsing with the lightning coursing through his body, his skin steaming in the cold air. Others would have dropped by now; he stood writhing in discomfort but withstanding it all the same. He was a general, more powerful than the others. She would need to do more.

She dragged herself toward him and threw her fist into his face, the strike sending him to the ground with a thud. Pain exploded through her knuckles, but she ignored it as she picked up her dagger and headed straight for the Valfae battling with Kalen and Torbin.

She didn't get far.

Venrhys's hand shot out, his fingers encircled her ankle, and with a sharp tug, she crashed to the ground face first, her dagger tumbling out of reach. The air was knocked from her lungs on impact, and before she could suck in a much-needed breath, Venrhys was on her, turning her onto her back.

"You're coming into your power. My master will be pleased to hear it," he told her with a sick grin.

Rexah threw her head forward, her forehead smacking into his nose. Venrhys cried out and loosened his grip on her. She planted her boot on his chest and kicked him off. Venrhys recovered quickly, and before she had the chance to scramble backward, he slid a wicked looking dagger from his belt and impaled the blade through her right thigh.

Rexah let out a scream of agony, and it sent a ripple of power through the air.

Venrhys chuckled as black blood slid from his nose, his dark eyes nearly brightening at the sound of her suffering. "That's it. Sing for me, Little Raven."

The pain was almost blinding, and when he pulled the dagger out, the burning agony spread through her leg like wildfire.

Venrhys rose to his feet, towering over her as he wiped the blood from his nose on the back of his sleeve. He opened his mouth to speak, but he was cut off by a blade imbedding itself into his chest. Venrhys stumbled back, gripping the hilt of the dagger.

"Step the fuck away from her," Kalen growled.

Rexah looked to see Kalen standing above her, a murderous look in his dark blue eyes.

"Quite the reunion." Venrhys groaned as he slid the dagger free from his chest, letting it fall to the ground as he clutched the bleeding wound. "My master's return is inevitable," he sneered. "I look forward to watching the agony in your eyes when he kills her in front of you." He took note of the dead soldiers lying around them before he disappeared in a cloud of inky black smoke.

Rexah's body trembled, confused between ice-cold and red-hot sensations.

"H-h-his blade ..." she said through chattering teeth.

Torbin dropped to his knees by her side, inspecting the wound. "Fuck," he cursed.

Kalen was by her other side in an instant, moving her hair from her eyes. "It's okay. You're going to be okay," he told her before looking at Torbin. "What's wrong?"

"His knife must have been laced with Valfae venom," he said, holding his glowing green palm above her thigh. "My magic will only do so much, we need to get her to Savindeer, *now*."

Rexah could feel the sheen of sweat coating her skin already. Pressure on her injury made her squirm, and when she looked down, Kalen was tying a piece of his shirt around her leg to stop the bleeding. When he lifted her off the ground and into his arms, she lay her head against his shoulder, unable to keep it up on her own.

"Let's go," Kalen said to Torbin.

As they rushed through the trees, Rexah kept her eyes on Kalen's face, taking in every little detail: the worried look in his eyes, the tightness in his jaw and the scrapes and bruises on his skin that were already beginning to fade. When he looked down at her and their eyes connected, butterflies went wild in her stomach.

"Keep those beautiful eyes on me, okay," he told her. "Don't fall asleep. We will go as quickly as we can, just hold on for me, darling."

It was easier said than done. Her eyelids were begging to close, just for one second. Maybe if she shut them for that one second, everything would be fine.

"Hold on for me."

She let them close.

24

VENRHYS

When he materialised outside the castle gates, Venrhys gave the two guards a look that threatened instant wrath if they didn't open the doors immediately and without request. The guards were smart and didn't hesitate, the doors opening with a groan as they were pulled apart.

Venrhys stepped over the threshold, his hand still clutching his bleeding wound. He had to find the castle healer before he requested an audience with the Elder. The last thing he wanted was to drip his black blood all over the ancient one's shoes. What a sign of weakness that would be, a stain on the trust the Elder had in his chosen general.

Various guards were stationed down the corridor, each one of them regarding the state he was in and giving him an irksome mix of shocked and surprised looks.

For now, he would ignore them all.

Greda didn't waste any time and quickly guided him into her healing room, closing the door behind her.

"You're very lucky the blade wasn't an inch further to the left or you'd be dead," she told him as she cleaned the wound.

"Thank you for your insight, Greda," he said through gritted teeth as she worked some herbal mixture into his injury.

Letting the herbs settle for a moment, she turned to her cabinet of concoctions. "It's been a while since I last had you in here," she said, reaching up and pulling out a small vial filled with dark-green liquid.

"As much as I enjoy your company, I tend not to make a habit of visiting," he replied. He could feel the herbs stinging in his chest, working by whatever magical healing properties they had.

She let out a laugh as she walked back over to him. "I'll take no offence to that," she said, pulling the tiny cork from the vial. "Now, this is going to hurt, so prepare yourself."

"Just get on with it. I have business with the Elder," he said.

Greda moved forward and tipped the contents into his open wound. As soon as the liquid touched him it felt like his chest had caught on fire. Black spots filled his vision as he let out a pained cry, grabbing the arms of the chair he sat in. The potion burned away the herbs already there, and he could feel his tissue fusing together, his skin knitting back into place.

"Settle down," she said as she used a clean cloth to wipe away the residue of blood and potion from his chest. "Stop being a baby, it's over now."

One thing he admired most about her was her lack of fear, her conviction in the face of those in higher rank. She spoke her mind, period. She was there to keep them all alive and fighting fit, and she fulfilled that role well.

Venrhys looked down, noting that the wound was gone and

all that remained in its place was a thin red line that he knew would fade over time.

"Thank you, Greda. Impeccable work as always," he said as he pulled his shirt back over his head.

"It's what I'm here for," she answered, cleaning her hands in a small bowl on her workbench. "Now fuck off."

He rose to his feet. "I mean this in the nicest way possible, but I hope I don't see you again any time soon."

She gave him a wide grin. "The feeling is mutual."

He nodded to her before he walked out of the room. His chest still ached but that would fade in a few days. A few days would be too soon; he deserved the discomfort. He couldn't believe he'd been so sloppy. He'd been so focused on Rexah, delighted with the dominance over her he had achieved, that he hadn't seen Kalen's blade coming. His soldiers should have taken care of the fae scum before anything like that could happen, but he blamed only himself. They were dead now anyway; he couldn't deal out punishment to them. Now he would receive his own reprimand from the Elder for his failure. He wasn't looking forward to hearing what his master had to say, or seeing what he would do, but he would accept whatever he gave him.

The guards nodded in respect as he walked by and down the familiar corridors. He practised in his head over and over again how he would explain what happened, but he knew there was nothing he could say that would make the situation acceptable.

The two Valfae guards glared at him as he approached, but he gave them his amazing smile, not letting the fear show on his face as they growled.

"I need to speak with the Elder. It is of upmost importance," he told them. The beasts looked to one another before turning their attention back to him, and he couldn't help but roll his eyes. "Do we really need to do this every single time?"

The one to the left huffed before they pulled open the heavy doors for him to enter. He tipped his head to them in thanks and stepped inside.

He could feel the apprehension rolling within him. No matter how hard he tried to dampen it down, it wouldn't be enough. The Elder would sense it regardless.

The master values honesty, he thought as he approached. *So, be honest.*

"You come to me with good news, I hope," the Elder's deep voice echoed throughout the chamber.

Venrhys bowed to him before standing up, straightening his spine. "I wish it were so, my lord, but unfortunately, the news is not favourable."

The Elder lifted his haunting gaze to him, studying his face. "Tell me everything."

Venrhys noticed he looked healthier still than the last time he'd visited. His skin was ever more youthful, his movement more deft than clumsy. The fae blood he was consuming was working its healing magic nicely. He wondered how many fae he fed from in a day to look as well as he did.

"We located the Chosen One and her companions, and we ambushed them. We did have the upper hand, however, the soldiers underestimated Rexah's fae protectors," he explained. "My main goal was obtaining the girl, and in my distracted state, Kalen managed to injure me. He and the other fae had killed all the soldiers that accompanied me, and I had no other choice than to … flee." The last words were hard for him to admit. He hated running from anything. It made him appear weak and incapable.

The Elder rose to his feet, walking to the fireplace and

placing his hand on the mantel as he watched the flames dance from within. "That is very unfortunate indeed."

Venrhys dropped to one knee, tipping his head down. "Please forgive me, my lord. Give me the chance to redeem myself, and I promise I will not fail you again." His pulse pounded as he waited for his punishment, praying for it to hurry up and begin.

"I am a reasonable individual. I am fully aware of the difficulties of this task. But I believe us more than capable of achieving our goals," the Elder said calmly, as though he meant every word. "Therefore, I am willing to give you another chance, but do not take this as forgiveness. I will offer you one final opportunity to bring her in. Do not fail me again."

His shoulders slumped slightly in relief as he looked up at him. "Thank you, master. I will not let you down again, I swear."

"I like you, Venrhys. It would be most unfortunate if I had to dispose of you." The Elder motioned for him to rise and he followed his command without question. "You've played around with her enough. It ends now." His eyes narrowed as they fell on Venrhys. "Bring her to me."

Venrhys nodded. "Of course, master. I will not return until I have her in my possession. If she doesn't have the sword, I'll force her to find it."

"Very good. Now go before I change my mind."

He didn't waste another second and turned on his heel, hurrying out the door.

I'm coming for you, Little Raven.

25

REXAH

The sounds of shuffling and clinking pulled Rexah from her slumber. When she slowly opened her eyes, an unfamiliar woman came into view. She knelt at Rexah's side, so focused on tending the injury that she hadn't noticed her rouse. The woman's hair was black with crimson feathers and beads woven through it. A small basket sat next to her filled with small jars of herbs, ash, and bloody bandages. Rexah noticed a vial in her hand filled with red liquid.

Is that blood?

"Oh, blessed be, you're awake!" the woman said, startling Rexah, and when she jumped the woman said, "Be still, my dear!"

Blinking a few times, Rexah looked around. Once she noted they were inside a tent, her eyes settled back on the woman. "Who are you?" she asked quietly.

"I'm Clarina, a healer and witch. You had a very nasty injury, and I was called upon to help."

Rexah nodded softly. Memories of Venrhys stabbing her flashed through her mind, the sight of the blade and the burning sensation it left in its wake. Gazing down at her wound, she was surprised to see that it was now nothing more than a thin red line.

"How?" she asked in wonder.

Clarina grinned. "With the right herbs and the right magic, any wound no matter how grave can be healed almost instantly. You might still experience some discomfort, but in a few days' time you'll be back to your normal self."

"One of these days you are going to walk into camp rather than being carried in."

Shifting her gaze to the tent entrance, she saw Sorana standing there, a smile spread across the fae's lips. Rexah smiled back at her. "Sorana."

The fae walked over to them. "Welcome back to Savindeer. It's good to have you back at camp. Everyone has missed you."

Rexah's eyes softened. "They have?"

"Yes, Elly especially," she replied, laughing softly. "She seems to have taken a shine to you."

Clarina rose to her feet, lifting her basket of supplies. "I will let you both catch up," she said, placing the small vial of red liquid into the box. "Try and take it easy for the next few days whilst your leg is in the final healing stages."

"Thank you for your aid. Let me know how I can repay you," Rexah said.

The witch smiled and dipped her chin. "Payment won't be necessary. I will see you both in the dining hall tonight," she said, bidding them farewell before slipping out of the tent.

Sorana sat down on the edge of the cot as Rexah slowly sat up. "How are you feeling?"

"My face hurts more than my leg at the moment," Rexah admitted as she gently touched her tender nose.

"You have a bruise on your eye as black as the night. It makes the violet in your iris stand out," Sorana told her.

"One of the soldiers got a solid punch in," she mumbled. Rexah carefully swung her legs over the edge of the bed and ran a hand through her tangled locks. She noticed she now wore a white top and grey leggings. "Where are Kalen and Torbin?"

"They're helping out around the camp. I had to force Kalen from your side," she said, smiling softly. "Both of them are okay. They were more concerned for your wellbeing."

Relief rolled through her. "Could I use the showers? I need to wash away the dirt and blood."

Sorana nodded. "Of course, do you need any help? Shall I go get Kalen?"

"No, it's okay. I think I can manage." Rexah took a breath before pushing herself off the cot. Much to her surprise, no pain shot through her leg. "Wow, what were those herbs Clarina used?"

Sorana laughed as she stood up. "She is a miracle worker. We are blessed to have her amongst us."

"I must repay her for her services. I don't have any coin, but there must be something I can do," Rexah said. "Also, what can I do to repay you? This is the second time you've allowed me into your camp. You've fed and clothed me, and I haven't returned the gesture."

The fae reached out and gently moved Rexah's hair behind her shoulder. "Seeing Kalen this happy is more than enough payment."

Rexah met her light-coloured eyes. "Well, if there's ever anything I can do for you, please don't hesitate to ask."

Sorana nodded and gently squeezed her shoulder. "I will keep that in mind. There are some fresh clothes on the chair over there," she said pointing to the corner. "You'll find clean towels in the bathing tent. Come to the dining hall when you're done, and I'll fix you something to eat."

"Thank you, Sorana, for everything," Rexah whispered.

Sorana bowed her head before she turned and left the tent.

Rexah took cautious steps towards the chair in the corner. The muscles in her leg ached slightly at the movement, but it was nothing she couldn't handle. Lifting the pile of clothing, Rexah slipped her feet into a pair of soft shoes that had been left at the foot of the cot.

As she was about to leave, she spotted a folded cloak sitting next to a pile of hot coals. When she tugged it on, the warmth from the material seeped into her skin and she let out a happy sigh. *It's the little things in life,* she thought as she pulled back the fly sheet.

Chilled air hit her as soon as she stepped out of the tent, and she was more deeply grateful for whoever had left the cloak as she hugged it closer. The camp had grown since the last time she was here, and it was nice to see it thriving. A few familiar faces came into view, and she waved to the fae who called her name and greeted her. The area of the camp seemed to have expanded, more tents and huts than she remembered now pitched and built. She took her time soaking it all in as she walked through.

Much to her relief the bathing tent was empty when she walked inside. Setting down her clean clothes, she hung the cloak up on one of the hooks on the wall. After lifting a clean towel, Rexah made one quick sweep of the tent to make sure she was definitely alone before stepping behind one of the curtains.

Rexah wasn't sure how to fill the tub with water considering they were out in the middle of the forest, but to her amazement, when she turned the mechanism, water began to pour from it like a fountain. She quickly put in the plug and thanked the gods, and Sorana, for the plumbing that had been installed.

More bath time, she thought.

Stripping out of her clothes, she stepped into the bathtub once it was ready, and she let out a blissful sigh as she sank down into the hot water. The heat soaked through to her bones and eased the ache in her thigh muscle. She stared up at the ceiling as she breathed deeply.

"My master's return is inevitable."

Clarina may have expelled the poison from her wound, but would she ever get Venrhys and his poison out of her mind?

"Sing for me, Little Raven."

She had been so close to being ripped away from Kalen and Torbin, and that thought terrified her. They'd been ambushed and outnumbered; Kalen and Torbin had taken out the soldiers before Venrhys could snatch her away, but how much longer could they go on? How much longer would they need to look over their shoulders for the enemy instead of living their lives without fear of ambush or attack? The enemy knew their strength now, and they would surely match or best it upon their next encounter.

Venrhys had been there to take her away, not only for breaking their deal, but because he was going to make her activate the sword once she found it. It wasn't simply about the sword anymore; Venrhys felt he'd been wronged, ignored, and his desire for vengeance was deeply personal.

"I don't like it when I'm lied to."

Footsteps approaching the bathing tent tore her from her thoughts. She sat up, pulling her knees to her chest in an attempt to cover herself as best she could.

"Rexah?" Kalen's voice rose from the other side of the curtain.

Her shoulders sagged and she let out a breath. "Yes, I'm in here."

"Are you okay?"

"I'm fine. I just wanted to wash off the blood and dirt," she told him, taking note of the muddy colour the water was turning.

"Do you mind if I sit out here and wait for you?" he asked.

A smile broke across her face. "Of course I don't," she replied, picking up the bar of lavender scented soap.

The sounds of shuffling filled the room as she assumed he'd sat down. Neither of them spoke as she cleaned her skin and hair in attempt to feel human again. The water rippling as she moved was the only noise echoing throughout the room.

"That was too close," he said, finally breaking their silence. "When I heard you scream …"

"Don't think on that." Rexah could hear the anger and the agony in his voice. "He won't get the upper hand on me again. I'm going to train harder to make sure."

"All I can do is think about it. The fear that coursed through me at that sound leaving your throat … it was the worst thing I've ever felt in my life," he told her.

She got out of the bath and grabbed the towel, wrapping it around her body before pulling the plug. When she lifted the curtain back and stepped out, Kalen was sat on the floor with his back against one of the cupboards. He looked up at her with tired eyes.

"Have you slept at all?" she asked him as she crossed the room and picked up her clothes.

"No, not really," he told her. "I tried, but I was too anxious about you."

Rexah went back behind the curtain to get dressed. "I'm okay, Kalen. Thanks to you and Torbin getting me here as fast as you did. Clarina is a miracle worker. It's like I was never injured," she said, stepping back out fully clothed in a burgundy jumper, black fur lined leggings and a pair of black boots that fit her like a glove.

These are so much better than the other ones.

Kalen rose to his feet. "It's good to be back here again. I just wish it were under better circumstances."

Rexah's eyes softened, and she nodded. "Me too. We always seem to arrive here after something terrible has happened."

She stepped around him and walked over to the mirror next to the cupboard. She almost gasped when she saw her face; Sorana wasn't kidding when she said she had a black eye. She had some slight bruising on her cheek and nose too.

Kalen appeared behind her, rage simmering in his eyes. "I hate seeing you hurt."

Her gaze met his through the mirror before she turned to face him. "I'm okay. It's not that painful. It looks worse than it actually is," she reassured him. She reached up and gently pushed his dark hair from his face.

"Tonight proved just how desperate they are to find the sword and the lengths they'll go to," he said, studying her features. "The danger increases with each day that passes."

"I know, but I can't find the sword on my own. I need Arelle's help," she told him. "We need to find her and the others before there's another attack. I need to find my family too."

Kalen gently cupped her face in his hands. "We will find your family, I promise. As for the sword? I believe you can find it without Arelle. You're so powerful, Rexah, more than you seem to realise or give yourself credit for."

"I'll try and do it on my own, but if it doesn't work I'll still need her help. It doesn't matter either way, we need to find her and the others regardless, okay?"

Kalen nodded. "Yes, okay."

Rexah moved forward and lay the uninjured side of her face against his chest, closing her eyes as she felt his arms wrap around her. She soaked in the feeling of security his embrace provided and took a deep breath. "One step at a time."

The dining hall was alive with fae and humans alike. Rexah noticed Clarina sitting at one of the tables with some of the older fae as she walked in with Kalen. The smell of cooked meats filled the air and her stomach growled. She hadn't realised how hungry she was until the delicious aromas filled her nose.

"Where's Torbin?" Rexah asked as they passed through the tables.

Kalen smiled and pointed to a table in the corner. "He's over there."

Torbin looked up and grinned, waving them over. Rexah smiled and walked over with Kalen. She slid onto the bench as she said, "I should have known you'd be here before us."

He chuckled. "I like this table. It's a good vantage point."

Kalen scoffed. "Don't lie. You get here before us so that Rexah doesn't judge you for having two portions of food."

Torbin glared playfully at him. "I love food, all right?"

"Having an appreciation for food isn't a bad thing," Rexah said, innocently defending him.

"Thank you, Rex," he said, inclining his head to her. "The food Arelle and Storglass made for us was very good, but nothing beats home comforts."

Her eyes softened as she thought of the many meals she'd eaten in the Grand Hall in Adorea. Her chest tightened. What she would give for just one more.

Sorana appeared at her side, distracting her from her thoughts. "I hope you're hungry," she said, setting down a tray with three bowls of stew and a large plate filled with vegetables and warm rolls.

Rexah almost licked her lips. "This looks and smells incredible. Thank you, Sorana."

"Enjoy." She grinned and walked off, leaving them to their repast.

Rexah didn't waste another second and picked up her spoon. A moan nearly slipped from her lips when the first splash of flavour hit her tongue. It was mouth-watering.

"Not that I'm in any hurry to leave, but what is our next plan of action?" Torbin asked mid-way through their meal.

Rexah explained the strategy she had devised with Kalen. "My family are out there somewhere too. There was no evidence of their demise. I'm hoping they managed to escape but finding them will be just as difficult as finding the sword."

"When we find Arelle, maybe she can help you find your parents and brother," Torbin suggested as he stuffed some vegetables into his mouth.

"I hope so," Rexah whispered, stirring the dregs of her stew. Her heart throbbed feeling Kalen's warm hand on her thigh, and when she looked up at him his cobalt eyes were filled with sympathy and understanding.

"I will help you any way I can with your meditation," Torbin said. "I'm no Seer, but I will do what I can, just like the last time we meditated."

She nodded her head in thanks to him before setting her spoon down. "I'm going to need all the help I can get. The last thing we need is to be ambushed again."

"We need to be more cautious," Kalen said. "We were unprepared for what occurred, but that won't happen again. We'll make sure of it."

Rexah wished she had their confidence, but the crippling pressure of finding the sword wouldn't let her have a moment of relief as it crushed her beneath its boot.

26

The next two days passed by and, as she had sadly suspected, Rexah was no closer to finding the sword, the location of the purple door still eluding her. The increased control on her power she displayed instilled confidence in herself as she attempted the search, but without Arelle's guidance through the void, she saw nothing she hadn't seen before. Even though her meditation sessions on her own and with Torbin hadn't brought her any closer to locating the Shadow Star, however, they weren't a complete waste of time; they helped calm her anxiety and deal with her grief. The monster in the cage deep within herself was shrinking. She had joined Kalen and Torbin in their training sessions, and much to her relief, her thigh had completely healed.

The night sky was filled with stunning, twinkling stars as she walked through the camp. It was the dead of night, and everyone was asleep in their tents, everyone apart from her. She'd tried her hardest to fall asleep but gave up after three hours of tossing and turning in her cot. Her mind was too active to shut itself off.

She had no destination in mind. She let her feet guide her and take her wherever they wished. The soft grass tickled her ankles, the frosted blades crunching beneath her soft shoes as she walked. The gentle breeze made her night dress sway softly around her lower legs. Tugging her robe closer, she cursed herself for leaving the comforting warmth of her tent, but she needed to try and clear her mind.

Rexah had missed Savindeer. Even though their last visit here had been a fleeting one, she'd quickly felt welcome and safe. She didn't know how long they'd stay this time, but once the evil was gone from the realm, she made a promise to herself to come back and stay longer than a few days. Helping the Vellwyndians with their daily tasks was something she thoroughly enjoyed, and she wanted to show her gratitude for letting her stay, not once but twice now.

She also looked forward to helping them and Kalen restore their home in Vellwynd to its former glory. She wanted to see where Kalen grew up, the home he shared with his family, and where he spent most of his time.

Rounding the corner, she spotted his tent up ahead. A large lit fire sat in the centre of the area, six tents in various sizes surrounding it.

Will he be awake? she wondered as she stopped outside it.

Rexah stood there for a few minutes contemplating whether she should just turn around and go back to her own tent, try to force herself to sleep again, but the tugging sensation in her chest wouldn't let her leave, not without seeing him first.

She gently pulled the fly sheet and was surprised when it opened with ease and that he hadn't tied it from the inside. Peeking around the material, she saw the shape of him under multiple layers of furs. Stepping inside as quietly as she could, she quickly realised this was a stupid idea.

Let him sleep. He needs as much rest as he can get. He doesn't need you sneaking into his tent in the middle of the night and disrupting it just because you can't sleep.

Rexah turned and stepped to leave when she heard his quiet, tired voice call out to her.

"Darling?"

Mentally cursing herself, she looked over to him. "I'm sorry. I didn't mean to wake you," she whispered.

Kalen sat up, the furs sliding down his bare chest as he ran his hand through his messy hair. Rexah's stomach fluttered at the glorious sight of him.

"It's fine. Is everything okay?"

"Yes, I couldn't sleep so I went for a walk and found myself here," she told him, fidgeting with the edge of her robe.

Kalen stood up from the bed and moved closer to her. "You can stay here with me if you'd like."

"Are you sure?"

He smiled tiredly at her and nodded. "Of course I am."

Rexah untied her robe and draped it over the chair to the right of her before kicking off her shoes. Taking Kalen's hand when he offered it to her, she let him lead her to his makeshift bed. The furs were already warm from his body heat, and she let out a content sigh as she slid under them, goosebumps flooding her skin at the warmth.

Kalen got in beside her and secured the furs around them as he gently pulled her into his arms. "There you go."

Rexah lay her head on his shoulder, her body tangling with his as they got comfortable. Her skin pebbled with more goosebumps as his heat transferred into her.

I could get used to this.

After a few moments of silence, Kalen finally broke it. "Why couldn't you sleep?"

"My mind won't shut down. There are so many thoughts going through my head right now that I can't pick one out from the next," she told him quietly. "I'm scared."

His finger hooked under her chin as he tilted her face up to his. "It's all right to be afraid. I am too."

"I feel so hopeless. It's like I'm in the ocean, under the water, and nothing I do brings me closer to the surface," she said, her voice breaking. "I feel like I'm drowning."

Kalen didn't respond with words. Instead, he leaned forward and captured her lips with his in a soft kiss. Rexah kissed him back without question. Her hand reached up and cupped his cheek as his tongue dragged across her bottom lip, and she opened for him gladly.

Rexah's body trembled, reacting to Kalen's hand as it slid down her side to rest on her waist. Their kiss grew hungry as her body pressed against his. She wanted more. She *needed* more.

Kalen slowly pulled away, leaning his forehead against hers. "Rexah," he breathed heavily. "If we don't stop …"

"I don't want to stop," she replied, her own breathing laboured. "Please … help me forget, just for tonight. Help me feel something other than this despair."

"Say it," he said, his eyes searching hers. "I need to hear you say the words."

"I want you," she whispered. "I need you."

Kalen gently ran his fingers through her hair. "If at any point you change your mind, or if I hurt you, say the words and I'll stop, okay?"

Rexah nodded, licking her suddenly dry lips, but when

Kalen kissed her again, all her nervous energy seemed to dissipate, and she melted into him.

Slowly, he moved his hand from her waist to her hip. His fingers found their way under the back of her thigh as he brought her leg up to rest against his hip. Her night dress rode up slightly at the change in position and she felt the hard length of him grind against her core.

Kalen grasped the edge of her dress as he pulled away. His eyes met hers in silent question, asking permission to take it off. With a single nod of her head, he slowly lifted her night dress up and off, throwing it to the side.

Rexah watched his reaction as he took in the sight of her nearly naked form. Even in the darkness of the tent she saw his blue eyes brighten before they turned the same shade as the sea on a dark night.

Her back arched when his hot mouth enclosed over her hard nipple, and she gasped in pleasure. The swirl of his tongue sent a thrill shooting straight to her centre. Her fingernails trailed down the rippling muscles of his abdomen, something she'd wanted to do since the first time she'd seen him shirtless, and she felt his powerful body shudder beneath her fingertips as she reached the waistband of his underwear.

Pulling away from her sensitive flesh, Kalen helped her rid them both of the remainder of their clothing. Now nothing separated them. His hand skimmed down her bare body, dipping between her legs. Bursts of pleasure erupted as his finger slid between her folds, gliding up and down the slickness that had gathered there. Rexah's breathing hitched when he pushed it inside of her. She gripped his arm as he stroked her. He kissed her, his lips soft against hers. Her other hand clasped the back of his neck as she pulled him closer, moaning against his mouth when he introduced a second finger.

Kalen intensified the kiss as he worked her, curling his fingers deep inside. Her muscles tightened as the familiar feeling of an orgasm began to build, but she didn't want it this way. She wanted him.

"Kalen," she gasped. "I need to feel you."

Withdrawing his fingers, he moved between her legs, the tip of his head brushing against her. Butterflies exploded in her stomach. If this was a dream, then she never wanted to wake up. Kalen placed one hand next to her head, bracing himself above her, as the other wrapped around his cock, lining himself up with her.

"I need to know," he whispered to her. "You're sure about this?"

Rexah's eyes softened, and she nodded. "More than anything," she said as she reached up and gently stroked his cheek. She widened her legs a little, getting into a more comfortable position.

Kalen moved his gaze to where they were about to be joined. She watched as his tongue swiped across his bottom lip, and her toes curled in anticipation. The first nudge of him sent her heart into a wild frenzy. He was bigger than Ryden, so when he took his time sliding into her, she welcomed the time he gave her to adjust. As he fully seated himself within her, his head tipped forward, leaning against hers as his chest rumbled a low groan.

Tears pricked Rexah's eyes, her mouth hung open as she felt every glorious inch of him. She wrapped her legs around his waist, gently pressing her lips to his as a way of letting him know she was okay, and she was ready.

Kalen slowly pulled back before thrusting his hips into hers. Every movement was slow and gentle, the feeling of their bodies colliding made her pulse quicken. Rexah could sense his restraint, like he was holding back.

She didn't want him to hold back.

Rexah placed her hands on his shoulders, moving them until he was under her, ensuring they didn't separate. She lay her hands on his chest, adjusting to the new position, her thighs resting at either side of his hips. He looked up at her with adoration shining in his cerulean eyes as his hands smoothed up her thighs to her hips.

She was in control now.

Rolling her hips forward, a new wave of pleasure washed over her, the position hit just the right spot and a breathy moan fell from her lips. Kalen's fingertips digging into her soft flesh encouraged her to move a little faster. Rexah managed to find her rhythm and let herself get lost in the feeling of him, of the way his cock stroked her most inner walls as she rode him.

"Fuck," Kalen growled as his hips rose to meet hers, intensifying the pleasure brewing in her lower stomach.

Digging her nails into his chest, she grinded herself on him, relishing in every single moment of this bliss. It had never felt like this before. It both terrified and excited her.

Kalen sat up suddenly, wrapping his arm around her waist, tugging her closer. He kissed her hungrily as his other hand squeezed her hip in a bruising grip, pulling her harder down on his throbbing cock. She wrapped an arm around his neck, the other resting on his chest as they moved as one.

"Kalen," she moaned loudly as his lips pressed against her neck. She gripped his hair as her hips moved of their own fruition.

"That's it, darling," he encouraged. "Come with me." His lips trailed down her neck, his breath hot on her skin, and when they touched the scar on her shoulder, it was enough to send her over that glorious edge with him.

Her head flew back, her eyes closing, and a cry of pleasure ripped from her throat as her orgasm crashed through her, setting every cell in her body ablaze. Her walls clenched around his cock as he spilled his release inside her with a guttural groan.

It was just the two of them. Nothing and no one else mattered. The world around them melted away and she swore she saw the night sky and its blanket of stars swirling around in a dance made only for them. Her blood sang and tingled in her veins as her body trembled with aftershocks. That tugging sensation she'd felt when she'd arrived at his tent intensified, like her soul was trying to leave her body and connect with his.

Neither of them spoke for a long while. They sat entangled in one another, breathing heavily, letting the blissful feeling run its course through their bodies. Once they came back to reality, Kalen carefully turned to the side and lay down with her in the furs, holding her close.

"Are you okay?" he whispered, gently running his fingers through her hair.

Rexah smiled tiredly. "Yes, I'm perfect."

And she was perfect, in this moment here and now, with him, she was absolutely perfect. There in his arms, she wasn't the heir to a fallen kingdom, a princess with no crown. She was just Rexah, a girl in love with a fae.

"What we did, I don't want it to be a one-time thing, or for it to happen now and again just because we feel like it," he said, his touch moving to her cheek, his fingertips caressing her skin.

"Neither do I," she whispered.

Kalen leaned closer and ran his nose against hers. "Be mine?"

Her violet eyes met his and she saw nothing but the truth

shining back in them. She'd given her body what it had wanted, now she would give her heart the same courtesy. "I'm yours."

Kalen's eyes lit up, and he pressed his lips to hers. She kissed him back, allowing herself to get lost in him for a fleeting moment. She pulled him close, never wanting to separate, her heart pounding with the feeling of him still inside her. When she finally pulled away, he kissed her nose, and her cheeks reddened.

I could stay here forever.

"I need to go and clean up," she said softly.

He nodded and pecked her lips as he slowly eased out. "Come back to me."

She slid out from under the furs and grabbed her night dress, tugging it over her head before pulling on her robe. As she secured the belt at her waist and went to exit the tent, Rexah looked back at him over her shoulder, smiling.

Judging by the sky, it was the small hours of the morning. Winter was here and so the early time of day was still dark, but Rexah could see hints of the first light of dawn beginning to shine through. Thankfully, that meant everyone was still sleeping, for now. To her relief, when she stepped inside the bathing chamber, it was empty, and she headed straight for the toilets situated in the adjoining tent to the left.

Once she had cleaned away the evidence of what they'd done, Rexah quickly cleansed the rest of her body, washing away the sweat that had clung to her skin. She picked up one of the towels after pulling her night dress back on and walked over to one of the sinks.

The mirror on the wall was fogged up with condensation, and when Rexah wiped it off with the towel, she almost jumped out of her skin when she saw Arelle standing behind her in the reflection. She spun on her heel, but the space was empty, and when she turned back to the mirror, Arelle was still there, staring back at her with worried eyes.

"Kaldoren," the Seer said, her voice a quiet echo. "Come to Kaldoren."

Rexah opened her mouth to speak, but Arelle shimmered before she disappeared.

What the fuck?

She grabbed her robe and wrapped it around herself before she raced out of the bathing tent.

When she rushed back into Kalen's tent, tugging back the fly sheet with haste, he shot up into a sitting position and frowned when he saw how flustered she was. "Rexah?"

"Arelle appeared to me! I know where they are!" she panted.

Kalen grabbed his underwear, pulling it on as he got to his feet. He closed the space between them, taking her hand. "Where?"

27

Kaldoren looked exactly as she remembered it, but it felt entirely different to her now. Once, the fog blanketing the kingdom had felt dreamlike, but now, abandoned as it was, it was a haunting picture. According to those at Savindeer, the Kaldoriens had fled after they heard about the attack on Adorea, fearing their kingdom would be next. The Dark Fae did descend upon Kaldoren but for whatever reason, after some light plundering of unlocked establishments, they left the city almost entirely as it was. Aside from some slight damage to the high stone walls surrounding the perimeter, it remained as it was before.

They'd left Savindeer with haste a few hours after Rexah had seen Arelle in the reflection of the mirror. It had taken them almost five days to travel here, and the gods must have been on their side as they never crossed paths with the Dark Fae or Valfae. Although, Rexah wasn't sure if she should feel relieved or worried about it.

Memories came flooding back as they cautiously made their way through the grounds, sticking to the shadows created by the tall, bare trees, and as they ascended toward the castle, the crisp winter air nipped at Rexah's face. The castle built within the mountain was known for being near impenetrable thanks to its tough, rocky surroundings, and like the rest of the city, remained unscathed. It wasn't situated too high up in the mountain, but the only way to access the main door was to climb six perrons, something she'd done many times before on visits with her grandmother.

Rexah tried to ignore the nostalgic ache in her chest. With every step she took, echoes of her childhood revealed themselves. As they began to climb the stairs, little Rexah and Ryden rushed past her, giggling as they ascended the stone stairway. Before they reached the top, the little royals faded, disappearing into the past once more.

"Rexah?" Kalen said softly beside her.

Blinking a few times, she looked up at him and realised that she'd stopped walking. "Sorry," she whispered. "This place holds a lot of memories."

Kalen comfortingly squeezed her arm. "Let's get inside. Hopefully the others have a fire going."

By the time they reached the top, Rexah's legs were throbbing, and her lungs were burning. She leaned forward with her hands on her knees, a sign that she needed to up her game in training as her fae companions hadn't even broken a sweat.

The dark oak doors of the main entrance towered over them. When she was younger, Rexah had thought these doors were once made by and for giants. Even as an adult, the doors had a powerful effect on her, and she shuddered with agitation. How silly she felt; the rightful queen destined to take back her kingdom still shrunk in the face of old memories and tall structures.

Get yourself together, Rexah.

Rexah pushed one of the heavy doors open with a groan. The wood creaked and the hinges squeaked at the movement. The foyer was dark. Dust coated every surface and dulled the shine of the grey marble flooring that was cracked in places. Cobwebs smothered the unlit sconces lining the walls.

"It saddens me to see it like this," Rexah whispered to them.

Torbin gently patted her shoulder. "I can imagine how grand it used to be."

Rexah guided them cautiously through the foyer, faint voices emanating from the door to the right caught her attention. Before she took a step towards it, the door swung open and Ryden appeared at the threshold.

"Rex," he said before rushing towards her, scooping her up into his arms.

She hugged him back, sighing with relief. "I'm glad you're okay."

Ryden pulled away, moving his gaze to Kalen and Torbin. "Are you all well?"

Kalen nodded. "We are. Where are the others?"

"In here, come on," Ryden said, beckoning towards the open door.

When they stepped into the room, Storglass was lounging on the sofa across from the roaring fireplace. Arelle stood by the bookcase to the right of it, an open book in her hands as her eyes scanned over the text.

Torbin strode across the room and grabbed Arelle by the waist, embracing her. It was an action that shocked everyone in the room, Arelle included, the book falling to the floor with a thump.

The Seer's arms slowly wrapped around him. "It's good to see you too, Torbin."

"You don't know how happy I am to see you unhurt," he told her quietly. "I feared the worst."

Arelle smiled and pulled away, looking up at him. "You never need to worry about me," she said, cupping his cheek.

Torbin realised what he was doing and cleared his throat as he stepped back from her briskly. Rexah smirked softly and made her way over to the fireplace to heat her chilled bones.

"Are the rest of you okay?" Arelle asked as she cast her gaze over each of them.

Kalen nodded. "Yeah, but we ended up in Dorasa."

"It was in ruin," Rexah said quietly. "A number of dead Valfae scattered across the square. My parents' home was destroyed too, but they weren't there. I … I don't know where they are. There was no evidence that they perished in the ambush."

"Maybe they managed to escape," Storglass said, his hazel eyes filled with sympathy.

"Wait … parents?" Ryden asked, confusion coating his words.

Rexah shifted her gaze to him. She slowly nodded. "Yes, it turns out my parents are still alive, and I have a twin brother."

Surprise filled Ryden's features. "When did you find out?"

"Not long ago. I can fill you in on the details later," she replied with a small smile.

"That's not all that happened on our journey here," Torbin said grimly, a frown deepening on his forehead. "Venrhys and his Dark Fae soldiers attacked us on our way to our people's safe haven. He injured Rexah."

Arelle's wide eyes moved to her. "Are you still hurt?"

Rexah shook her head as she rubbed her hands together. "No, there was a witch amongst the camp who healed me. It was quite remarkable."

"Venrhys was going to take her, so I put a dagger in his sternum," Kalen said, folding his arms across his chest as he leaned against the doorframe. His arm muscles strained against his shirt and Rexah forced herself to look away from him. Images of those powerful arms wrapped around her as she rode him filled her mind. *Gods, help me.*

"She's okay now, but it was too close." Torbin said, his tone serious. "Venrhys stabbed her in the leg with a dagger laced with Valfae poison. She could have died. We have to be more prepared."

"Is he dead?" Ryden asked darkly, leaning against the desk by the huge window to the right of Kalen, his jaw twitching.

"Unfortunately not. I missed his heart," Kalen told him. "I won't miss next time."

"I wouldn't have missed the first time," Ryden mumbled.

Rexah looked at Kalen and saw the exact moment his face contorted; his usually calm temperament made way for a rising anger, one that had been all too ready to surface.

So much for cordiality.

Kalen's dark gaze slid to him. "I'm sorry, but I was a little too busy trying to save Rexah's life. I fought off a dozen Dark Fae and then hurt a particularly powerful one enough for him to retreat. And where were you?"

Ryden opened his mouth to speak but Rexah interrupted. "That's enough. We've got bigger shit to deal with. We don't need a dick measuring competition between the two of you," she said, glaring at them both.

"Sorry, darling," Kalen said.

Ryden nodded his head to Rexah in apology.

"Okay, we need to make a plan," Storglass said, swiftly changing the subject. "We're safe here, for now, but it won't stay that way."

Rexah moved to the armchair and sighed as she dropped into it. "I just want a few days of nothing. No Dark Fae, no Venrhys, no sword searching," she said, wearily. "I want a few days where I can gather myself again. I'd even take a few hours of peace to read. I can't remember the last time I read one of my favourites."

"I wish you could have that; I wish we all could, but until the darkness has been dealt with, we don't have the luxury," Storglass told her.

"I know." Rexah nodded softly.

"I was very impressed with your harnessing progress back at the house, and now we are out of time." Arelle placed her hand on the mantel. "In the morning Rexah and I will meditate to find the sword, if that's okay with you?" she asked, her gaze meeting Rexah's.

"Yes, I need all the help I can get with it," Rexah replied, sitting back in the chair. "I'm ready."

"I've been experimenting in the medical wing of the castle over the past few days, and I've brewed some potions that will be useful going forward in our altercations with the Dark Fae and Valfae," Storglass said.

"What sort of potions?" Torbin asked, intrigued.

"Potions that cause explosions, blindness, all sorts of harmful reactions," Storglass replied nonchalantly. "I can concentrate on them and ensure we have enough to equip everyone."

"Remind me not to piss you off," Torbin murmured with a smirk.

"Torbin, Kalen and I will train. We need to be ready for anything and everything," Ryden said, both fae nodding their heads in agreement.

Rexah looked around the room, assessing the people who

had become family to her. Nothing about their future was certain, but one thing was for sure, they would always have each other's backs, no matter what. After losing her home, her family, Rexah never imagined she would have a family unit again. She would cherish the moments they had together and would never take any second for granted.

"Get as much rest as you can tonight. The next few days will be hard going, but we need to be prepared for this next phase of our journey," Arelle said.

With a collection of nods and supportive pats on the back, the group dispersed.

"I'm going to train a little before bed. Find some focus," Kalen said as he planted a kiss on the top of Rexah's head. "I'll see you tonight?"

She placed a soft palm on his cheek and offered him a smile. "I'll see you tonight."

"Come on, big guy," Ryden hollered, a mischievous look in his eye as he stepped past Kalen and walked toward the door. "Let's go work on our throwing."

Rexah stood by the window, gazing out at the mist slithering around the grounds. Knowing the kingdom had been abandoned, that they were truly alone here, had her ill at ease. How easy it would be to be crept up on here; how effortlessly the enemy could linger in the fog below. She hugged her arms as a chill ran through her.

"This was where you used to stay on your visits?" Kalen asked as he inspected the room.

Rexah turned to him and smiled softly as she watched him

open the wardrobe to have a nosey inside. "Yes, this was my room. Technically it's still my room."

"It's very cosy," he said, smirking at her.

She grinned at him. "Indeed."

Kalen walked over to her and gently pulled her into his arms. "What you said in the study about wanting a few days of peace," he said. "I can't give you a few days, but I can give you tonight."

Rexah's heart fluttered madly in her chest as she gazed into his eyes. "Then tonight is enough," she whispered.

He gently kissed her forehead before stepping back to kick off his boots and tug off his shirt. "Shall we?"

Once she was changed into a simple night gown from the wardrobe, she made her way over to the bed and pulled back the covers. It had been so long since she'd last been in this bed, and she'd almost forgotten how comfortable it was. Sliding under the sheets, she let her head sink into the fluffy pillow and her curves dip into the soft mattress. The sheets were cold and had her skin pebbling, but she soon felt the warmth of Kalen's bare torso on hers as he gently pulled her into his side, helping her to get into the position he knew she was most comfortable in: her head on his shoulder, one leg around his hips and her hand resting on his chest, glued to his side.

Kalen secured his arm around her shoulders, providing her with an extra sense of security. Taking a deep breath, she let her whole being relax in his strong arms. She wished they could stay like this forever.

"The night we shared in my tent back in Savindeer," he said softly, breaking the peaceful silence. "I haven't been able to stop thinking about it."

"Me neither," she whispered. "No matter how hard I try, I

can't seem to get it out of my head. But I don't see it as a bad thing."

"You don't?" he asked. She could hear the smirk on his face.

"No." Rexah tilted her head up towards him. "Because it's never been like that before," she told him. "I felt vulnerable, safe and content all at the same time, and it's a feeling I'll cherish forever."

"You know I would never push you into doing anything you don't want to do." Kalen's fingers gently skimmed her cheek. "And when you begged me to help you forget, I couldn't refuse you. I was worried you might have regretted it afterwards."

"It was my choice, and I don't regret a single second of what we did," she reassured him. "I've wanted to do that since the moment we met."

A seductive rumble sounded in his chest. "You don't know how hard it was for me to keep myself restrained," he admitted. "There were so many times I could have had you."

The muscles low in her stomach tightened at his words. "Well, now you can have me anywhere you like."

His navy gaze heated. "Don't tempt me."

Rexah swallowed the lump in her throat as the atmosphere between them charged. The want in her rose and Kalen's nostrils flared like he could scent it. "As much as I want you right now, I think it's best we get a full night's rest," she said. "We have a lot to do over the next few days."

His lips lifted into a heart stopping smirk. "I hate how right you are."

She laughed softly and buried her nose into his neck, breathing in his scent. When his hand slid to her lower back and began rubbing in those familiar circles, she gently moved her hand over his chest, up his neck, and pushed her fingers into the back of his hair. "Are you going to grow it back out again?"

"I might," he replied. "I haven't decided yet, this style is starting to grow on me."

"You could be bald, and I'd still like you," she said, grinning against his neck.

He let out a hearty laugh. "Could you imagine me bald?"

Rexah joined him this time, her stomach tightening with how hard she laughed. "No, please. I can't breathe!"

Kalen's laughter bubbled down to a chuckle as he buried his nose into her hair. "I'd just have to take some of yours. Do you think I'd suit the purple?"

"Hmm, that's up for debate."

"So, I should stick with the baldness then?" he asked, amusement dancing in his eyes.

"Absolutely not. Let's forget I ever mentioned it." She smiled tiredly up at him.

"Agreed," he said, kissing her nose.

Rexah moved her head back to his shoulder and let her eyes drift closed. It didn't take her long to fall asleep to the sound of Kalen's heartbeat.

28

The training room hadn't changed a bit. The memory of her first kiss with Ryden played in her mind. That was the day everything changed between them. They were no longer the *little royals* from the moment their lips had touched. The boy had become a man. The girl had become a woman. It felt so long ago that her heart ached, and she yearned to be close to the past where her grandmother lived, and her kingdom still stood.

Rexah's footsteps echoed throughout the large room as she walked towards the centre. She'd needed some time away to clear her head. If she was going to meditate again, she'd need to be as calm and open as possible. Arelle told her to take a breather and that she would be waiting for her whenever she was ready, but the question was, would she ever be? There was no room for error now in any part of their plan. One hair out of line and everything would collapse.

Pressure built on her shoulders whenever she thought about searching for the sword. The burden of finding it was hers and hers alone. She had the support of the others, yes, but they couldn't find it for her. This was something only she could do, and if she was being honest with herself, it terrified her.

"I thought I might find you here," Ryden's voice resounded through the room.

Rexah turned in time to see him walking towards her. "There aren't many places I can hide where you wouldn't find me, Ry. Especially when we're in your home."

He smiled widely. "That's true. You were rather terrible when we played hide and seek."

Rexah's eyebrow raised. "I wasn't *that* bad."

"You all but announced your hiding places. It was far too easy to find you," he chuckled, coming to a stop before her.

"Maybe I just *really* wanted you to find me." Rexah smiled wistfully. "Shouldn't you be off training with the others?" she asked.

His shoulders lifted. "They decided they wanted to spar outside, but I thought I'd leave them to it and come find you."

"Why?"

"Because I don't need to train. I'd rather spend some time with you," he said. "I've missed you so much, Rex, and when I thought you were dead, that I would never get to see you again, it tore me apart. I'm not used to the feeling of having you back yet. It still feels so tenuous. And after what happened recently … your leg …"

Rexah's eyes softened. "I've missed you too, Ry. When all of this is over we will go to the gardens and take a walk through the maze again."

Ryden's light-grey eyes brightened. "I can't think of anything more perfect." He took her hand and placed a gentle kiss to the back of it.

She cleared her throat and removed her hand from his, her cheeks growing hot.

"Sorry." He smiled weakly at her.

Rexah nodded softly before she turned and walked over to the bench below one of the arched windows and sat down. "I wanted to talk to you about my family."

Ryden nodded and joined her on the bench. "Your parents and brother."

"I haven't known about them for long. My grandmother kept it a secret from me until the day Adorea was attacked. She told me to go to Dorasa, so I did. That's where I found them," she said. "Xandyr isn't just my brother: he's my twin."

"Wow." His eyes went wide, and he shook his head in disbelief. "Do you look alike?"

Rexah nodded. "The only dissimilarity is he doesn't have the purple flashes in his hair and his eyes are blue. Other than that, the resemblance is uncanny."

"That must have been quite the shock. I can't imagine how you must have felt in that moment."

"It was a shock. It still is. I was angry at my grandmother for keeping them from me, but she did it to protect me and to protect them. Now they're missing, and I have no idea where they could have gone," she said, running her fingers through her hair. "I can't help but wonder if there were any other secrets she kept from me."

Ryden's eyes softened. "I hope not, but we will find out, and we will find your family, I promise."

She smiled at him and nodded softly before she sighed. "I can't believe how much our lives have changed."

"The gods like to keep us on our toes it seems," Ryden said. "Some of us get the better end of the stick than others."

Rexah winced at his words, feeling their sting. "I'm sorry for how things have turned out, truly I am."

He shrugged dismissively. "You can't help who you fall in love with," he said. "The heart wants what the heart wants."

She looked up at him, studying his face. She couldn't tell if he was annoyed or joking around, but the ache in her chest told her it was the former. "I know it's hard for you to see me with Kalen."

"We don't have to keep discussing this." His tone was sharp, and his features twisted. "I've told you it bothers me, but I've also said I'll get over it. We have been in love since we were sixteen. Our marriage was arranged, and we were going to live happily ever after, just like the stories we used to read," he said, his expression darkening. "That doesn't just go away overnight."

Rexah placed her hand on his arm. "I know you're hurting, grieving. I am too."

Ryden looked down at her. "You seem to be doing pretty well."

"What is that supposed to mean?"

"Come on, Rex, look around you," he said, gesturing with his hands. "The realm is falling apart, but you're busy playing happy families with Kalen and the others when your priority should have been to find the sword. You should have it by now."

Rexah rose to her feet, her gut wrenching. "What has gotten into you? You know I've been working hard on meditating, controlling my power, all so I can locate it."

"Nothing is wrong with me, as much as you'd like to believe that there is. You'd rather spend your time fucking a fae than finding the only thing that can save us all," he said, his voice and the look in his eyes full of disappointment and disgust.

His words felt like a slap in the face. Disbelief coursed through her as she shook her head. "You know that's not the truth. It's not as though I have a map that will lead me straight to it. We have to be smart about everything we do. We don't want to lead the Dark Fae straight to it. And while you don't seem to care about my wellbeing, Arelle doesn't want me to get hurt in the process!"

Ryden stood up. "The Rexah I knew wouldn't let anything stop her from achieving her goals. She never allowed anything or anyone to cloud her judgement," he said, his eyes regarding her in a way that made her feel so small. "Maybe she died along with her kingdom."

It happened before the thought even entered her mind. Her hand came up, and she slapped him across the face, the sound ringing through the room.

Rexah's eyes widened as they filled with tears. Ryden didn't say anything. He lifted his gaze to hers, giving nothing away of how he felt in that moment. Collecting herself, she looked him dead in the eyes. "The Ryden I knew would *never* have said the things you just did," she said, a tear escaping down her face.

She didn't wait to hear his reply; she spun and rushed out of the training room, adrenaline flooding through her as she fled down the corridor, needing to put as much distance between them as possible.

"Something is bothering you," Arelle noted with a tilt of

her head as they sat cross legged in the middle of the empty ballroom.

With Ryden's permission, Arelle had drawn a witch's circle on the floor in black chalk, directly under where they now sat facing each other. Candles surrounded them in a careful arrangement.

Rexah hadn't seen Ryden since their conversation in the training room, and she was glad. She didn't know what she was going to say to him. Her behaviour was unacceptable, but so were the things he'd said. The situation was tense at the moment, but that didn't excuse what transpired the day before.

"Ryden and I had an argument, and I ..." she trailed off for a moment, clearing her throat. "He said some harsh words, and I slapped him."

Arelle straightened her spine. "What did he say to you?"

"That I should be focusing my attention on finding the sword rather than on Kalen," she told her. "He said it more unpleasantly than that, though. I shouldn't have hit him. That's not like me."

"You shouldn't have, but everyone's emotions are high right now and when that happens, we sometimes do things out of character," Arelle replied, placing a comforting hand on her arm. "It's natural to feel this way given the current situation, but there are ways to handle it, and it seems he went about it the wrong way."

Rexah nodded. "I'm so angry with myself that I lifted my hand to him."

"It'll get sorted in the end. I get the feeling Ryden won't be able to stay mad at you for long and should apologise to you too," she said giving her a sympathetic smile. "If you're up to it, shall we get started on our meditation?"

"Yes. It'll help take my mind off everything for a little while," Rexah replied. "How do we do this?"

With the click of her fingers, the candles roared to life. "Take three deep, calming breaths to ground yourself and clear your mind."

Following her instructions, Rexah felt herself relax, remembering the little tricks Torbin had taught her about meditation. She shoved her anxiety out of her mind and focused on emptying every thought from her head until there was nothing left but the Shadow Star.

"Very good," Arelle said, her voice low. "Now, I want you to picture the door you saw before and once it's clear in your mind, take my hands. If you feel your magic surfacing at any time, control it. Like we practised."

Rexah placed her hands in Arelle's, hovering above the centre of the witch circle. "Will this hurt?"

"Not one bit. It might feel a little strange, but there's nothing to fear. I promise you."

"Okay."

She closed her eyes.

It took her a few tries, but after her fourth attempt, the darkness of her eyelids lifted to reveal the purple wooden door. She reached for Arelle and said, "I see it."

"Okay, now open your eyes."

Rexah frowned, confused at the instruction, but she did as Arelle told her. As she opened them, the door remained in view, the ballroom and Arelle both faded away. An unease settled low in her stomach, and her heart picked up as she stood and took a tentative step towards the door, it's shape warping.

"Stop," Arelle said, her image suddenly appearing beside her, her form translucent like a ghost. "Control your power."

Looking down, she saw her hands were laced with magic, itching to be released. She hushed it, promising she would allow it freedom later, and it responded, receding back into her body.

"Take a look around you. Do you recognise anything here?"

Scanning the area around her, Rexah took in the blurry surroundings. "I can't make anything out." She sighed in frustration.

"Try again," Arelle's voice echoed.

An unnatural warmth spread through Rexah's body. "What is that?" she asked, panicked.

"My magic," Arelle told her. "It'll help clear your mind further. Look around you, Rexah. Relax."

She slid her gaze to her surroundings once more, and instead of stepping toward the door, she took a small step back. As she did, the mist dissipated, bringing the visage into focus. Frosty grass crunched beneath her feet. Trees surrounding them reached the sky like giants. The stone structure, pristine and untouched by evil forces, was tall and intimidating as always. Two unlit lanterns hung at either side of the purple door. In the stonework above the door, the crest she knew so well sat proudly.

She knew exactly where this was.

Rexah lost her grip on the meditation, her mind no longer composed, and was ripped back to reality. Tears flowed down her face, but she was quick to wipe them away.

Arelle reached over and placed a gentle hand on her shoulder. "Steady."

"I found it." Rexah looked at her. "I can't believe I found it," she whispered.

Arelle grinned at her. "I never doubted you for a second," she said, moving a strand of hair from her face. "Where is it?"

It made so much sense to her now, and she almost laughed at the realisation. The Shadow Star hadn't disappeared when Riona died, it had followed her.

Rexah looked to Arelle, entirely dumbfounded, and when she answered, her voice was barely a whisper.

"Home."

29

"The Shadow Star is at the Ravenheart crypt."

All her ancestors were laid to rest there. It was where all Ravenhearts were entombed and reunited.

And they were so close.

Everyone dropped their cutlery, glasses and mouths. It seemed lunchtime was over.

"It's been there this whole time? We need to contact the Night Witches right away."

"Let's not do anything rash, Ryden" Arelle chimed in. "We're one step closer to victory now that we know where the sword is, but we cannot go running in blindly. We need to be extremely careful, now more than ever. As soon as we begin that journey, we *will* find trouble."

"Arelle is right. Just because we haven't seen any Dark Fae this last week or so doesn't mean they aren't there, hiding in the shadows, waiting for us to make our next move," Kalen said, giving Rexah's thigh another comforting squeeze before he pressed his lips to her forehead. "I'm so proud of you for finding the sword. I knew you could do it."

"Thank you," she replied timidly. "I couldn't have done it with you."

Rexah felt Ryden's eyes on her, and when she lifted her head to meet his gaze, it was filled with abashment. He looked away as soon as their eyes met, and Rexah was left feeling lost. She'd never been through anything like this before with Ryden, and she hated seeing him this way.

She looked back to Kalen and found a curious expression on his face. Had he picked up on her unease? On Ryden's? She watched as he slid his attention to Ryden, his narrowed eyes scrutinising as if he could see their argument written all over his face, but he said nothing. Rexah was grateful; the last thing she wanted right now was for a fight to break out at the dining table.

"I agree with Ryden that we should contact the Night Witches," Rexah said, shaking off the weirdness. "They swore an oath to the Ravenheart bloodline to protect their dead and they don't take too kindly to those who show up unannounced, Ravenheart or not."

"The Night Witches are an advantageous ally," Torbin said with a confident smile. "I've never met them."

Rexah smiled. "Neither have I; it was always my grand-mother who dealt with them," Rexah admitted. "But I've seen pictures in books, and they look like something straight out of a nightmare."

The Night Witches were feared by most. Despite their wraith-like appearance, and voices that were so harsh you felt each word they spoke scrape against your bones, they weren't evil beings. They only came out at night, conserving their energy during the day. Throughout Rexah's studies of them she learned that they made offerings to the Moon Goddess, Lunania, to show their devotion and gratitude to the Goddess who gifted them with their power.

The realisation hit her then: from now on she would need to deal with everything she was so used to her grandmother taking care of. She swallowed the lump of responsibility that formed in her throat before gulping down some water.

"I'm looking forward to seeing if the pictures are accurate," Kalen said. "I heard they like to eat babies."

Rexah burst into laughter, almost spitting out her water as she shook her head. "Whoever told you that was just trying to scare you. They don't eat babies, or any humans for that matter."

Storglass drank from his glass before asking, "How do we get in contact with them?"

"Leave that to Rexah and I. We will send word of our intended visit," Arelle confirmed as she tore off a piece of toasted bread and popped it in her mouth.

Rexah nodded her thanks to Arelle as she continued eating.

"Once contact has been made, we should start our preparations for leaving," Kalen said. "As soon as we have clearance from the witches, we need to leave as quickly as possible."

"What happens once we get there?" Ryden asked as he finished off his food. "What if we *are* being watched and the Dark Fae follow us there?"

"That's why we need to be on high alert and ready for anything," Torbin told him. "If we let our apprehension get the better of us all the time then we would never get anything done. It's a risk we need to take."

Rexah forgot how ruthless Torbin could be when he wanted to. "If we don't take this risk, then another one will present itself. We have two options: we either go to the crypt and get the sword, or the Dark Fae get their hands on me and force me to get it for them," she said.

She would die before she would let that happen.

Ryden nodded softly. "It's better we get our hands on it now," he agreed. "I just wanted to consider all the outcomes before we head out there."

Rexah's eyes softened. "There's nothing wrong with being overly cautious."

"Tonight, when the moon is at its highest, Rexah and I will contact the Night Witches," Arelle summarised. "In the meantime, we should ready ourselves, sharpen our weapons and pack up provisions. Are we all in agreement?"

Everyone nodded and the rest of the meal was sat in apprehensive silence that set Rexah's nerves alight.

Once the meal was over, Kalen and Rexah volunteered to wash the dishes and made their way to the castle's kitchen. Rexah felt very domesticated and fulfilled as she cleaned. She never did it growing up, and she found that she rather enjoyed it.

It felt strange cleaning up after themselves in a deserted kingdom, but she felt within herself an obligation to keep Ryden's home tidy. Too, if it wasn't for Storglass being able to conjure food, it would have been cold porridge for every meal; she was grateful for his effort, and it was only fair that they do their part too.

"What's wrong, darling?"

Rexah smiled as Kalen kissed the back of her head. "Retrieving it will be much harder and more dangerous than we anticipate. It always is. I'm afraid one day it will become too much for us."

"We've made it this far," he said softly. "We can do this."

"As long as one of us has a positive attitude then that's all we need to make it through."

Kalen huffed a laugh. "Positivity will destroy the enemy."

Rexah grinned. "If it were that simple then there would be no darkness cursing the realm."

Kalen moved beside her as he swiped the dish cloth across the plate, drying the water from its surface. "Ryden was quiet just now."

"He was."

"Do you want to talk about it?"

She didn't, but she wouldn't lie to him. "Ryden and I got into an argument. It really doesn't matter," she said dismissively.

Kalen stopped what he was doing, and she could feel his gaze on her. "An argument? Over what?"

"He said I should be more focused on finding the sword instead of ..." she trailed off.

"Instead of what, darling?"

She knew she would get nowhere beating around the bush, so she took a deep breath and channelled Torbin's bluntness. She lifted her gaze to meet his. "Instead of fucking you and playing happy families."

The moment the words left her lips Kalen's expression turned to complete and utter rage. He put the plate down on the counter with a thud.

"Kalen."

He turned to head for the door. "I'm going to kill him," he growled.

Rexah moved in front of him, placing her hands on his chest. "No, Kalen. Please, look at me."

Kalen stopped walking and looked down at her indignantly.

"Our emotions got the best of us in the moment. I slapped him after he said it. I regret it and I saw the emotion on his face that told me he felt the same. Please, don't do or say anything to him. I'm handling it."

He was quiet for a few moments before he ran his hand through his hair. "For you, I won't do anything. But if I hear him talk to you that way then I won't be held accountable for my actions," he told her.

She moved closer, burying her face into his chest as she wrapped her arms around his waist. "Everything is so tense right now. We both said and did things we regret."

Kalen slid his arms around her. "Promise me if it happens again, you'll tell me. He won't speak to you in that way thinking he can get away with it."

"I promise, but I know it was just the heat of the moment. It won't happen again," she assured him. "He's adjusting."

"Okay." He gently kissed her head. "Let's finish up here."

When they were done washing up, she kissed Kalen on the cheek and decided on a shower. She needed it to think; she needed it to figure out how she would fix things with her best friend.

How could you have been so thoughtless, Rexah?

On her way through the castle, ascending to the bathing chamber, she looked out a window and espied Ryden alone in the courtyard below, throwing daggers at a wooden pole. Between throws, as he went to retrieve his blades from the splintered wood, he pushed a hand through his hair restlessly. He must have thrown ten times in the time she stood there, peering down at him, and despite the desolation and disappointment etched across his face, not one of them missed.

The waxing crescent moon was stunning in the night sky, stars twinkling their stunning light around it. Rexah stood with Arelle on the main balcony that led back into the ballroom, as the Seer had suggested it was the ideal place to send their message to the Night Witches. From up here, Rexah could see the mist slithering through the tops of the trees, and it sent an ominous chill down her spine.

"What do we need to do first?" Rexah asked, hugging her arms as the cold night air bit at her skin. Even with a thick cloak around her, she still felt its frosty touch.

"It's quite simple. The first thing we need to do is write our message on this paper," she said, holding up a strange looking piece of parchment.

Rexah took it from her and watched in amazement as it shimmered with starlight. "Where did you get this?" she asked, running her finger down the page, feeling what she could only describe as tiny bubbles bursting under her skin as she did.

"Your grandmother wasn't the only one who communicated with the Night Witches." Arelle smirked as she pulled a quill out of the pouch at her hip. "I have stacks of them back home."

"I've never seen anything like it. I never saw this paper anywhere in the castle growing up," she said. "Then again, I didn't send messages to anyone."

"I'm honoured to be with you when you send your first." Arelle grinned.

"I have a question." Rexah looked up at her. "The night of the attack on Adorea, my grandmother received a message from the Night Witches, but she called it a shadow message, and this looks like the exact opposite. Are you sure we're doing this correctly?"

"When they receive a message, they absorb the starlight within the paper. Think of it like a peace offering. Once they take the starlight, all that's left is their shadow, and when they send their response, starlight will begin to shine through once again, but only if the person who the message was intended for opens it," Arelle explained with a giggle of excitement. "Sorry, I tend to get a little over excited whenever I do this. The Night Witches and I are *very* good friends."

Rexah's eyebrows hit her hairline. "You're friends with them?"

"Best friends, actually," Arelle confirmed. "They always invite me to their annual moon sabbath. It's such a fantastic event, but I can tell you more about that later. We should get this message sent as quickly as possible whilst the moon is in position."

Rexah took the quill from her. "Where is the ink?"

"No need for ink, just write to your heart's content," Arelle said, waving a hand at her to carry on.

No ink?

Taking her word for it, Rexah set the glimmering piece of parchment on the surface of the stone railing that encircled the balcony and began to write.

Dear friends,

It is with urgency that I write to you in this time of great need. I will be arriving in Adorea a few days from now to visit the Ravenheart crypt.

Please accept this as notice of my intended visit, along

with my companions. Your assistance upon our arrival would be greatly appreciated.

I look forward to officially meeting you and your clan.

Kindest Regards,

Rexah Ravenheart

R exah watched as her words bled into the paper, disappearing within the starlight. "This is magnificent. Did you enchant it?"

Arelle nodded. "It's a simple spell, but a very useful one. Could you imagine needing to carry ink around with you everywhere you went?"

Rexah grinned at her. "Magic is amazing."

"Next I need you to fold the paper as you would to place it into an envelope," Arelle instructed her, and she followed her direction without question. "Good, now hold the edge of the letter with your index finger and thumb up to the sky, in line with the moon."

Curious as to what would happen next, Rexah lifted the letter and aligned it with the moon. "Okay, now what?"

"Picture the Night Witches in your mind, focus your intent on them, and the letter will do the rest," she said.

Taking a deep breath, Rexah pinned her gaze to the letter, willing it to go to its destination, only to be read by the Prime. To her amazement, after a few moments of nothing, Rexah watched as the moon began to burn through the letter, the wicked points of its crescent shape prominent through the parchment. Rexah almost let it go, but shadows appeared as if from nowhere, snatching it from her hand and leaving nothing but ash swirling on the cold, frigid air.

"Holy shit." Rexah gasped, almost lost for words. "That was the most incredible thing I've ever seen."

Arelle laughed. "If I could have captured the look on your face in a painting, I would have. It was priceless."

"What happens now?"

"We wait for a response," Arelle said, leaning against the railing. "I don't know how long it will take, but we still have so much to prep for our departure."

"Maybe we will get our reply on the road," Rexah suggested.

"I think so." Arelle smiled proudly. "Well done, Rexah. You sent your first message by moonlight."

It was such a trivial thing to feel excited about, but Rexah couldn't help the grin that spread across her face. In some way it felt like her first duty as the future queen of Adorea. No matter how silly that sounded, it gave Rexah a boost of courage that she hadn't realised she needed.

30

Unease hung in the air as Rexah made her way down the stone steps, exiting the castle of Kaldoren. Ryden was waiting for her at the bottom, a sorrowful look on his face that filled her stomach with nerves.

"Are you okay?" she asked as she stopped in front of him.

His usual grey eyes were dull as they met hers. "It's never easy leaving home," he said. "I know it's empty and nothing like it was before, but it's still home."

Rexah gently placed her hand on his arm. "I understand, but once all of this is over, you'll be here with your people again, and you'll be king."

"I don't know if I'm ready for that," he admitted quietly, resting his hand on top of hers.

"I don't think either of us are ready to take the crown, but this is the hand that fate has dealt us," she told him. "Our people need us, Ry."

Nausea spread through her. Did any of her people survive the attack on Adorea? Would she have anyone to reign over?

Ryden squeezed her hand and turned to face her. "I'm so

sorry, Rex. I should never have spoken to you the way I did. There are ways to express thoughts and feelings, and how I presented mine was way out of line," he said, crestfallen. "I am so incredibly sorry for hurting your feelings like that."

She squeezed his hand in return, her heart throbbing with love for her oldest friend. "You did hurt my feelings, but that didn't give me the right to raise my hand to you. I'm so sorry," she said. "My emotions were all over the place, but that's no excuse for what I did."

Ryden wrapped his arm around her shoulder and pulled her against him, gently kissing the side of her head. "It's okay. I really shouldn't have said those things. The world is falling apart and it's affecting us both."

She nodded against his shoulder. "I forgive you. It won't happen again, I promise."

"Me too," he whispered.

They stood looking out onto the abandoned city in comfortable silence before Rexah spoke again. "Things will get better. The gods put us all on this planet to do good. The darkness can't prevail."

"Once you get that sword, it'll change the playing field and give us the upper hand," he said, running his fingers up and down her arm.

"What if I fail?" she whispered.

"The Raven God chose you for a reason, Rex. He wouldn't have blessed you if he didn't think you could do this," he said looking down at her. "He believes in you, and so do I."

A cold breeze brushed past them causing Rexah to bury herself closer to Ryden's warmth. "You're still my best friend, you know that?"

He smiled at her. "And you're mine. You always will be, no matter what happens."

Rexah turned her gaze back to the city. The mist swirled in the air like ghosts dancing on the wind.

"We triple-checked, and we have everything we need," Torbin said, descending the stairs. "We have enough food and water for the journey there, and we're stocked up on medicinal supplies just in case."

Rexah let go of Ryden's arm and turned to everyone as they approached. They'd decided against using portals to travel. It cost too much magic and they needed as much firepower as they could get, so they would travel on foot until they reached the nearest village where they hoped they'd be able to obtain some horses.

"Before we go, I'd like to say something," Rexah announced. When everyone focused their attention on her, she continued. "I didn't know what the future held after everything that happened in Adorea. Finding out that I'm the only one who can find the weapon to save us all was something I wasn't prepared for; I still don't know if I am; but the Raven God chose me, and I won't let him or the realm down.

"Getting to our location together and in one piece is the main priority. You *all* mean so much to me. I know we haven't all known each other very long, but our paths were meant to cross. I wouldn't be able to do this without any of you." Her hand brushed the hilt of her weapon, and a determination roused within her. "These monsters have had their fun. It's time for them to be put back in their place."

Arelle beamed at her. "You're getting good at these prebattle speeches."

Rexah's cheeks heated slightly, and her stomach fluttered when she saw the toe-curling smirk on Kalen's face.

"Like I told you before, Rexah Ravenheart, it's an honour to fight by your side," Storglass said, bowing his head to her.

Smiling at them, Rexah said, "Let's get going then, shall we?"

The sky filled with shades of brilliant reds and oranges as the sun began its ascent. It was a chilly morning, but Rexah was assured that once they started their travels, they would warm up quickly.

Kalen stepped closer and pressed his lips to her forehead. "You are so strong and so brave, darling," he whispered as he took her hand, threading their fingers together.

"Tell me that once the sword is in my hand," she whispered back, leaning into him.

As they made their way towards the treeline, Rexah noticed Ryden take one last look at his home, her heart aching for him as they crossed into the forest.

Rexah had been down this route many times going back and forth between Kaldoren and Adorea in the back of a carriage, but never before on foot with the world on her shoulders. Pulling the cloak closer as the icy breeze picked up, Rexah longed for the days when she was a little girl without any worries. What she would give to go back, just for one day, but part of growing up was accepting your responsibilities, and that was exactly what she was going to do.

Rexah almost groaned in relief as they reached the nearest village to Kaldoren. Her back ached from lying on a bedroll the past two nights, and she couldn't wait to sleep in an actual bed with a soft mattress and fluffy pillows. Maybe her expectations for the inn were a little high; the beds wouldn't be luxurious, but it was a step up from a bedroll, that was for certain.

The village was small but had a friendly aura, the lanterns lining the streets emanating a soft, welcoming glow. The hour was late, and it seemed most of the villagers had retired for the night. Rexah's boots clicked against the cobblestones as they made their way to their resting place for the night.

The inn was situated at the back of the village. Larger than she expected, it was a two-storey structure made from a mixture of dark wood and light stone and was called 'The Old Oak'. The interior was as warm and welcoming as the owner who greeted them with a cheerful smile. Sleeping arrangements were agreed between them when the owner announced she only had four rooms left. Rexah and Kalen would have one, Torbin and Arelle would share another whilst Ryden and Storglass each had their own.

Rexah faceplanted the bed once she got to the room. She heard a faint chuckle from Kalen and the door clicking closed and locked.

"As much as I enjoy taking in the scenery and breathing fresh air whilst travelling," Rexah said, her voice muffled against the cover. "I will never, *ever*, take a bed for granted."

"You've been spoiled by the time spent in Arelle's home," he said, and she could hear the grin on his face.

Rexah pushed herself up into a sitting position and looked over to him with an easy smile. "I think I have."

Kalen pulled off the bag that was strapped to his back and dropped it to the floor with a thud before unclipping his cloak. "I'll admit, I'm looking forward to sleeping in that bed tonight rather than the forest floor."

"See? I'm not the only spoilt one." She smirked as she stood up, removing her own cloak and kicking off her boots.

Kalen laughed as he hung up both of their cloaks on the hook on the back of the door. "Let's get settled."

Rexah took off her pack and dug out her night dress, setting it down on the bed.

"You won't be needing that tonight, darling," Kalen said deeply, his breath suddenly tickling the back of her neck.

Every hair on her body rose as his hands slid around her hips, pulling her back against his body. Swallowing the lump in her throat, she slowly looked up at him over her shoulder. His eyes were dark as they trailed down from hers to her lips, and Rexah's knees almost buckled.

Kalen's fingers slid under her tunic as he gave her a look that begged for permission. With a single nod, she granted it without hesitation, and he had it off in one smooth motion. The cool air sent a flood of goosebumps rippling across her bare skin, and she shivered slightly. His lips touched her shoulder as she leaned back into him; she lingered there, savouring the moment before turning to face him.

Lifting his shirt over his head, Rexah threw it, not caring where it landed. She needed to feel his skin against hers. She craved it. She was so addicted to him that it took no time at all to rid him of the rest of his clothing. Kalen followed her lead and tugged her leggings down. Soon their clothes were lying in a messy heap on the floor, but Rexah didn't care. All that mattered to her was for him to hurry up and make them one; she needed to feel him inside of her before she went insane.

Kalen swept her up into his arms with ease, and she wrapped her legs around his waist before he lay her down on the bed gently. "Gods, you are so beautiful," he mumbled before pressing his lips to her neck.

Rexah leaned her head back into the pillow to allow him better access, her fingers sliding into his dark hair, encouraging him. A soft moan escaped her lips as he sucked on her skin;

her back arched, causing her hips to brush against his hard length, the movement earning a groan from him.

"Kalen."

He pulled away slightly to look down at her. "Yes, my love?"

Her violet eyes met his. "I need you, right now."

A smirk pulled at his lips as his hand trailed between her legs, running his finger through the slickness there. "Soaked already."

Rexah's hips rolled reflexively, urging him to push his finger inside her. She gasped when he slid two fingers in, her body reacting to his actions as he slowly stroked her, teasing her.

Without warning, Kalen flipped her onto her stomach, gently pulling her up until she was on her hands and knees. Rexah's heart was pounding so hard in her chest she feared it was going to explode when she felt Kalen's calloused palm smooth over the skin of her backside. She felt him line himself up with her, anticipation slithering underneath her skin, and when he pushed himself inside her, a moan fell from her lips.

Curses left Kalen's mouth until he was fully seated, and hearing those words sent a new thrill through her body. Her hands gripped the sheet as he slowly thrusted, teasingly stroking her inner walls, and it was driving her crazy. She didn't need slow and gentle, she needed him to take her like it was their last night alive. She leaned into him, urging him deeper, praying he would understand.

With another irresistible curse, he gave her exactly what she wanted. His speed increased and his fingertips dug deliciously into the stretchmarks on her hips. His cock found that spot deep within and she almost saw stars.

"Hmm, that's what you wanted darling, wasn't it?" he groaned.

"Gods, yes," she moaned loudly.

She wanted this for the rest of her life.

Kalen reached down and pulled her up, her back against his sweat slicked chest. His lips pressed against her neck as he pounded into her. The room filled with the sound of their bodies, their skin, coming together with a symphony of blissful moans.

"Fuck, you take me so well," he said, his breath hot in her ear. "Such a good girl."

Rexah's hand snaked back to the nape of his neck. Her own hips began to rock in time with his, intensifying the orgasm that was brewing. No matter how hard she tried to hold on, she knew she wasn't going to last much longer. "Kalen," she breathed, warning him of how close she was.

"Go on, love. Let me see you fall apart." His hand left her hip and wrapped around her throat, tilting her head back against his shoulder.

The new angle Kalen hit was all too much for her. Rexah's back arched, pushing her backside harder into his hips, and stars exploded behind her eyes as a powerful orgasm crashed through her. His name tore from her mouth once more as her body convulsed with the force of her high. Her thighs pressed together as she clenched around him.

A few more hard thrusts and Kalen joined her over that heavenly edge, spilling himself within her with a deep growl that she felt vibrate through his chest.

Neither of them moved as they savoured every second of this feeling, of being joined as one. Rexah focused on the sound of their heavy breathing as she tried to calm down her racing heart. Kalen slowly withdrew from her and moved them to lay down on the bed.

"I'll be right back," Rexah whispered, rising from the bed and scurrying into the small bathroom attached to their room. It wasn't the greatest, but it had the essentials: a toilet, and a large sink. She cleaned herself up and looked at herself in the tiny mirror mounted on the wall above the sink as she washed her hands. Her cheeks were flushed, and her hair was all over the place. If anyone saw her now, there would be absolutely no mistaking what she'd just done. Her lips were swollen and tingling from Kalen's kisses, but a content look had settled in her violet eyes.

Kalen looked as comfortable and content as she did; he lay on his back, his blue eyes trained on her as she made her way back over to the bed, sliding in next to him. She moulded into his side when he pulled her into his arms and lifted the cover around them both. She could hear his heart beating a million miles an hour in his chest.

A thought suddenly creeped into her mind that made her body tense.

"Rexah?" he whispered. "What's wrong? Did I hurt you?"

She shook her head against his chest before lifting her gaze to meet his. "No, you didn't hurt me. I ... I just realised something," she whispered back.

Kalen didn't speak, but the look in his eyes told her he was listening.

"This will be the first time I've been in Adorea since the attack," she told him, her voice breaking as tears flooded her eyes.

He gently kissed her forehead, his fingers threading through her hair, his hand coming to rest at the nape of her neck. "I know how hard it will be. It's okay to be nervous or scared, but sooner or later you would have needed to go back and maybe sooner is better."

"I don't know if I'm ready to see my home in ruins," she admitted. "What if it breaks me to the point where I can't go on?"

"Look at me," Kalen whispered, and she lifted her eyes to meet his again. "The future is uncertain. You're still grieving a terrible loss. It's completely understandable for you to feel like this, but darling, you don't give yourself enough credit."

She frowned. "What do you mean?"

"Take a look back at everything you've overcome and achieved. Does that sound like someone that's so easily broken? I don't think so."

"How do you always find the right words to say?"

Kalen grinned softly at her. "It's easy when it's the truth. Everything you've been faced with you've never shied away from it. You've taken it head on, no questions asked."

"Things are only going to get much, much worse before they get any better," she told him with a sniff. "I hope you realise what you've signed yourself up for."

"My home was destroyed, just like yours. We signed up for the same fight. The Dark Fae need to be reminded that they have no place in this world. They must pay for every life they've taken, every home that's been destroyed, and I'll happily be there to ensure they don't forget," he said with conviction. "I'll be by your side every single step of the way," he promised her. "I made you a vow and I will honour it with my life."

Rexah reached up and cupped his cheek, her thumb gently stroking it.

"And I will do everything in my power to help you bring Vellwynd back to its former glory, I swear." Rexah leaned up and brushed her lips against his, solidifying her promise to him. She kept her eyes closed when he pulled away and leaned his forehead against hers.

"You don't know how much that means to me," he whispered.

Rexah lifted her head to look up into his beautiful blue eyes. "Your mother would be so proud of you; of the things you've overcome and the things you're about to achieve."

Kalen's thumb stroked her cheek. "I like to think she's helping me along the way. Sometimes I swear I feel her presence."

"She's always with you, Kalen. All of those we lost are never too far away," she said, emotion clogging the back of her throat. "We will put a stop to the darkness one way or another. The dark days will end," she said.

"The dark days will end," he echoed, burying his nose into her hair. "Promise me one thing before we get out of bed tomorrow?"

Rexah nodded, raising her eyebrow as she waited for his reply.

"Once this is all over and the Dark Fae are destroyed, promise me we will never leave our bed for anyone or anything?" he asked, innocently.

She giggled and nodded. "I promise, but for now, we need to go and save the realm, okay?"

"Okay." Kalen rolled his eyes and grumbled playfully. "If we have to."

31

orbin managed to secure them four horses from the stables. Rexah had no issues sharing with Kalen. It meant she could bury herself into his warmth for the remainder of their journey. Torbin offered to let Arelle ride with him which she accepted with a wink and a kiss to his cheek, leaving the last two horses for Storglass and Ryden.

It would take another three days to arrive in Adorea and an additional half day to get to the Ravenheart crypt. The funeral of a Ravenheart, much like a wedding, was no private or small affair. The body would be placed in a luxurious coffin which would be placed in the throne room for two days, and everyone would be welcomed to pay their final respects. From there, the body would be transported by royal carriage to the Ravenheart crypt, surrounded by the royal guard and the most senior officers in the Adorian army. The Adorian soldiers would accompany the family, protecting them on the road there. Finally, the coffin is laid to rest with the other dead royals with a short service performed by the royal priest, a ceremony witnessed only by the royal family members in attendance.

Rexah had never been to a funeral before, royal or no, and she was thankful. The thought of them made her feel uneasy, and from what her grandmother used to say of them, they were filled with heartache and sorrow. She didn't think she'd ever be able to sit through a service for someone she loved so deeply.

Rexah swung herself up onto the horse with ease as Kalen secured their bags to the saddle. Torbin and Ryden had purchased more rations for them from the market square to replenish their supplies, and they affixed everything to their own horses.

"Do you need help to mount?" she heard Torbin ask Arelle. Rexah shifted her gaze to them.

"I don't." Arelle smiled a delicious smile at him. "But I will take you up on your offer,"

Torbin returned her smile as he held out his hand for her. Arelle took his hand, grabbing the horn with the other. She placed her foot in the stirrup and pushed herself up. Torbin's free hand went to the small of Arelle's back, supporting her as she settled herself into the saddle.

Rexah grinned seeing it was Arelle's turn to blush when Torbin swung up onto the horse behind her, his chest pressed against her back.

"Those two need to hurry up and get together," Kalen whispered to her after getting onto the horse with her. "He's like a lovesick teenager around her and it's getting a little annoying."

Rexah laughed softly. "Leave him be. I think it's cute."

"He's shy. He always has been since we were children, but I think he just needs to find the right woman to bring him out of his shell," Kalen told her as he lifted the reins.

Rexah leaned back into him. "Well, I think he's found her."

Kalen pressed a soft kiss to her head. "I think so too."

"Is everyone ready?" Storglass asked, looking around at them all.

"As ready as we'll ever be," Ryden said as he shifted his grip on the reins.

The horses' hooves clicked against the cobblestones as they made their way towards the border. The village was livelier than when they'd arrived the night before, everyone going about their business. A few glanced in their direction, watching them with curious gazes, some with wariness written on their faces. A little girl caught Rexah's attention outside one of the butcher shops. She gripped her mother's skirts, tugging them to catch her attention.

The mother looked down at her. "Gilda, stop that. We will be home soon; I just need to buy some eggs."

"Mama, the princess!" The little girl beamed, pointing a tiny finger at Rexah.

The woman looked up and her eyes went wide when they fell on her. Rexah smiled at her before looking to the young girl, nodding her head to her as they continued down the street.

"Did you see mama?" the little girl continued excitedly. "She bowed to me!"

"She's never going to forget that for the rest of her life," Kalen mumbled in her ear.

Rexah smiled and nodded. "I know. Growing up I was always taught to respect everyone and show kindness no matter who crossed my path. It's the Ravenheart way."

"I always respected the Ravenhearts for that," Kalen told her. "Every royal house is different. I'm not saying the others are tyrants, but the Ravenhearts are unique in the best kind of way."

Rexah tilted her head to look up at him. "Do you really mean that or are you saying that to stay in my good graces?"

He chuckled. "I mean every word. There's never been and never will be a royal family like yours again."

"That's a very kind thing to say," she replied quietly. "My grandmother would have loved you."

Kalen's arm snaked around her waist, tugging her a little closer. She placed her hand on his arm, feeling completely secure in his hold. As they left the cobblestones and onto the dirt path of the woodland, Kalen said, "I would have loved to have met her."

The weather had been on their side since they left the village. The temperature was still freezing, but the icy wind had died down and the winter sun peeking through the canopy intermittently offered much-welcomed bursts of warmth.

Conversation flowed between the group, but they were sure to keep their voices low, not wanting to attract unwanted attention. Rexah noticed Kalen and Torbin scanning their surroundings and listening out for any sounds out of the ordinary. It eased her nerves a little knowing they would hear or see danger a lot quicker than she would.

They travelled until the sun began to set, at which time they took a break to let the horses rest. Torbin lit a small campfire, and everyone sat around it as they tucked into their rations and drank from their waterskins. They were soon back on the road, deciding against camping for the night due to the Night Witches being a nocturnal bunch.

Rexah's fear became a reality a few hours later when they

arrived in Adorea. She tapped Kalen's arm, asking him to stop. When the horse halted, she quickly dismounted. The frost covered grass crunched beneath her feet as she made her way to the edge of the cliff, staring down at her ruined kingdom below.

Parts of the once magnificent castle still stood but were smeared with soot. The area surrounding the ruins was nothing more than scorched earth, the green grass and flowerbeds completely destroyed. Large chunks of the castle walls were scattered across the gardens, and the trees that once stood tall and proud had been reduced to charred stumps.

Rexah's body began to shake. A crushing wave of grief filled her chest as tears leaked from her eyes. She knew it wasn't going to be an easy thing to see, but she didn't quite realise just how soul shattering it would be.

Kalen's arm wrapped around her shoulders as he brought her into his chest. His hand slid to the nape of her neck as he let her sob into him. The floodgates had opened and nothing she could do would close them.

"It's okay," Kalen whispered into her hair. "Let it out, darling."

Rexah gripped his cloak, trying to breathe in his scent between her sobs. The home she'd known all her life was destroyed and there was no saving it.

"It's gone, Kalen," she cried. "It was easy to put it to the back of my mind, but seeing it now with my own eyes, it … it's truly gone."

Kalen gently hooked his finger under her chin and lifted it until she was staring into his eyes. "Adorea won't remain in ruin," he said. "You will rebuild it to its former glory, and you will be its queen."

His words sank into her bones, forcing her grief back into

its cage. Her sobs eased and her breathing calmed as he pressed his forehead against hers.

"I'm making a vow, right here and now," she said, her voice low. "Never again will my kingdom fall. Those who try to attack will be reminded of how ruthless a Ravenheart can be." Her words were thick with conviction. A calm rage filled her blood, and she was determined now more than ever to get her hands on that sword and rid the world of the Dark Fae and their master for good.

"We will be by your side when you do," Ryden said behind her.

Rexah shifted her gaze to see he'd gotten off his horse and stopped a few feet away from them. She could see in his eyes that he shared some of her heartache for Adorea. He'd spent a lot of his childhood here, just like she'd spent time with him in Kaldoren. Her eyes softened and she nodded slowly.

"We should get back on the horse and keep moving," Kalen said. "We've got about an hour left of travelling, and the sooner we get there, the better."

She made her way back to the horse with him, and Ryden gave her arm a comforting squeeze as she passed. She didn't need any help getting up onto the horse, but she took Kalen's assistance with gratitude. Once everyone was ready to go, they set off, and Rexah didn't glance back at the ruins of her kingdom.

It took just over an hour to arrive at their destination. The Ravenheart crypt wasn't an easy location to access thanks to the Night Witches' protection. Magical wards surrounded the part of the forest where they crypt lay; they were so powerful Rexah could feel the magic skittering across her skin as though trying to determine if she was a threat or not.

"Maybe we should have waited for a reply to your message before coming here," Ryden said, his voice wavering.

It had crossed her mind to wait for a response from the Prime, but they didn't have any time to spare. She opened her mouth to speak but stopped when something in the corner of her eye caught her attention. Perched on one of the tree branches to her right was a raven. The bird was watching them, assessing their every move. A scratchy caw left its beak as it swooped down, and before it touched the ground, inky black smoke surrounded it, and when the smoke dissipated, a woman stood in its place.

A Night Witch.

The witch wore a fitted black dress that hugged her figure and fell to her ankles. Her dark hair floated at her waist, the skirt of her dress swaying in the breeze to reveal her simple black boots. Apart from the skeletal structure surrounding her right eye socket that looked as though the skin had been peeled back to bare bone, her features were delicate. The skin above the witch's knuckles was faded leaving nothing but bone so wickedly sharp at the ends that they looked more like claws than they did fingers.

"Rexah Ravenheart." The witch's voice was a haunting, high-pitched tone, each word lilting as she spoke, her pure white eyes focused on her. "Welcome home."

Rexah bowed her head in respect. "Thank you. May I ask your name?"

"I am Twyla," she replied. The headband made from bone that weaved through her hair signified that she was the Prime's Second in command of the coven.

"We sent a message by moonlight to the Prime. She should be expecting us."

Twyla nodded. "She is. She sent me ahead to greet you. I will take you to her."

Rexah thanked her and looked to her companions before they followed the witch through the woods. As they crossed into the woodland, the hum of magic from the wards became friendly, the defensive, skittering sensation replaced by a warm welcoming that drove the chill air away.

Bats clicked high up in the trees as they followed the footpath, walking in single file. Rexah was tailing Twyla with Kalen behind her, then Arelle, Torbin and Ryden with Storglass at the very back.

She didn't know if it was the wards, but Rexah felt safe here, back on her home soil. She had missed Adorea terribly, and a part of her fucked up brain had made her believe there was still hope that the attack was just a dream, a very bad dream. The evidence of the destroyed castle was proof enough that it wasn't, and it made her grief sink its claws into her a little deeper.

Nerves rolled around in her stomach the closer they got to the dwelling. She didn't know what to expect. People whispered about the Prime, some said she was the whore of the Dark Gods, others said she was the definition of a saint despite her frightening appearance. Rexah had only ever seen a drawing of her in her study book and wondered how much it actually captured the witch's likeness.

Well, I'm about to find out.

Ten minutes later they came to a clearing. The trees parted, giving way to a small hamlet. Rexah's eyes widened as she took in the scene before her. Several huts were scattered around the area. Tiny lights hovered above and throughout the woodland territory, and when she squinted, Rexah realised it was no ordinary light: it was starlight.

"The Prime's hut is just ahead. Keep up," Twyla said as she guided them through.

The other witches looked over as they walked by, talking in hushed voices so low that Rexah couldn't understand what they were saying. She kept her gaze forward, keeping up with Twyla.

They rounded the corner and the Prime's hut came into view. It was larger than the others and had a dark wooden staircase leading up to the front door. A crescent moon was etched into the door and painted a brilliant shade of white so it stood out and one knew exactly who lived here.

Twyla stopped a few feet away from the hut, and when the door opened, the witch held out her hands before her, palms facing the sky, bowing her head as the Prime stepped out onto the porch. Rexah's mouth almost dropped open as she took in the sight of her.

The Prime was tall and thin, and where the other witches had dark hair, hers was pure white and fell to her waist. A crown made from charred bone weaved through her hair, a dark, magical mist emanating from the sharp points. It looked similar to her own power. Much to her surprise, the leader of the Night Witches didn't wear a dress. The witch wore a corset made from blue goldstone, black leather leggings and a pair of black boots.

How on earth did she manage to make a corset out of crystals?

"Magic," the Prime answered as if she'd heard her thoughts as clear as day. She moved down the staircase, stopping once she got to the bottom. The moonlight shining down accentuated her features. Where only a small section of Twyla's face was bony, the majority of the Prime's face was skeletal, and her eyes were pools of swirling iridescent. The colour showing just how potent her magic was.

Swallowing the lump in her throat, Rexah bowed her head to her. "It is an honour to meet you, Prime."

The leader of the coven laughed softly. "There's no need for formalities here, Rexah Ravenheart," she told her. "And please, call me Esmeray."

Rexah lifted her head. "May we converse in private?"

Esmeray nodded. "We may speak in my hut. Follow me," she said, turning on her heel and heading back up the creaking staircase.

Kalen slid his hand into hers, giving it a reassuring squeeze, telling her without words that he would join her. The others held back, nodding for them to go on. She smiled her thanks and looked up to Kalen before they followed Esmeray inside.

It was the opposite of what Rexah expected to find when she stepped inside. A huge lit fireplace sat to the left on the main wall. Dark oak covered the floors, and the walls were painted a shade of dark grey. She'd expected to see a cauldron but was slightly disappointed when she didn't spot one.

Maybe she has a special room where she keeps all her witchcraft items.

"We have a main hut where we keep all of our magical tokens and tomes," Esmeray told her.

"How do you do that?" Rexah asked curiously. "Can you read minds?"

Esmeray laughed again and shook her head. "Not exactly, but I can read your energy. I felt curiosity and fear from you."

Rexah's cheeks flamed. "Apologies."

The witch shook her head, her bright locks shining in the

firelight. "I take no offense. It's only natural to fear us. We are witches of the night, after all."

"I need access to the crypt."

Esmeray nodded. "I appreciate you coming to me and not going to the crypt directly. Things would have gotten troublesome if that had happened. As you know, we swore to protect the crypt by any means necessary, Ravenheart or not."

"I understand, and I thank you for your continued loyalty to my family," Rexah told her.

"It is an honour to be allied with the Ravenhearts," Esmeray replied with a smile, the expression sharper on her skeletal face than it would be on any human. "It's been a while since anyone visited the tomb, but my coven continue to monitor it and ensure the weeds are uprooted and the wards are still strong."

"Did you lose anyone in the attack? My grandmother told me you sent her a shadow message, warning her of the Dark Fae," Rexah said as Kalen gently placed his hand on the small of her back.

Her bewitching eyes saddened. "Unfortunately, yes. I lost four of my best witches that night. They chose to stay behind so the others could retreat. Their yielding ensured the survival of many others. They will never be forgotten, and their sacrifice will not be in vain."

"My condolences to you and your coven," Kalen said softly.

"And who might you be?" Esmeray turned her quizzical gaze to Kalen and looked him over from head to toe.

"Kalen Vidarr," he replied with a respectful nod.

"You have a good soul, Kalen," she told him, her eyes softening. "A very good soul, indeed."

Kalen smiled at her. "My mother used to say the same thing."

Rexah's heart ached for him when he mentioned his mother. She could see the hint of sadness in his eyes, a brief glimpse of the grief he carried.

Esmeray turned her attention back to Rexah. "Please acknowledge this as my acceptance for you to visit the crypt. I do have one condition though."

Relief flooded through her. "Of course, what is the condition?" she asked.

"After a day's rest, you will go at first light, and you will only take two of your companions with you, as well as two of my witches," she said. "We still have a duty to protect the mausoleum, regardless of the time of day. It is sacred; I cannot fill it with warriors."

"I accept your terms," Rexah confirmed, nodding.

Esmeray smiled and dipped her head as she sat down in the huge armchair by the fire. She sighed as she sat back and got comfortable.

"There is one other thing I must ask of you," Rexah said.

"Yes, Ravenheart?"

"My parents and brother are missing," she told her. "They had to flee their home during an attack by the Valfae. I need your help to find them."

"I can do that." She nodded once. "Come find me after your visit to the tomb. I will get everything ready for your arrival."

The witch's hospitality and kindness brought tears to her eyes. "I will be in your debt. If there's ever anything you need, do not hesitate to ask."

"You are so much like her," Esmeray said so softly that it

was almost inaudible. She stood and walked over to Rexah; her head tilted in silent question. Her hand outstretched as though she might brush her long, terrifying fingers along her face, but she retreated with a small smile. "You are so alike that it would be so easy to mistake you for her twin. Your eyes are slightly darker and you're a little shorter than she was, but other than that you look exactly like her. You have her spirit and heart."

"You knew her?" she asked, shocked.

Esmeray's lips pulled into a tight smirk. "Who do you think I swore my oath to?"

"That's … that's incredible."

Kalen chuckled incredulously beside her.

"You must be tired from your journey – go and rest. My girls will show you to the spare huts," Esmeray said.

Rexah bowed her head to her. "Goodnight, Esmeray."

The Prime returned the gesture. "Goodnight, Rexah. Goodnight, Kalen."

Kalen smiled and nodded. "Rest well."

Rexah turned and took his hand before they saw themselves out. The others stood by one of the many fires lit around the hamlet, warming their hands against the flames. Arelle caught her eye and smiled at her, motioning them over.

"Have you spoken to your friends?" Rexah asked her as they approached.

"I have. It's strange to be here when there aren't any celebrations taking place," she replied. "But it's so good to see them again."

"Did you get permission to go to the crypt?" Torbin asked.

"Yes, Rexah is to go there after we are rested, but only two of us can accompany her," Kalen told him.

"I'd like Kalen and Torbin to go with me," Rexah told

them, moving her gaze to her fae friend. "It's the grouping that have fought together the most. If you want to, that is."

Torbin smiled at her. "I would be honoured."

She turned to Storglass, Ryden and Arelle. "You understand?"

"Of course." Ryden dipped his head respectfully. "I trust your judgement."

"As do I," Storglass agreed.

"Sorry to interrupt," a female voice rose behind them, and when Rexah looked around, a woman stood there. She looked eerily like Twyla but without the tiara in her hair. "I have been asked to show you to your huts for the night."

They followed her to two huts at the back of the area. Arelle, Storglass and Ryden walked into the hut on the left, leaving Rexah, Kalen and Torbin to take the one on the right. Torbin lit the candles and the fireplace using his power, and once the room was lit up, they noticed there were only two single beds.

Rexah grimaced. "Esmeray said she lost four witches in the attack on Adorea. This must have belonged to two of them."

Kalen gently rubbed her back and planted a soft kiss to her head.

"I'll sleep on the sofa," Torbin said, setting his pack down on the floor.

"Are you sure?" Rexah asked.

He nodded. "Absolutely. It also means I can be near the fire. The flames calm me," he told her sheepishly. "Probably because of my magic."

He bid them both a goodnight as he got himself ready to sleep, and it wasn't long before Rexah was curled up in the bed opposite Kalen. She lay on her side facing him, watching as he slid under the covers. Her heart fluttered when his blue eyes met hers.

"Get some sleep, darling," he whispered. "I'm right here."

She must have been more tired than she realised because her eyelids began to droop. "Goodnight, Kalen," she whispered before she let sleep take over.

32

When Rexah woke the next night, she couldn't believe she'd slept right through the day. Kalen hadn't left his bed either. Both their bodies had needed the rest. She certainly felt more energised than she did the day before, more mentally relaxed, but her stomach clenched, yearning for sustenance.

She shoved the covers off and slid out of the bed, stretching her arms above her head just as Kalen opened his eyes. "Good morning … well … good night, technically."

He chuckled; his laugh still laced with slumber which she found rather adorable. "I don't know about you, but I feel so good after that sleep," he said, sitting up, the cover sliding down revealing his toned abdominal muscles.

"Yeah …" Rexah practically ogled. His hair was dishevelled, and it made him look even more unbelievably hot. "I do too …"

"What are you thinking about right now?" he asked, a wicked gleam in his eyes.

Calm down, Rexah.

"Absolutely nothing."

"That's not what your body is saying." Kalen stood and padded toward her. He slid his hand down her waist, resting it on her bare hip where her dress had ridden up during the night. He smirked as he watched her squirm under his touch, goosebumps spreading across her exposed flesh.

"You are insufferable sometimes, did you know that?" she said, her voice coming out more seductively than normal.

Kalen chuckled. "You love it," he said, pressing his lips to hers. She kissed him back, shuffling closer as she rested her hands on his bare chest. She could feel just how much she affected him like he did her, either that or it was just natural morning wood. "We should get ready for breakfast," she said, reluctantly peeling herself away. "My stomach keeps growling at me."

Kalen kissed her tenderly before getting dressed. Rexah pulled on her own clothes and soon they both headed out of the hut. Torbin wasn't on the sofa when they passed through the living area, so they assumed he was already in the main hut. Food was his favourite thing after all.

The hamlet was buzzing with energy. The Night Witches basking in the power the moonlight and the stars provided them with. Some were gathered in small circles, chanting in Witch Word, others were dancing around the bonfire in the centre of the hamlet.

Rexah spotted her other companions sat around the bonfire, eating a meal as they spoke in easy conversation. Torbin was the first to spot them and grinned, waving them over. Rexah sat beside him, Kalen taking the spot on the other side of her.

"I saved some for you both," he said handing them small black bowls filled with mouthwatering stew.

"Thanks, Tor," Kalen said before tucking into his food.

Rexah smiled and took a small sip. Savoury flavours burst across her tongue as she swallowed the warm liquid, heating her throat as it went down.

"How did you sleep?" Arelle asked from the other side of Torbin.

"Very well," Rexah replied. "Feeling much better now."

Arelle grinned. "I'm glad to hear it."

"Did we miss anything whilst we slept?" Kalen asked.

The Seer shook her head. "The night's activities are just beginning," she told him.

Just as Rexah was about to enquire as to what the activities entailed, Twyla sat down by the bonfire, joined by another two witches.

"It's good to see you again," Twyla said.

Rexah smiled and took another sip of stew. "You too."

"These are my sisters, Lyra and Nyx."

Lyra had dark blonde hair and piercing green eyes. Nyx had inky black hair and her eyes were a stunning shade of sky-blue. Both women bowed their heads in greeting which Rexah returned.

Everyone fell into a comfortable conversation as Rexah finished off her food, her stomach settling down now that it had been fed. She listened to the women tell stories of their coven, both good and bad. Rexah was in her element, hearing the history from the witches themselves was so much better than reading about it in books.

"If you don't mind me asking, how is it you obtain your power from the night?" Rexah asked, her curiosity getting the better of her.

Nyx smirked. "Twyla *loves* telling this story."

"Lunania is our goddess," the witch began, excitement in

her eyes. "When the gods and goddesses created this world, Lunania created the moon and the stars. She passes her power to the moon, and during the night hours that power automatically transfers into us, her Chosen," Twyla explained. "To show our gratitude and loyalty to Lunania, we hold monthly celebrations in her honour."

"I thought you held the sabbath yearly?" Rexah asked.

It was Lyra who answered. "That's correct. The yearly sabbath is a celebration of the moon and is held on the night when it's at its strongest that year. The monthly celebrations are for Lunania."

"That's amazing. When is your next celebration?"

"Not for another two weeks," Nyx replied. "Maybe one day you can join our gathering and witness it for yourself."

"I would be extremely honoured," Rexah replied, amazed. "Once the Dark Fae are gone, I'd very much like to take you up on your offer."

Nyx smiled and nodded her head.

Rexah leaned into Kalen as the conversation stemmed off, the others joining in. Her pulse fluttered when he gently wrapped his arm around her and touched his lips to her forehead. She enjoyed the company around her, and how close Torbin and Arelle sat to each other didn't go unnoticed. Storglass was talking to one of the witches, summoning his green power into his palm to which the woman grinned and showed her own in return. She held out her hand; white magic swirled until it dissipated to reveal a full moon floating above her palm, sparkling like it were filled with stars. Rexah grinned seeing the look on Storglass's face. He was thoroughly impressed.

She watched as the other witches giggled with each other and danced in a circle around them. Rexah swore she could see faint traces of magic trailing behind them as they moved, and she watched them in awe. This was quickly becoming one of her favourite places, and she would definitely be visiting again, as long as she survived the inevitable war.

That last thought made her stomach churn, and she swallowed down the rising bile. There was a high chance that none of them would survive. There were no guarantees that they'd win. But she couldn't think like that.

"Positivity will destroy the enemy."

Shoving the negativity aside, she buried her nose into Kalen's neck, inhaling his intoxicating scent. Goosebumps rose along his skin, and she couldn't help but smile, loving the effect she had on him.

"Are you okay?" he whispered to her.

She nodded against his shoulder. "I'm fine."

Today, she was fine, but in reality she was on the edge of crumbling. Tomorrow she'd be going to the crypt to hopefully, finally, retrieve the Shadow Star. In the meantime, sat around the roaring fire, she prayed to the Raven God that it was definitely there waiting for her and that she hadn't led everyone into danger for nothing.

The crypt was exactly as she remembered in her vision, but now that she was here, the tomb had a heavy presence she hadn't anticipated. She wasn't afraid, but knowing the bodies of her ancestors were beneath her feet wasn't a pleasant feeling, and she couldn't escape the feeling that she was being watched by every single one.

Soft pinks and purples swam across the sky: the first light

of the sun rising. As fond as she was of the night sky, Rexah loved the pastel tones of the early morning.

"Are you ready?" Kalen asked beside her, his hand resting on the small of her back, his fingers moving in those slow circular motions.

"As ready as I'll ever be." Rexah nodded slowly. "We should head inside before my nerves get the better of me."

"We're right here with you," Torbin told her, giving her a gentle, reassuring smile.

The two young witches stood patiently at either side of the crypt entrance. It shimmered with magic, the wards powerful enough that Rexah could taste its bitterness on her tongue as she approached.

"We are ready to enter," Rexah told them.

The women bowed their heads in respect and turned to the purple door. Lifting their hands, they began to chant quietly in Witch Word, and Rexah watched in fascination as the wards began to ripple. First it rippled softly, like air around a hot surface, then it intensified, and like a rock thrown into a pond, it disturbed everything around it. Then, just as Rexah thought the magic might snap, a gust of wind blew past, and the ward protection was gone.

"It is done," one of the women said as they turned back to her.

"We shall wait here for you," the other said.

"Thank you." Rexah took a deep, grounding breath and stepped over the threshold before she managed to talk herself out of it.

Her footsteps echoed as she descended the stairs with Kalen and Torbin at her back. With each step she took, the knot in her stomach twisted tighter. So many thoughts raced through her mind all at once. What if she was wrong? What if the sword wasn't here at all? What if this was a trap that she had fallen so easily into?

Warm fingers tangled with hers, pulling her from her thoughts. "It's okay," Kalen whispered reassuringly.

Rexah nodded and continued down the staircase, and it wasn't long before they reached the bottom. The familiar room came into view, the overwhelming wash of dark-grey stone chiselled to sharp edges everywhere she looked. She hadn't noticed it in her vision, but now that she was here, Rexah spotted the names of the dead Ravenhearts engraved on the walls around the room. Her grandmother had told her that instead of burying the coffins in the earth, the Ravenhearts were interred within the walls of the crypt, sealed shut with magic.

Ryker Ravenheart.

Riona Ravenheart.

Arius Ravenheart.

When her focus fell to the centre of the space, her heart sank; she saw no storm of purple energy. There was only grey stone and the markings of her ancestors.

Was I wrong?

As she opened her mouth to speak, to tell Kalen how sorry she was for failing him, a memory – a voice – entered her mind.

"It calls to you," the Raven God said on a magical breeze. *"All you need to do is listen."*

"What do we do now?" Torbin asked beside her, his voice thick with concern.

Rexah looked to her companions. "We wait."

She closed her eyes, forcing her body to relax. She used every technique she had learned from Arelle and Torbin to empty her mind, to expel all doubt that her instincts might fail her, that she was inadequate for the role she had to fulfil; she dismissed everything until one thought remained, and her mind pushed it into the void, hoping it would be heard.

Shadow Star.

Shadow Star.

Shadow Star.

She waited patiently for its reply, repeating its name with conviction within her consciousness.

Shadow Star.

Shadow Star.

Shadow Star.

She stood, waiting in perfect nothingness, no thought in her mind except the purpose she had to fulfil. She was peaceful; her mind was free and open.

I'm listening.

"Rex…"

Torbin nudged her lightly, urging her attention, and her eyes opened slowly. She saw a small purple circular light had appeared in the centre of the room. It hovered, blinking, as though the magic were rousing from a long slumber.

Rexah smiled, assessing the light as it assessed her, and before she could decide what to do next, a voice rang in her mind.

Chosen.

Chosen.

Chosen.

A vapour began to spill out of the light, like a thundercloud travelling through a portal, until the room became lost to thick and humid air. Purple flashes of light followed, lighting the mist so brightly she felt herself floating within a violet abyss, and thunderous resonance filled the room.

She'd felt this before.

Finally, the mist dissipated – the crackling light reduced to a flicker and the booming quietened to a rumble – and it revealed the purple storm she expected to find. It swirled fiercely within the centre of the space; the room was charged with power.

"I've never seen anything like this," Kalen said, his mouth agape with awe.

The dagger began to vibrate against Rexah's hip, and she frowned down at it, unsure of its behaviour.

"It must sense the sword is near," Torbin surmised as he stopped at her left, his fiery gaze studying the weapon. "The blades must be made from the same steel."

Her eyes widened in realisation. "The dagger must have been made by the Raven God too." She brushed a light finger over the hilt as though attempting to calm the blade. "You are sisters," she whispered as she turned her attention back to the swirling energy. "Let's reunite you, shall we?"

Rexah looked up at Kalen and Torbin who both nodded encouragingly. She approached slowly, cautious in the proximity of such strong power. The hum of magic danced over her skin as though it were greeting her, welcoming her to join in its dance. She smiled. The closer she stood to it the less her worries ailed her. Her stomach no longer churned with anxiety; her hands did not shake at her sides. She'd imagined this moment often after having the vision and thought she would be a nervous wreck, but all she felt now was calm.

It's here.

A break in the magical mist revealed it, and the crackle of lightning within the energy cloud brought her attention to the weapon which lay within. The only hope for the realm within reaching distance. She felt a pull in her chest as her eyes ran over it. Raven wings splayed out across the black, purple jewelled hilt and fae runes decorated the steel, like the dagger.

This is it. This is the moment we've all been waiting for, she thought. *I can do this.*

Rexah lifted her right hand, her fingertips pressing lightly against the wall of power. It crackled against her skin, and her heart began to beat furiously against her chest, but she ignored it as she pushed her fingers through. She heard the muffled sounds of Kalen's voice behind her, but he felt a world away, unreachable. The magic was everything and it crashed over her in waves. She felt it swim through her as if testing her, ensuring she was the one, like an eel traversing a busy seabed. Gritting her teeth, she gathered her energy and thrust her hand forward, and when her fingers wrapped around the hilt, every-thing changed.

The purple energy exploded. Her head shot back as she gasped, her feet lifting off the ground as she hovered in mid-air, her gaze stuck to the stone ceiling. Magic filled her, mind, body and soul. Every cell and every nerve in her body sparked with the lightning shooting through her. The blood in her veins tingled as tears burned in her eyes. Her vision filled with storms and death, premonitions of the birth of the realm, of times gone by, and things she had yet to experience.

As quickly as everything happened, the energy dissipated and Rexah landed on her feet with a preternatural grace. The room was deadly silent apart from the crackle of lightning dancing down the blade in her grasp. Rexah slowly looked down at the sword, the fae runes glowing violet along the steel illuminating her face. The veins in her arm pulsed before returning to normal, but something wasn't right; something was different than it was before, she could feel it deep within her soul. She could see the dust particles dancing in the air; she could smell the faint remnants of magic.

"Rexah?"

Kalen's voice pulled her from her trance-like state. Her stomach fluttered when she noticed how crystal clear his voice was to her. How beautiful it was to hear his voice more clearly than ever before, each intonation a revelation. But how?

She slowly turned to see him pushing himself to his feet, Torbin doing the same. "Are you okay? What happened?" she asked.

"The blast of energy sent us into the wall," Torbin told her, rolling his shoulder with a slight wince.

"Darling," Kalen said as he took a step forward. "Are *you* all right?"

"I was terrified for a moment there, but I … I think I'm okay," she told him, nodding as she looked down at herself just to make sure. "I feel a little strange, though. I don't know if it's the magic, but it's like a light has been turned on. It's hard to explain."

"It's not so difficult to understand," Torbin said, his fiery gaze studying her like he could see something she could not.

Her eyebrows met in a frown. "What do you mean?"

Kalen walked forward until he was standing before her. He gently took her hand in his as his eyes roamed her face. "Do you remember what happened to Riona when she held the sword for the first time?"

Rexah cast her mind back to the story she'd been told many times growing up and nodded softly. "Yes. She lifted the sword and she …" she trailed off as her wide eyes met Kalen's. "No … no, that's … that's not possible."

Kalen moved her hair with one hand and gently lifted her

hand to her ear with the other. "It's happened to you too," he whispered.

Her chest ached. Bile rose to the back of her throat. The sword slid from her grip and fell to the ground with an echoing clang as her fingers glided over the now sharply pointed tips of her ears.

"Rexah, look at me," Kalen quietly commanded her, and her frightened gaze met his. "I need you to take a few deep breaths for me. Can you do that?"

Nodding, she did as he said and inhaled deeply, drawing oxygen back into her burning lungs. It had never crossed her mind that this would happen. She hadn't considered the fact that the same thing would happen to her that happened to Riona when she touched the sword.

"That's it, just keep breathing," Kalen soothed.

Torbin was quiet as he leaned against the wall, seemingly trying to digest what he'd just witnessed.

"I'm fae," she whispered once her breathing was back under control.

"Yes," Torbin said quietly, his dark brown hair falling into his eyes slightly as he nodded.

"We should head back. I'll get you a hot drink and we can talk about all of this in a more private setting," Kalen said, gently kissing her forehead. "We should get the sword out of here."

Rexah savoured the feeling of his lips against her flesh. She could feel her skin tingling under his mouth, reacting to the caress of his lips. Stepping back, she reached down and gingerly picked up the sword, afraid of what it might do, but her shoulders sagged with relief when nothing happened. She pulled the sword Storglass had given her out of its sheath and replaced it with the Shadow Star.

"Swear to me that you won't breathe a word of this to anyone for now?" she asked, looking between the two of them.

Torbin nodded softly. "You have my word, Rex."

"And mine," Kalen promised, taking Storglass's sword from her and sheathing it into his own weapons belt.

Rexah followed them up the staircase, fixing her hair to hide her ears as she went. She understood it was common knowledge that Riona had become fae when she wielded the Shadow Star for the first time, but Rexah needed a chance to let what she'd just experienced sink in; her life was never going to be the same from this moment on.

The two witches kept their word and were waiting in the same spot they parted. If they suspected anything had changed, they never showed it.

"Are you ready to head back?" one of them asked kindly.

Rexah nodded. "Yes, let's go."

The journey back was quiet apart from the occasional twig snapping or frosted leaf crunching beneath the witches' feet. Her own footsteps were silent, another sign of her new fae capabilities, and the birdsongs above now rang crystal clear. She felt like she'd been cloaked from the world her whole life, the veil now lifted, but she also felt overstimulated to each and every noise and sensation, and her head twitched with every new experience.

The hamlet was alive when they arrived. Everyone hurried around going about their business, none of them paying her any mind, much to her delight. The doors to the main hut were wide open and the smell of cooked meats wafted out, her stomach growling in response. After grabbing them some food, Kalen guided her to their hut. Torbin opted to stay and eat his breakfast in the main hut to give them some privacy to talk.

Rexah sat on the sofa by the roaring fireplace with Kalen

as they ate in a comfortable silence. She replayed the scene over and over again in her head, trying to come to terms with what had occurred. She wished now more than ever that her grandmother were here to give her advice. She stared at the Shadow Star; it lay on the coffee table before them, still sheathed, like it slept peacefully.

Any moment now, I'm about to wake up.

"I know I've asked you this already, and I know it's a stupid question, but are you okay?" Kalen asked her, his voice thick with concern.

Her eyes focused on the flickering flames as she searched for the words.

Am I okay?

"Today I woke up hoping we'd finally have the sword, but I didn't expect to not be human before the day had truly begun," she replied quietly.

"A fae body is different from a human one," he said. "It'll take time to adjust, and I'll help you any way I can."

An unexpected anger rose in her. "It's not enough that my home was destroyed, I find out my parents are alive, and I have a *twin*. To add to all of that, I'm the Chosen of the Raven God, and I'm the only one that can retrieve and wield the weapon that will destroy the Dark Fae and their master," she said. "And now I'm *fae*. When will I have a break in all of this? I'm so godsdamned tired, Kalen."

He took her plate, stacked it with his own and set it down on the coffee table before turning to her, wrapping his arm around her shoulders to bring her closer. "It's difficult, I know, but Renvian chose you because he knew you could bare this. He knew you were strong enough. None of this is fair, and if I could take on the responsibility and take the weight from your shoulders I would, but the best I can do is repeat my vow to you that I will never leave your side. Your enemies are my enemies, my sword is yours to command, and I will shield you with my life."

Rexah looked up at him, emotion clogging the back of her throat. "You don't know how much that means to me," she whispered and when he kissed her cheek, she asked, "Do I look different?"

Kalen studied her face with a small smile on his lips. "Apart from the sharp points on your ears, the violet of your eyes is more vibrant," he told her. "More than anything you will feel different in yourself."

She nodded. "Everything looks and sounds sharper. I can feel my magic sparking underneath my skin and through my veins. It's the strangest sensation."

"Like you said, it will take time for you to adjust, but one thing is for certain," he said. "You're a lot stronger now than you were before."

"What happens now?"

"Our goal is still the same," he said. "We have the sword now, so we move onto the next stage of the plan."

"What is the next stage? Defeating the Dark Fae? It's not something we can just *do*," she replied, running her fingers through her hair. "There aren't enough of us to take them on. We need an army."

Kalen's eyes moved to the sword. "It won't be easy gathering people to fight, but we need to try."

"We'll talk to the others about this, but can I have one day where I don't need to be the Chosen? I need one day to give my body and mind a chance to rest and process," she said, wearily.

Kalen's eyes softened. "Of course, but, darling, you don't

need my permission. I'll let the others know, and when I get back, we can have a relaxation day. How does that sound?"

"As long as I can drink my body weight in tea, then it sounds heavenly," she replied, a weak smile finally spreading across her face.

"I can make that happen." He pressed a kiss to her lips and stood up, lifting their plates before heading out of the hut.

Rexah looked to the Shadow Star on the coffee table once more. It needed her blood to unleash its full potential, and if the events in the crypt were anything to go by, the power locked within the blade would be a force to be reckoned with, and it frightened her.

She kicked off her boots and placed them underneath the coffee table. Wriggling her toes, she rose from the sofa and walked over to the mirror in the corner of the room. Nervously, she moved her hair away from her ear and her pulse jumped as she took in the sight of her new fae feature. Kalen was right when he'd told her that her eyes were more vibrant, but underneath it all, she was the same Rexah, determined to do whatever it took to save the realm and exact her revenge on the Dark Fae.

33

"Thank you for letting me have this day," Rexah said quietly. "I'm feeling better already."

Rexah was supposed to meet with Esmeray to search for her family, but Kalen had already let the Prime know she wasn't feeling great. He told her that Esmeray understood; they would take the day to recuperate before taking on the next thing. So, they'd dragged the covers from the beds into the living room – the coffee table moved and the Shadow Star still within reach – and spread the covers out on the floor next to the fireplace. There, they lay in each other's arms for hours.

They got to know each other more, talking about their hobbies and hopes for the future in more detail than ever before. She could listen to him talk for the rest of her life, his voice deep and soothing. She hadn't noticed it with her human sight, but now that they were relaxed and she could take in every little detail of his face, she could see faint swirling in his cobalt eyes, like the rippling waves of the ocean, and the butterflies in her stomach fluttered like mad.

His power.

Kalen shook his head. "No need to thank me. It's okay to admit when you need a break. Listening to your body is one of the most important things you can do to remain sane."

"Part of me is angry with myself because we're on a time sensitive mission and millions of innocent lives are depending on us, even if they don't know it," she admitted to him.

"You can't save the world if you burn yourself out," he told her. "You need to be ready and focused for what we're about to do. The Dark Fae will still be there tomorrow."

Rexah snuggled in closer. "You have a way with words, has anyone ever told you that?"

He chuckled, the laugh vibrating through his chest. "Torbin might have mentioned it before."

A smile spread across her lips. There wouldn't be many of these quiet, peaceful moments with him in the days, weeks and months to come, so she soaked up every small second she could, savouring it like her life depended on it.

In ways, it did.

"Things are moving quickly now," she said, her fingers gently tracing along the lines of his bare chest, watching as goosebumps flared to life across his skin where she'd touched.

Kalen sighed contently, his arms tightening around her slightly. "They are, but we'll be prepared for whatever the next part of our journey throws at us."

"Whenever I thought about my future, it never looked like this," she whispered. "All the death and destruction, I never once expected any of it."

Kalen gently hooked his finger underneath her chin, tilting her head up until their eyes connected. "No one looks for heartache and fear in their future. The gods and goddesses weave our paths, and we can do nothing but follow them," he said, his gaze so focused on hers it felt like he could see her soul. "I believe if I ever strayed from the road laid out for me by the gods, I'd have always found my way to you, because you're …" he trailed off, obviously fighting with himself whether or not to continue.

"Because I'm what?" she asked, encouraging him.

Kalen looked deeply into her eyes, his hand coming up to gently cup her cheek. "I've been wanting to tell you this for so long, but my fear gets the best of me every single time."

"You know you can tell me anything," she said, placing her hand on his wrist. "Talk to me."

He hesitated for a moment before he spoke again. "You're my mate. I've known since the moment we found you on that dirt road. Your scent hit me, and it was like I couldn't breathe; my body and soul surrendered to you, and from that moment on, I was yours."

Rexah's mind went into overdrive. The conviction in his voice sent a tingle through her body. Mates were a sacred thing in fae culture. Once you were mated it was for life. A few days ago, she might have questioned it, but now that she'd gone through the change and was fae herself, it made all the pieces finally click together. The way she gravitated towards him, how her body responded to the faintest of his touches, and how lost she felt when he'd been taken by Venrhys, it all made perfect sense now.

"My mate," she whispered as she studied his features.

"I know there are more important things to be dealt with right now, but I couldn't keep it to myself any longer. You deserved to know." He ran his thumb softly over the skin of her cheek. "How do you feel about this?"

She leaned forward and pressed her lips against his. She

sank further with him into the covers, showing him exactly how she felt.

Vast green rolling hills lay before her, darkened by the night sky above. The stars shone brighter than she remembered, winking in a familiar greeting. The grass beneath her feet tickled her ankles. A cool, gentle breeze brushed the skirt of her nightgown, lifting the ends of her raven hair into a slow dance.

Even though this place was unfamiliar, this was a safe space. She felt it deep within her bones.

A deep, hollow croak caught her attention. A beautiful black raven perched on a thick branch of the tree to her right. With her new sight, she noticed its feathers had a blueish tinge to them. Its powerful beak opened as it let out another croak and its black eyes connected with hers.

"Don't let her fool you," a familiar deep voice spoke behind her. "She's quite harmless."

Rexah knew instantly who it was. The power emanating from him alone was a clear sign as any. "She is stunning."

"That she is. She is loyal, fierce, and highly intelligent," Renvian replied as he stepped beside her. "She has been my companion since the very beginning of time."

Rexah's gaze slid from the beautiful bird to meet the Raven God's face. He did not look at her; his eyes settled on the view before them. It dawned on her then that the last time they met she'd never seen his face. He'd been obscured by swirling shadows, maybe simply by the limitations of her human sight.

His black hair was long and straight, falling to the middle of his back in a point. His features were sharp, bewitching in a way that made him devastatingly handsome, and when his eyes finally met hers, Rexah's breath caught in her throat at the stunning shade of indigo they were.

"I'm dreaming, aren't I?"

Renvian nodded. "Yes, you are. This is the only means of communication I can have with you."

She studied his face for a moment. "I thought the Gods weren't supposed to intervene."

His lips tugged up in a small smirk. "I am merely here to talk, nothing else. There are no rules against that."

"I found the sword."

"I watched you retrieve it," he said. "That's the reason why I brought you here."

Rexah looked around. "And where exactly are we?"

"This is a place I like to call the Other," he told her. "Not quite the heavens and not quite Etteria. Here we can speak freely without outside ears hearing our every word."

"I'm scared," she admitted.

"I know you are, and there is no shame in feeling afraid of the unknown. This road laid out for you is not an easy one, but only you have the strength to roam it."

Rexah looked up at him. "What if I can't? I'm not Riona."

"Exactly. You are not Riona," he said, turning to face her. His blackish blue leather armour reflecting the moonlight. "Once you stop comparing yourself to her, you will see the warrior in you that I do."

His words hit her straight in her gut. He was right. All her life she'd compared herself to her dead ancestor, setting impossibly high expectations for herself.

"You are Rexah Ravenheart, my Chosen," he continued, reaching out and tilting her chin up with his finger to connect their eyes once more. "And you do not bow down."

Goosebumps flooded her skin, his words washing over her in waves. "Now that I have the sword, what should I do?"

"Do what you were born to, what you were chosen to do," *he replied. "Bring an end to the darkness."*

"What happens afterwards?"

"That's a conversation for another time." He smiled softly. "Our time here is running out."

"Don't go; I need your guidance," she said, almost begged.

"Activate the sword with your blood. Only then will you feel its true power. The power to destroy the darkness for good." Renvian softly swept his fingers through her hair, moving it from her face. "It will show you how."

Rexah closed her eyes as he leaned forward, pressing a tender kiss to her forehead.

When she opened her eyes and found herself back to reality, she swore she heard the Raven God's voice echoing through her mind.

"I'm with you, always."

"I wasn't going to tell anyone, not right away, but I don't want to keep secrets from any of you. I needed some time to let it all sink in."

The main hut was empty apart from those sat with Rexah at the head table. Esmeray had instructed that no one disturb their meeting. Anyone who did would feel her wrath, and by the looks her witches had given her, Rexah knew none of them wanted to be on the receiving end, and all followed her command without complaint.

"I was there when this happened to Riona," Arelle said as she studied her. "It never occurred to me that it might happen to you too, but I didn't need to see your ears to know you'd changed. I could feel it."

Kalen's hand on her thigh was a welcomed comfort. "We understand, darling."

"No one is judging you or angry with you," Torbin said softly. "We've all been through a lot and the time we all had to rest was much needed."

"I can't rest for much longer. We have the sword now, and I'm worried the Dark Fae might be able to sense it. If that is the case, I've no doubt they would send every force they have to kill us and take it," she said. "I also need to find my parents and my brother."

"Leave finding your family to me, Rexah," Esmeray replied. "I will scry for them, but I will require a single drop of your blood."

Rexah nodded. "Of course, thank you."

"The Dark Fae will always be a threat as long as they walk the realm," Storglass said, his chair creaking softly as he sat back. "Whether they can sense you have the sword now or not, they'll always be after us until we take them out."

Ryden ran his fingers through his hair. His gaze was deeply troubled, and it had been that way since Rexah had filled everyone in on what had happened in the crypt. "Rexah has the sword. We should seek them out now rather than sitting here waiting for them to show up."

"You expect us to go charging at the Dark Fae? Just the six

of us?" Kalen asked, his features darkening and his eyes narrowing. "Are you really that stupid?"

Ryden's gaze snapped to Kalen. "We're putting everyone here in danger every second we linger. I say we make an offensive plan and take the fight to them for a change."

Rexah could feel the anger rolling from Kalen like a growing storm, and before he could answer, she said, "Ry, I understand where you're coming from, but I don't want to activate the sword and go rushing in there with no back up. I have the weapon now, yes, but it's useless if I get killed before I can use it." She looked to Kalen, reprimand in her gaze. "And nobody here is stupid."

Ryden didn't reply, but a look of understanding and appreciation flooded his steel eyes as he sat back in his chair.

"What is the plan then?" Arelle asked.

Rexah looked up at Kalen who gave her an encouraging nod before she turned her attention back to her companions. "Each one of us has connections throughout the realm. Given the current situation, I'm aware that the Dark Fae might have gotten to them first, but we should reach out and see who responds. We need as much firepower as we can get."

"I have a few friends I can talk to." Storglass nodded, his fingers rubbing his chin. "It's been a while since their last battle, but they are always itching for a good fight."

"My witches will be at your disposal too," Esmeray told her. "Give the word and they will be wherever you need them."

"What about the other covens?" Kalen asked.

Arelle's green eyes brightened. "Leave that to me," she said, her lips tugging into a small smirk. "They all owe me a favour anyway."

"We should head back to Savindeer. There might be some

fae warriors that would like to help and get their revenge at the same time," Torbin suggested.

The grin that spread across Kalen's face sent Rexah's heart into a spiralling mess. "Great idea, Tor," he said.

Ryden looked over to Rexah. "I will follow you wherever you choose to go, princess."

The use of the nickname filled her with a familiar joy now laced with sorrow for the life they once shared.

"So, it's settled then," Rexah said, her chair scraping against the floor as she rose to her feet. Her heart pounded fiercely against her chest, and her legs shook as she looked at each one of her friends.

They all gazed back at her with a mixture of hope and belief etched across their faces, and it sent a small burst of confidence through her veins before she spoke once more.

"At first light, we build our army."

EPILOGUE

He adored the forest at night. The sounds of the nocturnal animals calling and growling was like music to his ears. He'd always been drawn to the darker aspects of life. Nothing brought him more joy than satisfying his evil, masochistic nature, and he couldn't wait to properly serve his master once he was back to his full strength.

Looking up at the break in the canopy, he sighed. What was taking her so long?

Just as the thought entered his head, the sound of twigs snapping announced her arrival.

Finally.

Standing up from the tree he'd been leaning against, he turned to face the witch.

"I have what you requested," she told him, pulling the small vial from her pouch.

"Excellent." He held his hand out, grinning madly when she placed it into his open palm. He could feel the power humming within it. "Did anyone see you leave?"

The witch shook her head. "No, I was careful."

He chuckled. "How did you obtain this? There's more than I expected," he said, examining the red liquid.

"She arrived at the camp injured thanks to the nasty wound you inflicted," she explained. "It was easier than I anticipated."

"It's been a pleasure doing business with you," he said, tossing a small purse filled with coin to her.

Catching it with ease, she opened it to inspect the contents. "Of course. I'm here if you require anything else in the future."

Nodding, he turned and headed into the woodland; he only took two steps before she spoke again.

"Venrhys, you could have acquired her blood upon capturing her, why did you ask me to procure it?"

Looking over his shoulder, Venrhys smirked. "It's always good to have a plan b."

Venrhys turned and headed back through the trees, the vial of Rexah Ravenheart's blood thrumming in his palm.

Acknowledgments

Here we are again, this time at the end of book *two!* It's still so surreal that I'm publishing books. It's an absolute dream come true of mine, and I have so many people to thank for helping me along the way!

Mum, thank you for everything you've done and continue to do for me. I'm the luckiest girl in the world to have you as my mum. You've encouraged me to follow my dreams and never stopped believing in me.

Dad, I wish you were here to see that I've done it again! I know you'd be proud of me.

Christine, thank you for being the best, supportive big sister a girl could ask for. It means the absolute world to me.

Linzi, you have been there every step of the way. You've read countless chapters and drafts and gave your honest opinions that I value with all my heart. Thank you for being my best friend and alpha reader. Thank you for keeping my head above the water.

Amy, my amazing editor. Thank you, as always, for making my book look pretty! Also, thank you for all your advice and support. I couldn't do this without you!

Danielle, thank you for all the time and effort you put into making my stunning book covers! Can't wait to see what you do for the next one!

Ravenheart Hype Team, you guys are just the best! Thank

you for your continued support and promoting the hell out of my books! Every single one of you are amazing!

My husband, Nicky. You have been my absolute rock throughout this process, listening to me go on and on about the characters and story, even though you have no idea what I'm talking about. I am so lucky to have you in my life and you will forever be the Kalen to my Rexah. I love you, my sun and stars.

Elijah, my darling boy. You were in my belly the whole time I was going through the final draft of this book, kicking away, letting me know I wasn't alone. Thank you, my boy, for everything.

Finally, to my readers. Without you I wouldn't be able to do this. Thank you to each and every one of you from the bottom of my heart. I hope you enjoy the journey whatever it might entail.

ABOUT THE AUTHOR

Allie Brennan was born in Glasgow, Scotland and lives with her husband and son, Elijah.

When she's not writing, one of her favourite things to do is to sit with a big cup of tea and read. She also loves watching fantasy movies and fantasy/supernatural tv shows. She loves all things fantasy and witchy and loves her books spicy!

Follow Allie on social media to keep up to date with writing updates, book releases and more!

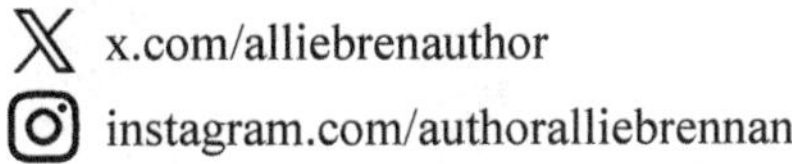

x.com/alliebrenauthor

instagram.com/authoralliebrennan

Printed in the USA
CPSIA information can be obtained
at www.ICGtesting.com
CBHW030229150924
14303CB00004B/50

9 781739 712631